praise for the way you love me

This is a wonderful contemporary romance story. *The Way You Love Me* is a fantastic read about forgiveness, second chances, and family.

—ALLYSON, GOODREADS

This is such a sweet story. It is a story of forgiveness and healing. A reminder that no one is too far gone and that there is a chance for reconciliation when we screw up. Which we all do. A sweet message of Christ's wonderful love and forgiveness for us.

—KIM, GOODREADS

The Way You Love Me is engrossing and sweet. It will touch your heart and leave you with a deep sense of how the words we speak have the weight to crush or build up . . . It proves Aleckson has a bright writing future.

—LISA, GOODREADS

Family conflicts, grief and loss, misunderstandings and past failures create intense emotions and situations, yet set the stage for the gifts of redemption, reconciliation, and healing.

—KIM, GOODREADS

D1600691

the way you love me

A Deep Haven Novel

Fox Family ❊ Book Three

michelle sass aleckson

Edited by

susan may warren

sunrise
PUBLISHING

To my Deep Haven sisters.
I never could've done this without you,
Andrea & Rachel!

For He has rescued us from the dominion of darkness and brought us into the kingdom of the Son He loves, in whom we have redemption, the forgiveness of sins.
Colossians 1:13-14 (NIV)

one

. . .

If they would just open the courtroom door, Oliver Fox could get this whole thing over with. He unfolded the paper in his hand and read down the list of names.

For such an ordinary sheet of notebook paper, it sure seemed important to the lawyer. It had sentimental value, of course. It was the last thing he'd done with his mentor Hezekiah. But would it really make or break his case?

"Ollie, sit down a spell before you make me dizzy with all your pacing. You need to relax."

Blanche's scratchy voice held a tone of sympathy. It was the only reason he listened and sat next to her on the hard, worn bench. Well, that and the fact that his sixty-year-old former-biker neighbor was still tough enough to take him down with force if necessary.

But she was wrong. He didn't need to relax. He needed this whole court thing settled and to get back to his daughter.

A beep from the security checkpoint and chatter from the people in the long hallway were enough to drive a man to distraction. He could pick out the lawyers in the crowd. Smart suits, expensive briefcases and shoes, smug expressions that said they held their clients' futures in their hands and they knew it.

Well, they didn't dictate *his* life. He would be in charge of his own destiny.

And to think at one point he'd thought he'd be one of them.

Although, that was a lifetime ago. Back before everything fell apart.

"So, what are you going to tell them?" Blanche leaned over, planting her elbows on her knees, setting the fringe on her leather vest swaying. Her white, spiky hair and black boots clashed with everyone around them, and he loved her for it. She wasn't going to let anyone, not even Kiah's aunt, try to take Kiah away from him without a fight.

Oliver shrugged and kept watch for his own lawyer. "The truth."

"The truth that you're getting kicked out of your home? Ace Plumbing is taking over the rest of the building in three weeks. You know that's gonna be an issue when custody of a five-year-old comes up."

Oliver threw an arm around her shoulder. "You don't need to worry about that. I'll find something soon."

"You could come to Florida with me." Behind that hardened expression beat the biggest heart and the closest thing Kiah knew to a grandmother. It was gonna be rough on them all when Blanche left the day after tomorrow.

But Oliver gave his head a small shake and leaned against the back of the bench. "You need this time to reconnect with *your* daughter. You don't need to worry about Kiah and me. Besides, I can't stand the humidity down there." He winked. Not that Mason City, Iowa, didn't have its fair share of hot, humid weather in the summer, especially now in the middle of August, but he liked his four seasons.

"I still don't understand why you don't go back ho—"

"I'm not going back." He clenched his jaw at the mere thought. It had been a long time since he'd considered Deep Haven home.

"The house is paid for and in your name. Why not?"

Go back to his hometown as a washed-up plumber to the place where everyone knew his history? Saw him as some pathetic kid whose parents had died?

No thanks.

His eye caught on the list again. Sure, a lot of the people he needed to talk to from that list were from Deep Haven. Okay, all of them. But he didn't have to move there to make amends. That was what phones were for.

Maybe a short visit if he had to.

Very short.

"Nice try, but I don't need the house. I've got her."

Oliver stood as he watched his lawyer approach. Blanche stayed seated on the bench. She didn't have much to say about the woman in the sharp pencil skirt and blazer, but Monica Emiliano was supposed to be the best lawyer in Cerro Gordo County. And nothing but the best was good enough for his little girl.

Monica nodded a greeting. "You have the list?"

"Of course." Oliver handed her the wrinkled paper. Her mouth tightened as she took in the frayed edges and chocolate smudge. He gave her a self-deprecating grin. "I probably should've typed it up, but I've been so busy with Kiah. Hope that's okay. Nice earrings, by the way. Are they heirlooms?"

Monica fingered the delicate pearls and softened her expression. "My grandmother gave them to me." She set down her briefcase and tried smoothing out the wrinkles in the paper. "We'll use the sentimental value of the handwritten note and Kiah's little doodle on here. Show the judge that you value your daughter's artistic expression. Anything else I should know about before we go in there?"

"Nope. I know you'll do great. Kiah and I are trusting you."

Her lips pursed again. "So no news on the job front?"

"Don't worry about that. As it is, we've been busy trying to get Hezekiah's affairs in order. Helping close out his estate and making sure Kiah is adjusting okay."

Monica sighed. "It would've been better for the case if you had a job right now." She tilted her head and stared him down.

"You have Hezekiah's reference letter for me, right? I can get a job with any plumbing contractor in a hot second. They're screaming for journeymen." He nudged her arm. "And with the best lawyer in town, this will be an open-and-shut case. We'll be out of here in no time."

Monica quirked an eyebrow as if to say *I hope you're right.* Blanche just huffed.

But they would see. This was *his* kid, for goodness' sake. Why was it even an issue? But he kept his grin in place—a show of confidence he couldn't afford to lose. All this hubbub simply because Jalisa's sister thought he wasn't a good enough dad. He had a lot to make up for, sure, but that didn't mean Cassandra could come in and take Kiah away.

A bailiff opened the door and called them in.

"Let's do this." Oliver straightened his tie and held the door open for the ladies. A typical courtroom lay before him with a judge sitting on a raised desk at the front of the room. Two long tables faced the judge, and an empty gallery of pews took up a majority of the space. Across from the table where Monica set her briefcase sat Cassandra with her lawyer, a tall guy who barely fit into his suit. His broad chest and shoulders dwarfed his client next to him. The guy had to be six and a half feet at least. Cassandra merely glanced at Oliver and wrinkled her nose as if she smelled something she didn't like.

The judge motioned for everyone to sit. She read off a tablet. "Let's get started. We're here with Ms. Cassandra Freeby challenging the custody of one Kiah Louise Jackson, currently with Oliver Fox." She set the tablet down and turned toward Cassandra. "Ms. Freeby, it's my understanding that Mr. Fox is the biological parent, and your sister, deceased Jalisa Jackson, was the mother, correct?"

"Yes, Your Honor."

"And why are you challenging custody? He is Kiah's father."

Oliver smirked. This might be easier than he thought.

"He isn't a father. He was a one-night stand, and my sister's biggest regret. But I've known Kiah since the moment she was born. I'm a stay-at-home mother of three, and my children and Kiah are more like siblings than cousins. My husband has a stable and good job. She would be better off with us. There's no way he should have custody."

The judge folded her hands on the desk in front of her. "And why is that?"

Oliver stood up. "With all due respect, Your Honor, I made some mistakes. No one is denying that. But I'm—"

"Mistakes? You're a drunk, Oliver."

Monica jumped to her feet before Oliver could say anything. "Excuse me, Your Honor." She handed the judge a stack of papers. "It was Jalisa Jackson's final wish before she died that my client have custody of their daughter."

"With stipulations." Cassandra's lawyer pointed at the papers.

Monica continued as if she hadn't heard him. "Obviously she could've left the girl with Ms. Freeby at that point, but she chose Oliver Fox, Kiah's *father*."

Cassandra popped up off her chair. "Jalisa wasn't in her right mind when she wrote that. She was sick."

Monica slowly paced in front of the table. "The will was documented and signed by a lawyer stating she was fully capable of this decision. She gave custody to my client."

Cassandra was about to say more as the judge read over the will, but Brawny the Lawyer stayed her with a hand on her arm.

The judge looked up from the document. "It says here that you were to be awarded custody, Mr. Fox, under the stipulation of completing a recovery program and continuing mentorship with a Mr. Hezekiah Jackson, Ms. Jackson and Ms. Freeby's uncle. Are you an addict?"

They'd known this would come up. No big deal. Still, the

squeeze in Oliver's throat gave him pause for a moment. "I'm a recovering alcoholic. But I've been sober for three years."

"And have you completed a recovery program? Where is Mr. Jackson?" The judge narrowed her eyes as she looked down on him.

"He died. Last month," Monica answered for him.

Oliver was still reeling from it. They all were. But he'd been through worse. And this court had another thing coming if they thought he would just sit here and let his baby girl be taken away from him too.

Monica moved toward the center of the room. "That's why we're here. Ms. Freeby here is using Mr. Jackson's death as a chance to spitefully take Kiah away from her own father."

Right on!

Cassandra stood. "I'm not being spiteful. I'm looking out for Kiah's best interests." She leaned over the table to look past her lawyer and face Oliver. "You don't deserve her. You know that."

Her words found their mark. But as much as it killed Oliver to hold back, he had to play this cool. For Kiah's sake. It had become his mantra since the caseworker showed up on his doorstep with her five months ago. And his girl's bright smile, her dark, curly hair framing her sweet face, was all he needed to think about.

Oliver smoothed down his tie and kept a pleasant expression plastered on his face as he met Cassie's fiery stare. "I'm her father. And like it or not, it was Jalisa's choice. Why are we even here?"

"Then why didn't you file for joint custody when Jalisa was alive?" the judge asked.

Oliver swallowed. Yeah, that sounded bad. But it wasn't like that. "Ms. Freeby failed to mention that I wasn't informed of Kiah's existence until she was almost two."

"Is that true, Ms. Freeby?"

Cassandra stared at the desk, answering with a quick nod.

"And what happened then, Mr. Fox?"

"Jalisa and I wanted to try to be a family. I married her. She and Kiah moved in. But it was quickly apparent that Jalisa and I weren't compatible. After a few months she wanted to move to Ohio, where she had a job offer."

"And you just let her go?"

"I love my daughter more than life itself, but what kind of man would I be to try to rip her away from her own mother when she was that young? I never wanted Kiah to have to choose between the two of us, and even though Jalisa and I were not a good mix, she *was* a good mom. When she left, I sent child support. I saw Kiah whenever I could."

"And how often was that? A few times a year?" Cassie huffed.

"I was working to support them." Not to mention trying to make something of himself, finishing up an apprenticeship so he could make a better wage. Trying to be the kind of dad his father had been. A dad Kiah could be proud of. Because the truth was, before she crashed into his life, he'd been spiraling fast. But meeting Kiah had been the wake-up call he'd needed to get his life together. He'd still been trying to wrap his head around the fact that he was a father when Jalisa left again. "And remember, I wasn't the one that moved seven hundred miles away."

Monica cleared her throat. "Your Honor, back to the issue at hand, my client has been sober for over three years. Here is Hezekiah Jackson's statement and letter of reference. They were close to finishing the twelve steps of AA at the time of Mr. Jackson's death. Mr. Fox is perfectly capable of caring for his daughter, just as he has been for the five months she's been in his custody."

"But he didn't complete the AA steps?"

Oliver could speak for himself on this. "No, but I'm close—"

"Close is not complete, Mr. Fox." The judge continued to scan the documents, barely looking at him.

Cassie smirked on the other side of the room. "Where are you even going to live? Or work? I saw Hezekiah's shop was up for sale. And we all know my uncle only gave you a job out of pity."

Now the judge looked directly at Oliver. "Are you currently employed?"

"Well, no, but—"

"No job? Now, that's a problem." The judge dropped the papers in her hand and stared him down. "What is your living situation? How do you plan to financially support your daughter?"

"We've been busy selling Mr. Jackson's business to pay for his medical expenses. I'm a journeyman plumber, licensed in three states now. I can get a job anywhere."

"And living arrangements? It says here you were living in apartments above the plumbing business. Were they sold too?"

"They were. So now I'm looking—"

"So let me get this straight. You haven't finished the recovery program. You have no job. And you have no housing. I fail to see how this is a good indicator of your ability to take care of your daughter, Mr. Fox."

Oliver wouldn't shrink under the judge's hard stare, but he was having a hard time finding the words to defend himself.

Blanche spoke up. "He has a home, Your Honor. And he's workin' on his steps. He has a list."

The judge swung her attention to Blanche. "And you are?"

"Blanche Middleton. I live in the apartments too and help watch Kiah when Ollie here is working. He's a good man. You can't take her away."

Good man? Not hardly. But he was willing to do anything for Kiah. He was trying. Didn't that count for something?

"And what's this home you have, Mr. Fox? And list?" the judge asked.

Oliver opened his mouth to speak, but Monica gave him a small shake of her head. She handed his list to the judge. "This is steps eight and nine of the twelve steps of Alcoholics Anonymous. My client made this list with his sponsor, of people he will make amends with. He is committed to finishing the process."

"If this is steps eight and nine, what about steps ten through twelve?"

Monica stood before the bench. "The next steps after this are simply to continue to take inventory of himself, to use prayer and meditation, and to reach out to other alcoholics. And, again, he's been sober for over three years."

While the judge read down the list, he tried not to fidget. Or yell. He'd rather take on Cassie's giant lawyer in a boxing ring than sit here waiting.

Kiah. He was doing this for Kiah.

Judge Clancy finally looked up from the smudged paper. "I'd like you to answer me directly, Mr. Fox." She waved the paper. "Who are these people on your list?"

Oliver cleared his throat. "My high school football coach, a couple classmates, people from my hometown, and the rest are"—as much as part of him wanted to drop eye contact under the judge's weighty stare, he didn't—"family. My brother, sister, and grandparents."

"You still don't have a home. Where is Kiah supposed to sleep? You don't have a job. How can I leave a five-year-old girl in your care when you don't have the basic necessities to support yourself?"

Cassandra leaned back in her chair and smiled like she'd already won. Her lawyer started packing up the papers in front of him. Monica even looked at him with that told-you-so expression. She was giving up too.

Blanche pinched his arm under the table. "Ollie!" she hissed quietly.

Fine. If this was what it took to keep his baby, he would do it. Even if his next words gutted him.

He jumped to his feet. "I have a house, Your Honor."

"And pray tell, where is this house? Because there's no way I can award you custody of your daughter without one." The judge waited.

Oliver clenched his jaw tight and got a handle on the churning within. "It's in Deep Haven, Minnesota. In fact, that's where most of the people I need to make amends with are."

"If you have a house, why aren't you there now?" the judge asked.

"My grandparents recently retired and moved south. They split up their properties and gave my siblings and myself each a piece. My sister got the family bakery. My brother received a city lot, and I got the family home. It all happened within the last few months, and that's when Hezekiah got sick. I wasn't going to abandon him in his time of need."

"And you plan to move there with Kiah?" the judge asked.

The air grew thick. Heavy. Everything hinged on his next words. Oliver scraped together the bottom of his reserves to spit out his answer. Probably the only answer this judge would accept. "Yes, Your Honor."

She held his stare a beat longer and then nodded. "All right then. I will award you *temporary* custody. I want you back here in three months with a statement from each person on this list that you have made amends. I want proof of housing and employment, and random welfare checks will be made for Kiah's sake at some point in these next months. During these checks, if it is perceived that Kiah is not doing well, she will be removed immediately. And if you do not have your affairs in order by the time we meet again, I will have no choice but to place Kiah where she can best thrive. Understood?"

Oliver nodded.

"I'll see you in November." The judge walked away and out a back door in the room.

Blanche clapped him on the shoulder. "I knew you could do it, Ollie."

Monica shook his hand. "It might not be a slam dunk, but

considering the circumstances, we'll take this as a good start. You've got some work to do."

Good thing work didn't scare him.

But now he had to move back home. And that would be his biggest battle yet.

🐺🐺🐺

DR. LENA LARSON WASN'T SAD TO BE IN THE JANOWSKIS' BARN staring at a mare's hind quarters rather than at the Dahlquist wedding back in town. The earthy scent of straw and animals surrounded her as she reached into the birth canal. Nick and Jae might be some of her closest friends, but with the rest of Deep Haven attending the sunset nuptials, she wouldn't be missed.

Here, she was needed.

This foal should've been out and suckling by now. The summer heat in the barn pressed in on her. Sweat trickled down her back.

Ah. There's the problem. Lena's fingers wrapped around the fetus's errant hoof and pulled it into place. The mare's flanks twitched.

"No wonder labor stopped. Thankfully the shoulder wasn't caught. Just the elbow." Lena backed away slowly. With the foal now in true "diving position," it would be a matter of moments and the mama would do the rest of the work.

Mr. Janowski's furrowed brows relaxed. "I'm glad you're here, Doc. I didn't know what to do for Cupid."

With a quick nod of acknowledgment, Lena joined him. "It was good you called. It's not a major complication, but it could've easily become one." Besides, Lena should be thanking *him* for rescuing the mixed-breed mare last year after she was found at a shack out in the sticks, malnourished and dehydrated.

But Lena didn't have the words, and Mr. Janowski didn't

seem to need them, intent as he was on watching the wonder before them.

Two hooves and a dark nose wrapped in the white inner membrane presented.

"One more push, mama," Lena whispered.

Within seconds the bay-colored foal lay on the clean straw. Lena helped clear the membrane away, and the foal drew its first breath.

Lena's heart squeezed.

Even Mr. Janowski teared up as they watched the mare nuzzle her newborn. "Well, doesn't that just beat all. Probably commonplace to you, but..." He leaned on the gate of the corral with a sigh of wonder. "Wow."

"Every birth is a miracle." Lena washed her hands in the bucket of soapy water next to the stall. "So, what will you call this little guy?"

"The grandkids already decided. They're sticking with the Christmas theme. Comet." He grinned like a proud papa.

Yes, Cupid, and now Comet, had found a good home with the Janowskis. And those were some lucky grandkids. If only—

Stop it, Lena.

No one could change their past or choose their family. At least she'd had Birdie and Howard Dawson when she was growing up. Like the Janowskis, they'd taken in a lot of strays.

Including her. Not that she'd ever lived with them, but she might as well have used their address as her own for as often as she was at their house.

After a quick examination, Lena gathered her bag and told Mr. Janowski what to expect for the rest of the evening. "And remember, if she doesn't pass that whole placenta in the next three hours, call me back."

"Yes, ma'am." He checked his watch. "Sorry you missed that wedding. I feel awful—"

"Don't. I'm glad to help. Besides, I'll still make it to the reception."

"Make sure you bill me extra for the house call."

No way would she charge extra or even send a bill. Not many people were willing to take a neglected, unwanted animal. Especially one as big and expensive as a horse. But they'd had this discussion before, so why bother saying anything?

They walked out of the barn together. "Don't worry about it. I should probably pay you for getting me out of having to sit through a wedding. Especially in this heat."

They might be in the north woods of Minnesota, but a heavy and hot wind bore down on them. The front of gray clouds moving in off Lake Superior didn't bode well for an outdoor reception.

"Not your idea of a good time?" Mr. Janowski asked.

"There's been a bunch of them lately. That's all." And truth be told they were getting a little old.

So much money and fuss. Nick Dahlquist might be a pretty decent guy, great with his sled dogs, but at the end of the day, he was still a guy. She certainly didn't need a man complicating *her* life, but hopefully Jae was happy.

After saying goodbye, Lena checked her phone. Speaking of fuss, twenty-two missed messages and five phone calls. All but one from her friend and next-door neighbor Robin Fox.

Lena called Robin from her truck as she left the Janowskis' long driveway.

"Where have you been?" Robin asked.

"Horse emergency."

"You sure you're not saying that so you could get out of the wedding?"

"It was a matter of life and death. I don't think you can say the same for Nick and Jae's wedding."

"Fine. But you're on your way to the reception now, right?"

"Do you really want me showing up in my mud boots and barn suit? And if you don't believe me about where I was, you should take a sniff of the boots. I don't wear them for mud."

"Ew! Just get changed and get over here. I'll save a spot at our table."

By *save a spot* she meant she'd drag a chair over, because there were only even numbers at reception tables, and Lena was the only single in their group. Not that she minded being single at all. But watching the others now that they were all paired up could get a little nauseating. Especially during the slow songs. Lena would be better off with a quiet evening at home.

Robin's voice cut through her musings. "And don't even think of backing out. You promised to help me with the cleanup afterward."

"Right." Because that's what good single friends did. Stayed 'til the bitter end and cleaned up the mess. So much for curling up with her pups and Korean dramas tonight. "I'll be there soon."

Lena ended the call with a groan. Looked like she still had to squeeze into that dress Robin left at her house after all. At least with it being a Dahlquist reception, she could count on some good food. And hopefully it was set up inside somewhere, since big raindrops splashed against her windshield as she made her way home.

Lena parked in her garage and opened the door to the kitchen. Wentworth, a big yellow Lab mix, pawed at her leg for attention while Jane, a fluffy but tiny mutt of unknown breeding, circled her feet.

"Hey, now. You both know how to behave. Sit."

They immediately sat and waited expectantly. She grabbed two treats, let loose a big grin, and crooned, "Now, who's a good puppy? Did you miss me?"

The two fur babies converged on her, licking her and wagging their tails. Definitely the best part of her day. Lena fed each one a treat. "I missed you too." She kissed them both.

"Have you been behaving yourselves?" She toed off the boots and did a quick sweep of the house. Kitchen was in order. The hardwood floors in the dining and living areas clean, the gray and black living room furniture all at right angles, and the rugs straight. One lone chew toy lay on the couch. Lena swiped it up and dropped it in the basket on the way to her bedroom.

She pulled down the hanger with the borrowed dress and grimaced. The navy beaded floral design wasn't really her style. Give Lena her scrubs and khakis any day. Even better, her soft Deep Haven sweatshirt, pajama pants, and a bowl of Cherry Garcia ice cream. Add her dogs and her latest entertainment obsession and it would be the perfect night.

How K-dramas sucked her in, she couldn't say. But one episode of *Cinderella and the Four Knights* and she was hooked. The dogs loved it too.

A loud boom of thunder shook the house.

Wentworth whined at her feet while Jane lay on the bed completely at ease.

"It's only a little thunder, you big baby." She kneeled down and stroked the Lab's blocky head. "You know I would rather stay here too, but I've got a wedding reception to get to. You'll be okay."

Her phone rang from the kitchen. Was it bad that she hoped for another animal emergency?

Probably.

She checked the phone. Why would Birdie be calling? Lena hit the green icon to answer.

"Lena, you have to come, quick!"

Definitely sounded like an emergency.

"Where are you? Are you at your apartment?"

"We need you at the shelter!"

"The shelter? What happened? Birdie?" The call must've cut out.

Lena jumped back into her boots. After grabbing her raincoat, she rushed for her truck and left.

Maybe she shouldn't go wishing for emergencies.

Lightning lit the sky in bursts followed by more thunder. Sheets of rain blew against the truck as she drove down the hill and into town. As Lena pulled up to the block where Deep Haven Animal Shelter was located, she spied the flashing red and blue emergency lights. Firefighters were here?

That couldn't be good. She ran from her car and yanked the door open. Water from the lobby gushed out and onto her boots. Inside the building, the only lights were the emergency exit signs casting an eerie red glow on the mismatched plastic chairs and reception counter. Water covered the floor. Voices over radios and chatter sounded from the back of the building.

"Birdie? Where are you?" Lena skirted around a cardboard box floating through the room.

"Back here!"

Lena sloshed through the hall to the kennel area. Birdie and Jensen Atwood herded a calico cat into a pet carrier. In the corner of the room, water poured down the wall through an opening in the roof that had been covered with a tarp.

"How did that get there?" Lena pointed at the gaping hole. "Where is Gavin?"

"I don't know." Birdie had to yell over the fire alarms going off and three more cats meowing in angst from carriers on the counter that ran along one side of the room. Birdie's long gray hair hung in wet strands. Her T-shirt and pants clung to her thin frame as she shut the carrier. "Haven't seen him since Monday."

"He was supposed to fix that roof. You mean he hasn't been here at all this week?"

Seriously, were there no reliable men in the world? Lena reached for the last cat in the enclosure, a gray tabby, and scanned the room, taking in the peeling paint on cinder block walls, the chipped counters, and worn linoleum floors. Sure, she wanted to bulldoze the place every time she walked in, but for these animals it was better than nothing. And thankfully, Birdie and the other volunteers made up for what the building lacked with a lot of love and attention.

And now, thanks to Gavin, they had nothing. Good thing he wasn't here so she couldn't wring his neck.

But really, it was her fault. She knew better than to depend on a man.

The tabby cat scratched Lena's hand and almost bolted out of her grasp.

She couldn't blame the poor thing one bit. Lena carefully placed the cat in the remaining carrier.

"Where are the dogs?" she asked Birdie and Jensen.

Jensen took the carrier in hand. "Two are in the back of Birdie's car. They're scared, but they're dry at least. A couple more are in my SUV. The three bigger dogs are in the outdoor fenced area. They have that small shelter, but they're probably still getting wet. I didn't know where else to put them."

Peter Dahlquist, fire chief and—guessing from the tuxedo he wore and the fact that he was Nick's cousin—best man at the wedding, rushed in. "Everyone okay?"

"It's raining inside the building," Lena said, "so, no, we're not okay."

Peter ignored her sarcasm and waved them toward the door. "You need to get out. Now."

"What's going on?" Jensen asked.

"We've got tornado and hail warnings. Not to mention the structural integrity of the whole roof is compromised."

Birdie's expression went from frantic to pure terror. "What are we going to do? The animals. If I still had the house—" She pushed the wet hair out of her face.

But she didn't. Once Howard passed away last year, Birdie had moved from their remote little house in the woods down the road from Lena to the senior apartments in town. Apartments that would not allow animals.

There was only one solution. "We'll take them to my place."

"But, Lena, they'll tear your place apart. It's so small," Birdie said.

Peter stepped farther into the room and grabbed one of the cat carriers. "We don't have a choice. We need to go. Now."

"It'll be fine. We'll set up some temporary kennels in the

garage," Lena yelled over the yowling and thunder to Jensen across the room. "Help me load the big dogs in my truck." Turning to Birdie, she pointed to the cat carriers. "Load them in your car and any bins of food you can carry. Peter can help."

By the time they had the various animals loaded into three different vehicles, Lena was soaked. She drove carefully on the slick and muddy roads with Peter, Jensen, and Birdie following behind her. She breathed easier once the caravan of vehicles all made it to her house. In the garage, they set up two temporary kennels with extra fencing they'd managed to free from the shelter. One of the bigger dogs, a mastiff Birdie called Bruce, absolutely refused to go into the kennel with the other dogs.

He darted away every time Lena tried to coax him in. He finally lay down at Birdie's feet and refused to move.

"He does this at the shelter too. He barely tolerates being in a kennel alone, and he's fine with other dogs outside a kennel, but he won't do both."

"Fine, I'll take him inside for now." He easily followed Lena into the house, instantly putting Wentworth and Jane in a tizzy. He jerked out of her hold and lunged for her light-gray couch.

"No!"

Too late. With his huge muddy paws and sopping wet body, Bruce leaped for the couch and shook. He made himself at home while Wentworth cowered in the corner and Jane barked from under the coffee table. She couldn't leave them like this while she went back out to the garage.

"Come on, big boy." Lena brought the big rescue dog to the main bathroom and set out food and water in the tub for him. He was happily chomping away when she closed the door and went back to help the others.

Jensen and Peter finished securing the kennels while Birdie and Lena found towels and blankets. By the time they were all situated, most of the animals had quieted down and were sleeping.

"Lena, you can't keep them here forever. What are we going

to do?" Birdie squeezed her hands together and blew on them. She'd lost so much weight since Howard passed away, and now she was soaked clear through.

"I'll think of something." Lena grabbed her winter coat from the labeled container on one of the shelves and draped it over Birdie's thin shoulders. "Go home and rest. Everyone's okay for now."

"But Bruce, he needs—"

"Birdie, go home. Bruce is fine."

"We just haven't found the right person for him. He's a lot, I know—"

"We'll take care of this tomorrow."

"I don't know how you stay so calm, Lena." Birdie squeezed Lena in a tight hug—the only one who ever dared to do so.

Apparently, Lena had Birdie fooled, because with all the problems with this arrangement screaming at her, she was anything but calm inside.

But no need to let anyone else see that. Lena thanked the others and went back into the house. Bruce barked from behind the bathroom door. When Lena opened it, he shot out and down the hall. In the thirty minutes she'd left him alone, he'd pulled down the shower curtain, ripping holes in it, chewed a corner of the cabinet raw, tipped over the small garbage bin, and made a steaming mess on the rug.

Lena grabbed her cleaning bucket and mop.

Maybe a wedding wouldn't have been so bad.

two

. . .

HEZEKIAH'S OLD PLUMBING VAN—THE ONLY THING ACE PLUMBING *didn't* want—rumbled down Highway 61 toward Deep Haven. Based on his glance in the rearview mirror at the frown on Kiah's face, Oliver still had a lot of convincing to do. The sulking wasn't much better than the tears she'd shed yesterday. Tears at the Duluth Zoo. Tears at the waterpark hotel they'd stayed at last night. Tears every time he had to buckle her back in her booster seat. With all she'd been through, including Blanche's departure for Florida two weeks ago, how could he blame her for being upset? He just wished he could find a way to reach her. As much as he'd tried to bond with her since she'd moved in last March, Kiah still held back, treated him more like a stranger than a father.

Not the greatest first impression for his family to get when they meet Kiah. Of course, it also might help if his sister, Robin, knew Kiah existed, but it was a little late now.

His thumbs tapped the steering wheel. "Hey, cupcake, what do you think?" He pointed out her window at the afternoon sunlight glinting off the sapphire blue waters of Lake Superior when they passed a break in the trees. "This is where Daddy grew up."

She squeezed her stuffed elephant and mumbled.

"What was that, sweetheart?"

"I said, it's just a dumb lake."

"Look at those bikers on the bike path though. It goes for miles and miles along the lake. Won't that be fun? We can go for a ride, maybe even have a picnic. We're going to have lots of adventures up here."

She gave him a half-hearted shrug and looked away.

Nope. Not impressed at all. And the road to Deep Haven was only getting shorter.

Even if they wouldn't be in town long, it would be nice if Kiah could create some good memories here. Like the kind he had from back in the day when his best friend had been his brother Grayson and their favorite pastime had been teasing Robin and her friend Lena, who'd lived next door. Back when they'd spent hours in the woods behind Grandpa's little barn. Or when Dad had taken them on camping trips and they'd fished off the dock at Flour Lake. Back when they'd been a real family.

Of course, his parents were gone and the Fox children were all grown up now, hardly in contact. Just add it to the list of all the things he'd messed up.

Yeah. He should've called. The house might be in his name, but Robin was the one living there and paying utilities. Why had he thought surprising her would be a good idea?

"Are we almost to Deep Haven?" Kiah asked.

Considering they'd already passed the ski lodge and swanky luxury resort a ways back, yup. "We're almost there."

Looked like Moose Ridge Resort had gotten a new sign in the last twelve years. And the supper club had closed? Oliver stared at the sign in the window. When had that happened? The place had always been busy back in the day.

And there it was—Deep Haven, the little town nestled along the bay. Lazy boats bobbed on the water. Tourists were scattered along the rocky shoreline. He didn't remember it being so busy on a weekday before. And were those new streetlights?

He couldn't avoid it now. He was fast approaching his hometown after having been gone over a decade, and nothing was the same.

"Daddy!" Kiah screamed.

Oliver whipped his focus back to the road, where a small black-and-white goat pranced into the middle of his lane and stood. He slammed on the brakes. Tires squealed and the van slid to an abrupt stop.

Had he hit it?

With a glance to make sure nobody was behind him, Oliver jumped out of the driver's seat and ran around the van. There in the road lay the goat.

Kiah's sobbing carried out the open driver's side door. "Did you kill it?"

"Kiah, stay in the car."

He hated to use such a sharp tone with her, but he needed to keep her safe. Watching her through the windshield, he waited until she nodded.

Oliver squatted down and studied the black-and-white goat. There was no blood, no injury he could see at all. But the animal didn't move. It lay on its side with four legs sticking straight out. Weird yellow eyes stared at Oliver, but the goat didn't make a sound. The van wasn't even touching it.

Sheesh. Two seconds in town and already Oliver had a disaster on his hands. A couple cars sped past, honking. Kiah's sobs continued.

"It'll be okay, sweetie. Stay calm."

Maybe he needed those words more for himself than for his daughter. He for sure needed to get this animal out of the road. Did Dr. Johanson still have an office down near the library? Oliver ran to the passenger side door and snagged his jacket off the seat.

"Is it dead? Did you kill it, Dad?"

Oliver took a moment to look his girl in the eye. "It's not dead. We're going to get some help. All right?"

She sniffed. "Okay."

He scooped up the goat with his jacket and laid the stiff animal in the seat before getting back behind the wheel. Ignoring the goat's accusing eyes and more honking cars, Oliver focused straight ahead and started driving. He passed a new brewery and the old ice-cream place.

"Where are we going?" Kiah asked.

Before Oliver could answer, the goat shot up and stood on the seat and gave a loud bleat.

Kiah screamed.

Oliver braked.

The goat jumped to the floor of the van, went stiff-legged again, and fell over like a toy figurine being knocked down.

What in the world? Oliver glanced at the animal on the floor of his passenger side, then scanned the sign on the last building on the block.

Pet Haven Veterinary Clinic.

Finally. Oliver pulled up to the curb. Dr. Johanson must've changed the name of the place. Once more he gathered the stiff goat in his arms. Kiah unbuckled.

"Follow me," he told her as he crossed the sidewalk and used his back to push open the door of the clinic.

He stood in the middle of a clean lobby with gray and lime-green furniture. An empty reception desk to one side blocked access to a shelf full of immaculately organized medications, supplements, and an assortment of pet supplies. But not a person was in sight.

"Help. Please?" The goat wasn't heavy, but with its legs sticking straight out like rigor mortis had already set in, it was awfully awkward to carry.

Someone certainly had brought Dr. Johanson's place into the modern age. No more linoleum flooring or old posters for flea and tick meds with the corners curling. Instead, the floor was tiled and the walls held framed black-and-white pictures of dogs and cats.

Oliver turned in a slow circle. "Hello?"

The goat went limp in his arms and bleated again. His little goat legs started kicking, one of the hooves catching Oliver in the groin.

Umph!

Oliver dropped the creature and bent over in pain.

"Oh, for the love of—" he groaned.

The goat must've been fine. It landed on all four legs, leaped onto the nearest green chair, and proceeded to prance from seat to coffee table and back to the seat, bleating as though it was enjoying Oliver's misfortune. Another hop and it landed on a counter with a coffee pod machine. Little hooves knocked over a stack of disposable coffee cups and lids.

Kiah stared. "Dad, do something!"

Stirring sticks and packets of sugar and cream flew through the air, landing all over the seats and the floor.

"I'm trying," he said through clenched teeth. He managed to stand straight.

"She's making a big mess. You have to catch her!" Kiah backed up and moved behind a chair.

"Easier said than done, kiddo." Oliver reached out to grab the goat but missed. It jumped onto the table. Bending over, the goat bit off the cover of the magazine under its hooves.

"No!" Oliver lunged toward it before it could destroy anything else.

The goat stopped mid-bleat, stiffened, and then fell once more into Oliver's arms with its legs straight out and half a Maybelline ad in its mouth.

"What's going on out here?" A familiar voice, a little shrill and very annoyed, carried over Oliver's shoulders as he spun around with the goat in his hold once more.

"And what happened to my lobby?"

Lena Larson.

Number five on his list of people he had to make amends with.

Out of all the things that had changed over the years, he couldn't help but smile at one of the things that hadn't.

Her scowl as she stared at him.

And oh, how he had loved to make her scowl.

Although that facial expression hadn't changed, a lot about Lena had. She had matured from a stick-thin teenager with braces to a woman whose scrubs couldn't hide her curves. Straight brown hair framed big green eyes and full lips. Lips that pinched into a straight, unrelenting line.

"Oliver Fox." She released a short breath. "I should've known it was you."

He chuckled. "Whatever do you mean?"

"Who else could destroy a perfectly ordered lobby in the ten seconds I've been gone? And what have you done to that poor animal?" Using the stethoscope around her neck, she examined the goat while Oliver continued to hold it. A whiff of a sweet lemony scent hit him as Lena leaned in. It wasn't the same fragrance she'd used when they were in high school. No, this one fit her better. Clean, but like the tart fruit, there were underlying notes of sweetness. A smattering of freckles scattered across her nose and cheeks. Those were new. And as she felt for a pulse on the animal, her eyes and lips softened.

Well, that was new too. A softer side of Lena Larson?

She glanced up at him. "You didn't answer my question. What did you do to the goat?"

"Uh." He cleared his throat. "I might have hit it with my van."

"Might have?"

"It came out of nowhere and was standing in the middle of the highway. I tried to stop."

Her pursed lips and glare said she didn't believe him. "Let me guess. You were by the putt-putt place?"

"Yeah. Since when did they add barnyard animals to the attraction?"

The goat grew heavy in his arms and went from stiff to

mobile once again. Oliver trapped its legs quickly before they could kick, but it was like wrestling with a greased pig. "Never mind. Don't answer. Come on, Lena. You've got to help me." He spoke through gritted teeth as the goat bleated and squirmed. Adjusting his hold, he caught three of its legs in his hands. One back leg kicked free. "Please!"

He looked up to see the tiniest smirk on her face.

"You're enjoying this, aren't you?" he asked as he grabbed for the kicking leg.

"What are you doing here, Oliver?" She was all serious now as she continued assessing the goat.

"I'm...bringing you a goat."

"No, really, what—"

The goat's leg caught him in the stomach. The air in Oliver's lungs whooshed out. "Lena!" He grunted and caught the hoof before it could kick again. "Is that really important right now? This animal needs your help."

"Are you talking about you or the goat?"

Yeah. She was enjoying this.

"And for the record, I *am* helping it. I had to make sure it didn't have any broken legs. You can put it down now. It will be fine."

"Dr. Larson, do you need anything?" Another woman in green scrubs walked into the room.

The clattering of princess dress-up shoes on the tile floor drew everyone's attention to Kiah. "Dad, is the goat okay?"

Lena's jaw dropped. She stared from Kiah to Oliver. "Did she say—"

"I'll pay whatever I need to pay. Just tell me you'll help this goat. There's gotta be something wrong with it, the way it keeps falling over."

She lost the amusement that had crept into her tone before the others came in. "Of course I'm going to take care of the goat." She turned to the other lady. "Sheila, can you take our new patient back to Exam Room One?"

"Sure, Dr. Larson." She reached into her scrubs pocket for a small treat and held it out to the goat. It followed her obediently out of the room.

Lena looped her stethoscope around her neck. "It's most likely a fainting goat. It's normal behavior for the breed, but I'll check it over thoroughly."

"What's a painting goat?" Kiah asked.

Lena gave his daughter a tiny sliver of a smile. "Fainting goat. When startled or scared, they go stiff and fall over. And after a little while, they get up again. It doesn't hurt them."

"But Daddy ran into it."

"We're going to check it out and make sure it's okay."

Oliver rested his hands on Kiah's shoulders. "Thanks, that—"

"Does Robin know you're here?" Lena lost her ghost of a smile and speared him with a look, eyes narrowed. "I talked with her this morning. She never mentioned you were coming."

"I wanted to surprise her. So, no, we haven't seen her yet. But we're on our way, right, kiddo? This is Kiah, by the way."

Kiah nodded with a shy smile. It was more than she gave Oliver lately. Hopefully it boded well for meeting Robin.

Lena showed her a basket of stickers and some coloring sheets in the far corner of the room. "Go ahead and pick some out to take with you."

While Kiah decided which ones to take, Lena walked back to him. "Surprises, huh? You're definitely full of those, Oliver."

He quirked his eyebrow and grinned. "What can I say—"

"I didn't say that was a good thing."

Oh.

"But I hope you're going home to see Robin next. I won't keep you any longer."

The passive-aggressive dismissal. He was definitely in Minnesota.

While Lena said goodbye sweetly to Kiah, she tossed him one last glance of accusation and disappointment as she left the room.

Yep. That was still the same too.

"So, that lady is going to fix the goat?" Kiah tugged on Oliver's hand.

He nodded as he scooped her up. "Yup. She's going to fix the goat." But now he had a lot of fixing of his own to do.

⊱⊱⊱

She had an animal to treat and a business to run.

It didn't matter that Lena could hear her own pulse thundering in her head. That her past had just waltzed through her door, upsetting her lobby and her precarious handle on her emotions.

Everything was fine. Just. Fine.

Maryann, her vet tech who was only a few years younger, stood across the exam room table from Lena in her matching green-and-gray scrubs, her dark-brown hair pulled back in a ponytail. She stared at Lena rather than the goat on the table between them. "Was that Oliver Fox?"

"Yes." Lena focused on sliding her hand into the latex gloves she'd grabbed.

"Didn't you two have a thing back in high school?"

A thing? Was that what one called it? A relationship dating back to childhood that included Oliver tormenting her throughout her elementary years? One that had developed into a fierce rivalry throughout high school and a horrible teenage crush, then ended in utter humiliation? What kind of label did one put on that?

Something like "the biggest mistake of her life" would be close but still didn't encapsulate it all.

Lena swallowed down the bitter memories.

Memories she had no intention of sharing. Now, back to

picking up the pieces he'd left behind... "Let's make sure the goat isn't injured."

Lena checked each limb, carefully sliding her hand down the legs while Maryann still stared.

"Really? We're not going to talk about how the extremely handsome prodigal son of Deep Haven has returned after how many years? And has a daughter?! How did—"

"Maryann, we have more important things to do here than gossip. The goat."

Her vet tech rolled her eyes. "We both know it's one of the fainting goats from the mini-golf place. They fall down at the tiniest little scare. It's probably fine."

As if to prove her point, the goat hopped off the table. It wandered around the room and made a puddle in the corner.

Lena snagged paper towels by the sink to clean up the mess. "Yes, it's most likely a myotonic goat. But 'probably fine' is not the way we do things around here. Oliver hit it with his vehicle. I need X-rays to make sure there's no internal organ damage or broken ribs. Have Sheila help you."

"Whoa-kay." Maryann snapped on gloves and grabbed treats from the counter. "Come here, goat." She held a treat in her hand, and the goat followed her out the door, bleating down the hall to the X-ray room.

As soon as the door shut, Lena slumped against the table and closed her eyes.

Oliver Fox was back.

And he had a daughter.

Not that it mattered to her. Not anymore. The slight tremor to her hands only meant the AC was working.

Probably.

But Ollie's return would be a big deal to his family—even if Robin was the only one in the house next door to Lena now. Jim and Elaine Fox had moved to Florida earlier this year, but Elaine still kept in touch. The few times Elaine had heard from Oliver throughout the years, she'd always told Lena.

Like she cared or something.

But Elaine had *never* mentioned a great-granddaughter. And she would've. She would've reveled in being a great-grandma. Which meant she didn't know. And come to think of it, Elaine had never mentioned a career for Ollie.

He was probably a wildly successful lawyer, like he'd always said he'd be. And she couldn't deny that he looked good. Like a young Ryan Reynolds.

What was wrong with her that she'd even noticed his dark-brown hair long enough to see the natural wave to it? Brown eyes that mocked and teased, fringed with thick lashes. She hadn't thought to check for a ring, but with a beautiful daughter like that he must have an equally beautiful wife somewhere, making them the picture-perfect family.

Not that he deserved any of it, but the man had always lived a charmed life.

Lena shook herself. Whatever. It didn't matter what Oliver Fox did. They weren't in high school anymore. He probably wouldn't even be in town long. But it had better be long enough to see his sister. It was about time he stopped taking his family for granted. His stupidity had driven Grayson away, and it killed Robin to have her two brothers at odds with each other.

"Dr. Larson." Cheryl, her receptionist, popped her head into the room. "There's a call for you. Line one."

She had bigger problems than Oliver. Like what to do with all the animals still living at her house two weeks after the storm had wrecked the shelter.

"I'll take it in my office. And while I do that, please call Melvin at the Green Acres Mini Golf and tell them we have one of his goats."

After Lena finished her last appointment, Gordy Dahlquist walked in with two scruffy-looking dogs. As bad as she felt for the dogs, the lack of sleep from dealing with Bruce last night was catching up with her.

"We're done for the day, Mr. Dahlquist. Cheryl can help get an appointment for your dogs—"

"These aren't my dogs! They chased my poor Petunia up a tree. Scared her half to death."

As the only vet in town, she knew Petunia's health history. The obese cat could probably use the exercise.

"If they aren't yours, whose are they?" Lena moved toward the small terrier mix with fur that might've been white at some point. Now it looked gray and was filled with burrs and tangles.

The other fared worse. It didn't have any fur on its black-and-pink-spotted body except for the scraggly tufts of white hair on its head, chin, and tail, like the Chinese crested breed. The shorter legs and snout were very pug-like. But it was the blind, completely infected right eye and the left ear that'd had a bite taken out of it at some point that tugged at Lena's heart. The poor thing also had a rather long scar along the torso and multiple scratches on her stout body.

"I don't know who they belong to, and I don't care. They've caused me enough grief today." Gordy dropped the leashes and marched out the door before Lena could say anything.

But—

Ugh. Did all the infuriating men in her life have to show up in one day?

The crestie-pug at her feet circled her legs and whined. Lena picked her up and she cuddled right in, hungry for affection. "Well, aren't you a sweetheart." The dog licked Lena's chin.

Cheryl grimaced. "She might be sweet, but she sure isn't very...pretty. In fact, she's probably the ugliest dog I've ever seen."

Lena cuddled her closer. "Why should that matter? She still needs care." And why was she so offended for the dog's sake? Cheryl wasn't wrong. Lena must be more tired than she realized. "Sheila, come help me get these two cleaned up."

Sheila grabbed the smaller terrier. They met Maryann in the back washroom.

"What? I thought we were done for the day." Obvious frustration on her face melted at the sight of the dog in Sheila's arms. "Aw, where did these guys come from?"

Lena held back a sigh and focused on the job. "Two more strays. Come on. You help me with this one while Sheila washes the terrier."

As Maryann lifted the crestie-pug out of Lena's arms, her eyes widened. "Oh my. Like my granny used to say, you have a face only a mother could love."

"She might not look like much, but she's very affectionate," Lena said. Someone had to speak for the strays of the world.

"Well then, let's call her Darling, cuz we definitely can't call you Fluffy, huh?" The dog barked and rested its head on Maryann's shoulder.

"Aw. You're right, Dr. Larson. She is a sweet little thing."

"She may be sweet, but we're gonna have a heck of a time getting someone to adopt her." Sheila set the terrier in the washing station sink. "This one isn't so bad. Can we name him Scamp?"

"Sure." She'd worry about trying to adopt them out later. For now, they needed to be cleaned up and given a good meal. Lena pushed her exhaustion aside and reached for Darling again. "I changed my mind. Why don't you help with Scamp, and I'll bathe Darling here. I need to get a good look at her eye." And being hairless, she would need a gentle touch.

Not that Maryann and Sheila would be rough—they were both dedicated and competent vet techs—but the poor thing had obviously been through so much already. And something about Darling drew her. This one needed a special home. Someone who could give her lots of attention.

Together they washed and fed the newcomers, gave them new collars, a much-needed flea medication for the terrier, and a soothing lotion for Darling's irritated skin.

"Now where are we going to put them?" Maryann asked.

They looked at the full kennels, the myotonic goat taking up one of them.

"Why is the goat still here?" Lena asked. "Mel should've picked it up. Then these two could share that kennel space."

Sheila shook her head. "I couldn't get ahold of him."

"Great. So we have a stray goat." Lena pushed her bangs back. "Maryann, can you—"

"Oh no. I'm not taking a goat home. My husband would flip."

"Then what about one of the dogs?"

"I can't. He's allergic. That's why I always have to change clothes here before I go home."

"Darling doesn't have hair. She's great for someone with allergies."

Maryann shook her head. "He won't go for it. He's not an animal person."

They turned to Sheila, who was already shaking her head. "Don't look at me. I love my job, but the animals stay here. My house is full."

Lena looked around the room. Each kennel was occupied by strays. Not patients recovering from procedures. Not pets waiting to be picked up by owners. These were the unwanted. Lost creatures she kept hoping someone would call about. Frank the cat meowed from his perch above the dog enclosures. He'd been here so long he roamed freely throughout the clinic, kind of like a mascot.

But she couldn't exactly do that with these two strays or the goat. And with the shelter still out of commission, Lena already had seven other dogs, six cats, a bunny, and a bearded dragon filling her own house, all left behind by their previous owners and forgotten.

A little like her.

"What about you, Dr. Larson? You've already bonded with Darling."

"She needs a lot of attention. Someone who is home during

the day. And I'm worried about what Wentworth and Bruce would do while I'm gone."

"What we need is a new building for the animal shelter," Maryann said as she scratched Frank's head. "We can't hold out much longer without one."

Yeah, but how could they pay for it? "We didn't own the old building, so we're waiting to see what the Landrys are going to do before we decide anything," Lena said. But what did she do with a stray goat in the meantime?

She handed Darling to Sheila. "I'll take the goat to Melvin's. Can you two lock up here? And make sure Darling gets an extra blanket in her kennel. Without fur, it would be easy for her to get too cold."

Lena clipped a collar and leash on the goat. "Let's get you back to your home." She used a large dog carrier in the back of her truck to transport the little black-and-white goat to the putt-putt place. Being a seasonal business, it stayed open late for the tourists in the summer. Giggles and squeals sounded from the barnyard-themed mini-golf course. In the middle of it all was an enclosure with a tall platform Melvin had made for his goats. It was the perfect home for them. At least she could get this little girl back to her home and family.

The goat pranced alongside Lena as she walked into the building.

Melvin himself was behind the counter. "Howdy, Doc. Whatcha got there?"

"What do you mean? I've got your goat. She had a bit of a scare, but after her examination I've determined she's good to join the rest of your herd."

The goat bleated. She found the slack in the leash and started to chew on the length of nylon.

"Sure is nice of you to check out the goat, but she's not mine."

Lena tried to free the leash. "But she was found right outside here on the highway. She must be yours."

"No, ma'am. I know my animals. She's not mine."

"Well then, who else has myotonic goats around here? I need to get her home."

"No idea." Melvin shrugged.

"Can't you add her to your—"

"I can't help ya, Lena. I'm at max capacity."

"What about your barn? The one you keep the animals in all winter. Surely you have room there."

"During the summers, Sandy uses it for her furniture restoration projects. That's our deal. It's full of dressers and wardrobes and chairs right now. No room for a goat. Even a little one like this."

Great. One day back in Deep Haven and already Oliver was complicating her life. Now she was stuck with a stray goat.

three

· · ·

If Lena's "welcome" was any indication, Oliver had his work cut out for him. And fine, maybe he was dragging his feet, still sitting on the banks of Lake Superior in the harbor park rather than facing Robin.

But another five minutes wouldn't hurt anything. Not with the thin, wispy clouds sweeping over the water and Kiah happy for the moment. Not with him, per se. No, she was still aloof with him. But she seemed to enjoy throwing rocks in the bay and chasing seagulls. Amazing what a couple of hours in the sunshine and some ice cream could do for her, even if he couldn't get his own stomach to unclench.

Kind of like the way he couldn't get Lena's last expression out of his head. Nothing like running into an innocent animal to announce he was back in town. Just another thing piled onto his growing list of Things Oliver Messed Up.

He tugged his ball cap lower to block the late-afternoon light.

Kiah ran up to him. "Daddy, I'm hot. Can I swim?"

"Swim? I can't have you sopping wet to meet your aunty."

"But I'm hot." She stuck out her bottom lip. "And we've been here forever. When can we go swimming?"

Never. Not in this lake, anyway. It had stolen enough from him.

"This water is way too cold. We'll swim at a different lake another time."

"But I'm hot now." The whiny pitch to her voice was back.

Guess there was no putting it off anymore. "Then we better get out of the sun and go see our new home."

"What's so great about that?"

"That means no more tiny apartment. We'll have a whole house. The house I grew up in. And it has a big yard. And a barn out back."

Kiah narrowed her eyes and said nothing, like she was sizing him up.

He knelt down in the rocks and took her hand. "We'll go swimming a different time. At a different lake. One that's warmer." And safer.

"When?"

"Tomorrow."

"You promise?" She held out a pinky.

Oliver linked his own pinky with hers. "Promise. But for now, why don't you grab your Ellie-phant and we'll get ready to go."

The promise didn't erase all the skepticism from her eyes, but it was progress. And he'd better face Robin while Kiah was still somewhat in a good mood.

They walked back to the van parked in front of a souvenir shop. A wave of heat hit Oliver as he opened the sliding van door. He stepped back onto the curb, bumping into someone on the sidewalk.

"I'm sorry—"

"Oliver Fox?"

Nathan Decker stood there. His short brown hair had more gray to it than a decade ago, but he still dressed well, in his snazzy blue polo and tan slacks. His handshake was as firm as ever.

"Hey, Mr. Decker. Nice to see you. Actually, I was hoping to run into you."

"Please, call me Nathan. And who is this lovely lady?" He grinned down at Kiah.

Remembering Lena's reaction, Oliver braced himself. "This is my daughter, Kiah."

Nathan's grin didn't fall. He didn't seem surprised or shocked. He simply shook Kiah's hand and asked her how old she was.

"I'm five," she answered.

Huh.

"So, what were you hoping to see me for?" Nathan asked, looking back at Oliver. "Anything to do with your house here in Deep Haven?"

"You know the house is in my name now?"

"I helped your grandparents with distributing their different properties and changing the titles. Your grandmother always knew you'd come back. And here you are. I'm sure she's thrilled."

"Here I am." Oliver gave a half-hearted chuckle. "But I'm not sure how long I'll stay." Or how thrilled Grandma would be with what he was about to do. "That's why I need to talk to you."

Nathan's brow wrinkled. "Are you wanting to sell the house?"

Yes.

One simple word.

So why couldn't he spit it out?

Maybe because of Nathan's mention of Grandma. Selling the house would break her heart. And what about Robin? She was still living in it. And if Lena's reaction was anything to go by, this trip to make amends with everyone on his list might take longer than he hoped.

He should've stayed in Iowa. Everything seemed so much easier from hundreds of miles away.

Oliver grabbed the back of his neck. "I'm not sure. Guess I was wondering what the options are."

"You can sell it, of course. You'll probably get more bang for your buck if you do some remodeling first. There's always renting. But my best advice, which I admit is biased, is to move in and stay awhile. It's a great place to raise your kids. And no, your grandparents didn't pay me to say that." He winked down at Kiah.

"Stay?"

"Why not? Annalise and I have loved raising our kids here."

"Right. I suppose they're all grown up."

"Yeah, Henry is in grad school now. Jason and his family are in Duluth, but Colleen is engaged and lives here in town. She's a flight nurse."

"Sounds like they've all made something of themselves." Unlike him. But he still didn't see judgment in Nathan's gaze. "After"—he looked down at Kiah listening to every word— "everything that happened, you really think I should stay? I thought this town would send me packing as soon as I stepped over the city limit line." Oliver tried not to choke on the chuckle he forced out.

"Your past is the past, Oliver. Besides, selling your home is a big deal. I tell all my clients to make sure they're doing it for the right reasons. It wouldn't hurt for you to take some time and see if that's what you really want. And if it is, I will do everything I can to help."

Time to think about it. It made a lot of sense. He hadn't even seen his sister yet. "Okay. I'll think about it some more and let you know."

"Good. You take care now." He leaned over to stage-whisper near Kiah's ear. "I'd better get home before Annalise gives my dinner to the dog."

Kiah giggled.

Wow, she really was in a good mood.

After Nathan left, she tugged on Oliver's hand. "Can we go meet my aunty now?"

He set her in the van. "Let's do that."

In the twelve years since he'd been home, the roads to get there had changed little. Thick forests of timber still lined the gravel lanes. They passed a few more clearings and houses than the last time he'd driven this route.

He turned on to his street, and a hundred memories flooded him. Riding bikes on the dirt road. Mowing the lawn in the summer, and Grandma bringing out lemonade and cookies. Raking leaves from the maple tree in the front yard.

Oliver parked the van in the driveway and took in the old blue farmhouse.

His grandparents' personalities were so evident in the whole setup of the property. The perfect symmetry of the yellow door in the exact middle of the porch, flanked by two large windows, was all Grandpa. The flower beds filled with friendly daisies and pots of petunias were all Grandma. She was the one who'd picked out the cheery Robin's egg blue paint too.

"This is where we're going to live?" Kiah's voice filled with awe.

He shouldn't let her get her hopes up too much if he was going to sell it, but something ignited inside to have his daughter sounding impressed for once. Like maybe he could really redeem his past, make something of himself here. Have her look at him with trust and affection rather than the suspicion and uncertainty she had worn so often since she'd moved in.

"You like it, Kiah?"

"It's like a storybook house!" She ran out of the van and up to the porch.

Storybook house? He followed her to the front door. She obviously didn't have the memories coloring the vision or Grandpa's voice in her head.

You're too old to be playing and sledding with Grayson and Robin. You need to clear the driveway.

No, you're not going! When you decide you can act with honor and uphold the Fox family name instead of joking around during church, maybe we'll talk about next year's Boundary Waters trip.

When are you going to stop this foolishness, Oliver, and make something of yourself?

The man had gone from being his favorite fishing buddy and hero, the man that'd always laughed at his antics and slipped him a stick of gum in church, to a substitute father and disciplinarian overnight.

Of course, that'd been Oliver's fault.

So no wonder Gramps had lost the smirk and sparkle in his eye at a shared joke. What used to be an affirming and comforting hand on Oliver's shoulder had morphed into a cold, heavy weight after Mom and Dad died.

The playful sound of wind chimes rang, pulling Oliver back to the present.

Wind chimes? Since when had the Larson home gotten wind chimes? Oliver looked past his garage to Lena's house. No longer tan like it had been when he'd seen it last, it was still a respectable gray ranch. But never had there ever been anything as whimsical as wind chimes sounding from next door.

"Dad, are we going in?" Kiah tugged on his shirt.

Whether Robin would react like Lena or Nathan, he couldn't say. But like it or not, this was home for the foreseeable future. Oliver swallowed down the bitter memories and knocked on his own front door.

🦊🦊🦊

WHAT IN THE WORLD WAS LENA SUPPOSED TO DO WITH A FAINTING goat?

Ugh! This was all Oliver's fault.

She stood in her own driveway, holding tight to the goat's

new collar as she opened her garage door. The dogs inside barked, probably anxious for their evening walk and dinner. Most of the cats, in true feline fashion, barely blinked at the noisy door sliding into place. The goat bleated, following Lena.

What was Oliver even doing back in town. With a daughter?

Stop.

No use giving the guy any more mental space than he had already stolen. She had bigger things to worry about. Like a garage full of animals needing to be fed.

"Hi, everyone. I know you're excited and ready for a nice long walk, but first things first. We need to make room for the rookie here."

Lena moved to the middle of the two-car garage. She could admit Peter and Jensen had done a good job following her plans and setting up one side into two big fenced-in kennels for the dogs. Her high shelves above the area weren't disturbed, and the dogs had the length of the garage to move. But even with Bruce still inside the house, there were seven of them. No room for the goat.

She turned to the other side. The cat enclosure might only be six feet wide, but the fencing went all the way to the ceiling. With all the vertical space to use, they'd made carpeted shelves and hung boxes on the walls for the cats to climb and lounge on. She could already picture the goat kicking up the litter boxes in the corner and chasing the cats off their perches. No room here either.

A car pulled into Lena's driveway. Birdie. She smiled as she walked up to Lena, but it didn't hide the dark circles under her eyes. No shelter and thus no job was doing a number on her.

"Hello, dear." Birdie hugged her. Her hands stayed clasped on Lena's arms. "How are you?"

"Me? All right. What about you? Still not sleeping well?"

"It's been a bit of a blue day, but it's always better when I come here." She squatted down by the goat and rubbed the black-and-white furry body. Birdie's eyes brightened. "And who's this sweet thing?"

"Another stray. I'm trying to figure out where to put her. I spent an hour trying to call around the few people that have farms, but no one is claiming her." And no one wanted her.

Thanks a lot, Oliver.

"Why don't you put her on the dog run set up in the front yard while we feed and walk the dogs? Then we'll figure it out."

"Good idea." After attaching a leash to the goat's collar and then the leash to the line set between the two pine trees in Lena's front yard, she went back to the garage where Birdie was scooping fresh litter into the cat boxes.

"Is Robin having plumbing problems?" Birdie asked.

Lena added cat food to their dishes. "Not that I know of. Why?"

"There's a white van with a plumbing logo in her driveway."

"Oh." The van she'd watched Oliver and his daughter drive off in. Lena gathered the water dishes and threw them in the laundry sink for a quick rinse.

Birdie paused what she was doing. "What's wrong?"

"Nothing's wrong." Lena turned on the water and scrubbed.

Birdie must not have believed her, since she walked all the way over and leaned against the counter by the sink. "Who does that plumbing van belong to?"

Focusing solely on scrubbing the dish, Lena could still feel a laser stare boring into her.

Fine. It didn't have to be a big deal if she didn't make it a big deal. "Oliver."

"Oliver Fox?"

"Yup." Lena filled the dishes with fresh water and carried them back to the cat enclosure.

Birdie followed and opened the latch for Lena. "Do you want to talk abou—"

"So, did you hear from the Landrys yet? What are they going to do with the building?"

"I'll take that as a no," Birdie said.

Hello! Of course she didn't want to talk about Oliver Fox. Seeing him in person only brought up unnecessary emotions like invasive weeds sprouting from humiliating memories. Talking about it wouldn't change a thing.

They closed the cat kennel. Birdie moved to the dogs and pulled out an older Maltese named Oscar, then settled him in a dog stroller.

"And the Landrys?" Lena asked again.

"I did finally get a call back from Abe." Birdie said the words with a deep sigh.

"What did he say?"

Birdie's shoulders slumped. "They're going to condemn the shelter building and tear it down. They'll most likely build a new strip mall." She looked up at Lena with such a lost and defeated expression.

Lena snatched the dog leashes from the wall and handed three to Birdie. The dogs barked louder, anxious to get out.

"So we need a new building. Not ideal, but now we know what we're up against." Not that she blamed the Landrys for finally bulldozing the place, but her garage was already full, and more strays came in every week. And what about Birdie's job?

"Where are we going to find another building? The only way the last one worked was because the Landrys donated the space and we only had to pay utilities." Birdie readied the three dogs in the one kennel and waited for Lena to finish attaching the leashes to the others.

"I don't know. But I'll figure it out. Don't worry."

Worrying was Lena's job. She mulled on the question as they walked down the driveway and turned right. Because no, Lena did not want to walk past the house next door with Oliver there. But she forgot what was down this direction until minutes later, when Birdie stopped in the middle of the road. She stared at her own property and the burnt shell of a house that stood on it.

"I'm so sorry, Birdie. I shouldn't have come this way." Lena stood next to her, the dogs straining against the leashes.

Tears made their way down the older woman's cheeks. "It's okay. Howard and I had a lot of good years here." She smiled at Lena with wet eyes. "And we had a lot of love."

Which she'd lost, leaving an almost hollow version of the Birdie Lena had grown up with.

Lena cleared her throat, not quite sure what to say. "Howard was a good man."

The paltry words didn't come close. Because Howard had been more than a good guy. Probably the only man Lena had ever felt truly comfortable around. As a science teacher, he'd taught Lena about biology and anatomy, sparking her whole career. And since Lena had grown up without a dad, he'd been as close to a father figure as they came. And he'd adored Birdie. Lena owed it to him to take care of her, and she was failing miserably.

The black Lab mix barked, wanting to move on. "I promise you, Birdie. We'll find another place. We'll open a new shelter." The thought struck her. "Maybe we could even do it here. On your property, in honor of Howard."

Birdie's face lit from within. "Here? That would be... amazing. But where will we find the funds to build something here?"

"Leave that to me. I'll figure something out."

"Lena, you do too much as it is. It's not healthy. You're so young. You should be out enjoying life. Finding love—"

Lena snorted. "I have more important things than wasting my time on some guy." It certainly hadn't worked out for her mother. And the animals were so much more...predictable.

They started walking again, Birdie pushing Oscar in the stroller. "Speaking of guys...I take it you already spoke to Oliver if you know that van belongs to him. When did he get to town?"

"Today. But back to the animals, I think—"

"Oh no you don't, young lady. We were talking about Oliver. He hasn't been home in…well, I don't know how long—"

"Twelve years. He was back for Grayson's graduation." Not that she'd spoken to him then. In fact, she'd made every effort to avoid him at the ceremony and open house. So technically, it had been fourteen years since she'd had an actual conversation with Oliver. Too bad she'd broken the streak this afternoon.

"So, what is he doing back? Is he staying?"

"I hope not."

Birdie was quiet for a moment. "Still not over what happened? It was so long ago. I'm sure he's a different boy than he was back then."

"Not over it?" Lena planted her feet. The dogs tugging on their leads jerked her arm. "Birdie, he utterly humiliated me."

"I know, but—"

"In front of the whole high-school football team." Lena started walking again. Fast.

Didn't Birdie know how traumatic that had been? "And he *hasn't* changed a bit. He hit a goat with his van, and now I'm stuck with yet another stray animal no one wants to take care of. I don't know how he manages to take care of his daughter, but I feel sorry for his wife."

Birdie looked confused. "Daughter? Wife? Oliver's married? Elaine never said a thing."

"I don't know about married. But he had a little girl with him at the clinic, and she called him Dad."

"I see." Birdie grew quiet.

They walked in heavy silence. Lena didn't want to know what Birdie thought she "saw." If it had anything to do with Oliver, it didn't matter. Birdie mattered. These forgotten, castaway animals mattered. And that, Lena could do something about.

"So, what do you think about building the new shelter on the property? Having the land means we would only need money for a building. You have the infrastructure already here."

"Do you really think we can find the funds to do that?"

Lena wanted to keep the spark of hope in Birdie's voice alive. "Let me worry about the finances. But I want to be sure. That's still your land. Do you *want* to build the shelter out here?"

"I can't think of a better way to honor Howard's memory. But—" Birdie stopped walking.

"Seriously. If that's what you want, I'll find a way to make it happen. And until we can build it, I'll find a home for each and every animal. Just like Howard always did."

"I love your determination, dear. But remember, you don't have to do it alone. You have a whole community here. Friends. Neighbors. And it wouldn't hurt to let them help you."

But letting others help got messy and complicated. Lena didn't do messy and complicated very well.

After their two-mile walk was finished, they settled the dogs in for the night. The goat bleated from the yard.

"What will you do with her?" Birdie asked as she stood by her car, keys in hand.

Lena glanced over at the plumbing van next door.

"She'll be settled by the end of the night. But you should get back to town before dark." She said goodbye to Birdie.

The goat would be taken care of after she scrounged up a few things. Now to figure out how to scrounge up enough money for Birdie's shelter too.

four

. . .

HE JUST WANTED TO MAKE HIS GIRL HAPPY. OVER THE LAST FIVE months they'd been together, he'd tried so hard to connect with her. But she wasn't that bubbly toddler he'd first met anymore. Like Blanche would remind him, she was a little girl who'd just lost her mother, her home, and her great-uncle who'd been more like a grandfather to her.

Now the poor kid was stuck with only him.

"Where's my aunty? We've been here forever," Kiah grumbled from the other side of the kitchen peninsula. Obviously the ice cream and excitement over staying in the "storybook house" had worn off in the hours after breaking in with the hide-a-key. And still no Robin.

So much for a warm welcome.

"I bet she'll be here any minute." Oliver pulled the pot of elbow noodles off the burner and emptied them into the strainer in the sink. "And when she gets here, we'll have a yummy dinner all together." Nothing like his mom's mac and cheese recipe to smooth things over. It was the one thing he never messed up.

"Did she text you back?" The accusation in her tone nipped.

Oliver checked his phone. Nothing.

"Like I said, any minute she'll be walking through that door." He poured the milk and butter and grated cheese into the saucepan. "Do you want to stir?"

She shook her head.

"Are you sure? I could use the help. I even got the step stool out for you."

"No, thank you."

Guess they were back to the polite stranger routine.

The doorbell rang. Kiah perked a tad. "Can I answer it? Is it my aunty?"

Oliver peeked out the kitchen window. What was Lena doing here?

Probably something for Robin. Or she had the bill for treating the goat and the destruction of her lobby all ready to go and slap in his hand. That hadn't taken long.

"Can I, Daddy?" She hopped off the barstool.

Funny how it was always "Daddy" when she wanted something. But he was desperate enough to take what he could get.

"Sure. It's Lena—I mean, Dr. Larson. She probably has something for me. You can thank her and bring it over. I don't want my sauce to burn." And if it brought a slight thaw to the current funk his daughter was in, even better.

Muffled voices from the entry carried over as Oliver added the noodles to the sauce. Kiah squealed. And if his ears weren't mistaken, that was a happy squeal. What was Lena saying? He'd have to run over there later and beg her for the secret.

He poured the cheesy pasta into the baking dish and sprinkled the butter-breadcrumb mixture he had ready. Footsteps on the wooden floors grew louder.

He quickly slid the dish into the oven and wiped his hands. He turned to see Kiah standing there, holding something in her hand. A leash?

But she had the biggest grin he'd yet to see on her beautiful face. She was happy. Honest-to-goodness happy. Wow.

A loud bleat announced the presence of something else.

No. She wouldn't.

A familiar black-and-white goat pranced into the kitchen and jumped onto the step stool Oliver had gotten out for Kiah.

"What is that?"

"Look, Daddy! The goat is all better. And she's ours. I want to name her Oreo." Kiah hugged the furry little menace.

"We can't keep a goat." What was Lena thinking?

Kiah's grin faded. "But we have to. You said whatever the doctor had to bring it to you." Kiah dropped the leash.

"I know, but I didn't—"

"The goat doctor said she was ours. And she had a message."

Did he even want to know? He clenched his jaw. "What was the message?"

"She said, 'You break it, you bought it. Welcome home.' So see, we have to take her. You can't give back a present."

And thanks for that, Lena. Oliver pinched his nose.

"Baby, we can't keep a…goat."

As if offended by his comment, the goat leaped off the stool and made a run for the living room. It pulled one of the floral throw pillows off the couch and started chewing on it before Oliver could reach it.

"Stop!"

The goat froze and tipped over. Again.

"Dad, don't yell at her." Kiah rushed over and kissed the goat's furry head. "She needs a home. She needs us. Mommy always said I could have a pet. Why can't I keep her?"

Oliver took a second to compose himself. Expelling a deep breath, he knelt down by Kiah. "I know you miss your mom, and I know you want a pet. But we can't keep the goat. We don't even have food for it. Where would it sleep?"

"But Dr. Lena gave us food. And straw. She left it in the barn. She said Oreo would be happy there." Kiah sniffed. "Please, Daddy." She looked at him with her big brown eyes, tears clinging to her thick lashes. One simple word and he could make her happy.

He stifled the groan building inside. It was getting late. There wasn't anything they could do tonight anyway. "Here's the deal. The goat can stay, but—"

Kiah leaped into his arms. "Thank you, Daddy!"

He didn't get the rest of the sentence out, the important part about it being only until they could find the goat a new home still stuck on his tongue. But how could he say that now when Kiah was hugging him? Voluntarily. The warmth from having her in his arms went straight to his heart. Sheesh, he was tearing up himself.

"All right, let's go get this animal settled."

"Her name is Oreo." Kiah beamed.

If this was what it took to make his grieving daughter happy, he might consider buying a hundred goats.

Oreo popped up as if nothing had happened. Before the wily creature could get back to the pillow, Oliver scooped her up and they went out the back door. Across the grassy yard lay the red barn. It wasn't a big structure, only meant to hold a few cows and maybe a horse or two back in the day. At one point Grandma had kept chickens, but those days were long gone.

The big door creaked as they opened it. They passed the old dairy parlor and walked through the big open space to the very back where the stalls were. Like the hayloft above, where he and Grayson had always been tasked with stashing the Christmas decorations, two of the stalls had been repurposed for something other than farm life. They now held fishing tackle and lifejackets, old sleds, and a rusty wheelbarrow. The one in the middle, though, was empty except for the bale of straw and a bag of feed. A handwritten note gave feeding instructions and was signed with a simple *L*.

There was no doubt about who *L* was. The handwriting was too similar to the letter that haunted him, still in his wallet.

Lena.

At one time, she'd liked him. But he'd destroyed that too.

Oreo kicked, pulling Oliver out of his haze. "Here's your place for the night, kid." He nudged Kiah's arm. "Get it? Kid? Like the name for—"

"I know what a kid is, Dad." Kiah rolled her eyes.

That was short lived.

Oliver cut the twine around the bale and spread out straw in the stall. He left Kiah and Oreo to search for a water and food dish. Grandma used to keep a few in the dairy parlor for the barn cats. There. And what was this big mound under the tarp? Probably more junk. Oliver lifted a corner and froze.

Grandpa's fishing boat. There on the bow lay a faded orange life ring. Oliver's chest squeezed.

Why in the world did they still have that?

His hand shook. This was why they needed to leave. Soon. Too many memories everywhere he went.

"Dad, did you find water? Oreo's thirsty." Kiah wandered into the room. "Dad?"

Oliver dropped the tarp. "Water is coming right up."

"Are you okay?"

He plastered on a smile. "I'm good. Let's get Oreo some food and water." He shook off the dark memories, and they settled the goat in for the night. Oliver shut the gate for the stall. Kiah reached through the wooden slats and stroked Oreo's neck.

From the big open barn doors, the faint sound of an alarm carried in.

Was that a smoke alarm?

The mac and cheese!

"Kiah, stay here," Oliver called over his shoulder as he sprinted for the house. He scrambled up the steps to the back porch and threw open the dining room doors. Smoke poured out of the kitchen. Oliver ran through the rooms opening more windows. He flipped the hood vent over the stove on and pulled the burnt mass out of the oven. The sound of a slamming door cut through the alarm blaring overhead. Waving a hand towel over the blackened dish, he coughed, trying to clear his lungs.

Once again, footsteps approached the kitchen. "Kiah, I asked you to stay outside. You shouldn't breathe in smoke."

"I'm not Kiah. And I don't know who you are, but you better get out of my kitchen."

Finally the smoke started clearing. Standing there with a fire extinguisher pointed straight at him was a woman he barely recognized with curly auburn hair and a green sundress. But the eyes were exactly like their mom's.

"Hey, sis."

"Ollie?" Robin dropped the extinguisher. "Is it really you?" She studied his face a moment. "Oh my goodness. What are you doing here?" She pulled him into a tight hug.

"Yeah, it's me. I was trying to make you dinner." Two hugs in one night. Both turning him into a blubbery mess. Man, it had been too long.

"That's what you call it, huh?" Robin laughed, pointing at the disaster-in-a-pan.

"Daddy?" a shaky voice called from the back porch. "Did you get the fire out?"

Robin's jaw dropped. "Did she just call you—"

"I'm okay, Kiah. You can come in."

Kiah ran over and hugged his leg. Her little body trembled.

"What's the matter?" he asked in a gentle voice.

"I was a-scared you would be killed in the fire."

Oliver scooped her up. "Oh, baby. It's okay. No fire. I just burned dinner." He held her close.

Sweet girl. She really did care. And for one second he just soaked in her concern for his well-being. Maybe they would be okay after all. "Look, my sister is here."

Kiah lifted her head off his shoulder and gave Robin a shy look. Oliver held his breath. His family could do whatever they wanted with him, but he wanted them to accept his little girl.

"Robin, this is my daughter, Kiah Louise Jackson."

Robin managed a brave smile, but the wide eyes and forced laugh gave her away. "Wow. Your...daughter." She seemed to gather her thoughts. "You mean, I'm an aunt?"

Oliver nodded.

"And she's named after Mom? Louise?"

He nodded. One of the few thoughtful things Jalisa had done. She hadn't thought to tell Oliver she was pregnant, Kiah didn't have *his* last name, but Jalisa must've remembered how much he'd wanted to name his first daughter after his mother.

"I'm glad to meet you, Kiah. And if this"—Robin pointed to the smoking mac and cheese—"is how your father feeds you, it's a good thing you're here with me now. Are you hungry?"

Kiah nodded.

"We'll have some pizza ready in no time." She speared Oliver with a look over Kiah's head. "Then your dad and I are gonna have a long talk tonight catching up on *all* I've missed."

Yeah, he was in for it.

After a late but lighthearted dinner and settling one very tired girl into his old bedroom, which now apparently was an unused exercise room complete with treadmill and stationary bike where his dresser and desk used to be, Robin dragged Oliver back downstairs and into the living room.

She faced him with hands on her hips and hissed, "You have a daughter? A daughter?"

"I do. So say whatever it is you need to say to me tonight, but don't take it out on her."

"Honestly, Ollie, do you think I would do something like that?"

"Well, no, but it's been a while—"

"And whose fault is that?"

Yeah. She was mad. And rightly so.

"I know. I've been gone. But I'm here now."

Robin folded her arms across her chest. "How old is she?"

"She's five." Oliver cracked his knuckles and stared at the

rug they stood on. He deserved Robin's wrath. But when he looked up at her, it wasn't anger behind her stare. It was hurt.

Her eyes filled. "Why didn't you tell us? And where is her mother?"

"It's a long story."

"You mean the story of the last twelve years? Yeah, that's a long time, and obviously a lot happened. But I can't believe you didn't tell us you have a daughter!"

Oliver released a pent-up breath slowly. "Look, sis, for a long time I was in a bad place. I didn't want you to see me that way. But I've been sober three years now, and I was trying to get my act together, ya know? And the truth is, I didn't even know about Kiah until she was two."

Robin tilted her head. "That's still *three* years ago."

"I know. But it was a lot to adjust to. And it pushed me to get sober."

His sister seemed to consider his words. She dropped her arms and sat on the couch, pushing aside the chewed pillow. "Then what happened? Who's her mother?"

Oliver sat in the recliner Grandma had always liked. He perched on the edge of it, not wanting to settle into it until he got the story out. "Her mother is a woman I went out with a few times. Her name was Jalisa. And even though we tried once I found out about Kiah, her mom and I couldn't make it work. She took Kiah and moved back to Ohio. Then Jalisa passed away in March, and now I have custody. And even that is contingent. So I'm here. Trying to make amends."

"Yeah, but you're my brother! And you just…left. I don't care how low you get. Family should stick together. We could've helped." She wiped a stray tear. She lifted her chin, and Oliver remembered that stubborn look on her face. He was in for it. "How long are you here?"

Huh? She wasn't kicking him out? It might be his own house on paper, but she had every right.

"I…don't know."

"Come on, Ollie. Give me a ballpark. Are you sticking around for good or is this a visit?" She stilled. "Wait. You're not going to sell the house like Grayson did the lot, are you? I mean, I know it's yours, but it's our family home. It's been in the Fox family for generations."

He'd already failed Robin so much. He hated to disappoint her any more than he had. "We're here for now, at least the next week or two. And we'll have a great time."

She stared him down. "Make it a *month* or two. Then you can help me with Grandma and Grandpa's big fifty-fifth anniversary party in October."

He cracked his knuckles again. "I can't—"

"I want a chance to get to know my niece. A niece you hid from us! A few weeks isn't long enough. And the girl is five. She should be starting kindergarten next week."

Now wait. "Kindergarten? I didn't start until I was six."

"Oliver, she sounded out the word *milk* at dinner. She's ready. Besides, she needs stability right now. A home. A family. And what are these contingencies that your custody is based on?"

"You don't need to worry about that."

"No. We're done shutting each other out. Like it or not, I'm gonna be involved, Ollie. So spit it out. What do you need to do to keep Kiah?"

Oliver clenched and unclenched his jaw. He was prepared to shoulder this load alone. It was *his* mess. *His* daughter.

But maybe Robin was right. Maybe a little longer here *would* be good for Kiah. Watching the two of them interact over dinner had done his heart good. It'd felt like a real family meal. Robin had had Kiah giggling over their childhood antics.

He blew out a long breath. "I have a list of the people I've wronged that I need to make amends with as part of my recovery program. Almost everyone is here in Deep Haven."

"That's it?" Her eyes narrowed. It was almost eerie the way she looked exactly like his mother had when she didn't believe he'd finished his homework like he said.

"And a few other things."

"Like what?"

She wasn't going to let it drop. He'd better just spit it out. "Normal stuff. I have to prove I have a job, a home, that kind of thing."

"But don't you see? This would be the perfect place to raise Kiah. This *is* a home. And I can offer you a job right now at the bakery. Register Kiah for school and we'll work around that schedule."

But that wasn't the plan. Staying in Deep Haven?

"I admit staying in Deep Haven to regroup might be good, at least until I get through the custody hearing in November, but that's all I can promise."

"All right. So who do you need to apologize to?"

"You to start with." He stared down at his shoes. "I wasn't here for you like I should've been. And I know I made some dumb mistakes and hurt you."

She nodded slowly with a sad smile. "I could've been a better sister. So I guess we're even. But I can't be the only one, so who else?"

Oliver walked over to his duffel bag, still sitting in the entryway. He pulled out the list and showed it to Robin.

"Coach Presley?"

"He was like a dad to me, and I never even went to talk to him after his accident. I blew him off when he asked about my drinking. Lied straight to his face."

"He's actually recovered quite a bit. He's in a wheelchair now."

Something loosened in Oliver's gut. Maybe he should see Coach next.

Robin continued reading the list. "Peter Dahlquist, Edith Draper, Grayson, Grandma, Grandpa, and…Lena." She winced. "You've got your work cut out for you, bro."

"I know."

"Register Kiah for school and promise to stay until your

court date and you can cross me off too."

"I don't think that's how it works." He chuckled. "Besides, you said we were even."

But Robin didn't budge. She folded her arms and waited without a word.

Oliver groaned. "All right. But please don't say anything to Grandma and Grandpa about Kiah yet. I'll tell them when I'm ready."

"Fine. I don't like it, but it's your place to tell them. Now, you're not going anywhere until you catch me up on everything. And I mean *everything* else." She shocked him as she stepped over and gave him another hug. "I've missed you."

"I missed you too, sis."

LENA NEEDED TO CALM DOWN IF SHE WAS GOING TO MAKE IT through the interview in an hour. It was bad enough with Oliver crashing into her life three days ago. Even though she rarely saw him, it was nerve-wracking just knowing he was next door. Birdie's phone call was not helping either.

"Are you sure you're okay to do the interview alone?" Birdie asked. "I feel awful that I told you I would be there and now I can't."

"I'll be fine." At least, Lena hoped she would be. She stood in her pajamas in front of her closet, flipping through the few shirts hanging there. "I just need to find something here that's not scrubs or flannels. You need to be there for Mrs. Campbell's surgery."

"She doesn't have anyone else. And she's so worried."

Lena could picture Birdie wringing her hands and pacing. Sure, her own heartbeat might be in panic mode, but she didn't want to worry her friend. "Birdie, you don't have to explain.

We've got the plan all laid out for the committee. I know it backward and forward."

Bruce barked from the living area.

"It's a brilliant plan. But I know how much you hate public speaking. I should be there."

"You're doing the right thing staying with Mrs. Campbell."

Birdie paused. "Howard would be so proud of you."

Lena swallowed hard. And that's why, despite her phobia, she needed to do this.

"Let's just hope the committee sees the potential as much as we do and will give us the grant."

The barking grew louder as Wentworth and Jane joined Bruce.

"I'll be praying, dear," Birdie said.

"Thanks. I better go. The dogs are upset about something."

After saying goodbye, Lena pulled down a white button-down shirt and tossed it on the bed on her way to the living room.

"What's going on ou—"

The three dogs were lined up at the large picture window, barking at the chaos happening in the front yard. Oliver's fainting goat chased Darling and Scamp in circles around the two pine trees.

"How did they get out?"

Poor Oscar cowered in the bed of hostas that lined her driveway, while the black Lab mix they'd been calling Rascal barked at a squirrel up in the trees at the wooded edge of Lena's property.

Lena ran for the door. As she opened it, Bruce bolted out, shoving her aside before she could grab him.

No! She quickly shut Wentworth and Jane in and jumped off her porch into the yard. Lena lunged for the closest animal—the goat.

"Stop!"

The goat paused midair and keeled over. As she bent low to

check it out, a little girl's scream sent Lena's heart into overdrive. Oliver's daughter stood in the swath of grass between the two driveways, eyes wide as Bruce bounded straight for her.

Lena sprinted but wouldn't reach her in time. "Bruce, stay!"

It was completely ridiculous to expect the dog to obey the command when he'd yet to do so in their training sessions. But instead of barreling into the kid and running her over, the big lug skidded to a stop right at Kiah's feet and sat. He gave her a slobbery lick on her cheek.

And then he kept licking until Kiah giggled.

He'd been living with Lena for a couple weeks now and barely tolerated her, despite all the treats and attention. And here Kiah wrapped her little arms around his massive neck and kissed him back. He couldn't get enough of her.

Oliver bolted out of his house. "Kiah! What's wrong—"

Before Lena could spit out the words *she's okay*, Bruce jumped back to his feet and stood guard. He barked at Oliver. A deep warning bark.

Lena forced a calmness to her voice she didn't feel. "Ollie, wait. She's fine. But Bruce doesn't react well to men."

"She is not fine—"

Bruce barked again, and Oliver thankfully stopped approaching.

"Daddy, look at the doggy. He's so cute." Kiah laughed and ran for Oliver. She took him by the hand and brought him over to Bruce. Apparently, that was all the permission Bruce needed to accept Oliver's presence. But he didn't care when Oliver gently patted him on the head. It was Kiah's attention he wanted. He lay at her feet and rolled over to his back, exposing his belly.

Kiah plopped down and obligingly rubbed it. "Hi, doggy. You're such a good puppy."

Lena couldn't believe it. The dog was enamored with the girl. He was a completely different animal.

Oliver watched a few more seconds, then marched over to

Lena, his voice low but gruff. "What's up with your dogs? And why was my daughter screaming?" He pointed at the melee behind Lena with Scamp and Darling still barking and running in circles and the goat coming out of another fainting spell.

"My dogs? Hello? What about your goat? What is it doing in my yard?"

Rascal's squirrel jumped to the pine tree in the yard, and now the three dogs and goat broke the circle they'd had going before and scattered. Oscar whined and started pawing at the hostas.

Lena glared at Oliver. "Great. Now look what you did."

He ran after Rascal. "What *I* did? These are your animals."

Lena made a break for Darling. The always-hungry-for-attention crestie-pug came and jumped into her arms. "They're not mine. They're just staying here temporarily." She carried Darling over to her open garage door. The kennel gate swung in the breeze. How had that opened? She set the dog in the kennel, and Oliver followed with Rascal. Kiah had Bruce under control, so Lena carefully approached Oscar next.

"Come on, boy. It's okay." He didn't come toward her, but he didn't back away when she stepped closer. "Ouch!" Lena stepped on something sharp. Oscar bolted under her truck in the driveway.

"Oscar, come. I wasn't yelling at you." As Lena tried coaxing the old dog out, Scamp zoomed through the yard. "Ollie, go get him before he runs out in the road!"

As if Lena's words had put the idea in his little doggy head, Scamp indeed ran straight for the road and out of sight. Oliver sprinted after him.

After ten minutes of bribes with treats and promises of cuddles, Oscar eventually crawled close enough for Lena to reach him. She scooped him up just as Oliver walked up the driveway breathless, holding Scamp. They kenneled them with the others and went back to the front yard. Kiah and Bruce happily played on the lawn. Wentworth and Jane still barked from the window, probably wanting some attention too. And the goat nibbled on the pansies cascading down from Lena's porch.

Oliver was still trying to catch his breath. "You owe me for that one."

"Owe you? Your goat is probably the one that started the whole thing."

"I don't know how Oreo got out, but there's no way the goat could open up your garage door."

"I had it open for the animals to get some cool air. It's hot."

Oliver nodded at her pajama shorts. "Is that why you have firefighter kitty-cat pj's on?"

Looking down at her ensemble, a ratty science club T-shirt and shorts, Lena groaned. Of course Oliver would have to see her like this, because he hadn't embarrassed her enough in life.

Before she could come up with any sort of dignified response, he chuckled. "Why do you have so many animals anyway?"

"Not that it's any of your business, but the shelter in town closed. There's nowhere else for these animals to go."

It seemed to sober Oliver quickly. "Oh."

"Daddy, can we keep this doggy? He likes me." Kiah trotted up to them with Bruce at her side.

Oliver groaned. "Sweetie, we have Oreo. Let's get used to one animal at a time."

The girl's face fell. Lena waited for a fit of some sort. Wasn't that what kids did when they didn't get what they wanted? But the girl's quiet and obvious disappointment was the silent type. And somehow it was worse.

Maybe it was knowing now—thanks to Robin—that Kiah had recently lost her mother. Maybe it was just that Lena never could handle seeing any creature hurting. But she needed to do something to alleviate Kiah's pain.

"You could always come visit him though," Lena offered. "I could use your help training him. He responds to you."

Kiah looked up at her, a little smile peeking through. "Really?"

Oliver cleared his throat.

Right. "If your dad says it's okay."

"Why don't you show Lena how great you are with Oreo by putting her back in her pen?" Oliver said. "Then we'll think about when you can help."

"Okay." Kiah took his suggestion and skipped off with Oreo toward their barn.

Lena wished she could cross her arms over her chest, but it took both hands to hold Bruce back from following Kiah. Lena had managed to avoid Oliver since he'd moved in, but now she really should be thanking him. She could've lost Scamp for good if Ollie hadn't chased after him.

But she couldn't find the words.

"If you really need help with the animals, Kiah and I can help out."

Lena shook her head. "I'll be fine." No use letting down her guard. Not with him. With pasts so entwined, it was too easy to fall back into that same pattern and habit of trusting Oliver Fox. But in the end, she had to remember: he didn't want her. She couldn't let her heart be pulverized like that again. Even now, his brown eyes drew her attention. It wasn't fair, and it certainly wasn't wise to spend any time with him.

"Lena, I really need to talk to you abo—"

Her smartwatch buzzed with a notification. Lena looked down at her wrist. The interview! She still needed to get ready "I have to go. Sorry." She ran inside with Bruce and did her best to forget all about Oliver while she took a quick shower.

After changing her clothes five times to find the right outfit—one that looked professional but not over the top, something that wasn't her usual khaki attire or scrubs—she settled on the black blazer over her white button-down and nice jeans. She drove to Ella Vassos's soap shop, where the grant committee was meeting. Good thing she hadn't eaten anything or she would've lost it before she walked in.

Ella looked up from behind the counter. "Lena, nice to see

you. Come on over and tell me all the news while Adrian finishes setting up for the interview."

News? She meant Oliver. It was all anyone in town wanted to talk about.

Lena grabbed one of the light-green bars of soap on display instead and sniffed. "This is nice and light. Is it lemongrass?"

"It is. And it's one of my best sellers this summer."

Voices from the big open room attached to the shop pulled Lena's attention away. She still didn't know who was on this committee.

"So, you have a couple of new neighbors, huh?" Ella asked. "That's exciting."

"I wouldn't say exciting." Different, maybe. It would've been hard not to notice the difference over the last week. After a long stretch of quiet years, the Fox home was once again full of laughter and delicious smells. Even last night, the aroma of barbecued chicken had wafted over as Oliver manned the grill while Robin and Kiah played a card game on the deck. Ella didn't need to know that Lena had cracked a window in her own dining room to be able to hear and smell it all. For a moment she could pretend she was there too. She could imagine what it felt like to be a part of a real family.

"I think I remember Robin saying you grew up together, right?"

Lena nodded.

"So, what is Oliver like? I haven't met him yet, but the town is buzzing."

"Uh, he's...outgoing." How did Lena explain? Ollie would never comprehend being on the outside. He was always well-liked and easygoing. So different from Lena. "I'm sure you'll meet him at some point."

"And he's a dad?"

"He has a daughter named Kiah. She's five." And she had to admit, everything she saw and heard pointed to him being an excellent father. Hadn't Robin said someone else wanted custody of Kiah? He could've easily skipped out on fatherhood if he'd wanted.

But he hadn't. He was fighting *for* Kiah. It was more than Lena's father had ever done.

Besides, she should know by now. Plumber, lawyer, baker, or father—whatever Oliver Fox chose to do, he would be wildly successful and brilliant at. She had only herself to rely on, and now she had Birdie relying on her too. So she should quickly forget the niggling picture of a family that constantly tugged at her heart. She had real-life problems to fix. Like securing funding for a new animal shelter.

Adrian came into the soap shop. "Lena, we're ready. Come on in." He waved her into the next room. "We're waiting for a few more to arrive. Would you like coffee?"

"Water, please. I'm jittery enough as it is."

Adrian laughed. "Don't be. It's just a chance to hear more about your project and get to know you better."

Lena found an empty chair. The mayor, Seb Brewster, was deep in conversation with Ed Draper. Those two wouldn't be so bad. Ed was a dog person.

Gordy Dahlquist walked into the room, munching on a donut. What was it Birdie told her to do?

Connect with people. She could do this. "How's Petunia, Gordy? Is she doing okay on the diet cat food?"

"I admit, I was skeptical, but she's doing all right. She even jumps on the couch again instead of waiting for me to pick her up." Gordy took one of the seats across from her.

That was a good sign.

Lena thanked Adrian for the bottle of water he set in front of her. The woman standing at the coffee maker turned around. Constance Burkowski. Aw, great. She'd always had something against Lena's mother. Unfortunately, Valerie Larson had been a vault of secrets, and she'd taken them to the grave with her four years ago.

No surprise when Constance sat at the table without a word to Lena. She struck up a conversation with Gordy instead.

If this was everyone, maybe it wouldn't be so—

A gaudy animal-print dress appeared in the doorway, accompanied by a heavy perfume filling the room.

Lena bit back a groan. Gertie Thurber.

Lena couldn't deny Birdie's assessment of the woman.

She's a grump, that one. Not even the golden streets of glory will please that woman.

"Come on in, Gertie. I think we're ready to start." Seb stood as she walked into the room. The only spot was right next to Lena.

Lena's nose immediately started running. Goodness, was the woman drenched in the cloying perfume? Lena dug through her purse for tissues.

This was no time to wimp out. She had Birdie to think about.

The reminder infused some much-needed confidence. Lena straightened her back and focused on what Seb was saying.

"We looked over your application and I have to say, I'm impressed. I don't know if anyone has ever color-coded their business plan before."

"I find that it makes it easier to follow."

"Sure," Ed Draper said. "So, we see that it's well thought-out, but now we want to see your heart, your passion for this project. Why should we give *you* the grant?" The kind smile was probably meant to encourage her, but it didn't. She might throw up.

They wanted heart? Passion?

Why? The business plan had everything laid out. She wasn't trying out for one of Vivien's plays here.

"Uh, I'm sure you can see on page five of the report I included that the stray pet population—"

"We went over all that." Mrs. Thurber's nasal voice bounced around the room.

Adrian picked up where she left off. "And we know you can

run a successful business. Now we want to hear why this project means something to you."

What did that have to do with it? If there was anything she dreaded, it was speaking in front of a group, and now they paired that with needing to hear her "heart"?

Some would even say she didn't have one. Didn't they know her nicknames? Robo-Lena. Ice Queen. Lonely Frump-a-Lena. Or her great-grandmother's favorite, Cold Fish. That lovely one stuck her every time.

You have the personality of a cold fish.

The blunt declaration had shot a barb into her brain at the tender age of seven, and she had yet to find the way to remove it. All because she wasn't a people person.

And what did this committee want? Some passionate speech about why she wanted to rebuild a pet rescue and shelter? Shouldn't that be rather obvious?

She wasn't sure why, but Oliver's face came to mind. She could picture that particular smirk he would wear, and suddenly there was something Lena could grab on to. She couldn't let that smirk best her. She would scour the depths for something touchy-feely to convince this committee.

Birdie.

Everybody loved Birdie.

"I've watched Birdie and Howard Dawson care for sick and injured animals most of my life, and with each rescue they reminded me that every creature deserves a second chance." Her voice shook, but she powered through. "We're finding more and more strays in our county, and these pets deserve their second chance. I know you want to see heart and passion. Well, I don't have much of that, but Birdie does. She's the heart of this non-profit, and I'll be the brains."

Lena's gaze flitted from face to face.

"Well, then I'd say your chances are good at receiving it," Ed Draper said. "Especially since you're the only applicant so far this year."

Lena finally caught a full breath. Yes!

Gordy Dahlquist tapped the papers in front of him. "That doesn't mean it's a given. We could hold out until next year and give two grants or business loans."

"Stuff it, Gordy. There's no reason why we couldn't offer the grant to Lena."

Mrs. Burkowski was on her side? Lena held her breath.

"We still have over a month before the deadline though. Someone else might still apply." Mrs. Thurber made a mark on the business plan, like she was crossing something out.

Lena clasped her hands under the table. "But other than that? If no one applies, we get the grant?"

"We can't guarantee anything before the deadline, but yeah, if no one else applies, looks like you'll be opening up a new shelter," Seb said.

Everyone stood up. Finally, the break she needed. The chance Birdie needed.

They all gathered their things and moved toward the door. Lena pulled out her phone as she walked. She couldn't wait to tell Birdie.

"And I, for one, will be looking forward to your community presentation." Mrs. Burkowski smiled at her again.

But Lena's pulse stopped along with her feet. "Excuse me? Presentation?"

"Right," Adrian said. "The last requirement. Because the non-profit or business receiving the funds has to show how they will benefit Deep Haven, you'll have to inform us when you'd like to schedule your community-wide event or presentation." He made it sound like it was no big deal.

She, on the other hand, could start hyperventilating any second now just thinking about it.

Seb chimed in. "It needs to be open to the public. Usually we find an interactive event is best. And if by chance someone else applies, your events will most likely be the deciding factor on who gets the funding."

Another public-speaking thing. That was just great.

But she had time. And she would figure this out. Maybe together with Birdie she could come up with something that didn't include making a complete fool of herself in front of the whole town of Deep Haven.

Maybe.

five

· · ·

"It's a first day for the both of us. Are you ready, peanut?" Oliver asked his daughter as he double-checked her seat belt. She looked ready in her brand-new cotton dress and sweater. The day after Labor Day, and already he needed long sleeves this morning.

Kiah kicked her new sparkling tennis shoes together to make them light up. "All ready. And remember, I want to walk in the classroom all by myself."

"Right. All by yourself. I'll wait in the hall." Oliver shut the door and hopped behind the wheel.

"And no hugs goodbye."

He turned around to see her. "Are you going to at least wave?"

"I guess." She shrugged. "But why is it your first day?"

"It's my first day at the bakery."

"We been there lots of times. It's not your first."

"But this is the first shift Aunty Robin is leaving me alone." A chance to prove to her he was a different guy. He was a man she could count on now. "And I won't have my best helper there because she will be too busy at school." He started the ignition.

"Dad, you're gonna have to get used to it." She gave him a look of pity and a melodramatic sigh.

She was growing up way too fast.

Most of the trees Oliver passed on the way to Deep Haven Elementary were still vibrant green, but a few hinted at the yet-to-come autumn colors. It would be a short-lived but impressive show in a few weeks. And then a long, cold winter would set in. By then they'd probably be long gone.

"Look at that tree, Dad. It's already turning yellow. That means it's a deciduous tree."

He laughed. "Are you sure you're only starting kindergarten? Or am I dropping you off at the high school?"

"Daaaad."

Wasn't sure what was worse. Watching a daughter he barely knew growing at the speed of light, hardly needing him, or all the memories waiting for him in his old school building. Memories of when his family had been whole. When he'd been naive enough to think the worst thing in the world was the kids who wanted to pick on his brother and sister or Lena. He'd grown big enough to put a stop to that. Back then he could take on anything.

Until life had shown him just how wrong he was. Because there was no way to put a family back together after he'd failed so drastically.

As he pulled into the school drop-off line, Kiah suddenly grew quiet watching the groups of kids hopping out of cars and rushing toward the building.

"This is it, darlin'." Ollie manufactured some enthusiasm and injected it into his words as he joined the line of cars.

He looked over his shoulder to wink at her.

"I don't remember where to go." Her voice quivered from her booster seat. "What if they don't like me?"

Without another thought, Oliver pulled into the first spot he could find and jumped out. He opened Kiah's door, and his daughter fell into his arms, squeezing his neck and cutting off his breath, but he didn't care.

His little girl still needed him. He held on to her and breathed in the scent of her coconut lotion. As much as he wanted to whisk her away and wait a year, it wouldn't do her any favors.

"Kiah, you're going to do great. You'll make new friends and learn a ton. You'll probably be smarter than me by the end of the day."

"I can help you at the bakery instead. I don't wanna go!"

He knew the feeling. But he also knew how giving in to something once could become a vice of destruction.

"I'll tell you something my dad once told me when I was scared. He said, 'Put on a brave face, Oliver, and remember who you are.' You can do that, right?"

"I don't have a brave face." She mumbled the words into his neck.

"Oh, but you do. Making your brave face helps remind you that you can be a hero even if you're a little scared."

She pulled back and stood on her own two feet. "What does it look like?"

"You need to tilt your chin up like this." Oliver lifted her chin. "And then you pull your shoulders back and stand tall."

She crinkled her nose and frowned. "But I'm not tall like you."

"That's okay." He squatted down in front of Kiah. "The last part of your brave face is your secret weapon. And I happen to know you have a very powerful one."

"What's my secret weapon?"

"Your biggest smile."

"Dad. That's not a weapon." But she lost the scared pouty face and couldn't hold back the glint of humor as she stared him down with her hands on her hips. They were getting there.

"Sure it is. Your smile is the best thing about *my* day. It scares away all my yucky feelings. That's pretty powerful."

"Really?" She must've learned that look of skepticism from

Lena. His girl had the form right on from the quirked eyebrow to the slight pucker on one side of her mouth.

"Really. I bet there's someone else who is nervous about starting school. You can help them be brave too."

"You really think it will work?"

"I do. Now, let's see your brave face. And don't forget the smile."

Kiah stood straight, lifted her chin, and released a big grin.

"That's it! You've got this." He held out a hand toward her.

Kiah grabbed it. "You really think other kids are a-scared too?"

"Yup. But it's okay. A lot of new things are scary at first."

It was only helping her face her fear and walk in to her first day of school, but Oliver felt like a conquering hero. Together they found Kiah's kindergarten classroom. She ran to her cubby and proudly showed him how she could hang up her backpack. No more trembling lips or teary eyes as she pointed out her name. Kiah Jackson.

That's my girl.

A young woman with long, dark-brown hair, glasses, and a tight skirt came up to them. How did she teach in that? And why did she look familiar?

"Oliver Fox? It really is you." She shook her head and smiled. "I wondered when I saw Kiah's registration."

This had to be the teacher. What was her name? Kiah had said it a million times after Robin took her to the open house, but he was drawing a total blank.

"Uh, yeah. This is my daughter."

"And I have my brave face on. See?" Kiah grinned up at her.

The teacher chuckled. "It's nice to see you again, Kiah. Why don't you find your name tag on the table over there." She pointed to the far side of the room, where a few other kids gathered. Kiah skipped over and immediately started talking to a little boy with red hair and freckles.

She was going to be just fine.

"So, I noticed you don't have another parent listed for Kiah on her parent contact form." There was something suggestive in the teacher's tone. "Is that right?"

"It's just the two of us." He continued watching Kiah as she mingled with the other kids. So far, so good.

"Are you back in Deep Haven permanently?" The teacher stepped closer, swept a lock of hair over her shoulder. Oliver stopped watching his daughter and made eye contact.

Oh.

Oh!

Was she flirting? He almost laughed out loud at himself. So, it had been a while since he'd done this song and dance.

"Not sure yet. But we're here now." Aw, that was lame as all get-out. He cleared his throat. "So, how about you? You're…still in town?"

Before she could answer, Kiah ran up to him. "Dad, you can go now." She practically shoved him out the door with one last hug goodbye.

The teacher wiggled her fingers. "See you around, Oliver Fox."

All right then. Maybe coming back wasn't so bad. But who was this teacher and what was her name?

Oliver read the red apple cutout by the door.

Miss Zimmerman.

Like that helped. There were a bunch of Zimmermans in this town. But she obviously knew him. And she wasn't scared away. If anything, she was maybe a little too welcoming, but there were worse ways to start the day.

Within a few minutes, Oliver hummed while walking into the Fox Family Bakery. He slipped an apron and hair net on.

Robin bounced up to him. "Well, how'd she do? Was she nervous? Did she cry?"

"It was a little touch and go at first, but she did great. Practically shoved me out the door before I could catch her teacher's name."

"Misty Zimmerman."

"Misty! That's right. I thought she looked familiar. Wasn't she in your class?"

"Yup, but I have to run. Sammy's waiting for me. Are you sure you can handle this? Because I can—"

"Robin, go. I've got this. It's in our blood, right? I've done it before."

"Once, Oliver, and I was here."

"I can handle it." He picked up the piece of paper she'd left for him.

She walked backward toward the exit and pointed at the paper. "That's the recipe for the walnut raisin bread, but I need you to double it."

"Double it. Got it."

"You have to get it going right away. I'll be back in time to make deliveries to the resorts, but we're cutting it kinda close. After the loaves are started, move on to the cinnamon rolls. The dough is already rising."

Oliver turned his sister around before she ran into the mixer. "Stop worrying. Go."

She hugged him and left. Oliver cranked up the country music station on the radio and read over the recipe. Basic stuff. Flour, milk, eggs. Throw in some raisins and walnuts and he would be good to go.

Thirty minutes later he stood over the big mixer. What had he done wrong?

The dough was completely crumbly. It didn't stick together at all like when Robin did it. He picked up the paper from the counter, and flecks from the cinnamon sticks fell off it.

Oh. It was three packages of flour. Not eight.

And then he'd doubled it.

But that was fine. He'd simply compensate. Divide the mess in the bowl and take out two thirds. They could even save it for tomorrow's batch of loaves. Then he could eyeball it and add some extra liquids until the consistency was right. How hard could it be?

He should've never asked the question, because after adding more milk, eggs, and water, he now had a brown soupy mess on his hands. He stared at the clock over the door. These should've been in the oven by now.

The oven! Oliver groaned. He ran to the fancy oven and set it for three hundred seventy-five degrees. Something he should've done before he'd even started.

But he could still salvage this. He slowly added more of the crumbly surplus mixture from before as the huge dough hook spun. Once the texture looked right, he let it mix for five more minutes. He separated the dough like Robin had shown him last week. He was behind schedule, but maybe if he moved these closer to the oven, they would rise faster and he could make up some of the time.

But when Robin walked in three hours later, he only had a dozen half-baked loaves, ten burnt loaves, and three sheet pans of soggy cinnamon rolls to show for it. Robin looked at the flour spilled on the floor, the still-messy kneading table, and a sink overflowing with dirty dishes.

"Are you early? I was hoping to have this—"

She held out her hand to stop him. But her tight lips didn't open to say a word. Instead, she pulled her hair back with the binder she wore on her wrist.

Oliver's gut clenched. "I'll fix this. I will. You can tell all your customers your big bro—"

"This is my fault. I shouldn't have given you so much responsibility on your first day." She didn't look him in the eye as she grabbed a broom.

"Here, let me clean." He tried to take the broom from her. "I can at least do that."

She shook her head. "Why don't you take a break? I'll get this."

She still hadn't looked him in the eye. But even if she did, all he would see was a pile of disappointment bigger than the dishes stacked in the sink, because once again he'd proved to his little sister she couldn't count on him.

He pitched his soiled apron in the laundry bag and left. He sped out of town in his van heading west. Mile after mile, Robin's expression haunted him.

This was why he hadn't wanted to come back here.

Seeing the sign for the Cascade River, Oliver pulled over at the state park and followed the fast-moving river water down to where it emptied into the blue of Lake Superior. He raked up a handful of stones and, one by one, chucked them out into the deep. Not far enough.

He picked up more and pitched them out too.

What he wouldn't do for a drink right now. To just get deliriously drunk and forget—

His mouth went bone dry. He tried licking his lips. The amber hue of the river water looked so much like a good bourbon he almost dove in.

He had to get out of here.

With shaky hands, he found his phone and called Blanche as he walked back to the van. He didn't even let her finish saying hello. "I need help."

"Where are you?"

"I'm at the river, but…" Everything in him yearned for an escape. The need for a shot of something hard and strong sank its fangs into him and wasn't letting go.

"Find a meeting, Oliver." Blanche's raspy voice was his lifeline.

"It's early afternoon. And I'm out in the middle of nowhere—"

"Those are excuses. I want you to keep me on speakerphone and look it up right now. You've fought hard for this, Ollie. You're not gonna give up now."

"What am I doing here, Blanche? I can't even help—"

"The meeting, Oliver."

Right. He looked up the nearest AA meeting. There was one starting in two hours, but— He groaned.

"What? What's wrong?" Blanche must've heard him.

"There's a meeting not too far away. But it's in Deep Haven."

"So? That's good. It's close."

"I'll know everyone there. That's what I'm trying to avoid. They're all looking down at me enough as it is."

"What makes you think that?"

"Because my own sister can't even trust me to do my job. What am I even doing at the bakery? Everyone here thought I would be a big hotshot lawyer. *I* thought I'd be a hotshot lawyer. Now I'm coming back with nothing but a plumbing license—"

"Stop the pity party right there. Yeah, you're a plumber. A plumber who worked his butt off to put food on the table and care for not only your daughter but Hezekiah and myself too. That's nothing to be ashamed of."

"I know that."

"Do you?" Blanche's long-suffering sigh came through the line. "Don't you think the bigger problem might be all the stuff you haven't dealt with?"

"What are you talking about?"

"You gotta deal with it sooner or later. Go to that meeting. You need to find a support network there. Monica will be keeping tabs on you, so you'd better have something in place."

Right.

The urge to hit the closest liquor store lost a little of its grip while he hiked along the river killing time. But he couldn't shake it completely. At least out here in the wilderness, tempted or not, he wouldn't be able to find a drink.

When he arrived back in town later, he made do with the weak coffee they served in the church basement. He sipped from his Styrofoam cup and checked out the group gathered in what must be a kids' Sunday school room with Bible verses painted in bright colors on the wall.

That had to be Elton Zimmerman setting up chairs. And

sweet Mrs. Phelps? An alcoholic? It seemed so normal for her to be setting up cookies on a tray like she had when she'd worked in the school cafeteria. But he didn't recognize the five other people there. Including the pastor who greeted them and called the meeting to order.

Oliver found a seat in the back and bowed his head in the opening prayer.

"Lord, You know our weaknesses. You know our temptations. You know we are powerless against alcohol. Nothing is hidden from You. Bless us now as we come together to encourage each other to continue the path of sobriety. Amen."

Weaknesses. Powerless.

Oliver squirmed in his seat. He hated those words. He'd come to accept them—they were straight from the twelve steps—but he still despised them.

The pastor invited Elton to share. Like many of the Zimmermans, he was a hulk of a man towering over the small podium. He'd been a football legend when Oliver was growing up. He had to be related to Kiah's teacher. Bet the next time Oliver saw her she wouldn't be flirting.

"I'm Elton. I'm an alcoholic. For a long time, I couldn't admit it. But a couple years ago my boy, he got into some trouble. Drugs. My wife told me he was taking after me. And I didn't see it. Until she kicked me out."

He paused and took a sip of water, his hand trembling slightly, but he continued. "She changed the locks. She took most of the money out of the accounts, and I was left with nothing. I was too ashamed to tell anyone. I slept at one of the hotels we owned, but those were dark days. And I didn't have anywhere to go. Until Charlie there invited me to this meeting. I thought I was the only one, you know? The only one that couldn't stop. But I'm not. And…I guess I just want to say, if you're here, you're not alone either. Today is my one-year anniversary of being sober."

Not alone. It sure felt like he was alone with Hezekiah gone.

Blanche was almost two thousand miles away. Oliver was here with a daughter who was still adjusting to life with him and grieving her mother, and a little sister who couldn't count on him. But if big Elton could stand there and admit his struggle, maybe this group would help keep Oliver on track too. Because coming back home might just be the biggest threat to his sobriety yet.

🐕 🐕 🐕

LENA SCANNED THE TOP FILE MARYANN HAD LEFT OUT FOR HER while she scarfed down two bites of her peanut butter and jelly.

Oh no. Not today. Didn't she have enough problems? It'd been over a week since her interview, and she still didn't have an idea for a community event. Her garage was overflowing with unwanted animals. She'd had the weirdest dream about Oliver last night, and now this?

Maybe it was a mistake.

She stuck her head out of her office and into the clinic hall.

"Maryann, why is Mrs. Thurber's file here? She wasn't on the schedule earlier today." Lena kept her voice down in case anyone else was in hearing distance.

Her vet tech rolled her eyes. "Why else? Her precious Charles is deathly ill and needs to be seen immediately."

First Lena had to deal with Mrs. Thurber on the committee. Now in the clinic too? The last time Mrs. Thurber had insisted the Yorkshire terrier was on his deathbed, he'd simply been refusing to eat a new brand of dog food he didn't like. Before that, she'd been adamant he was violently ill when he'd gotten into the groceries and eaten half a bag of brown sugar, causing a bad case of gas. "This better not be like last time."

"She insisted. I didn't know what to say."

"Fine, I'll see Charles, but not before the two patients that actually had appointments." Lena moved the file to the bottom of the pile.

Maryann grimaced. "Are you sure? She's really upset already. That's why I put her on top. And I already talked to the last three patients scheduled today to explain that we're delayed so they could know to come in later."

"That's fine for them, but I'm not going to give her preferential treatment and make my other patients that are here and already waiting wait any longer. If she wants to be fitted into the schedule, she'll have to wait her turn. I'm already behind because of the emergency call at the petting zoo."

Not that there wasn't extra pressure with Mrs. Thurber being on the grant committee, but it wouldn't be right to treat her differently because of it. Lena continued down the hall to Exam Room Two and treated Isaac Frank's bulldog for the infection in its paw, carefully cleansing the wound and prescribing antibiotics. Then to Exam Room Three, where a rabbit had a bad case of ear mites. Now she could see what mischief Charles had gotten into.

She paused in the hall and braced herself for the wrath she was sure to face, when Sheila rushed out of the exam room where Mrs. Thurber was waiting.

"Dr. Larson, you need to come quickly." Sheila's voice rarely sounded that shrill.

"What's wrong?"

"Charles. He's seizing."

"Other symptoms?" Lena opened the door and snatched clean gloves.

"It's about time you—"

Lena blocked Mrs. Thurber's tirade and focused on listening to Sheila's response as she crouched next to the Yorkie. He was unconscious on the floor, mouth open, body stiff.

"Loss of appetite, weakness, some diarrhea," Sheila said.

"Evidence of icterus?" Lena pulled out her stethoscope.

"Possibly. I haven't checked yet," Sheila said.

After checking for injury, Lena carefully lifted the dog to the exam table.

Mrs. Thurber railed at her side. "I told you something was wrong. Do you know how long I've been waiting? Two hours!"

Lena used a light to check the Yorkie's eyes and gums. Yup, a yellow tint to both. Icterus. "Mrs. Thurber, when you're done yelling, you could help here. Is he drinking and urinating more?"

"You're the vet. You tell me. And if you'd done your job—"

Lena listened to the dog's heart and lungs. Breathing good. Heartrate high. "Any changes to his diet?"

"What does that have to do with anything? You know how picky he is."

Lena stopped everything and stared directly at Mrs. Thurber. "It has to do with giving you a proper diagnosis. Have you been feeding him fatty foods? People food?"

"Of course I give him people food. Have you smelled the dog food you tried to sell me last time? It was disgusting. He likes pork rinds instead."

Charles started to rouse.

"Oh, Charles!" Mrs. Thurber scooped him up. But Lena had seen all she needed.

"We'll take a blood sample for some labs, but I'm fairly certain Charles has a portosystemic shunt."

"And what does that mean? I'm not the one that went to veterinary school, because if I had, I certainly wouldn't be here."

Lena clenched her jaw, holding back all she really wanted to say. She couldn't afford to lose her cool. Not with her professional reputation at stake. Once she could steady her voice, she explained. "There's a shunt obstructing blood flow to the liver. I believe we caught it early enough that we should be able to treat it, but you'll have to monitor his diet very carefully, and we'll need to look at surgery. For now, we should get him some fluids and do the blood work."

"You want to cut him open?" With Charles under one arm, she moved to the door and yanked it open.

"Mrs. Thurber, we still need to discuss surgery—"

"If you would've seen us when we arrived this wouldn't have happened. I'll be looking for another veterinarian." She yelled the whole way down the hall and into the lobby, where Lena caught up with her.

"But he still would've—"

"I don't want to hear another word." She stopped by the reception desk. "You'll be hearing from my lawyer. And there's no way you should get that grant—"

"This has nothing to do with the grant."

"It has everything to do with it. You want to be in charge of a shelter for animals when you neglect the ones in your own practice? It won't happen under my watch. I promise you that."

"Mrs. T? Is that you?"

Lena whipped around.

Oliver Fox. What was he doing here? And why was he always present during the worst moments of her life to witness her humiliation?

Ollie sidled up to Mrs. Thurber and gave her Yorkie a scratch between his ears. "And who is this handsome fella?"

Mrs. Thurber melted a bit when she gave Oliver a weepy smile and introduced Charles. "Oh, Ollie, you just wouldn't believe the day we've had. But how are you, dear? Your sister told me you were back in town."

How in the world had Ollie befriended Gertie Thurber? She hated everyone. And here she was acting like a doting grandmother. Did she just squeeze his arm?

"Aw, what's a-matter, Mrs. T?"

"My poor Charles has been horribly neglected. I need to find a new veterinarian." She dropped her voice. "Let me warn you away now, Oliver. I should've left a long time ago. I don't know why I stayed."

Neglected? Lena fumed. She never neglected her patients.

With all the pork rinds and meat scraps Charles was eating, his liver would have already been struggling, causing toxins to build up in his blood. The seizure had been a result of hepatic encephalopathy, not neglect on her part.

Lena ripped off her gloves and threw them away. The worst part was that after all she'd done, she'd probably just thrown away Birdie's chance at the shelter too.

six

· · ·

IT MUST'VE BEEN DIVINE TIMING THAT'D BROUGHT OLIVER INTO THE clinic right after this week's Thursday AA meeting. If he could help smooth things over for Lena, maybe then she would finally let him bring up their past.

Not that he'd meant to eavesdrop, but the drama happening in the lobby of her clinic was on full display. She always masked her feelings well, but he knew that particular twitch in her eye and slight flaring of her nostrils as she threw away the gloves she'd been wearing. She was ticked.

And she might be many things, but she wasn't neglectful or sloppy as Gertie accused.

He scratched Charles behind the ears. "Dr. Larson was the top of her class at the University of Minnesota. And it's one of the top schools for veterinary medicine in the country. We're pretty lucky to have her here in little old Deep Haven."

"I didn't say she wasn't smart." The older woman sniffed. "Just neglectful. Charles almost died. So I will be looking for another vet. And if you know what's good for you, you'll take your animals elsewhere too." She stomped out of the clinic with her Yorkie in her arms.

Whoa-kay, so maybe they needed to let Gertie cool off first.

Watching her leave, Lena didn't move, but her assistant standing next to her rolled her eyes and exited the room, leaving an awkward silence in the waiting area. The lady sitting with a small pet carrier at her feet grabbed a magazine and started flipping through it, while a teenager with a bunny cage went back to doctoring a coffee drink.

"Don't worry about her, Lena. She always did love being a victim. The next time Charles needs something, she'll be back," Oliver said.

"That's not my biggest problem right now." She marched toward the back of the building.

He jogged down a short hallway after her. "Is the dog going to be okay?"

"I can't discuss another patient's condition—"

"Lena, stop." Surprisingly enough, she did. But she didn't turn to face him. He moved in front of her and stilled. Her lips pinched together tightly, like she was holding back tears.

There was only one other time he'd seen her cry, and like then, all he wanted to do was make it better.

"Ignore Gertie. She's just a cranky lady with nothing better to do."

Lena's eyes sparked. "Ignore her? She accused me of negligence. And that was after we rearranged our whole schedule to fit her in. Her dog is going to suffer because she won't listen and feed it properly. How am I supposed to ignore that?"

She walked through a door with her name on it. "She blames me for his condition. And if she spreads the word, leaves a bad review, what then? I lose even more patients. And none of it is true. I mean, yes, I made her wait her turn, but that's not what caused his seizure."

Oliver followed her inside. The office was typical Lena style—everything on her long white desk in neat piles and at right angles. But the pictures in here were in color rather than the black-and-white ones she had in the lobby. They were pictures of Lena with various cats, dogs, horses. There was even one with her standing next to a Holstein cow.

"Are you actually grinning in this one?" He moved in closer.

"Oliver, stop staring at the picture. What are you doing here anyway?"

"I was on my way to see…someone, and I wanted to ask you—"

What he really needed to talk about was their past. But this probably wasn't the best timing. Not while she was still upset. "—about goat feed. We need more."

Lena's form relaxed slightly. "You can ask Cheryl at the front desk. She can order it for you if you like, and they'll deliver to the house. Now, if you don't mind—"

"But what are you going to do about Gertie Thurber?"

"What more *can* I do? She's impossible."

"If you really don't want her to spread bad reviews, why don't you try to smooth things over?"

"Easy for you to say." Lena plopped into her office chair. "You're the king of charm. You waltz in and, poof, all is forgiven. Everything comes easy to you."

"Not everything. Didn't Robin tell you about my bakery disaster?"

"You? Involved with a disaster? Gee, doesn't surprise me."

"Ouch. Although, given our history, I—"

Lena jumped out of her chair. "Our history is not what we're here to discuss. If you don't mind, I have work to finish."

Oliver blocked the door. "Wait." Obviously, she wasn't ready to talk. But he could still help her.

He *needed* to help her.

Work wasn't going well. Kiah liked school, but she was acting up at home. And like Seb reminded him at the AA meeting, sometimes it was the smallest accomplishments that kept him going. He needed a win here.

He leaned casually on the doorframe. "What if I helped smooth things over with Gertie?"

"Why would you do that?" Suspicion lingered in her words.

"I came back to Deep Haven for a reason. I'm not the same guy I was back then. Let me help."

Lena stepped closer. "How would you accomplish that? Gertie is one of the most cantankerous people I know. She won't listen."

"She's lonely. And I think if you went to her house, maybe offered a discount, it would go a long way."

"A discount? Are you kidding?" Her lips thinned to almost nothing.

"You're gonna have to give something to entice her back."

If Lena were one of her patients, her hackles would've been raised. "I didn't do anything wrong. Giving a discount implies that I did."

The high-and-mighty Lena never could stand to be wrong. In anything. This would be a tough sell. "You have to be the bigger person here, Lena. Charles is the only good thing in that woman's life. She doesn't have friends. She lives alone. She's miserable and enjoys making others feel miserable too. You can rise above it. And while we're on that subject, this should be a warning for you."

"About what?"

"Getting out and enjoying life a little so you don't end up like Gertie Thurber."

She huffed. "Not all of us can drift through life on laughter and charm. Some of us have to work."

"Yeah, but there has to be more to life than that too."

"And what do you suggest?"

"You could come over sometime. We play a mean game of Old Maid and Slap Jack." And maybe then she'd see he wasn't such a bad guy.

Because as much as he hated to admit it, it was tearing him up that Lena still hated him. Not that he didn't deserve it, but everything inside wanted to change the way she saw him. At one point she'd really cared about him. He had proof. He had her letter.

"I'm busy." She counted off on her fingers. "I've got the clinic, and Birdie and I are trying to get a new shelter going, and—"

"I get it." She allowed him to come closer without backing away. "You're one of the hardest working people I know. But it wouldn't hurt to have some fun every now and then too. And when it comes to Gertie, I can come with you if you want."

Lena's expression softened. "Use your powers of persuasion for something good?"

"Something like that."

There was so much more to Lena Larson than she ever let on. He wanted to pull back the screen and see all that she hid inside. He wanted a chance to be friends again. At one point, she'd been as close to him as his own brother and sister. He'd teased her mercilessly when they were kids, but after his parents died, she'd been one of the only people he could be real with. At least, until he'd failed her.

"What do you say?" He tried not to fidget while she considered.

"I'll think about it. But for now, I should get to work."

"Sure." Better than a complete rejection. Thinking about it meant he had a chance.

Oliver stepped toward the door. They both reached for the knob at the same time. Their fingers entwined for a mere second, but the sensation from the connection rocked him. He missed her touch as soon as she pulled away.

That was weird.

"Ollie, don't you have someone to see?"

Right. His next errand. "Coach."

Lena stilled. "You're going to see Coach Presley?"

Oliver nodded, his gut suddenly churning.

"Did you ever…after the accident?" She studied him, not with judgment but something like empathy in her steady gaze.

Almost like she could see how difficult it would be, and that she...cared.

The churning inside eased a bit. "No, I never did. I...have a lot to make up for."

She didn't say anything, and she didn't look away.

Maybe he had a chance here. "Maybe I could come over tonight and we could talk—"

Lena's shoulders stiffened. She opened the door farther. "Coach is doing a lot better, you know. He's not on a ventilator anymore. He has movement back in his upper body. He loves having visitors. Might even enjoy *your* company. You were close once."

Message received. He was dismissed.

"Yeah, we were."

Coach Presley had believed in him. Oliver could remember with perfect clarity the moment the man had sat him down in his office.

You've got a choice here. I've seen the kids you're hanging out with, and I know what they do in their free time. But you're a good kid, Oliver. I know you can do better. So I'm giving you a chance to be a real leader here. I'd like you to be our defensive team captain. But you're gonna have to keep your nose clean. Do me proud, son.

And oh, how he'd wanted to do just that.

And for a while he had. He'd found other things to do instead of the parties, until Jeremy had dragged him to a seniors-only bash. He'd tried so hard to play it cool, but when all his friends had circled him chanting "Keg stand! Keg stand!" he'd caved. Let Coach down.

The very next day, Coach's car had slid into an intersection and been hit by another driver, killing his wife, traumatizing his daughter Izzy, and robbing him of mobility and his career. It'd rocked the whole town. And when the man had needed the community and the team the most, Oliver had never had the guts to see him. Not once.

"I hope you have a good visit," Lena said, her words jolting him back to the present.

Right. He had his own work to do. But the sincerity in Lena's voice spurred him on all the way to the nursing home where Coach now lived.

Oliver waved to the nurse at the desk inside the entrance. He couldn't recall her name, but she looked familiar and thankfully didn't stop him. He tried to ignore the sharp antiseptic odor of the hallway as he counted down the rooms. This was it. Room 12. Someone had decorated the door with cardboard football cutouts and Husky memorabilia. A picture of Coach in his glory days surrounded by previous Husky players was front and center.

Oh, how Oliver wished he'd listened to Coach, been stronger back then.

He rubbed his chest, trying to loosen the tightness squeezing the breath right out of him. Coach had every right to dismiss him, but he had to try. Oliver knocked and jammed his hands into his pockets.

He'd made some progress with Lena. Hopefully he could here with Coach too.

The door opened. How strange to see a man that had once towered over him, larger than life, now confined to a wheelchair. There were more wrinkles and sagging skin where muscles had been, but his eyes were sharp and clear as recognition shone. Coach knew exactly who he was.

Oliver held his breath, waiting for his response.

Coach opened the door wider. "Oliver Fox. It's about time you came home, son."

🐺🐺🐺

COULD THIS DAY PLEASE BE OVER? BETWEEN THE EMERGENCY callout at the petting zoo, falling behind with her appointments, and the fiasco with Mrs. Thurber, Lena's nerves were shot. And she was all out of ice cream at home. That would have to be remedied as soon as she left the clinic to go home.

And then there was Oliver.

Oliver wanting to talk about the past she wanted to erase. If only she could go back and stop herself from writing that stupid letter. She wanted to forget how naive she'd been to lay it all out there, against her better judgment, against all her mother's advice to never let a man take hold of her heart. She never wanted to relive that humiliation again.

Ever.

Lena plopped down in her office chair and gave it a full spin.

But she had to admit, the boy who'd run away with her heart had come back a different man. She would never tell him, but she wished she could've seen his meeting with Coach Presley. And he had a good point when it came to Gertie Thurber.

She needed to go and make things right. Birdie deserved this shelter. Lena couldn't let Gertie stand in the way.

But she would do it without Oliver's help. No need to recall how everything inside her had gone berserk when their hands accidentally touched on the doorknob. Where had that curiosity about running her fingers through his thick, dark waves come from? Or the strange desire to see what it would be like to kiss him?

This was Oliver Fox, for goodness' sake!

He was obnoxious. Irritating. They had nothing in common except a property line, and even that she didn't like.

But his deep voice still rang in her head.

Dr. Larson was the top of her class at the University of Minnesota. And it's one of the top schools for veterinary medicine in the country. We're pretty lucky to have her here in little old Deep Haven.

How did he know she'd been at the top of her class? Or that the U of M was a top vet school? It almost sounded like he admired her.

Obviously the hunger was messing with her brain now.

She scarfed down the rest of her sandwich and finished the appointments for the day. After the others had clocked out, Lena grabbed her laptop and left. She might as well get the unpleasant task over with.

She drove to Gertie's cottage, a few blocks away from the clinic, with Oliver's voice in her head.

You have to be the bigger person here, Lena. Charles is the only good thing in that woman's life.

Be the bigger person.

Lena knocked on the door and waited. Nothing. She knocked again, this time harder.

"Who is it?" The muffled voice behind the door sounded like a Midwestern Fran Drescher.

"Dr. Larson."

"What do you want?" Gertie finally opened the door. Charles was still tucked under her arm, but the woman's hair was mussed. Dark makeup was smudged under her eyes, like maybe she'd been crying.

Lena would never say this to his face, but Oliver might've been right. Maybe behind all that crankiness was a hurting woman.

"Well? What are you standing there for? I have better things to do than let all the cool air out."

"I came to apologize for your long wait at the clinic."

Gertie lifted her chin. "You're only saying that for the grant."

"I'm saying that because I want Charles to have the best care possible. And if you're willing to come back and let me treat him, we'll work to get him healthy so you can have him for as long as possible. I don't want you to have to drive over a hundred miles away if there's an emergency."

Her eyes narrowed. "Oh, so you want my money. Or are you trying to avoid a lawsuit?"

It took every ounce of self-control Lena possessed to keep her tone even and spit out the next words. "I'm willing to give you a ten percent discount for today's appointment. If you don't want to come back to the clinic, fine. But please get Charles care somewhere soon. He needs it."

Mrs. Thurber held the Yorkie closer to her. "If we come back, it will have no bearing on whether or not you get that grant. I'll email you what I decide."

"I understand." Lena had offered what she could. The rest was up to Gertie.

But now she was completely spent, and she still had groceries to buy if she wanted to eat tonight. After a day like this, another peanut butter and jelly sandwich was not going to cut it. It was too hot, and she was too tired to cook.

If Oliver invited her over for dinner, she might actually cave.

Better grab some hot fudge to go with the ice cream. Not the most nutritious of dinners, but it would do.

Lena drove to the grocery store and parked. Before she got out of her truck, the phone buzzed with an incoming message. Lena checked the screen. Her work email? Maybe Gertie had already decided what she was going to do for Charles.

But it wasn't Gertie's name in her inbox. Brad Fowler?

No. It couldn't be the same… After all this time?

Lena's finger hovered over the message. She closed her eyes for a moment and clicked.

She opened her eyes and started reading.

Dear Leann,

I know this is rather impersonal to contact you through your business email, but this was the only way I knew to communicate with you. I'm not sure if you know about me. While your mother was alive, I did as she asked and didn't intrude in your life. But I know that situation has changed, and I hope that finally I can meet you.

I'm your father. I knew Valerie in college, and although things didn't work out between us, I hope that you and I can have a fresh start. If this is something you would be open to, you can reply to this message or reach me at this number.

I look forward to hearing from you.
Sincerely,
Brad Fowler

Lena's whole body went cold.

Her dad. The one who'd abandoned her mother before she was born. The father she'd never met. Contacting her.

She'd only been dreaming of this for the last thirty years.

And now it was happening.

Yeah, he hadn't gotten her name right, but with autocorrect, it was bound to have been a simple typo. More importantly, he wanted to meet with her.

She had so many questions. So many sensations running through her at once that her brain might explode. She needed help.

With a quick text to Robin, she arranged to meet her at the VFW for burgers. Too jittery to sit still, Lena walked the three blocks and found a table near the back. The background music over the speakers couldn't distract her from the loud thoughts racing through her mind. She forced herself to sit in the hard plastic chair and read through the menu she knew by heart.

She had to get these feelings under control. She needed to think clearly. The next steps were crucial.

Her father had contacted her.

It wasn't long before Robin walked in wearing denim shorts and a cute striped tank top. She settled into her chair. "What's going on? You said it was urgent."

Before Lena could say anything, Melissa Ogden walked over with waters for them. "What will it be tonight, ladies?"

Robin ordered a burger and fries.

Melissa looked at Lena. "And you?"

"I'll take a bacon cheeseburger, onion rings, and a chocolate shake."

"What size shake?"

"Large." Lena handed Melissa the laminated menu. "No. Make it extra large."

Robin frowned. As soon as Melissa left, she leaned across the table. "An extra-large milkshake? What's going on?"

"This." Lena handed her the phone with Brad's email on the screen.

Robin's eyes grew big. "This is your father?"

"Yeah."

"Are you sure? He didn't even get your name right."

"It's him. And he sent this from his phone. It was probably just an autocorrect typo. But I know that's his name. Grandma always threw it around like a curse word when she was angry with Mom."

"But why did he wait so long to contact you?"

"Like he said, and like we always suspected, my mom didn't want him to have anything to do with us."

"Your mom's been gone for four years." Robin probably didn't mean to sound so accusing.

"I know that."

The sharpness that slipped into her voice sounded a little like a bark from a wounded animal, even to her own ears.

Get ahold of yourself, Lena.

So, this was not the reaction she'd been expecting from her friend. Then again, how could she count on Robin—coming from a real family, raised by two parents and two grandparents and surrounded by her two brothers—to understand the scope of this situation? That finally Lena, who had zero family, had now found one person she was actually related to by blood.

She reined in her tone of voice to something more clinical. There was a logical explanation. "Maybe he found out about her death only recently." Lena folded her napkin in half and traced the crease.

"I know this is something you've always wanted, but I'm just a little suspicious. I don't want you to get hurt."

"I supported you when you went to Paris, when you came

home again, in your relationship with Sammy, and then when you went back to France. Why can't you just be happy for me?"

Lena started to rise and Robin laid a hand on her arm. "I *am* happy for you. Please don't be mad at me for having a few doubts. I would hate for you to set your heart on something and have it all fall apart. Believe me, I went through that with Victor in Paris. You think a guy is gonna do the right thing, not scam you out of a career, but it happens. I'm trying to look out for you."

Maybe she had a point. She'd been pretty shaken up after the whole Paris bakery debacle. Lena sank back down.

"I get that, and believe me, I have my own questions and doubts too. But for this one moment I want…"

She wanted to revel in the fact that finally, finally her father had come looking for her. Wanted her.

The words sounded needy and foolish in her head, but she couldn't deny what her heart was crying out for.

"You want me on your side. And I am," Robin said.

"But maybe you're right. Maybe this is all too good to be true."

Maybe that's why her mother had always told her to rely on facts not feelings. But something inside was not going to let go of this opportunity. It had been denied too long.

"I'm not saying I don't have questions too." Lena folded the napkin in half again. "I do. But you of all people know what this means, how much I've wanted this."

"I do." Robin smiled. "And if he's legit, no one will be happier for you than me. But—fair warning—if he's not, I'll be the first in line to rip his heart out for hurting you. Deal?"

Lena nodded. "Deal."

"So, how are you going to respond? Are you going to text him? Call?"

"I'm not sure. That's why I need your help."

Because this could be one of the most important moments in Lena's life, and she wanted to get it right.

seven

. . .

THE PHONE CALL OLIVER HAD BEEN DREADING HAD COME. HE stepped into the garage and looked down at his lawyer's name on his ringing phone. Best get it over with so he could get back to his project.

He injected cheer he didn't really feel into his voice. "What do ya know, Ms. Emiliano?"

"I know you were supposed to be giving me weekly updates and I haven't had one since our court date. What's going on?"

"Aw, do ya miss me already? I could've sworn that was only yesterday." He opened up the garage door, allowing a warm breeze to blow in.

"The last communication I have from you is a text with your forwarding address in Deep Haven. That is not an update, and it was the last week of August. It's now the middle of September."

"Right, and I've been busy. Busy doing *all* the things that the judge asked for. How are you doing?"

"Where are you at with the list? Do you have a job yet?"

He grabbed his toolbox out of the van. "Of course I have a job. Kiah—"

"Wait. Where are you employed?"

He could hear the clicking of typing on a keyboard. "At the Fox Bakery."

"I assume this is your family bakery?"

The way she said *family* grated on his nerves. Did she know how hard it was to own a business in a small town? He set his toolbox down in the kitchen next to the oven.

"Yeah, it's a family business. My grandparents started it, and my sister runs it now. I help her." Which might be a little bit of a stretch. He did stuff, but he didn't know how much help he was to Robin.

"Is it enough to support Kiah? I'll need copies of paystubs."

"I'll be getting something else soon that pays more, but it's giving me the time I need to help Kiah settle in." It put groceries on the table, but not much more than that.

"Address?"

He rattled off the business address as he walked back out to the garage.

"Have you been attending AA meetings?" she asked.

"Yes, ma'am. Twice a week."

"Good. Do you have a new sponsor? Someone to vouch for your sobriety?"

"Not quite. But Kiah is in school—and doing great, by the way. She's been my first priority." Oliver adjusted the wrench hanging on the pegboard wall.

"Wonderful." She spoke with all the warmth of a frozen waterpipe. "Where are you on making amends?"

"I made amends with a few alr—"

"Define 'a few.' I need numbers."

"Two. My sister Robin and Coach Presley."

"That's it? Do you have signed statements from them?"

"Well, not yet, but—"

"Let me remind you that you only had three months to finish *all* the requirements the judge asked for. And because of some medical procedure scheduled, she just moved up our court date to November first. If you want to continue to keep custody of

Kiah, you shouldn't be dragging your feet. You're down to less than two months."

"I read the email notice. We'll be fine."

"Great. Then I will expect an emailed update next Friday. Remember, I can only help you if you do your part. I want you to keep custody of Kiah."

"Believe me, I do too. I'm working on it."

"Sounds good." She hung up before he could say anything more.

Sounds good.

She'd said the words, but the whole conversation had sounded more like *not good enough.*

Not a good enough dad. Not a good enough job. Not good enough to keep his daughter.

Or maybe it was Grandpa's voice still in his head.

Oliver opened up the back door of the van and hefted a new farmhouse sink up on his shoulder and carried it in. The porcelain basin easily weighed over a hundred pounds, but it was still lighter than the memories knocking around in his head.

Grandpa Jim hadn't cared that Oliver made football captain, or won first place at a debate competition and did okay in classes. It was always, "You can do better."

He'd never harped on Grayson for his grades or Robin for being late. Grandma had tried to smooth things over or make excuses, but deep down Oliver knew.

Grandpa still blamed him.

Even now, when Ollie tried to point that out to Robin, she didn't believe him. Grandpa doted on Grandma, was an elder at church, respected in the community. He was a man to look up to. And for a long time, Oliver had. But it had never been enough.

You're a Fox, Oliver. Start acting like it.

Carefully, Oliver set the sink on the kitchen floor next to the box with the faucet in it.

Those words had been thrown at him right after Oliver had been caught fighting again, this time over a guy in the locker room threatening to put the moves on Robin. But it hadn't mattered to Grandpa *why* Oliver had punched the guy in the face. Only that he'd gotten caught and been suspended.

After Oliver disconnected the waterlines and drains under the old stainless steel sink, he removed it with a grunt. He made the adjustments on the base cabinet and set the new sink in place.

Maybe that was why he'd quit trying to meet Grandpa's expectations and started drinking. First, out of spite for being grounded when he missed curfew by five minutes. But then he'd found he liked the buzz and people liked *him*, especially when he was drinking. He'd liked the freedom to be uninhibited. Until it became its own kind of prison.

It had taken years before he could climb out of the pit he'd found himself in. Thank God he'd found Hezekiah.

Well, more accurately that Hezekiah had found him. Though Jalisa had originally introduced them, and Oliver had worked for the man at various times, when Oliver had been at his worst, Hezekiah had offered him a home, a steady job, and some much-needed truth. Unlike Grandpa's version of it, this truth hadn't been laced with judgement and disappointment.

Oliver sighed. The grief of missing his mentor hit hard. His mouth went dry, and everything inside screamed for his favorite whiskey. Just a shot. To feel it burn going down and scraping the edge of the pain off with it.

He pulled out his three-year token and held it tight in his fist until the hard metal bit into his palm.

He was trying to be a better man. Each step brought him closer to showing his grandfather that he wasn't that failure anymore. That wussy twelve-year-old kid who couldn't throw a life ring far enough. The kid who'd let his own parents drown in the summer storm.

He had changed. He was stronger now. He just needed to prove it. The token went back in his pocket.

Once Ollie had his bearings again, he finished assembling the new faucet and reconnected the lines. He stood back to look at his work. With the new white subway tile backsplash and now the sink, the kitchen looked brighter. Hopefully Robin would like it and it could make up for his shortcomings in the bakery.

He gathered up his tools and was stowing them away in the van when Lena pulled up in her truck. He crossed over to her driveway.

"Hey, Doc. Late night at the clinic?"

Her hair was pulled back in a braid, but a few wisps of her light-brown hair framed her face. "What are you doing here?" she asked suspiciously.

"Can't a guy be neighborly?"

"You're not just any guy, Ollie."

Was that good or bad?

Whatever. He would show Lena, too, that he was a better man than the one that'd hurt her in high school—if she would let him.

"So, what is it you want?" Lena pulled something out of the truck and opened the garage door. Inside, multiple dogs of various colors and breeds barked in their kennels. An orange tabby cat jumped from a carpeted shelf on the wall to the floor and meowed.

"Still no word on the shelter?" Ollie followed her in.

"I'm working on it." She scooped food into the cat dishes. "If you're gonna stick around, make yourself useful." Lena handed Oliver the water dish. "Fill this in the sink over there."

Even in the chaos of animals overtaking her garage, the laundry sink was meticulously clean and all the shelves on the wall neat and orderly. Lena always did have her life put together.

Oliver handed her the full container of water and moved to the dog food container. "Any special instructions for feeding these guys?" He carried the food over to the dog kennels on the opposite side of the room.

"Put two scoops in each bowl. In the next kennel they'll need three each."

Oliver scooped the dog food. The canines barked excitedly. When he finished feeding and watering the dogs, he looked over at Lena. She held a long-haired gray cat. It nuzzled her neck. She looked affectionately at it as she stroked its back. She had a lot more heart than people gave her credit for.

This was a good time to get the ball rolling. "So, I was thinking—"

"There it is."

"What?"

"The real reason you're here. What do you want?"

"Seriously, Lena, can't a guy—ow!" He'd moved closer and reached out to pet the cat, but it suddenly swiped at Oliver's hand, then jumped out of Lena's arms and back to its perch. "What did I do?"

"I've always said animals have good instincts." Humor lurked in her voice.

"And that's why most animals love me. Something must be wrong with that one." Oliver shook his hand. The cat had left a scratch that was puffy and already dripping blood. "Great. Now I'll probably get some sort of infection—"

"Don't be such a baby. Let me see." Lena took his hand, her touch warm and surprisingly gentle. "Better come with me. It needs to be cleaned out and bandaged. I have a first aid kit in the bathroom."

She led Oliver through the garage door into her kitchen. Inside her meticulously clean house, two more dogs welcomed them. And Lena actually grinned at them. She bent down to give them treats and crooned at them in a voice Oliver had never heard from her.

He stared. She should definitely do that more often.

Deep barks sounded from somewhere farther in the house. "This is Wentworth and Jane. I need to let Bruce out, and then I can clean your cut. He's destroyed my guest room, but I don't have another place for him yet."

He followed her down the hallway. As soon as she opened the door, the huge apricot mastiff ran past Lena and jumped on Oliver, knocking him down to the floor. The dog licked his face.

"Now that's a welcome. But down, boy. I don't think Lena wants me bleeding all over her floor." Oliver sat up, but Bruce lay down on his lap, his body stretching across the hallway.

"Wow. He really likes you." Lena stood over him, a confused look on her face. "He didn't act like that last time he saw you."

"Don't act so surprised. I'm not so bad if you would get to know me."

Lena paused, hurt reflecting in her eyes. "I do know you, Oliver." Her voice was soft. "That's the problem."

"A lot can change in the fourteen years since we graduated, don't you think?"

"And some things never change."

"I did. And that's what I want to talk about." He nudged Bruce off his lap and stood. The dog stayed glued to his leg. "I want to show you I'm not the same jerk I was back—"

"Let's get that hand cleaned out." Lena practically ran into the bathroom and started digging through her medicine cabinet and drawers.

He followed her. "I'm trying to—"

"The past is the past, Ollie. Leave it there." She wet a washcloth and picked up his hand. She gently wiped the blood away.

Up close as she assessed his wound, he studied her. Her eyes picked up the green in the shirt she wore—a pretty, mossy kind of green. Her cheeks were slightly flushed, her lips full. In the small bathroom, he was very aware of her proximity. He breathed in her sweet lemony scent.

A burning sensation stung his hand.

"Agh! What are you doing?" He pulled his hand away, but she held it tight.

"I've got to clean this out. Stay still." She continued to treat his hand, applying ointment with a gentle touch she seemed to reserve for hurting creatures.

She didn't show this side of herself to others much. But he couldn't be fooled. She had strong emotions all right. Emotions she hid well.

Like she had when they were kids.

"Remember the last time you bandaged me up?" He hoped his question would draw her gaze back to his own.

She stilled a moment but didn't look up. "That was a long time ago. We were children."

But he needed to remind her there'd been a time when she'd trusted him. When he *had* been there for her. Dumb boys on the bus had been at it again. Older boys teasing her for not having a dad.

"You were always so strong, even back then, holding it together and acting like you didn't care a whit what they said. I always admired that."

"They were just big bullies."

But their words had wounded her. He would never forget how she'd run straight for the woods after they were dropped off. The girl who'd acted like the cruel taunts didn't bother her had wept against the big oak tree as if her heart had been shattered. When he'd approached, she'd glared at him.

What do you want, Ollie?

He'd wanted to make it all better. He'd wanted to comfort her. And he'd promised himself then, he'd always protect her. He'd made sure those boys had never messed with Lena again.

She finally looked up at him. "You got in a lot of trouble that day."

"It was worth it." He'd take all the detentions and bloody knuckles in the world if it meant Lena bandaging his hands and looking at him with shy admiration like she had back then.

But the one time she'd actually offered him her heart, he'd failed.

So what was happening here? He didn't have the right to want her anymore. He wasn't trying to start something here. He just needed to make amends.

"Why are you looking at me like that?" Her familiar scowl was back.

He laughed. "You're right. Some things never change."

"I think I need that in writing."

"What?"

"It's about time you realized I'm right. Only took you thirty years to admit." Her completely deadpan expression made her humor all the funnier. But there was just enough spark in her eye to show it was in jest.

And he wanted to see it again. Maybe even be the reason her green eyes danced.

"So there's hope for us, Doc?"

Her body stilled. "Us?"

"Yeah. Think we c—"

"Let's get one thing straight. There is no 'us,' Oliver Fox, and there never will be." She stretched a bandage over his cut and slapped a tube of ointment into his palm. "Keep the scratch clean and put this on it three times a day."

She walked out of the bathroom.

Bruce was still next to him, pawing at his leg for attention.

Oliver sighed. "That went well."

Bruce barked as if in agreement.

SERIOUSLY, WHAT WAS GOING ON? LENA SCRUBBED HER HANDS AT the kitchen sink. And why was Oliver still here? She'd been pretty clear. He needed to leave. Now.

But she couldn't look at him again long enough to kick him

out. Not when looking at him scrambled all reason and logic and left her slightly breathless.

After all this time, he still had some kind of hold on her, just as he had ever since she'd found out he beat up Bobby Zimmerman and Danny Olson for making fun of her in the fifth grade.

She squirted more soap into her hands and rubbed them together until they were covered in foamy suds and stinging.

It wasn't right. In fact, it was so very wrong.

The way her heart had leaped at his words.

So there's hope for us, Doc?

She should've screamed "No!" She should've shoved him away. She should've done a million things.

But she was mostly horrified at herself and the overwhelming desire that had washed over her in that one brief moment.

She wanted there to be an *us*. With Oliver Fox!

At least, until she'd finally grabbed hold of her senses and realized what was happening.

She would not fall for those big brown eyes that had looked down at her and made her go gooey down to her core. She couldn't do that again. Oliver was all charm and no substance. So how could her heart betray her so fully?

Bruce barked from the bathroom.

Right. The dogs. She shut off the water and grabbed the leashes. She'd take the dogs for their nightly walk and get some fresh air and oxygen to her brain, which obviously needed it.

She clipped the leashes to Wentworth and Jane and braced herself to face Oliver. "Bruce, come."

Oliver came out of the bathroom with Bruce firmly set at his side.

"Bruce, come on. Let's go on our walk." She wiggled the leash, his cue to do one of his favorite things.

The stubborn dog refused to leave Oliver.

"Why don't you hold him back and I'll slip out the door?" Oliver said.

That's what she wanted. For Oliver to leave. So why this disappointment swirling inside?

Lena nodded and grabbed Bruce's collar. "I've got him. You can go." But as soon as Oliver stepped away, Bruce lunged after him, taking Lena too.

"Stay, Bruce!" Lena used her alpha voice.

It didn't matter. He barked and whined as Oliver tried once more to separate himself, and the dog was too big for Lena to hold back. She wanted to scream.

"Can he come home with me for the night?" Ollie knelt by Bruce and scratched behind his ears.

"That's not fair for him to grow accustomed to you if he's going to have to find another home."

"Then why don't I adopt him? Kiah's been begging for her own dog since she met him."

"Since when did you decide you were actually going to stick around?"

"I'm here now."

"I won't let him grow attached to you and then have you up and leave him. That would be cruel."

"Yeah, but—"

"Mastiffs are very loyal and protective. He's been through enough."

"Lena."

She'd done well to keep her eyes fixed on the dog and away from Oliver's face. But the tenderness in his voice drew her eyes to his whether she liked it or not.

"I'm not going anywhere." His voice was steady, deep. Like the calming cadence of the waves of the lake hitting the shore.

He held her gaze. She adjusted her grip on Bruce's collar. But could she really believe him?

"Besides, you were the one that said I was capable of caring for a goat. And we've had Oreo for a couple weeks now. Don't you think I can handle a dog?"

"I know very well what you're capable of."

His eyes blinked and he flinched at her words like they'd actually met soft flesh and drawn blood. "Maybe you should give a guy a second chance. Let me prove to you I've changed."

She wanted to laugh. Or cry. It was hard to say which with everything swirling inside, overwhelming her senses. She wanted to believe him, and yet it would most likely end up being the biggest mistake of her life.

Bruce whined and lunged toward Oliver once more.

"It will be okay." Oliver eased Lena's fingers out from the collar and gave them a light squeeze. "Give me a chance."

She stood and pulled her hand out of his grasp. Bruce drooled on the floor and pawed at Oliver's leg, asking for more scratches.

"Looks like I don't have a choice."

"Or you could look at the bright side and see that you can have your guest room back." He grinned as he scrubbed Bruce's blocky forehead.

"Don't make me regret this." She stood and watched the pair leave and then spent the next two hours cleaning up all the messes Bruce had left behind, hoping she hadn't made a big mistake trusting Oliver Fox.

eight

· · ·

IT HAD PROBABLY BEEN A BAD IDEA TO BRING BRUCE INTO THE
school building, but the dog had serious separation anxiety even
though he'd only been with them a little over a week. Neither
Kiah nor Oliver had had the heart to leave him home after all the
whining and barking when they tried to leave for the parent-
teacher conference. So hopefully Miss Zimmerman would be
back in her classroom soon.

At the moment, Bruce lay like a perfect gentleman in the
"quiet corner" while Kiah lounged against him, humming and
flipping through the pages of a picture book. It was as if his
daughter had a secret power over the dog. She could get him to
do whatever she wanted. Everyone else he merely tolerated. The
night Oliver had brought him home, he'd realized it wasn't him
Bruce wanted. It was Kiah. Oliver had merely been a means to
an end.

Finally Miss Zimmerman sauntered in with a silky shirt and
another short skirt. Instead of sitting at her desk, she slid one of
the kiddie chairs right up to Oliver's and joined him at what
Kiah referred to as the reading table.

"Sorry for the wait. I needed to make some copies for

tomorrow." She flipped her long wavy hair over her shoulder and leaned closer. "I'm glad we could meet this afternoon."

Oliver averted his eyes from her low, scooping neckline. "Thanks for letting us bring Bruce."

"Kiah adores that dog. Bruce is all she's talked about the last few days."

"Being an only child, she can get lonely. Bruce has been a good companion for her."

Misty slid the pendant on her necklace back and forth. "Being a single father must get lonely too."

Wow. She wasn't subtle, was she?

"Uh, yeah. I mean, no, we're good. Kiah's my first priority. And she's been through a lot, so I just wanted to see how she's doing."

Miss Zimmerman didn't lose the sultry smile or seem put off by his stumbling words. If anything, she moved closer, her strong floral perfume flooding his senses.

"Kiah's doing great. She knows her letters and leads the class in reading skills. She must've had a good preschool program."

The best his financial support could buy. But Jalisa had also been a smart woman. Kiah had inherited her good looks, smooth dark skin, and her brains from her mom.

"But how is she doing socially? Does she behave? Listen well?"

"I have no complaints. She gets along well with the others. She's a great kid." Misty dropped her gaze to Oliver's hand on the table for a moment. "Although, she could probably use a woman's influence in her life. Especially as she gets older."

Oliver tugged at the collar of his shirt. "Good thing we live with my sister."

"And Dr. Lena lives right next door." Kiah set her book down and joined them at the table with Bruce right at her heels. "She teaches me all about animals."

"No wonder you take such good care of Bruce." Miss Zimmerman stood. She scribbled on a notepad. "As you can see,

Kiah is doing wonderfully, but here's my number. Feel free to call me anytime." She handed the note to Oliver. "It doesn't have to be school related."

Oliver stared at the paper. A little flourish at the end of *Misty* almost looked like a heart. He wasn't sure how to respond. A beautiful woman. Small-town girl. Good profession. Great with kids.

At one point he would've jumped all over this. What was his deal?

"Can we go to the park now, Daddy?" Kiah tugged on his shirt. "You promised."

"Park. Yes. I'm sure Bruce needs to stretch his legs." And Oliver wouldn't mind the fresh, non-perfumed air.

They said goodbye to Misty and drove to Harbor Park. Kiah threw a stick into the water for Bruce. They watched him paddle out for it over and over again.

At one point she looked up at him with a contented smile. "I like it here."

"You do?"

"Uh-huh. And I love Bruce. He likes it here too."

He watched Bruce bound toward them dripping wet. The dog dropped the stick at Kiah's feet and she threw it again.

"Can we stay here forever? I'm doing good in school. Miss Zim said so. You're not going to make us move again, are you?"

Oliver knelt down and took Kiah's hand. "You really like it here, peanut?"

She nodded.

"I have friends at school. Aunty Robin is teaching me how to bake. And I take good care of Oreo and Bruce. Dr. Lena was telling me all about when the lake freezes. I want to see it. I don't want to go somewhere else."

"I guess that's something to think about."

He didn't want to make a promise just yet, but with watching Kiah thrive, it was hard to find a reason to leave anymore. Being back in Deep Haven hadn't been easy, but they'd found a good rhythm for the most part.

Although, if he was going to stay much longer, he'd need a better job. A baker he was not. And Monica hadn't been impressed by the paystub he'd emailed her.

No judge will consider this a living wage. Need to do better.

So add that to the things he needed to do.

Bruce butted in between them and shook off the water, making Kiah squeal with laughter. Oliver soaked in the moment.

She really was happy.

Robin joined them on the shore. "Now that was a great photo opportunity missed. You should've seen your faces."

"Aunty Robin, watch this." Kiah proceeded to throw the stick, and Bruce swam in after it.

Robin and Oliver settled on a bench and watched the show.

"So, did you ever in a million years think this would be your life—washing dishes at the bakery, taking care of your daughter, a tiny fainting goat, and a giant slobbery dog?" Robin bit into an apple she'd brought.

He laughed. "No, but it's not so bad. Especially with Kiah settling in so well. But now I've got my lawyer breathing down my neck."

"About what?"

"She thinks I need a better job. Not that I don't love working at the bakery, but we both know you don't need me. And I have to get letters from everyone on the list."

"You already talked with Coach Presley, right?"

"Yeah. I have a statement from him. I'm starting to make some progress with Lena. But I've gotta track down Peter Dahlquist at some point."

"Shouldn't be too hard. He's the fire chief. He's probably at the station."

"Perfect. I'll try to find him there."

"So…you talk to Grandma and Grandpa yet?" Robin asked.

Not this again. "I'll get to it when I'm ready."

"Ollie, they deserve to know. You need to tell them about Kiah. They might hear it from someone else if you don't. And you need a letter from them too. They're on your list."

"And I *will* tell them about Kiah. In my own time."

"What's holding you back? They'll love her when they meet her."

"There's some things I need to get settled first. As soon as Grandma knows, she'll rush up here, and I need to be ready to face them. I want them to see that I've got my life together. And I'm getting close." But he wasn't there yet.

Six months since Jalisa's death, and he was only starting to bond with Kiah himself. Why bring more drama in right now?

Robin plucked the stem from her apple and threw it. "What about Grayson?"

"I was hoping you would help me with that one."

"I did. I gave you his number last week. Did you call him?"

"I tried texting first, but he won't respond. When I called, he didn't answer. I was hoping to have that settled too before facing Grandpa."

But if Grayson wouldn't even talk to him, how was he going to face Grandpa with a great-granddaughter he didn't know about and no job?

"I don't know what you expect me to do." Robin took another bite of her apple.

"Can't you talk to Gray? Smooth the way for me?"

She shook her head. "I'm not getting in the middle of you two. And I'm not going to pick sides, so please don't ask me."

"I just need you to—"

"No, Ollie. I'm sorry. I love you both, and I want our family to be close again. But you and Grayson have to work through your own issues."

She was right. It wasn't fair to expect her to fix his mistakes.

"So what are you going to do?" she asked.

"First, I'm going to find a job. You mind taking Kiah and Bruce home?"

"Of course not. And you know you can work at the bakery as long as you want. Maybe you'll enjoy more of the business side of things, help with the accounting?"

He stood and ruffled her hair. "Na. It's your baby. I'll find something."

"Good, then get out of my hair." She swatted his hand away. "But for the record, I'm still glad you're here." She gave him a quick hug.

After saying goodbye to Kiah, he left and found the latest copy of the *Deep Haven Herald*. He didn't see much in the way of employment opportunities, but he could make some progress on his list and hunt down Peter Dahlquist. Being from one of the Deep Haven dynasties, he'd probably know of some good job leads anyway.

Oliver drove up the hill a few blocks and parked by the white metal building. The crisp sunshine reflected off the metal roof, a hint of woodsmoke in the air. One of the big doors was open, and a familiar-looking guy in a DHFD shirt and cargo pants hosed down a tanker truck.

"Seth Turnquist? That you?" The man was built like the lumberjacks of old, with a barrel chest and a thick mane of dark blond hair.

"Oliver Fox." Seth continued hosing off the truck. "You're back."

"Is Peter Dahlquist around?"

"He's down at the CRT HQ."

"CRT?"

"Crisis Response Team." Seth aimed the hose at the front tires, a spray of water bouncing off the treads and almost hitting Oliver.

Oliver jumped back. "Where is that?"

"Where the old Westerman Hotel used to be."

"That's what that new building is?"

"Yup. I'm sure you don't need any help finding it."

Ah. Seth probably wasn't over the conference game that

would've taken them to state that Oliver had single-handedly tanked. The whole team later found out it was thanks to a pregame bender Oliver and his buddy Jeremy had thrown at the Westerman.

"Dude, you know I'm kidding, right?" Seth set the hose down and walked over to him with an outstretched hand. He grinned like he'd done back when they were teammates. "It's good to have another Husky player back in town. We should get the gang back together sometime."

What?

Oliver shook his offered hand and tried not to sound so surprised. "Yeah, that would be great."

"Good. I've gotta get back to these trucks, but like I said, if you need to talk with Pete, he'll be at the headquarters."

"Thanks, man."

Oliver drove to where the old hotel used to be. Sure enough, a large and impressive new building complete with helicopter pad out front sat on the edge of the bay. After asking a couple people in the big open bays with the ambulances, he found Peter in the break room.

Peter Dahlquist had filled out and grown his hair long since Ollie had seen him last. One of the fittest on the football team, he'd obviously stayed in shape since they graduated.

"Is that you, Fox? What are you doing here?" Peter stood and shook his hand with a friendly grin.

"I was looking for you, actually."

"What's up?"

This was harder than he'd thought. He didn't mind a physical challenge or project, but somehow he had to get these words out and might as well jump right in. "I...uh...I'm trying to make amends for my past."

"Amends?" Peter looked confused. "For what? I haven't seen you since we graduated."

"I've got regrets. Like when I let you take the blame for crashing into old man Atwood's shed."

"Wow. That was a million years ago." Peter laughed and shook his head. "So that was you? I always wondered."

Okay, so he must not be too upset by it if he was laughing. The weight across Oliver's shoulders eased. "I should've manned up back then, but I didn't. I was going to use your truck for a dumb prank, but I'd been drinking and ended up denting the side of the shed instead. Then I ran away. I know Mr. Atwood came down hard on you."

Peter crushed an empty water bottle and tossed it in a recycling bin. "Yeah, I spent a hundred hours doing lawn work and menial labor for him."

"That should've been me."

Peter's eyes narrowed as he studied Oliver for a beat. "So, what brought this on? It's kinda out of the blue considering that was over a decade ago."

He took a breath. "It's part of a recovery program. I'm an alcoholic."

There. He'd gotten the words out. It was one thing to admit it to others who understood in a weekly meeting, who were in the same boat. But this was the first time he'd admitted it to anyone else besides Robin.

He waited for Peter's reaction.

It wasn't much of one, just a slow, thoughtful nod. "So this is one of your steps."

"Yeah, make amends to people I harmed in the past."

"That's why you're back in Deep Haven."

"Yup. But I have a daughter too now. She just started school. She loves it here. I'm thinking of sticking around for the school year, then see what happens."

"Deep Haven has a way of not letting you leave. You should stick around longer. Join the volunteer fire department and first responder crew."

So Peter wasn't going to laugh him out of town? Chastise him? If anything, he showed a good dose of respect. Maybe there was more for Oliver in Deep Haven than he thought.

And Peter had connections.

"You guys need help? I'm looking for a job."

"What kind of a job?"

"I've done a variety of things in the past. I'm not afraid to work hard."

"So what was your last gig?"

"I'm a plumber. Got a master license in Iowa, Minnesota, and Wisconsin."

"Really? We need a good plumber. We've got some bad leaks at the fire department, and Mack Hill is gone half the time. He wants to sell his business and retire, but there's no one to buy it."

"You think he'd sell to me?"

"Maybe. And while you're at it, you could join the firefighter-first responder class coming up next week if you want to start. We need more help."

Oliver Fox, a business owner? Even more, a rescuer?

It was almost heroic, something that said *I've got my life together and I'm not a screwup.*

"You might be on to something there, Pete. Sign me up for that class. And while you're at it, do you have Mack's number?"

🐺 🐺 🐺

LENA WASN'T SURE WHAT TO DO. SHE SAT DOWN ON HER PATIO chair and breathed in the sun-sweetened evening air with Jane in her lap. There probably wouldn't be many more warm days this late into September. Wentworth lounged in a patch of sunshine at her feet. Oh, to be at such ease. Lena stroked Jane's back as she looked down and stared at her phone screen.

BRAD

Can we meet in person?

Had it only been a couple weeks ago she and Robin had

crafted that first email response and sent it off to Brad? She'd lost count of how many emails and then texts they'd sent between them. Now he wanted to meet her in person.

Everything she wanted was finally falling into place. Her father coming back into her life. Wanting to get to know her.

Why was she even hesitating?

Because she could still hear her mother's voice.

He's no one worth knowing, Lena. Don't waste your time on him or any other man. You're better off without him.

But what if her mother had had it all wrong? He'd been nothing but kind and thoughtful since they'd been in contact. He'd had no problem showing her copies of identifying documents and doing a quick paternity test. And he wanted to fly from Nevada now to meet her.

So why shouldn't they meet? It was the next logical step.

"Whatcha doing, neighbor?" Oliver walked over with Bruce. He wore a brown-and-green flannel over his gray T-shirt that brought out a warmth in his eyes.

"I told you no returns—"

"Relax. I'm not bringing Bruce back. Kiah would kill me. Just trying to be neighborly."

"Annoying is more like it."

Kiah ran through the grass after him. "Hi, Dr. Lena. Can I say hi to the bunnies?"

"Of course."

She ran to the far end of the porch where the rabbit hutch was. Lena should be moving them soon to their winter shelter. Another thing she'd have to find room for in the garage.

Oliver joined her. "I know you missed me. And I'm fine, thanks for asking." He held up his scabbed hand where the cat had scratched him.

He seemed chipper tonight. That extra twinkle in his eye, his dimple a little more pronounced with his familiar smirk. And somehow it made her own sanctuary feel a little emptier. In fact, her once cozy home was feeling uncomfortable more and more, which was why she'd come out to the porch to think in the first place. And now Oliver had to come and invade her space.

Why didn't that bother her more?

Without an invitation, Oliver moved closer and scratched Wentworth's chin.

"Don't you have better things to do tonight than to bug me?" Lena asked him.

"Not really. I was wondering if you wanted to come over for dinner?"

"What?" Those were the last words she'd ever thought Oliver would say to her. Need help with something? Sure, that she could expect. But a dinner invitation?

Something was up. "What's the catch?"

"No catch. Just dinner. I'm celebrating a new job."

"What happened to the bakery?"

"The bakery is fine, but it's not enough hours, and I'm more harm than help there. So I'm working for Mack Hill. And we have an arrangement where I'm buying the business from him."

That sounded like Ollie would be sticking around on a more permanent basis. She schooled her expression to reveal nothing. It didn't matter what Oliver decided. At all.

Bruce nudged his new owner's hand. Ollie obliged him with a few scratches, but his direct gaze didn't leave Lena's.

"I've got steaks to grill, but Robin is ditching us for Sammy. So Kiah suggested you join us for dinner. What do you say?"

"Oh. I..." Lena scrambled for an excuse. Why did Oliver always have to throw her off course? Just when she had him figured out... "I have stuff to do."

"Come on, Lena. Whatever dinner you had planned can't be as good as my rib eye. I've also got a salad and some baked potatoes. Oh, and to entice you further, Robin felt so bad for ditching us she made pumpkin bars. So you can't say no. Then I'd be facing two rejections in one night—one from my own sister—and you wouldn't do that to a guy."

He probably hadn't experienced two rejections in his whole

life, let alone one night. What would he know about it? She didn't need his pity invitation. Even if her salivary glands had perked up the minute he'd said *rib eye*. "I've got a lot to do."

He gave a dramatic sigh. But was that real disappointment in his eyes? The usual spark of challenge was still there—like always. But he almost had her convinced he really wanted her to come over.

"Lena. Don't make me break out my secret weapon."

"And what's that? You'll sic Bruce on me?"

The spark grew brighter and the corner of his lips creeped up. "Oh no. This weapon is much more effective."

And the smolder he sent her was almost her undoing. But no. She had to remain strong. She would not fall for him again. It didn't matter that his clear brown eyes reminded her of a crisp fall hike along the Temperance River. That the scent of him was better than any bottled air freshener she could find. That being in his presence she felt…seen. Not exposed, though, but noticed and protected.

She fought against the gaze that held her captive. Why couldn't she get the words out of her mouth to send him away?

Noise from the rabbit hutch interrupted the heated stare down.

"Dad, is she coming?" Kiah asked.

"Come on over and help me convince her, kiddo." He turned to Lena. "Here comes the secret weapon."

"Really, Oliver—" Because he'd just played his trump card, and she was sunk.

And the look on his handsome face said he knew it.

Kiah ran over to Lena. The braids were out, and her thick, curly hair was held back in a bright purple headband tonight. "Are you coming Miss Lena? Daddy said I can get out the fancy glasses if you do."

How was Lena supposed to say no now?

And fine, there was nothing appealing about the microwave meal on Lena's dinner plan. But as much as everyone considered her a heartless robot, she wasn't. She couldn't disappoint this beautiful child begging her to come to dinner so she could put out the fancy glasses. Even if she hated that it would mean Oliver getting his way.

Again.

Lena pocketed her phone. "I guess so—"

"Yay!" Kiah bounced up and down. After Lena put Jane and Wentworth back in the house, Kiah grabbed Lena's hand, practically dragging her across the yard and into the back door of the Fox home.

Kiah completely forgot about setting the fancy glasses out and showed her every room of the house.

Ollie had been busy in the few weeks since they'd arrived. He'd put in a new backsplash and sink in the kitchen. Kiah's toys added a touch of whimsy in every corner of the place. After so many years of it just being Jim and Elaine Fox, the house seemed full of life again.

It was nice.

It was more than nice.

Of course it was. This was Ollie's life. He had it all. But temptation abounded, and she needed to get a handle on it quick. So she would enjoy this moment of pretending to be a part of a real family, but as soon as the meal was done, she'd leave.

Oliver stepped out to the back porch with a plate of meat. "Ki, why don't you give Oreo her dinner while I throw these steaks on the grill?"

"Can Dr. Lena help me?"

"As long as you do the work. That was our agreement in keeping Oreo, right?"

"Right." Kiah ran across the lawn, calling over her shoulder, "Come on!"

Lena followed her to Oreo's outdoor pen. Kiah unlatched the gate and led the goat into the barn.

"This is where Oreo sleeps, Dr. Lena." She showed her the

goat's pen, gave her fresh water and a couple scoops of feed. "I want to get some chickens too. I would put them here." She ran to the corner where some old nesting boxes were still attached to the wall. Bruce followed everywhere they went.

Lena reached out to pet him. He stood still for a moment and allowed it, but as soon as Kiah moved he was right there with her, leaving Lena in the dust.

Oliver called out across the yard, "Dinner's ready."

They sat at the patio table, set with Elaine Fox's goblets and Corelle plates.

"I remember this pattern." Lena traced along the pink-and-blue design around the edges.

Kiah looked at her with a question in her eyes.

"My mom worked late, so I came over here after school almost every day when I was growing up. We always had a snack, usually cookies or muffins, on these plates."

"You growed up with Aunty Robin and Dad?"

Lena nodded.

"And you went to my school too?"

"I did. Do you like school?"

"I love it. Jack is my best friend. And Lacie." Kiah went on to tell them all about her classes and friends.

Oliver said little as they ate, but he hadn't lied about his steaks. The rib eye was every bit as delicious as he'd promised. He seemed to enjoy Kiah's chatter as much as Lena did.

"You should ask Lena about the time she pushed me from the hayloft," he told his daughter.

"I never pushed you. You jumped." Lena reached for one of Robin's pumpkin bars and spoke to Kiah, sitting across from her. "Your dad tricked me, saying there were kittens up in the hayloft."

Kiah's forehead bunched. "Daddy, that's not nice."

"I wanted Lena to see how fun it would be swinging from a rope and jumping into the big pile of hay. She was scared."

"It wasn't safe!" Lena had never been much of a risk-taker, even then.

"Robin even came up and jumped with me. You wouldn't even try until I tricked you into coming." Ollie narrowed his eyes in a playful tease.

Kiah didn't look convinced. "Did you do it, Dr. Lena?"

Lena dabbed her lips with her napkin. "Yes. I eventually did try it."

"Was it fun?"

Oliver challenged her with one quirk of an eyebrow. She'd never get away with lying to the girl.

"It was." She could practically feel the adrenaline surging through her as she remembered flying through the air, the freedom of letting go of the rope and landing on a soft pile of fresh hay. Having a safe place to land had changed everything for her.

But there was no hay in the loft now, and the longer Lena stayed, the more she risked her heart. Oliver had always been too convincing for her own good.

She finished off her pumpkin bar and stood. "I can help with dishes, since you did all the cooking."

"Oh no. You're the guest. I'll throw these in the dishwasher real quick." Oliver took the plate out of her hand and started stacking them.

"Can you read me a story?" Kiah's big brown eyes were impossible to deny.

"Sure. I can do that before I go." She'd always loved reading. Lena settled on the floral couch in the living room. Kiah rummaged through a basket of books and brought one over. She plopped it in Lena's lap and cuddled in next to her, then laid her head against Lena's arm and held her hand.

Lena blinked as tears surfaced at the sweet gesture. How long had it been since she'd experienced the simple pleasure of holding someone's hand? And here Kiah did it like it was the most natural thing in the world.

Like Lena belonged.

Like maybe she really wanted Lena to be there, and not just as an excuse for setting the dinner table with fancy goblets. She swallowed hard past the tightness in her throat.

Lena read the cute story of the mama duck looking for her lost babies in Central Park. She could get used to this all too easily. And that was the danger. Because Oliver might beat up bullies for her, convince her to fly into a pile of hay, and cook up a delicious dinner, but he didn't want her heart.

"I should probably go home." Even though Oliver had made no advances throughout the meal, Lena couldn't help but feel pulled toward him. Her internal alarm system was failing. She stood up to leave.

"But I want you to read me another story." Kiah clasped her hands in front of her. "Pleeease?"

"Stay, Lena. I was hoping we could talk once this little Chatty Cathy goes to bed."

Her breath caught. Yeah, that wasn't going to happen.

"I really need to get back. I've got a lot to do at home." She squatted down to Kiah's level. "But maybe we can read together another time. My friend Beth used to work at the library, and she showed me where all the best animal books are."

"Is she at the library tomorrow? I don't have school."

"No, she's out in Oregon with your unc—"

Wait. Did Kiah even know about Grayson? Lena had been so busy with work and looking for funding for the new shelter that she hadn't talked with Beth since Ollie came back to town.

"My what?" Kiah asked, bringing Lena back to the present predicament.

Oliver scooped up his daughter. "She's talking about my brother Grayson. Your uncle."

"The one in the picture with you and Aunty Robin?"

"Yup." There was a hint of sadness in his voice. "Why don't you say goodnight to Miss Lena, go upstairs, brush your teeth, and get ready for bed. I'm going to walk her back, and I'll come tuck you in after."

"G'night, Miss Lena." Kiah wiggled out of her father's hold and opened her arms for a hug. When Lena bent over, Kiah squeezed her tight. "Sweet dreams."

"You too, kid." Lena's throat squeezed tighter. Her family hadn't done this. It had just been Mom and herself. They hadn't said goodnight with cuddles and stories. They hadn't hugged. Lena had watched the Foxes and other families show affection and wondered what it was like.

Now she knew.

And she almost wished she didn't, because this was the way it should've been all along, and there was no way to go back and change it. There was no way to make it right.

No wonder she'd been such a freak growing up.

She walked out the patio door and turned. "Go be with your daughter, Ollie. I know the way back."

"I really need to talk to you, Lena. About the past. I want—"

"No."

And now it all made sense. So that was what this dinner was about. A little wining and dining so he could make his move with whatever this need of his was to dig up their ugly history.

She did not need to relive that utter humiliation ever again.

Lena turned and walked toward her yard, calling behind her, "Leave it in the past. And…congratulations on the new job."

She rushed back to her house, stepping into the quiet. The slightly stale air, the sanitized counters and stark floor. Nothing sparkly pink and girly. No smell of grilled steaks and spiced pumpkin bars or sounds of little girl giggles. There was no rumbly voice teasing her.

This was her life.

She lay down on the couch. Jane came and cuddled by her side. Wentworth hopped up and covered her feet, resting his big head on her hip. She'd always known she was missing out growing up. Now it was all too real. Tonight she'd had a tiny taste, a few hours of playing house, and her heart would never be the same.

What had Lena done that was so wrong to have missed out on it all? Maybe Birdie was right, and she needed to let people in a little more.

She couldn't change the past, but she could do things differently now.

She pulled out her phone and stared once more at the screen with Brad's text message. Before she could talk herself out of it, she typed out three letters and hit Send.

LENA

Yes.

nine

. . .

Oliver tucked Kiah in tight with her fluffy comforter and stuffed elephant. The princess lamp Robin had bought, the one feminine piece in the place, cast the room in a cozy glow and allowed enough light to read a bedtime story. Kiah graced him with a drowsy smile as he finished the last page and closed the book.

These were the kinds of moments he lived for, and yet something was still lacking.

He kissed her sweet head. "What was the best part of your day, kiddo?"

"I liked having dinner with Miss Lena. She's smart, Dad. Did you know that goats have four stomachs?"

"No, I didn't." But at the mention of Lena's name, he immediately knew what was missing.

"Yup. And she's gonna show me where the animal books are at the library. Do you think I could be a betrinarian when I grow up?"

"I know you can." He tweaked her nose.

"What was your favorite part, Dad?"

"Definitely dinner. Maybe we should do that again. Have Lena over." Because he wanted more time with her.

And Kiah seemed to agree. "That's a good idea. I think she's lonely."

"Why do you say that?"

"Cuz sometimes she looks hungry when she looks at our house."

"Hungry?"

"Yeah, like when Aunty Robin makes those caramel rolls I love, but I have to wait and I get so hungry for them. Dr. Lena looks like that."

His daughter saw way more than a five-year-old should. Lena had had a rather lonely childhood. Did she see something she liked as she looked over from her house? Something she wanted for herself?

The thought that Lena *might* see something in him stirred a deep desire. Desire that was harder and harder to ignore the more he spent time with her.

"Get some sleep now, darlin'. Daddy loves you."

"Thanks." She hadn't ever said the words back to him yet, but she did give him a hug. They were getting there.

In the kitchen, he grabbed a can of pop and bowl of pretzels, then went to the family room and settled on the couch with Bruce. From the sofa, he could see out the dining room window to Lena's place. She was right next door with her own dogs. He couldn't help but wish she were here. He didn't want her to go back to a dark, lonely house next door. And there was more to it than simply needing to make amends.

Here in the dark, he could admit it. He'd always been drawn to Lena Larson. She had this tenacity about her he couldn't help but admire. Even after his parents died and everyone had been so awkward or pitying—or worse, like Grandpa Jim, who'd stopped talking to him—she'd treated him like she always had. She hadn't stopped challenging him in school or treated him with kid gloves. She'd seen him as a worthy opponent and given him something to fight for.

Her consistency when everything else had been out of control and changing had gotten him through the worst days of his life. She was the kind of woman that worked hard and didn't give up when things got tough.

The kind of woman who would probably stick by a guy through the hard times, unlike Jalisa.

And what if he was crazy enough to want more than a friendship when he looked at his next-door neighbor?

Because he did. Maybe he'd always been half in love with Lena Larson and just too stupid to realize it. He should've recognized a good thing when he'd had it back in the day. Back when his only concern had been finding his next drink and escaping Grandpa's disapproval and rules. When Oliver had just wanted to live life on his own terms.

A lot of good that had done.

And if she couldn't get over his past, how would he ever repair his family? What hope did he have with Grayson? Or his grandfather?

A rattle of the front door had him sitting up straight. Had Lena changed her mind?

Wow. He was further gone than he realized, because there was no mistaking the pang of disappointment when Robin walked in the door with the same dopey face she always had after seeing her boyfriend, Sammy Johnson.

"Aw, did you wait up for me?" She plopped down on the couch next to him and gave Bruce's head a pat.

Oliver relaxed once more against the cushions at his back. "Yes, and did you look at the time? You're ten minutes past curfew."

"Go ahead and punish me. It was totally worth it." She blew a dreamy sigh and lounged against the couch with her hands behind her head.

"You really like this guy."

"I hope so. I'm gonna marry him someday."

"He better deserve you."

"He does." She reached for a handful of pretzels on the coffee table. "How was dinner?"

"Good. We invited Lena."

The pretzel froze halfway to Robin's mouth. "You had dinner with Lena?"

"Why is that so surprising?"

"Oh, I don't know. Maybe since you were the thorn in her side growing up and you relished it. Always fighting for the top of the class, student body president, and homecoming your senior year…? Let's not forget how that ended."

Right. That. "I've grown up a little since then, don't you think?"

"Maybe." She munched on her pretzel. "So how did it go?"

"It was great, but when I tried to talk to her alone, she rushed back home. I want to make amends and she won't let me."

"What do you expect? You humiliated her and broke her heart. In front of the whole football team." She threw a pretzel at him like they were back in elementary school or something.

"I was an idiot. I know."

He hadn't been able to see what was right next door.

But he did now. "So how am I supposed to make amends if she won't let me talk about it?"

"For one, don't do your typical bulldozer move."

"I don't know what you're talking about."

"Clueless. You're completely clueless." She rolled her eyes and shifted her body to face him. "You can't run over there and demand she make amends with you. You're gonna have to be patient. Have a little finesse."

"How?"

She lost the playfulness in her tone. "If you really want to reach Lena, you're going to need to be vulnerable, Oliver."

Something inside sank to his gut at her words and raised all his defenses. "Oh, you mean weak."

"No, I mean vulnerable. There's a difference. She poured out her heart to you, told you she was in love with you in that letter, and you let Jeremy Stanly read it in front of the team. And then you all laughed and called her Lonely Frump-a-Lena."

"He took it from my locker. I didn't know—"

"You did! Lena and I were there. We heard you guys on the field because there was a note telling Lena to meet you there. We were behind the concession stand waiting."

"That's how she knew?"

"Yeah."

"I didn't write any note telling her to meet me. I never even saw her letter until Jeremy pulled it out and read it to everyone." But the sadness and disappointment he saw in his sister's eyes still hit him like a punch in the gut. This was not a little thing he could gloss over. He needed to make this right.

"Maybe you didn't. But I know you liked her back then. Why didn't you admit it to those jerks and stand up for her?"

"Can we chalk it up to me being young and dumb?" The beers he and Jeremy had chugged down before practice probably hadn't helped.

Because he *had* wanted to stick up for her. He'd wanted to take on the whole team and smash every one of their smart mouths for mocking her, but if they'd known the truth—that he really did have a thing for the brilliant girl next door—they would've massacred him socially. All he'd had back then were his friends and his social life. And so he'd gone along with them. And he hadn't thought Lena would ever know.

But she did.

And he didn't really have words for that. Just shame. So much shame. He'd failed the people he cared about the most.

Guess it was a habit with him.

Maybe this was what Hezekiah had meant when he said facing the past was going to be the hardest thing he'd ever done. It was harder than the withdrawal. It was harder than the hour-by-hour temptation to turn back to a drink to feel better.

But Oliver was breaking habits now.

He was three years sober. He had a daughter. He had a job, a home. He had a lot worth fighting for.

And a lot to make up for, especially with Lena. But he would do it. He could be in it for the long haul.

He just had to prove it to her.

"Eh-hem." Robin cleared her throat. "Earth to Ollie. Did you hear me?"

"What did you say?"

A slow smile spread across his sister's face. A dangerous smile. "You still like her."

The urge to deny it rose.

No. He could do this. He could be…vulnerable. Even if he did gag on the word.

"Maybe. But that won't matter if she won't let me talk to her."

"Keep trying. Eventually she'll listen. Just drop the charm and be real with her."

Right. He had to keep at it and not give up.

🦊 🦊 🦊

LENA WOKE TO THE SOUND OF BARKING. FRANTIC BARKING. JANE licked her face until she sat up in bed while Wentworth barked by the door. The morning light filtering in from the window was still rosy and gold. What time was it?

And was that pounding?

Lena ran to her living room. Sounded like the noise was from the front of the house. She stepped onto her front porch, her feet freezing the instant they hit the cold wood. Oliver stood on a ladder in her driveway, reaching the light at the peak of her garage.

"Oliver, what are you doing?"

He smiled down at her, a layer of dark scruff covering his jaw and chin. Still, he looked way too fresh and chipper in his flannel and vest for this early in the day. "I'm helping. What does it look like?"

"I didn't ask for your help." The chilly morning air raised goosebumps on her crossed arms.

He chuckled. "It needed fixing. Why are you grumbling?"

"You riled up all the dogs. I was going to get to the light eventually."

"Well, now you don't have to."

"Come on, Ollie. Why are you doing this? What's the catch?"

"No catch." He stepped down from the ladder. "I want to help. Show you I'm not the same guy I used to be."

"And you thought waking me up at six thirty on the one morning I could sleep in was a good way to do that?"

He paused as if he hadn't considered that. "I'll make it up to you. Wait here." He ran off toward his own house.

"Like I'm going anywhere now." She yawned and made her way to her porch swing. Wrapping herself in the throw blanket she left folded across the back, she rocked back and forth in a lazy rhythm. The grass of her front yard was frosty. Leaves had started turning gold and amber in the wooded area across the road and on the side of her property. It'd been a long time since Lena had simply sat and enjoyed the view from the porch.

After a few minutes, Oliver jogged back with a to-go coffee cup and something wrapped in a napkin, which he handed to her.

"Here. This will wake you up."

She braced herself for whatever bitter brew Oliver was offering and sipped. But her first taste was sweet and creamy with a hint of coffee flavor. "How did you know I like my coffee like this?"

"You're surprised I got it right."

She wouldn't give him the satisfaction of letting him know *how* surprised she was. "Maybe. Did Robin tell you?"

"Nah. Some things stick with you."

She unwrapped the napkin and found a pumpkin bar from last night's dessert. The cinnamon aroma of the cake with the cream cheese frosting smelled divine. She bit into it. It tasted even better.

"Well?" Oliver asked.

She shrugged. He'd done well, but she'd better not let him get too big of a head. Or reveal how quickly his thoughtfulness was melting her resolve to keep him at arm's length. "I'd still rather be sleeping." She sipped the coffee and stared toward the garage, where the dogs were barking again.

"Do you need help feeding them?" Oliver asked.

"I will in a little bit."

The poor dogs shouldn't still be here. She should've found homes for them by now. Accusation pricked her, stealing some of the beauty of the morning. If Oliver could get this impromptu breakfast right, maybe he could assist her in the biggest issue weighing on her mind.

I want to help. Show you I'm not the same guy I used to be.

"If you really want to help, why don't you put that Fox charm to good use and help me figure out a community event to help the animal shelter."

"What kind of event?" He sat down on the porch, his leg swinging over the edge as he sipped from his own cup, looking as comfortable and confident as always.

"That's the problem. I don't know. I need a community-wide event open to the public to help promote the shelter and secure funding for a new building. And we both know how great I do with people, especially public speaking. But these poor dogs and cats desperately need homes, and I can't come up with anything."

"Why don't you do an adopt-a-pet day? Then you can do both—find homes for the animals and make it a big community-wide event."

An adopt-a-pet event? "The shelter is demolished. It would

be a logistical nightmare in any of the city parks, and the clinic is too small."

"Have it here."

"In my garage? That's a terrible idea."

"No. In my barn. There's plenty of space in there for the animals and for people to wander around. We could throw some tables in the yard, have some games and face-painting for the kids. It would be great."

She started to speak and then stopped.

"See. I have good ideas. So good I rendered you speechless."

"I didn't say it was a good idea. But...it's not horrible."

"Of course not. It will be fun. And if we can do it during the homecoming weekend, we'll get lots of folks who are back in town looking for something to do. We can have some other things to help raise funds too. Sell some bakery items, have a raffle. We could have businesses donate items for giveaways."

The more she thought about it, the more she liked it. But could they pull it off in so short a time? He was right. Homecoming weekend would be perfect.

"We'd need to clean out the barn and build some temporary pens. Make flyers. Find tables and chairs."

Ollie shrugged like it was no big deal. "We can do all that."

"You'll help?"

"Why do you look so skeptical? Of course I'll help. Now admit it. You like my idea."

I want to help. Show you I'm not the same guy I used to be.

Maybe he had changed. There was definite potential in this idea. "I'll reserve judgment until after the fact. I can organize it, but I still have the clinic. And now you have a full-time job. How are we going to pull this together in two weeks?"

"We'll be a great team. You organize. I'll get the barn ready and work the crowd. We'll get all those animals out of your garage and into their forever homes." He sat up straight, his voice and face animated. His enthusiasm always was contagious.

She could admit it. "It might work."

"It *will* work."

"We'll see." She took a bite of her pumpkin bar and rocked in the swing. "But for now, stop talking and let me enjoy my coffee in peace."

"You got it, boss."

Lena relaxed into the rhythm of the porch swing and swallowed the last bite of the dessert breakfast Oliver had provided. It would probably spike her blood sugar and she'd be even more tired later, but it sure did taste amazing. All the bad things for you did.

But maybe this surge of energy would be good, because if they were going to pull off a big event, there would be a lot to do in the next two weeks. A never-ending to-do list ran through her mind. There wasn't any time to waste. Lena brushed the crumbs off her hands, finished her coffee, and handed the cup to Oliver.

"Thanks for the breakfast. If you're serious about helping, give me twenty minutes to get ready. I'll take care of the animals, and then we can walk through the barn and talk about what we need to do. I can put a plan together."

Oliver saluted her and walked away whistling.

Time would tell if he had really changed. And while he was quickly filling empty places in her schedule, she needed to be on guard. Friendship was a possibility. But she had to stop herself from wanting anything more. Oliver Fox was still sly and charming.

She gave herself a stern talking to as she quickly changed and threw her hair back in a ponytail. After taking care of the animals, she grabbed a clipboard and notebook and headed to the Fox barn.

Together she and Oliver walked through the building and made a list of all that had to be done. By the time they'd finished, Kiah had joined them, wondering what they were doing.

"What does *adopt* mean?" she asked Lena as Oliver measured the empty stalls.

"It's when a person or an animal doesn't have a family but

you bring them into your home and they become part of yours. Like what you did for Bruce," Lena told her.

"And Oreo!"

Lena nodded. "Right. All those dogs and cats in my garage need good homes and new families. We're going to help them find them."

"Where's your family?" Kiah asked.

The innocent question threw her off guard. "Uh, I...don't have one."

"Daddy, can we adopt Miss Lena?"

Oliver laughed. "It doesn't exactly work that way with grownups."

"But she doesn't have a family. Can't we be her family?"

Yeah, let's air out all the ways Lena is deficient and lonely.

But before she could find the words to steer the conversation to something else, Oliver squatted down by his daughter. "Lena might not have a family, but she's got some great next-door neighbors."

"You mean us?" Kiah asked.

"Yup."

"And she has all the animals too. I want to have a bunch of animals when I grow up."

"That's great. Why don't you take Oreo to her pen for the day."

"Okay." Kiah skipped over to Oreo's stall and took the goat outside.

Oliver stood back up. "Sorry about that." He looked at her intently. "I'm sure she—"

"It's fine. Really. And...it's not that I don't have any family at all. I just found my...father. Well, he found me. And—" She clamped her mouth shut. Why was she babbling?

Oliver lost the playful smirk he usually wore. "I didn't realize you were in contact with your father."

"It's recent."

"He contacted you out of the blue?"

Lena picked at the corner of her notebook page. "Is it so hard to believe that he'd want to get to know me?"

"Not at all. It's just surprising that he waited so long. I thought—"

"You thought he was a deadbeat dad. Like my mom always said. But he's not. He's a really nice guy."

"Good, good. That's...good." But the awkward silence overtaking the barn space made his assurances sound hollow.

Why did she even care what Oliver thought of him? "He lives in Nevada. Vegas," she said.

"What does he do?"

Her cheeks burned. "We're still getting to know each other, so I don't know yet, but I'll find out."

Oliver had exposed this weak spot, and she waited for him to pounce on it.

Instead, he relaxed his shoulders. "I can't say much. I have no idea what my only brother has been up to the last twelve years."

He was sympathizing? But she latched on to the change in subject and deflected the attention back to something else. Anything else. "You guys used to be close."

"Until I put his life in danger."

"You mean the accident after his graduation?"

He nodded. "It's a miracle he only broke a couple ribs."

The pain in his eyes and remorse in his tone revealed a wound. And Lena hated seeing any creature hurting. Even a predatory animal like a fox. "Accidents happen."

Ollie's gaze dropped to the pile of dirt and old straw on the floor. "Especially when the person driving is impaired."

"Impaired how?"

And maybe trying to be sympathetic herself did help, because he lifted his head once more and looked at her tentatively. "I was drunk. And...so stupid." He palmed the back of his neck. "I can't tell you how many times I've wished I'd been smart enough to realize just how bad I was that night. And I'd like to say I learned my lesson, but it took a while—until I found AA and my mentor. Now I can thankfully say I'm three years sober."

She didn't understand everything, but fighting any kind of addiction took a lot of courage and strength. Maybe Ollie really was trying to change. Be better. Maybe she could help him the way he was helping her with her event. "So, aren't there some steps or something they do at AA?"

"I'm working on step nine. Making amends with the people I've harmed."

Ah. So that's why he kept wanting to talk about the past. "Is that why you came back here?"

"That, and Kiah and I needed a home. But I also need to make up for the years I've lost. Fix all the things I broke. But Grayson won't even talk to me. I've tried calling and texting. He doesn't answer. I'm not sure what to do. Robin doesn't want to get in the middle of it, and I can't blame her for that."

Probably she shouldn't get in the middle either, but she also knew what it was like to miss out on family. If there was any way to help Oliver make things right with Grayson, she should.

"He and Beth are coming back here for homecoming."

Oliver's head popped up. "Really?"

"Yeah. They're staying until the anniversary party for your grandparents. Beth said he'll be out at Trinity Horse Camp, while she's going to stay with her dad. I can't promise anything, but maybe you can make some inroads then."

"You think so?" He looked so hopeful. It tugged at her heart and threw her thoughts into a tailspin.

"Well, you're harder to ignore in person."

The rumbly laugh that burst from Oliver's chest warmed Lena to the bones. She let a small smile escape. Being Oliver's friend wasn't so bad.

She just had to make sure it stayed that way and she didn't start wanting something more.

ten

. . .

THE NEXT TWO WEEKS PASSED IN A BLUR. ANY TIME OLIVER WASN'T working with Mack Hill or taking the volunteer firefighter/first responder classes, he was getting ready for Lena's big event. Basically, he didn't sleep.

But it felt good to be useful again. To be fitting into a community again. And the more time he and Lena spent together, the more he wanted to see her.

They cleaned out the barn until they could practically do surgery on the floor. There were times they butted heads, but eventually they would come to an agreement. It usually meant she won, but the debating was fun. A slight flush to her cheeks and pursing of her lips were often the only hints of emotion as she would calmly make her argument.

She had high standards, no doubt. If he really wanted to rile her up, all he had to say was something was "good enough." Boy, did she hate that expression. And he made sure to say it at least once a day when they were together. Eventually she caught on and just shook her head at him, knowing he was helpless but to do her bidding.

They'd been up until late the previous night, stringing lights across the high ceiling and under the hayloft floor. And looking around in the early morning light, he had to say it'd been worth it. She'd turned his vague idea into an amazing reality.

What had once been dusty cow stalls were now pens for the dogs. For the cats, they'd sectioned off the small dairy parlor with temporary fencing and chicken wire. Oliver had brought over the carpet-covered tower and built a new one where the cats now lounged and scratched. Lena had tables in the yard covered with red-and-white checked cloths. They had face paints and coloring sheets at two of them. Robin was set with cookies, pies, and apple cider for sale at another. Birdie was ready to fill out adoption forms at the fourth table, and Kiah tested out their little hay bale climbing area near Oreo's pen.

Lena had even set up picturesque spots with cornstalks and pumpkins in little corners of the barnyard. She'd turned Grandpa's old tractor into a photoshoot-worthy backdrop. The Instagram moms would go nuts over it. And hopefully a lot of them would be coming. Kiah had already invited her whole class to the event, so chances were good.

Lena walked into the barn. She looked like she belonged here in her brown, puffy vest over a green-and-orange plaid shirt, jeans, and cowboy boots. The slanted sun coming through the double doors glinted on the silky strands of light-brown hair that fell across her forehead and cheeks. She had an understated beauty that didn't need heavy makeup or short skirts to draw attention.

She yawned as she checked her ever-present clipboard. "Did you get—"

"Good morning."

"Huh?" She stopped and looked up at him.

"Usually it's customary to greet someone before you start bossing them around." He handed her the coffee he'd made earlier, purposely brushing her fingertips with his own.

A slight blush brightened her cheeks as she took a sip. "Sorry." She blew out a long breath. "I might be a little nervous."

"I couldn't tell. You're always so calm."

She looked down at her boots. "Let's just say there's always a lot going on under the surface. And I need this to go well."

"It will. Don't worry. I mean, look at this place. It could be in a magazine."

She took another slow drink and looked around. "It does look nice. But I should've—"

"Nice? All that hard work we did, and you come up with 'nice'? You can do better than that." He stood at her side and leaned on one of the posts. He could smell the sweet, citrusy fragrance she used. He leaned a little farther and nudged her arm.

She didn't back away. In fact, she leaned his direction a smidge. "Wouldn't want it all going to your head."

"It's too late."

She quirked up her lips into a half smile. "You did good work, Ollie."

The urge to do a victory dance welled up inside. Why not go for the win? "Does that mean you'll go to the homecoming game with me when this is all over?"

Her eyes widened. "The game?"

"Yeah. It's this thing where guys toss a ball—"

"Dad, there's people here!" Kiah ran into the barn and grabbed their hands. "Aunty Robin said it's time to start."

"But they're early." A flash of panic crossed Lena's face as they walked out of the barn.

"It's okay. We're ready, right? That's why we stayed up late finishing everything on your list. Now you and Kiah go help Robin bring out the cookies while Birdie and I greet everyone."

"Cookies. Right." His confident Lena was a little frazzled, but she marched away. Once she and Kiah disappeared inside, Oliver met Seb Brewster and his wife Lucy as they came around the side of the house, following the signs Lena had put up yesterday leading to the backyard.

"Oliver, think we're set to win tonight? We can't have our boys losing the homecoming game." Seb shook his hand.

"I'm sure they're ready."

"Good." Seb looked around the yard, where people had started to trickle in and mingle at the tables. A young mom had already found the tractor and was positioning her husband and toddler for a picture. "This looks great."

"Yeah, it's all Lena's doing."

"Speaking of Lena, I'm surprised you're working together on this."

Most people probably remembered them as fierce rivals, but Ollie was hoping for something more.

"We've had our differences, but that's in the past." They moved toward the barn. "So, did you get the application I sent in last week?" Oliver asked.

"We did. The committee doesn't meet for a while though. Your application said you'll be teaching a community ed class?"

"Yeah, simple plumbing fixes for homeowners. I've found a lot of people don't even know how to clean a measly faucet filter. Does wonders for your water pressure, and you don't have the labor and call charge for a professional plumber."

Lucy's eyes perked up. "Please tell me you're going to this class, Seb. Then you can fix our showerhead I've been complaining about."

He laughed. "Sounds like your idea is a good one. I'm looking forward to it. And it's good to see you're not letting the competition get between you guys."

Before Oliver could figure out what Seb was talking about, Lucy walked toward one of the dogs. "Honey, come here. Look at this little guy."

"See ya at the game, Ollie." He left to join his wife, who was petting a little black-and-white dog Lena had been calling George.

The tractor couple with the toddler wanted to see one of the cats, so Oliver brought them into one of the spaces they'd created for families to see the pets up close. They didn't need much convincing that the long-haired gray was their next fur baby. Ollie's scabbed hand was not sad to see it go.

An older couple browsed the stall with the small dogs, Darling and Scamp. Oliver sauntered up to them. "Ready to find your next best friend?"

The woman, a petite lady with silver hair and bright blue eyes, gestured toward Darling. "What's the story with that poor thing?"

"Now, honey, we live in an RV. We don't have room for a dog." The man tucked her hand in the crook of his elbow. "We're just here for the bakery items."

"But look at her, Bob. She's a little thing."

Oliver leaned casually on the post next to the stall. "Not only is she little, but she's very mellow and affectionate."

The man grimaced. "She doesn't have hair, Mae. If we're getting a dog, I want one with hair. And what happened to her eye?" He looked at his wife. "Do you really want one with health issues?"

Oliver reached down and picked up Darling. He bounced her lightly in his arms. "She's very healthy now. When we found her, the eye was already infected and had to be surgically removed. And not having hair is just her breeding. It means less dander and shedding for you to clean." He passed Darling to the woman.

Darling licked her cheek and nuzzled right into her shoulder. "She is the sweetest little thing. What do you say?"

Oliver knew that look. This was a done deal. After a short discussion, Mae had Bob agreeing.

As Oliver led them to Birdie at the registration table, Lena came up to him and grabbed his arm.

"Did I see you talking to Seb earlier? What did he say?"

Her hands clutched his bicep. She was more nervous than he'd thought. But he certainly didn't mind the tight hold she had on him.

Laying a light hand on top of Lena's, Oliver took a step

closer. "Seb was impressed. Look at him. Lucy has him posing by the pumpkin with George."

Lena concentrated on Seb and Lucy. "They look…"

"Happy, Lena. They're happy. Relax."

"Right." She nodded and loosened her grip on his arm.

But she didn't let go completely.

"Did you really convince that couple to adopt Darling?"

"Of course I did. I told you this would work." And while she was impressed and looking at him with a hint of wonder… "So, what did you think about my other idea?"

"Oliver, it's too late for a chocolate fountain, and I already told you, it's too messy. We centered everything around a pumpkin theme."

"Not that. I mean the homecoming game."

Lena's gaze snapped up. "You were serious?"

"Why does it surprise you that I'd want to spend time with my smart and beautiful neighbor?"

She rolled her eyes. "You're so full of it." Her attention snagged on the other side of the yard. "I better go tell those kids not to feed Oreo too much."

She walked away shaking her head.

He followed after her. "Hey, I was serious."

"I am too. If they feed her too much, she'll—"

"Lena, the goat is fine." He jumped into her path to get her attention once more. "I mean I'm serious about you and me. Maybe I wasn't clear. I'd like to go to the football game with you. What do you say?"

Her jaw dropped. "You want to go with me?"

"That's what I've been trying to say. I was hoping maybe we could meet up with Beth and Grayson."

"Oh. You want me to help smooth the way. Now this is making sense."

"No, that's not it. I mean, yes, I want to see Grayson and try to talk to him, but mostly, I…I want to spend some time with you. Kiah would be there too, of course, but I've really liked hanging out with you these last few weeks."

"You mean where I bossed you around and made a general spectacle of myself?"

"I mean when you made this old barn and a simple event into a community-wide festival. I overheard someone say we should make it an annual thing. You did a fantastic job."

Lena's hand slid up to her face to hide her smile. She mumbled something he couldn't hear.

"What was that?" He gently drew her hand away from her mouth.

"I said…I couldn't have done it without you."

"So is that a yes to the game?"

She stared.

"If you really don't want to, I won't make you. I know I've got a lot of baggage, and I've got a kid and—"

"Yes."

He froze. "Yes? You'll go with me?"

She nodded.

"You're sure?" He leaned closer to her.

She shoved him away but didn't hold back a grin like she usually did. "Pick me up at six."

"Sure thing, boss."

Kiah came up to show them the unicorn painted on her cheek. He picked her up and twirled her around.

They had a date.

IT WAS ONLY A DATE WITH OLIVER. OR WAS IT? IT WAS A FOOTBALL game. She didn't know a thing about the sport. Seemed like a big waste of time, but maybe she should try it before she knocked it.

Lena walked in her bathrobe to the closet, toweling off her wet hair.

So she didn't date much. Or ever. She never had the time. Surely the fluttery sensation in her middle making her want to puke was all normal. Or maybe it was the worry for the animals that hadn't been adopted today. Poor Oscar. And Scamp still needed a home. And Gypsy, the cranky calico, now had the whole cat enclosure to herself.

Why had she agreed to go with Oliver? She should be finding homes for these pets. Besides, he'd probably only asked out of pity. Or maybe a culmination of their work together over the last two weeks. One last hurrah before they went their separate ways again.

So no reason to worry about what to wear or attempt makeup. She dressed in comfy jeans and a Deep Haven Husky sweatshirt. She was drying her hair when the doorbell rang.

She opened the door to find Beth, who looked her up and down and shook her head in disapproval. "You're wearing that on a date?"

"What's wrong with this?" Lena pointed to her sweatshirt. "I don't want to be cold. And it's a football game, not a date."

Beth moved in for a hug. She was one of the few Lena didn't feel like a complete awkward moron hugging. And she had missed her.

"Come on. Let's see what else you have in that color-coded closet of yours. And then you can tell me how it came to be that you're going on a date with my boyfriend's brother."

"Again, not a date. And I'm not exactly sure how it happened. We were at the adopt-a-pet event, and I was trying to stop some kids from overfeeding the goat, and the next thing I know I'm agreeing to go to the homecoming game with him. It's not a big deal."

"Um, it's a really big deal. It's the unofficial high-school reunion. Everyone will be there." Beth opened the closet door and started flicking through the outfits. "You have way too much khaki in here."

"It doesn't show the dirt."

"Yes, very utilitarian, but not super cute."

"I'm wearing jeans. That's not khaki."

"Stained jeans from 1992. We can do better."

And here she thought she'd done pretty well on that mud stain on the thigh. "So, how's Oregon?"

"Amazing. I do get homesick for Deep Haven, but the mountains and the ocean and Grayson make up for it." She pulled out a charcoal-gray sweater and the one pair of skinny jeans Lena kept because they tucked nicely into boots. "Let's try this."

Lena changed into the chosen outfit.

"Much better."

"What should I do with my hair? Low ponytail? Braid?" Lena tugged on one of the long strands.

"Leave it down. It looks nice." She swept Lena's bangs to the side. "When is Ollie coming to get you?"

"In an hour. But maybe I should go help finish putting things away from the event. Robin forced me to leave, but I should be able to sneak back—"

Beth raised her hand to stop. "You're staying here. They can do without you."

"But—"

"Nope. Let's enjoy a glass of iced tea I know you have in your fridge, and tell me how it is I leave for a little while and come back to you and Oliver dat—doing whatever it is you're doing."

"You've been gone over two months." Lena pulled out two glasses and filled them with ice.

"You know what I mean. And this is Oliver we're talking about. The one who broke your heart and almost killed Grayson in a car accident. He left and came back with a kid, so Robin said."

"And is a recovering alcoholic." She poured tea and handed a glass to Beth.

"You're not winning me over here."

Settling in the living room with their glasses, Lena tried to make Beth see. "I know. None of this makes sense. Except that I do think he's changed."

"You said he's an alcoholic though."

"Recovering alcoholic. He's been sober for three years. And you should see him with his daughter. And Bruce."

"Who's Bruce?"

"A rescue dog."

"Ah, so that's how he got through your armor. He takes in strays."

"There's no armor to get through. And we're not dating. He's all wrong for me. I'm just trying to help smooth things over with him and Grayson. He deserves a second chance."

Beth didn't look convinced. "I don't know if it's going to happen. Grayson's been resistant to communicating with Ollie. He never said so, and he won't talk about it, but I think he doesn't want to be hurt again. But I did encourage him to see him face-to-face. He'll try to talk to him at the game."

It was a start at least. And Lena could understand Grayson's hesitancy. But over the last month, she'd seen a different side of Oliver Fox. And he wasn't so bad. Grayson just needed to give his brother a chance.

Beth set her drink down. "Enough about those guys. What's going on with your dad? I couldn't believe it when you forwarded me his email."

"It took me completely by surprise. But Robin helped me, and I wrote back to him. So we've been communicating for a few weeks now."

"And?"

"It's good. He wants to meet. And you know how I've spent my whole life wondering about him, feeling like I was missing a huge part of myself."

"So are you going to meet?"

Lena nodded. "It's been hard to wait. Brad tried a few times to push the date up, but I couldn't fit it in. He even offered to drive here, but we'll meet up in Duluth next Saturday. I don't want the first time I meet my father to be in front of all of Deep Haven."

Beth chuckled. "I can understand that. But, wow. Two men who broke your heart coming back into your life. I don't know how you're staying so calm."

Easy. She wasn't. She wasn't sleeping much and lived on a steady diet of antacids, but her mother had taught her well. She knew how to put on the mask to hide it all. And the best thing she could do now was turn the tables. "Tell me about Oregon."

After talking about Beth's new apartment and job, Lena grabbed her vest and they moved to the front porch. Beth promised to meet up at the game. "We might need to pull the brothers away if things get tense."

"I hope it doesn't come to that. I know Oliver has been working hard to reconcile with people he's hurt."

"Including you?"

Lena shoved her hands into the pockets of her vest. "He wants to talk about it all, but I haven't let him."

"If you're going to have any kind of relationship with him, Lena, you need to. I know it hurts to dig all that history up, but you can't really go forward until you deal with it."

Beth might have a point. But before she could say anything, Oliver and Kiah pulled into her driveway. Her friend said goodbye as Ollie walked up to the front porch.

His slightly damp hair curled in tousled waves across his forehead. He smelled fresh and clean and masculine. Her pulse kicked up a notch.

This was wrong. So very wrong.

But then Oliver smiled. "You look amazing."

The sincerity in his warm brown eyes cut through the fear and melted her reservations. He held out his arm like a true gentleman. "Are you ready? I've been looking forward to this all day."

Words failed, so she nodded and gave him a wobbly smile of her own. In the van Kiah chatted, rehashing the pet adoption event. She still had the unicorn painted on her cheek and was excited to meet up with her friend Jack at the game. Her little voice helped break the ice and set Lena more at ease. This wasn't a big deal. Just a friendly outing. Could she even call it a date with a kid along?

It kinda felt like a date though when Oliver insisted on paying for tickets. As soon as he did and they walked in the gates, Kiah saw her friend Jack Mayer. They ran off together with Jack's mom, leaving Lena and Oliver all alone. Ollie wove through the crowd and led Lena up the bleachers to the very top. He laid down a thick quilt before inviting her to sit.

"I'll be right back with some hot dogs and popcorn."

"I can wait in line with you."

"You have to stay here and save our spot. These are the best seats in the house."

Oliver made his way back down the bleachers, pausing multiple times to greet people. He was such a natural. He'd really worked his magic on the crowd earlier in the day. Even Mrs. Thurber had come. He'd had her laughing as they watched Oreo in her pen. Laughing! She hadn't believed Mrs. Thurber capable of it until she'd seen it with her own eyes. She might begrudgingly allow Lena to treat Charles, but there was still an air of mistrust.

Oliver was standing in line for concessions, chatting with newlyweds Nick and Jae Dahlquist, when Misty Zimmerman joined them.

What was she doing there? She'd been in Robin's class in school. She'd always been popular and pretty. Looked like that hadn't changed.

She was acting pretty cozy too, flipping her auburn-highlighted waves and laying her hand on Oliver's arm. She giggled at something Ollie said and playfully batted his shoulder. She stood there in tight jeans and a yellow cropped sweater. When she raised an arm to pull her hair over to one side, her trim waist was displayed.

Heat infused Lena's cheeks.

But Oliver looked away. With a wave to Nick, Jae, and Misty, he left the line and started winding his way back up the bleachers empty-handed. By the time he reached Lena, her face had cooled a tad but still felt flushed.

Oliver sat down next to her.

How did she play this? Because this was not a date. She licked her lips and tried to relax her hands. "Were they out of hot dogs and popcorn?"

"Not exactly." He scrubbed his face and leaned closer, dropping his voice. "Kiah's teacher found me. She's nice and all, but she comes on a little strong, if you know what I mean."

"A *little* strong? You think?"

"So you saw that, huh?"

"It was kinda hard to miss."

Oliver quirked an eyebrow and smirked. "Are you jealous?"

Lena reared back. "Nooooo. I mean, go for it. If Misty is your type—"

Oliver moved in close, his gaze direct and heated. "She's not."

It didn't make sense. She got the distinct impression that Oliver was trying to communicate something, but she didn't know what. What man alive wouldn't want cute crop-top Misty with the perfect hair and tight jeans flirting with them? Who would choose Lonely Frump-a-Lena over that?

His warm touch on her hand stilled all the swirling questions.

"I want to be here with you."

Oh. Her breath caught in her chest.

He didn't let go of her hand, and she didn't mind it. The high-school band started playing, and Lena lost herself in the excitement of the moment. She stopped worrying about everything else. Oliver explained the game once it started. And when the Huskies made their first touchdown, Lena stood with the crowd and cheered.

For once, she got it. She wasn't on the outside, looking in. She was part of it all. And the more Oliver spoke in her ear so she could hear over the surrounding noise, the more this was feeling like a real date.

And crazily enough, she didn't mind that either.

eleven

· · ·

OUT OF ALL THE THINGS THAT OLIVER HAD THOUGHT WOULD BRING out Lena's ever-elusive emotional side over the years, never had he thought it would be high-school football. But when the Huskies finally took the lead with a running pass touchdown to Tommy Zimmerman, she stood next to him with her hands in the air, screaming at the top of her lungs with the rest of the crowd in the bleachers.

Suddenly her arms were around his neck. He turned his face, and before he could say anything, she kissed him.

On the lips.

Oliver froze. By the time what was happening registered, she'd whipped back around and continued cheering. Like it hadn't fazed her at all.

But it struck him with the force of an avalanche.

Lena Larson had kissed him.

For the first time in his life, he watched the game but couldn't concentrate on anything.

Anything except her.

They found their seats once again as the row in front of them sat down. Oliver grabbed her hand and held it. She didn't pull away. He didn't dare look at her. Just relished the feel of her soft skin, her long fingers entwined with his.

He was falling in love with her.

There had been some sizzle with Jalisa at one point, but with the drinking, he didn't remember a whole lot, and it certainly hadn't lasted. This was different. Lena knew him. She'd seen him at his worst and she was still here. She'd believed in his idea for the pet adoption, listened to his input. She was smart and caring, even though she hid her affectionate side well. She challenged him to bring his A-game to whatever he did.

After the kick, she leaned over. "I'm hungry. Think we can get those hot dogs now?"

Yes. Food. Something he could do to keep his mind occupied. Because all he wanted to do was a little kissing of his own, and this was not the place.

"I'll go grab us something to eat."

"I'll come with you this time. The quilt can save our spot."

He wasn't going to argue with that. Especially if Misty was still on the prowl. He kept hold of Lena's hand as he led her down the bleacher steps and to the concession stand. Even then he didn't let go. He stood there with what he knew was a giddy grin, waiting in line.

"Oliver?"

Ollie turned. His mouth went dry.

Grayson.

His brother stood there in jeans and a light-brown Stetson. Grayson had filled out since his high-school graduation. His tan face under the hat had matured, but he still had those same serious eyes.

Lena nudged him. He should probably say something.

"Hi." It came out raspy and thin.

Grayson nodded. Beth Strauss stood by his side, watching the two of them intently.

Oliver swallowed and found his voice again. "I've been wanting to talk to you."

"So you said."

"I, uh, think I'm going to go find the ladies' room. Lena, want to come with me?" Beth asked.

The girls walked off, and the men continued to stare each other down.

Oliver stepped out of the concession line. "I know I don't deserve a second of your time after what I've done, but I'd like to talk to you."

"We're talking now."

"Can we meet up for coffee tomorrow? Or maybe after church on Sunday? I've got some things to say. Things to make up for."

Grayson waited a beat. "I can meet on Sunday."

"I'd appreciate that."

The awkward silence broke as Grayson cleared his throat. "Robin said there's someone you brought back with you. Someone I should meet."

"I have a daughter. Kiah."

Grayson's jaw twitched. "I guess a lot can happen in twelve years."

"If you want, I can introduce you."

"Let's see how Sunday goes before we do anything else. See you then." Grayson walked away, but for the first time since the accident, Oliver hoped.

Maybe there was still a chance to redeem his relationship with his brother. He'd do whatever it took. Because nothing hurt like seeing the kid he'd shared so much with treat him like a stranger.

Oliver joined the line again. Someone jostled him from behind.

"If it isn't Jolly Ollie!" A strong hand clapped his shoulder and swung him around.

"Jeremy Stanly?"

"The one and only, brotha!" His once lanky friend wore an old Huskies jersey, now tight around his soft middle. His face was puffy and red, the blond hair a lot darker. He'd always been ready for a good time.

Apparently that hadn't changed. A whiff of Jeremy's breath and the glazed look in his eyes were still the same. He was drunk.

And like triggering muscle memory, seeing his old friend sent a signal to his brain that it was time for a drink. Oliver slammed his hand into his pocket to find the sobriety chip.

I admit I am powerless over alcohol. My life became unmanageable.

I believe in a Power bigger than myself which can restore me to sanity.

The recited steps helped him fight through the sudden dryness in his mouth and the urge to quench it.

"What are you doing in town, Mr. Fox? I thought you were loooong gone." Jeremy laughed.

"I'm back. Got a daughter now and thought this would be a great place for her. What about you? You married? Got a family?"

Jeremy blew a raspberry. His spittle flew into the air, hitting Oliver's face. "No way. I'm free as a bird." He flapped his arms. "I mean, I was with someone. Do you know Candace?"

Oliver shook his head.

"Yeah, she was cool, but then she got clingy and wanted a commitment, and that's just not the kind of guy I am." Jeremy stumbled as they stepped forward in line.

Oliver caught him under the arm and waited until he was steady once more. "You okay?"

Jeremy's drunken mirth slipped a bit. "Yeah. All good. But we should catch up. You look good, man. You work out?"

"Not really. But yeah, we should get together." Get a head start on the last step of AA.

Having had a spiritual awakening as the result of these steps, we try to carry this message to alcoholics, and to practice these principles in all our affairs.

Obviously Jeremy could use some help.

"Gimme your phone." Jeremy took Oliver's phone and added his number. He sent a text. "Now I got your number. I'll call you."

"Sure."

"But I gotta go." He walked away without a goodbye. "Go, Huskies!" he yelled randomly to the crowd.

Oliver's heart went out to the guy. That so easily could still be him. Jeremy probably wouldn't remember this little encounter, but maybe Oliver should try to get ahold of him later and see if he'd be interested in going to some meetings. Ollie could use one right now with the way the temptation for a shot of whiskey or a case of cold beers still had him by the throat.

At the concession window, Oliver ordered hot dogs and pop, knowing it wasn't going to quench the thirst he had. He reached for Lena's Coke, his hand shaking a little.

Then suddenly she was there.

Lena stepped up and steadied the drink, and Oliver found the light again.

She gave him a shy smile. "Need some help?"

"More than you know."

But he had a meeting with his brother on Sunday and a beautiful woman by his side right now. A beautiful woman who'd spontaneously kissed him.

So for tonight, he'd call that a victory. And it was better than any touchdown he'd ever made.

∗ ∗ ∗

KIAH JOINED LENA AND OLIVER AFTER THE HALF-TIME MARCHING band performance and requested a seat on Lena's lap. Lena happily obliged and focused on the action on the field. Maybe if she pretended that kiss hadn't happened, she wouldn't have to explain herself. She could go on acting like everything was normal. That the rush of attraction for Oliver was all a fluke.

Because that's what it had been. A momentary loss of her faculties resulting in a catastrophic lapse in her judgment.

And maybe Lena had had it all wrong back in high school. She'd hated the preferential treatment the sports teams got. She'd fought for more money for STEM labs and science clubs as her platform when she ran against Oliver for student body president.

Of course, she'd lost and had thus boycotted the games out of principle. Games he'd played in.

But sitting here in the bleachers with Oliver, she could see the allure. Families cheering on the players. The banter back and forth with the announcers. The strategy and teamwork it took for the Huskies to fight back their rival. As Oliver explained the plays, it made so much more sense.

And it didn't hurt to sit here with Kiah snuggled close, Elaine Fox's yellow-and-purple quilt wrapped around them, sheltering them from the autumn chill in the air. They shared popcorn and sent Oliver back for more drinks. Something warm this time.

But honestly, even though her feet were blocks of ice, it was the coziest Lena had been in a long time. She didn't spend much time around children, but Kiah made it easy. When Oliver handed her a paper cup of hot apple cider and sat close next to her, it seemed so natural. So right. Like it could always be this way.

Robin and Sammy found them and joined their row. "What do you think of the game, Kiah?" Robin asked.

"The purple team is winning. And Miss Zimmerman's cousin made some points."

Sammy squished in on the end. "You have Miss Zimmerman as your teacher?"

Kiah nodded as she munched on another handful of popcorn. "Daddy's gonna be a teacher too."

"What are you going to teach?" Lena asked him.

"I'm doing a basic plumbing course for Community Ed. I thought it would be a good way to introduce myself to the town as the new plumber and establish a foothold for the business."

"So you're really going to stay?"

"Mack Hill and I are having a contract drawn up. I need a down payment, and I'll have to make continuing installments over the next two years as I work. Then it will be mine."

So he *was* sticking around. Buying a business, joining the fire department, and teaching a class.

"Who are you?" The question fell from her mouth before she could snatch it back.

Oliver just looked amused. "What do you mean?"

"You've changed."

"That's what I keep trying to tell you." He scooped Kiah off Lena's lap and plopped her on his own. "Now, if you don't mind, I need this warming pillow back that you stole from me." He wrapped his arms around Kiah and hugged her tight.

"Daddy! You have to share." She laughed and wiggled out of his hold to find her way back to Lena. Then she made the rounds to Robin's and Sammy's laps too. But by the end of the game—a Huskies' victory—the little girl was in her daddy's arms and her eyes were droopy. When it was all done, Oliver carried her while they all walked to the parking lot.

"Why don't we take Kiah home with us?" Robin held out her hands, and Kiah didn't hesitate to go to her. "Then you don't have to hurry back, Ollie." She winked and walked away with Sammy.

Lena looked to Oliver as he held her door open for her. "What was that all about?"

"I don't know. Maybe she saw you kiss me." He shut the door before she could say anything else.

So much for pretending it hadn't happened.

As soon as Oliver sat in the driver's seat, Lena turned toward him. "I didn't kiss you—"

"Oh yes you did. What else do you call it when you put your lips on my lips—"

"I was caught up in the moment. It wasn't a real kiss."

"Admit it. You like me." He grinned as he turned on the ignition and joined the line of cars leaving.

"I...no...wait." She took a moment to gather her scattered thoughts into a sentence. "Like I said, I was excited about the touchdown. It doesn't count."

"Yeah, it does."

"Ugh. You are so irritating."

He tilted his head toward her. "And you love me for it."

"Where do you get these idiotic, completely false ideas?"

"From your mouth. Literally. Like when it kissed mine."

"Oliver!" She slugged him lightly on the arm.

"Lena, it's okay. The first step is always denial. But admit it. You had fun tonight."

She turned to look out at the clear sky sprinkled with stars. They were so bright and beautiful from far away, but one could never get too close to them. The nuclear fusion reactions at their core would consume anyone that tried. "That doesn't mean anything. Fun is fleeting. And feelings get you in trouble."

"Spoken like a true scientist. Which is probably why I never did great in biology. But it's a good thing you have me to remind you of the finer things in life."

"No. It's a good thing you had *me* to tutor you so you could pass bio."

"That too." He turned onto their road.

"You're incorrigible."

"I'm taking it as a compliment."

"It's not."

"Well, I'm going to take it as one anyway. Because I know the truth." He paused, probably knowing it would drive her nuts. "You like me. And I have scientific, *biological* proof."

"What proof?"

"Your kiss."

Lena shook her head and laughed. At least she didn't have to worry about him taking anything seriously.

"It's nice to hear you agree," Oliver said.

"I didn't agree."

"It kinda sounded like you did." He grinned at her, his dimple poking through. "And by the way, you should laugh more often."

"I laugh."

"No, you don't. Not as much as you should."

"You think I should laugh more? Why?"

"Because…you have a great laugh, and the world is missing out not hearing it." His tone grew serious. "You really shouldn't hide so much of yourself. And if you want to cry, you should. Or yell. Or cheer. Just let it all out. Like you did tonight."

"Easy for you to say. It's not the way I was taught." Her voice sounded small in the darkness of the van.

They reached the Fox driveway. Oliver parked and turned toward her. "But I hope you know…you can be real with me." She'd rarely heard Oliver speak so gently. So sincerely.

Be real? Where did she start?

He hopped out of the van and ran around the front of it to open her door. As she got out, Oliver held out his hand. She gave him hers as he walked her to her own yard and up the steps to her porch. His warm grip was comforting and yet so dangerous at the same time. She could very easily find herself wanting it too much.

At the door, he looked down at her with those deep-brown eyes. He lost the teasing glint, the ever-present charm and smirk. "All joking aside, I had a really nice time tonight. With you."

Her breath caught. Okay. She could start with that. Honesty. "I never understood sports, but thank you for taking the time to explain the game to me. I can see why you liked it so much back in high school."

"Does that mean you'll go out with me again?"

She started to tug her hand away. "Ollie…"

"C'mon, Lena." He didn't let her hand go. A hint of desperation laced the air between them. "Give me a chance. Please."

A brisk wind kicked up, blowing leaves onto the porch and invading the cozy moment. "I'm not sure we should set ourselves up for disappointment."

He would probably be fine, but she hadn't fully recovered from the last time he broke her heart.

"I just want to spend some time with you."

Time with her? Alone? Tempting and terrifying at the same time. And the way he gently tugged her closer, temptation might be winning here. "I can't promise you anything."

"I'm not asking for promises. Just a chance." He held both hands now, his voice so sincere.

"What makes you so sure you want this? You say people change, but I haven't changed much from the person I was senior year, and you certainly didn't want me then."

Oops. She hadn't meant for that to come out. She pulled away and sat on the front step. This was why it was so dangerous to let herself go and start sharing things. It lifted the floodgates, and it was so much harder to hold everything back once she started. A tear slipped down her cheek. This was why Oliver was so wrong for her.

He joined her on the step, his head hung low. "You haven't changed much because you didn't need to. But I did." He picked up a stick and started twirling it in his hand. "I was a complete jerk back then. I...I liked you. I always have. You were the one person that always put me in my place. You pushed me to be better. But also, you were always there for me. And I can't tell you how many times I've wished I'd had the guts to admit that I liked you back then."

Words she'd always hoped for back then tickled her ears. Was she dreaming? "You liked me? For real?"

He blew out a long sigh. "Truth is, I know I didn't deserve you then, and I know I don't deserve you now. But I want a shot,

Lena." He turned toward her and reached for her hand again. "When I'm with you, it feels like it's possible."

"What's possible?"

"To be the man you deserve. The guy I *want* to be. Someone Kiah and my family can be proud of again."

And suddenly she saw it. The guy underneath the charm and the dimpled grin. The guy who was an amazing father. The guy who took neglected animals into his home and took care of them. The guy who was trying to rebuild relationships with the family he'd spurned. The neighbor who gave up his barn and free time to help her with her project.

Maybe it wouldn't be so bad to spend some time with that guy.

"All right," she whispered into the night.

A slow smile spread across Oliver's face. "All right." He leaned in. "So, do you want to seal this with another kiss, or—"

Lena chuckled. "Don't press your luck, mister. Let's call this starting over as friends. That's all I can offer."

Oliver caught her hand and pulled her up to standing. "Taking it slow. Got it. And I know I'm hard to resist, but you'll just have to try." He twirled her around and kissed her hand. "Good night, fair Lena." He bowed low like a knight from a fairy tale.

"Good night, Ollie."

And it really was a beautiful night, with the Milky Way and a riot of stars against the velvet sky. With her high school dream of being with Oliver Fox within reach.

He walked away, giving her a wave as he crossed onto his own property. Oh, the man was way too charming. Someone should remind her that he'd devastated her heart last time. She shouldn't be so willing to jump in blindly this time. But yes, she could give Ollie a chance.

She lifted her hand and waved back.

twelve

· · ·

OLIVER COULDN'T QUITE RELISH LAST NIGHT'S VICTORY YET. IT WAS only a foot in the door. He needed a game plan if he wanted any chance of proving to Lena he was serious about them.

"I've got a great idea." Robin set down a plate of maple-pecan waffles in front of Oliver and Kiah.

Oliver buttered Kiah's waffle and poured syrup over it.

"Aren't you going to ask me what my idea is?"

"I figured you would tell me anyway." He made a silly face at Kiah, who started giggling.

"I'm only trying to help you. But if you don't want any help making amends with Grandma and Grandpa…" Robin sipped her coffee.

Oliver doctored his own waffle. "Okay. I'll bite. What's your grand idea?" He looked over at his daughter. "Get it? Grand?"

She shook her head and rolled her eyes. "Dad, that was totally lame."

"Since when did you become a teenager?"

She shrugged and stuffed her mouth with a bite of waffle.

"Since you asked"—Robin sat down with her mug—"I think you should organize the fifty-fifth anniversary party for Gran and Gramps and have Lena help you."

"I thought we were doing a small get together at church with one of your fancy cakes."

"I'll still make a fabulous cake, but think how far it would go if you helped throw a big shindig. They would love it. They would get to see all their friends, how involved you are in the community again, and you would get all the credit."

"What do you mean by 'big shindig?'"

Robin focused on cutting her own waffles. "The barn is already cleaned out."

"So?"

"Why not have the party here?"

"We only have a couple weeks, and it's getting colder every day."

She batted away his concern with a wave of her hand. "You threw the adopt-a-pet event together in two weeks. And we could rent those big outdoor heaters."

Oliver took a big bite and chewed slowly.

"You could ask Lena to help organize it. It would give you an excuse to spend more time with her." Robin's relentless stare didn't budge.

"I want to help with the party. And I like Miss Lena." Kiah chugged her orange juice. "I still think we should adopt her."

Oliver tugged on her pigtail. "It doesn't quite work like that, kiddo, but I like her too."

Robin popped up off her chair and started stacking waffles on a platter. "Great. Then you should take her some breakfast and start planning the party. We'll need to send out invites right away."

"I didn't say—"

Robin shoved the plate at him. "Wrap this in foil and head on over. I happen to know that Lena has a particular weakness for waffles. Something about the symmetry and squares."

"Yeah, Daddy."

"Isn't it kinda early?"

"Trust us," Robin said.

"Yeah, trust us," Kiah echoed.

Being overpowered by the women in the house, and hoping they knew what they were talking about, Oliver headed to Lena's. He knocked on her front door. A sudden attack of nerves hit him. Was this too early? Last night, in the dark, he'd bared a part of his own heart to her, but maybe that had been too much too fast.

Yeah, this was a bad idea. She was probably sleeping still. Wentworth's deep bark sounded behind the door.

Now he'd done it. He'd started to turn away when the door opened and Lena poked her head out. Her hair was pulled back in a messy braid hanging over her shoulder. She rubbed her eyes. She stood in a light-pink robe, looking adorably disheveled. "Ollie?"

"Hey…" He held out the platter. "I have waffles."

The confused look on her face softened. "You brought me waffles?" A hint of wonder in her voice said Robin was on to something.

"I did."

"Okay." She opened the door wider to let him in.

So far, so good. He'd butter her up with breakfast and then ask for help. Because Robin was also right about the party. Showing his grandfather that he could execute an event in his honor would go a long way in proving to him that Oliver had become someone he didn't have to be ashamed of anymore.

"You mentioned some baking disasters. Should I be worried about these waffles?" Lena pulled out plates and silverware and carried them to her small dining room table.

Oliver poured coffee for both of them and doctored hers the way she liked it. "Robin made these, so nothing to worry about."

She seemed satisfied with the answer as she carefully laid out the silverware on place mats and added cloth napkins and plates. Unlike him with his mostly paper-plate meals, this woman didn't do casual.

He sat down at the table and lifted the foil off the platter. "Looks like I came to the right place."

"Don't start yet. I still need to warm up the syrup." She set the butter dish and knife on the table in front of him. "But you can tell me what brought you over here this early."

"I thought we should team up again."

She looked over her shoulder at him while placing the syrup in the microwave. "Team up how?"

"No need to look so suspicious."

"I'm always suspicious with you."

He sent her a grin and plopped a still-hot waffle on her plate. He waited for her to set the warm syrup on the table and sit down. She buttered the waffle, making sure every square was covered before slowly pouring a steady stream of what smelled like one hundred percent pure maple syrup. Not the fake stuff he always bought.

"Okay, spit it out. Tell me the real reason you're here."

"Can't I just enjoy breakfast with your sunshiny company?"

She snorted as she cut into her waffle straight along a ridge. "You're funny. The waffles were a smart move though. So spill it while I'm still in a good mood and before the coffee kicks in and my brain starts working again."

"I need your help to plan a party."

"For whom?" She stirred her coffee and sipped.

"My grandparents. Their fifty-fifth."

"When?"

"Party would be October twenty-eighth."

"That's only fourteen days away."

"We did the pet adoption event in fourteen."

"True. So where will this party take place? Are you thinking sit-down dinner? Buffet?"

"Robin thought we could use the barn again. Everything else is open for debate."

She didn't look thrilled with his answer. "What kind of budget are we talking about?"

Oh. Money. "Not sure." He bent down to pet Wentworth, who at some point had settled by his feet.

"Do you at least have a theme?"

"Do we need a theme?"

She speared him with a look and took another bite.

Whoa-kay. "The theme can be whatever you want."

"Something green."

"Green?"

"Yes. The fifty-fifth is the emerald anniversary."

"Didn't know that. But sure. Let's do something green."

Lena set down her fork. "So basically you came here because you want me to plan it all."

"It's not like I don't bring anything to the table. I brought you waffles. I bring the brawn and a willing attitude. I'll do the wheeling and dealing to get the best prices. And most importantly, I'll be completely at your beck and call. I've never planned a party before."

Her eyes narrowed as she dissected his argument points. "That's not true."

"You mean the event yesterday?"

"No, my birthday party."

Oliver scrambled to remember what had obviously been a big deal to her. "Which birthday party?"

"The only one I've ever had. Don't you remember? My mom had an out-of-town conference over my birthday, and I was staying with you guys. You and Robin and Grayson threw me a Crocodile Hunter party. We had cake. There were presents. And Robin told me she wanted to invite others, but you knew. You knew I would want it small and just the family. And…it was perfect." She looked across the table at him, something shy in her expression.

And he remembered. "That's right." He laughed. "Do you know that I made the first cake?"

"What do you mean by 'the first cake?' I only remember one cake."

"I wanted to help, but I was no good at decorating or buying presents for a girl. So Mom suggested I do the cake. I insisted on doing it myself."

"Hmm. Why am I not surprised? So what happened?"

"I left something out and it ended up flat, burnt, and inedible. Grandma and Robin stayed up all night and made another. I think they let me add sprinkles to it the next day though."

Lena stared at him in wonder, almost like she was seeing him for the first time. "It was a really good cake. And my favorite birthday by far."

"So, does that mean you'll help? You wouldn't want another cake disaster for my grandparents." He leaned in, determined to sweeten the deal. "And you get complete control over planning. Think of all the spreadsheets and flow charts. I do the executing and schmoozing. The people stuff you hate."

"I don't know…"

"You *do* know. This is the way we roll, and you like ordering me around."

The corner of her lips slowly curled up. "Maybe."

"I helped you with your event. And look how great it turned out. You said it yourself. I did well."

She picked up her fork once more. "Your grandparents deserve something nice. I'll do it for them."

"But part of you is really doing it to spend more time with me. Because you can't resist—"

She threw a piece of sticky waffle at his face. "Don't make me regret agreeing."

He laughed loud and long until she joined in. "You are full of surprises, Lena Larson."

"Don't you forget it." She stood and grabbed a notebook already on her counter. "Now, let's get started. We don't have a lot of time. And I'm meeting someone in Duluth later, so I can get started on shopping."

"Who are you meeting?"

"Brad." She avoided his eyes and took another bite.

"Brad? Who's Brad?"

"My biological father."

"This is the guy that left you and your mom high and dry?" All his protective instincts flared. "You're meeting up with him? I'm not so sure that's a good idea."

Lena tilted her head and glared. "You want me to give you a second chance. Why not him?"

"But how can you be sure this guy is legit? He could be running some sort of scam."

She huffed. "Give me some credit. I insisted on a test. DNA says he's my father."

But that didn't mean he was a good man. This guy had caused Lena a lot of grief. And no one knew who he was. "That doesn't mean he's safe. Maybe I should go with you—"

"You're worried." Lena's whole face softened. "And it's sweet that you're acting all protective, but I'll be going alone. You're going to be busy." She tapped her notebook. "I'll give you a list before I go."

"But—"

She shook her head. "I'm a big girl, Ollie. Let it drop."

The stubborn lift of her chin brought back enough memories to know she was serious. And the more he pushed, the more she would dig her heels in.

Fine, he'd let it go for now. But that didn't mean he had to like it. Oliver might not be considered a good guy with all of the things he'd done in the past, but he was trying to make up for it. What kind of man was Brad?

🐕 🐕 🐕

LENA MIGHT HAVE TOLD OLLIE SHE WAS A BIG GIRL AND THAT meeting her father wasn't a huge deal.

Well, she'd lied.

Big time.

Why else would she still be sitting here in her truck in a parking lot in Canal Park? He was in that coffee shop somewhere. She'd waited her whole life to meet him. But she couldn't move.

A huge barge cut smoothly through the Duluth canal, and the lift bridge lowered back down. People walked along the sidewalks happy, chatting, walking their dogs and enjoying the gorgeous fall weather, completely oblivious to the life-changing moment she was about to embark on.

Too bad she hadn't brought Wentworth and Jane. Maybe they could've calmed the trembling in the pit of her gut. Or maybe Oliver coming along wouldn't have been such a bad idea. Because being with him lately made her feel...empowered. He didn't mind that she liked organizing things, called things like they were, wasn't super girly or emotional. It was kind of cute how jealous he'd gotten when she'd mentioned Brad, almost like he really did like her.

Then again, Oliver could be passionate and impulsive, and she certainly didn't need any more of that right now. She was barely keeping down her breakfast as it was.

Get it under control, Larson.

With a long inhale, she opened her driver's side door and wiped her palms on her pants. This was it.

She walked into the coffee shop and scanned the crowd. The man in the corner could be him. But he looked older than the picture he'd sent her. A big group of college students and a couple with two young kids sat in different corners of the room.

No one else came close to the right age or gender. She kept the man in her peripheral vision as she ordered her vanilla latte. By the time her drink was ready, he stood and approached.

"Lena?"

She lost all words as her throat constricted. She wrapped her hands around the drink, trying to absorb some of its warmth.

The man facing her wore khakis and a thick fleece jacket. He smiled like he was glad to see her.

Lena swallowed past the tightness. "Brad?"

He nodded. "I've got a spot over here."

She followed him to the small table and sat, hating that her back was to the door. But she studied the man before her. She might have her mother's frame, but the hair, eye color, the shape of his nose were undeniably like her own. His green eyes were clear, framed by wrinkles. His forehead was lined more than she would've expected for a man in his fifties, and he had a lot more gray hair than brown, but the biology of aging could be weird like that.

"Wow, you look so much like your mother," he said as he took his seat. "It's almost like stepping back in time." The hint of a smile must mean that was a good thing. Right?

Mom was the one thing they had in common. She could start there. "How did you two meet?"

"College. We were in the same dorm. She knocked on my door to tell me to turn my music down."

"Was it one of those instant romances?"

He shook his head. "No, believe it or not, we didn't quite hit it off at first. And she was dating someone else. But later, after she was in grad school, we ran into each other, and one thing led to another. At that point we both fell hard and fast."

"Oh." What did one say to that? Lena sipped her drink. Where were all the years of questions she'd stored up? She couldn't come up with one.

But Brad didn't seem to mind her silence. He quietly studied her, maybe gauging her reaction or something. He finally broke the silence. "I was sorry to hear she passed away."

"Then why did you wait so long to contact me?" Okay, that might've been blurted out a little fast, because now the questions flooded, and that particular one had been bugging her.

And it looked like it threw him off guard. "I didn't know what to say, what she told you about me, or how you would take my sudden appearance after such a loss. I was torn between wanting to respect her wishes and wanting to see you."

He sounded sincere. Honest.

After a silent moment he looked up. "So, what did she tell you about me?"

"That I shouldn't waste my time asking questions."

"Ah." He played with the string on his tea bag hanging out of the cup in front of him. "That sounds like Valerie."

Lena could go on with other statements she'd heard from her mother over the years in regard to him, but it probably wouldn't make for good conversation.

Don't waste your time crying over him or any man, Lena.

They promise you the world, but in the end they follow their dreams and leave you pregnant, broke, and alone.

But sitting across the table, the man didn't look so horrible. He looked…contrite. Apologetic. Humble even.

"I'm sorry. I did try to stay in contact. Did your mother ever tell you?"

Lena shook her head.

"I was afraid of that. I begged her to give me another chance, and she turned me down. And when I asked to get to know you after you were born, she outright refused. Did she ever…find someone? Do you have a stepfather?"

"She was happy with her career. She didn't need anything else." And the one man who'd lived with them for a short while when Lena was young had only ended up breaking both of their hearts, so why mention him?

Brad nodded like he got it. "Did she become a doctor like she always wanted?"

"She was a physician's assistant." It wasn't the same, and her grandmother had never let Lena's mom forget it.

And honestly, she wasn't here to defend her mother. She was here to learn about this man. "What about you? What do you do?"

"I develop websites and podcasts."

"In Nevada?"

"Yeah, in Vegas."

"You mentioned you like cooking?"

It was a good question. Brad talked for the next twenty minutes about the gourmet cooking course he'd taken last year. As he did, he lost a little of the pastiness in his face.

See, this wasn't so bad. The more he talked, the more Lena relaxed.

"So, tell me about yourself, Lena. What is life as a vet like?"

"It's different every day. I see everything from cats to cows and horses. Not that there's a lot of farms in the area, so mostly I'm in the clinic and seeing small animals. I like the variety and the challenge of working with different species."

He asked some good questions, and before she knew it, an hour had passed. She gathered her purse and looked for her keys inside. "I better go. I have some more errands to run before the long drive back."

Brad looked disappointed. "I was hoping to take you to dinner. We have more to talk about."

"I already have plans."

"Then when can I see you again? I could come up your way tomorrow?"

The earnestness of his plea almost had her reconsidering, but she had a lot to process as it was. Then again, maybe she should make the most of his time here, since he'd come all this way. "I guess you have to get back to Nevada soon."

"I'm here in Minnesota for the next month. Maybe longer."

"That long?"

"I can do my work remotely, and I wanted to be here. Close to you. We've got a lot of time to make up for. So what do you say? Tomorrow?"

As glad as she was to have spent some time with him, she still wasn't ready to have him invade her home world. But eventually...maybe. "I'm busy. But we could meet up halfway for dinner next week. There's a place in Silver Bay. I'm free Thursday night."

"I'll try to be patient until then." He stood up and smiled. What did one do in a situation like this? Hug? Handshake? Nothing felt right, so she simply waved goodbye and left.

She breathed a little easier as she drove away. For the first face-to-face meeting with a man she had always wondered about —okay, almost obsessed about—it hadn't been too bad.

Oliver certainly had nothing to worry about. The only thing Brad wanted was to spend time with her. It had to mean something that he would stay a whole month in state so he could get to know her. And now that the first awkward meeting was done, the next one would be better.

Lena spent the rest of the afternoon stocking up on items for the clinic and home. It was amazing how many cleaning supplies and paper towels the clinic went through. She picked up invitations, priced out party supplies and different options for the menu she'd already started thinking through. Lena arrived home exhausted, but perked up to find a sweet picture of Oreo from Kiah and a mason jar with branches of bright-colored leaves on her front porch.

She opened the little note tucked into the jar.

Hope you had a great day. We took the dogs for a walk already. Love, Oliver.

Love, Oliver.

They were only words, but knowing that he'd thought of her, taken care of her animals, meant so much. And now her father was wanting to know her. All the things she'd hoped for were finally coming together.

But walking into her garage, she found a different kind of note and Darling circling in the kennel with Oscar, Scamp, and a new stray.

The black poodle mix jumped and barked. "Who are you? And, Darling, what are you doing back here?"

Lena read Birdie's note. The retired couple Oliver had

convinced to take Darling at the adoption event had brought her back, and Birdie had found the newcomer wandering in town, lost and hungry.

Well, that was just great.

Darling whined until Lena let her out of the kennel and picked her up. Her scar from where her eye had had to be surgically removed had healed nicely, but it didn't help her looks any. She longed for affection and cuddles. And with Lena's hours away from home, she couldn't provide what these dogs needed long term. Thank goodness Birdie came and checked on them during the days, but Darling needed more.

Lena held her close. "Looks like we still need to find you a home. Someone who will give you all the love and attention you need. Huh, girl?"

Darling licked Lena's chin and settled against her shoulder.

"I won't stop until we do."

thirteen

· · ·

Trapped in the lobby of Deep Haven Community Church, Oliver smiled and nodded at whatever it was Edith Draper was saying to him. Sure, it was the first time at his home church in over a decade, and everyone wanted to welcome him back. But after catching up with Nathan Decker, meeting Colleen's fiancé Jack, and Peter Dahlquist's wife Ronnie drilling him on the first responders' class prep work, if one more person stopped him on his way out to see the one woman he wanted to see, things were gonna get ugly. After making sure Kiah was safely with Robin, he finally broke away from Edith and headed for the exit.

"Lena!" He jogged across the parking lot to her. She spun around, her hair—down for once, just like at the game—caught the sunlight and fell softly around her face. Her green eyes were luminous, her lips shiny. Why had he ever thought she was plain? He couldn't take his eyes off her.

"Hey, Ollie." She smiled shyly, completely catching him off guard. "Did you want something?"

He wanted her. Not that he could admit it out loud. "I just wanted…to see how it went yesterday."

"With Brad?" She looked confused. "I already told you when you texted last night."

"Yeah, but I thought you might elaborate a little more than the 'good' response you took so long to type out."

"It was fine. Why are you so worried?"

"The guy's been MIA your whole life and he suddenly shows up. It's suspicious. Did you have Cole Barrett or Kyle Hueston run his name in their system? They would know if he has a criminal history."

"That's a complete invasion of privacy, not to mention unethical. And there's no need. We had *coffee*."

"I know, but—"

"Oliver. He didn't kidnap me. I'm not worth any money. There's nothing he could scam out of me, so down, boy. I don't need a big brother stepping in here."

Good, because he didn't want a brotherly type relationship with her. "I know you're capable." But he did wonder how it was affecting her. "So it was…okay?"

She lifted her shoulder. "It was weird. But we had a good conversation."

"Weird how? Was he a sicko or something?" His blood pressure started to rise.

"He was completely normal." She twisted her watch around her wrist absently. "It's just…awkward. I'm thirty years old and meeting my father for the first time. There's no book on how to do that. I'm not quite sure what to expect."

"Oh." As much as he was tempted to do so for Lena's three decades' worth of heartache, it didn't sound like he needed to track the guy down and rough him up. "So now he goes home and you go back to your life?"

"Actually, he's sticking around. He wants to meet again."

Oliver stifled a groan. He shouldn't begrudge her this. She'd taken a lot of grief for not having a dad in her life. Obviously she wanted this, so he kept his mouth shut and nodded. But he didn't mind when she changed the subject and told him about the party stuff she'd picked up in Duluth.

"And I was able to get invitations. I'll print them out as soon as I get the guest list from Robin. Did you get everything on your list done?"

"Yup. I talked to the rental center about tables, chairs, heaters, and the big tent. We got it all reserved. They also have the lights if we want more."

She looked down and fiddled with her truck keys. "Maybe we can get together for lunch and discuss the rest of the details."

Was she…oh yes, she was. He grinned. "Are you asking me out?"

Her head snapped up. "No! It would be a *working* lunch. As *friends*. We've got a lot still to do for your party." Her cheeks turned a pretty shade of pink and her eyes sparked. "That's all."

Man, he loved it when she got snippy. Especially when she blushed and spoke in italics.

"I better check my calendar…" He pulled out his phone. The words under today's date blared up at him.

Meet w/ Gray.

Shoot. Visions of a romantic lunch and more teasing fizzled. "I've got something already."

"That's fine." She opened her truck door, but Oliver burst forward to stop her.

"I'd rather have lunch with you. Believe me, I would. But this is my shot with Grayson. I'm meeting him out at the camp."

"I understand. I've got a lot to do anyway." She paused and her gaze softened a tad. "I hope it goes well."

Warmth infused him. And hang it all if his focus didn't catch on her lips again and get stuck.

"So…I'll see you later?" she asked.

"I'd like that."

Because he couldn't get enough of her. He wanted to see the woman she hid behind that cool exterior. A chance to unravel the mystery, to experience something true and rare. Maybe experience a real kiss.

But he let her drive away. He couldn't waste this chance with Grayson. He jumped in the van and headed out of town.

He followed the dirt road that cut into the forest wilderness. At the sign for Trinity Horse Camp, he turned, memories of the summer he'd attended replaying. Grayson had loved it here and took to it immediately. Oliver had been kicked out when he missed dinner and chapel one too many times. Taking one of the horses for an unapproved solo trail ride had probably had something to do with it as well. But he'd just lost his parents that summer. He'd been too angry and hurting to want to be around people then.

He parked and strode toward the stables, where Grayson had said to meet. Walking in to the smell of hay and horses, he let his eyes adjust to the dark interior.

"Hello?"

Grayson stepped out of a stall, hefting a saddle. "Hey." He set it down on a straw bale. "So you decided to come after all."

"Sorry I'm late. I got caught up in the after-church chitchat."

Grayson's gaze slid over to him for a second, but he said nothing as he shook out the saddle blanket. It stirred up a cloud of dust.

Guess it was up to Oliver to get this started. "I'm surprised I didn't see you at church."

"We had a service out here with the guest group."

"Oh." The words he'd planned stuck in his throat. He looked around the stable. "The camp looks great. Do they need any help around here?"

"Not from you."

"What's that supposed to mean?"

Grayson tossed down the blanket on the saddle. "Look, say your piece and let's get on with it so you'll feel better. But let's not pretend you're here for me."

His brother's words felt like a punch in the gut. "But I *am* here for you—"

"Don't kid yourself. You do only what's good for you."

"Hey, I came out here to talk."

"So talk." He stared Oliver down in the middle of the aisle, his arms folded across his torso like a barricaded gate. "Get whatever you want off your chest, and we'll play nice when the party rolls around."

Oliver clenched his jaw. "I was hoping for something more—"

"You thought I'd play 'Hail the Conquering Hero'? Fat chance."

"I'm not expecting—"

"Then what do you want?" Grayson's lips went taut, and his stare could've burned the whole barn to the ground. Gone was Ollie's best friend and brother. They were meeting on a battlefield now as enemies, and like acid, it was tearing him up inside.

"You're my only brother, Gray. I was hoping we could set aside the past and…I dunno. Start over." Oliver took a step toward him.

"You mean pretend you didn't walk out on our family? That I haven't seen you in over a decade?"

"I was messed up."

Grayson marched up to him. "That was obvious. But you know what isn't? Why you left without a word. You didn't even come to the hospital after you—"

"I did!"

A big chestnut horse whinnied and poked its head out of the stall.

He probably needed to lower his voice and not completely spook the animals.

Grayson turned away and walked over to the stall, clucking his tongue. He stroked the horse's forehead and crooned in its ear.

He had all the patience in the world for the animal, but he wouldn't give Oliver the time of day.

How could he get him to listen?

"I was in the waiting room at the hospital all night long, but they wouldn't let me see you. Then cops showed up and threw me in the holding cell at the jail. Grandpa had me released that morning, but when I asked him about how you were, he—" Oliver clamped his mouth shut.

"He what?"

The words were burned into his brain, but he didn't want to repeat them. He didn't want them spoken out loud ever again.

Even if they were true.

"What did he do, Ollie? Is this another one of your excuses? Because it wasn't Grandpa who put me in that hospital and then left me behind. That was all you. So how do you blame that on the old man?"

"I didn't leave you behind!" He'd failed in a lot of ways as a big brother. And the accident was his fault, no doubt. But there was more to the story than Grayson knew. Maybe it was time to stop protecting him, let him hear what Grandpa really thought. "I was commanded to go. And I was told to not contact you again."

"What are you talking about?"

"Grandpa. He told me I didn't deserve to be a part of the family. That I'd brought shame to the Fox name, and that until I could clean up my act, I wasn't a part of it. He wouldn't let me see you. He said I was too bad of an influence."

Grayson frowned. "That doesn't sound like him."

No, it didn't. Because Grayson and Robin hadn't been the ones responsible for their parents' deaths.

Not that Grandpa had ever yelled at Oliver like that before the incident. Usually his judgments came down hard but in a solemn voice of disappointment. But that night, it hadn't surprised Oliver when the man's true feelings came out in that awful moment. Because deep down, he'd known. Grandpa was right.

Oliver *didn't* deserve to be a part of them. So he'd walked away and hadn't looked back. Until now.

But it wasn't ever going to be enough, was it? He was never going to be able to atone for his past.

"Why are you here, Oliver?" Grayson still glared.

What did he have to offer the brother he'd almost killed? "I have a daughter now. I want our family back together. I'm trying to make amends."

Grayson studied him a moment. "That's a nice sentiment, but I'm not sure I trust you, Ollie. There's a lot of water that's passed under that bridge you burned." Grayson walked away.

Ollie stood there in the dark stable.

God must've had some mercy on him though, because no one was home when Oliver arrived except Bruce, who met him at the door. But once the dog realized he wasn't Kiah, he lay back down on his rug. He wouldn't even lift his head off his paws.

"Disappointed it's me? Join the club. I thought you were supposed to be man's best friend. Loyal."

Bruce lifted his eyes at the comment but made no move.

Fine. But Oliver desperately needed something to do. He grabbed his toolbox from the closet. Bruce met him at the back door and followed him as he marched out to his barn. He sniffed around while Oliver cranked up the old radio. Lynyrd Skynyrd blared as he started in the dairy parlor/cat cage. He wedged a screwdriver under the staples holding down the chicken wire he'd used to section off the area. One by one, he pried the staples out of the wood frame.

"I guess it didn't go well, huh?"

Oliver turned. Lena stood in the doorway. A breeze slipped in with her, carrying her lemon scent. It cooled his ire for a moment, like a long sip of lemonade on a hot day.

"You could say that." He ripped another staple out.

She turned down the music. "What happened?"

"Let's just say he's not interested in anything I have to offer."

"What exactly did you offer him?"

"Does it matter? I was kidding myself thinking there's anything I could do to make up for the past."

"You're right. You can't." She looked straight at him without a blink.

"Gee, thanks. Why didn't you say that in the church parking lot before you drove away?" He went back to the staples. "You could've saved me a trip." He drove the wedge of the screwdriver under the next staple, but only one side popped loose. The other stuck firmly in the wood and didn't budge.

Forget this piddly stuff. He dropped the screwdriver and yanked on the chicken wire, ripping it down.

Lena moved inside the room and leaned against a post. "Nothing is going to change what happened. Not throwing parties or volunteering with the fire crew. Or cleaning out this barn."

What kind of nonsense was she spouting? And how could she stay so calm?

"Hey, I'm trying. Do you think it was easy to come back here? To face everyone after everything that happened?"

She slowly shook her head. "No, I don't." Her voice stayed steady and even. "But you can't expect us to just forget either and act like it didn't happen."

"Then why did you decide to give me a shot?"

Lena paused. "I'm not exactly sure. I keep asking myself the same thing."

"If it's not enough, you're free to go."

Her eyes narrowed and she stepped closer, but she stayed so irritatingly cool. Like he didn't affect her at all. Was he the only one all fired up right now?

"You want me to go?" she asked, her voice monotoned.

He dropped the chicken wire in his hand and stood to face her. Of course he didn't want her to leave. He wanted her to stay. Fight with him. He wanted to ruffle up her perfect hair. He wanted to affect her, make her feel the inferno she set off in him.

He grabbed her hand before she could turn away. "No, I don't *want* you to go."

"Then what do you want?" Her voice was calm, but her eyes betrayed her. She was testing him.

"You!"

Her eyes widened but the rest of her body was deadly still. He stood inches from her, his chest heaving and jaw clenched tight.

"I want to kiss you, Lena. I want you to stop hiding who you really are. I want…you."

There. He'd said it. He'd exposed what he'd tried so hard to protect. Because everything inside him wanted to tear down her walls and see the passion she kept hidden inside. To see this amazing woman pulsing with life.

She swallowed hard and took a step back.

Right. She should step away. Far away. Because like drinking a scotch on ice, if he started kissing her, he'd be completely at her mercy. Powerless.

Before he did anything more he'd regret, he turned and walked out of the barn and over to Oreo's pen with Bruce following. Oliver fisted a hand and gave the fence a solid pound. If he got splinters, it would be the least painful part of the day.

"You're trying to make amends by doing all the things. But have you stopped to simply take responsibility and say you're sorry?" Lena's voice carried over his shoulder.

He spun around. That was what she'd gotten out of that conversation? Fine. Safer than thinking about kissing her. "Of course I have." Bruce barked like he understood. Maybe there was some loyalty there after all.

Lena folded her arms across her chest, like maybe she was exposing something too and needed to shield it. "You didn't apologize to me."

"Yes, I did."

"When? Because I think I would've remembered hearing words I've been waiting to hear since we were seniors in high school."

"The other night after the game. On your doorstep. I told you how much I regretted things. I told you I was a jerk."

"But you never once said 'I was wrong. I'm sorry.'" Her voice cracked.

"It's the same thing."

"It's not." Her nostrils flared, and there was an actual bite to her words.

"Well, it was implied. I fixed your light. I helped with your event. Actions speak louder than words."

"Words still matter!" Her voice yelled so loudly it echoed off the side of the barn. She stomped up to him and shoved her finger into his chest "You can't undo hurting me or drinking and causing Grayson's accident or walking out on the family. But you *can* start with an actual apology. If you're going to do it, do it right."

It was about time.

For once she wasn't holding back. He couldn't help the pride that surged through him for chipping away at that robotic shell she hid behind and seeing the flesh-and-blood woman he'd always known was there.

But her words...? Everything in him cringed at them. He didn't accept defeat. He'd had to fight for everything—for every day of sobriety, for every cent that he had, for a way back into his family. For his daughter's sake as well as his own.

And now Lena was saying none of it mattered? That he needed to simply apologize?

It didn't sit well inside. At all.

"You asked why I'm giving you another chance. It's because I know you're not the same guy you were. I see how you care about others. But you hurt a lot of people, Ollie. The least you could do is admit that to them and say you're sorry."

So she had noticed he was trying, that he'd changed.

And he *was* sorry. More than anybody knew. Shame and regret were relentless companions. He'd tried shaking them for so long.

It was just so flippin' excruciating to admit. To expose his weakness for all to see, not knowing if they'd kick him to the curb or take advantage and destroy him.

But he owed it to Lena. And if he had a shot with her, he was gonna take it.

He dug deep and looked her in the eye.

"Lena, I was wrong for hurting you. And I'm sorry."

She pursed her lips to the side for a moment, then finally spoke. "Thank you."

"Does that mean you forgive me?"

"It means…I'm starting to. There's just a lot there to process."

Oh. Something inside deflated. "Let me know when you decide." He snapped his fingers to get Bruce's attention, and they headed back to the barn. But there was one more thing. He turned and called to her.

"And by the way, you should yell more often too."

LENA WATCHED OLIVER WALK AWAY, HIS BROAD SHOULDERS PULLED back but his head drooping. He reached down and scratched Bruce between the ears.

He'd apologized. Finally.

He didn't mind that she'd lost control and yelled. He liked it when she laughed. It didn't matter how much she tried to fight it, he had this direct line to her heart. An invisible hold on her.

And when she'd asked him what he wanted and he'd spoken that one word, it'd cracked what was left of her defenses.

He wanted *her*.

It was everything she'd wanted back then. But was it what she wanted now? He was irritating and joked around too much. He was loud and relentless. Spontaneous and passionate. So unpredictable.

But he was also the kind of man who wouldn't tell her to stop crying if she wanted to cry. Someone who wouldn't leave if she wanted to yell. Someone who didn't let her take life too seriously. And more than all that, he was a really great dad who did everything he could for the sake of his daughter.

And in truth, she still wanted that man, the one who still lived in her dream. The boy who stood up for her.

"You really want to kiss me?" Her voice carried out into the barnyard.

He stopped but didn't turn. "It's your fault," he said over his shoulder.

"My fault?" She marched up and spun him around. "How is it my fault?"

He looked down at her with a challenge in his eyes. "You started it."

"Then what are you waiting for?"

His dimpled smirk was the last thing she saw before he pulled her in close and kissed her.

And oh my, what a kiss.

It was every bit as passionate, heated, and yet sincere as the man himself.

He pulled away for a moment. "Does this mean you forgive me?"

"Oliver, shut up and kiss me."

A low moan of pleasure—something that sounded like "Yes, ma'am"—and he dove right back in. His hands cradled her face, and Lena lost herself in the wonder of his touch. Why had she ever thought she wanted a stuffy, straitlaced kind of man when this was what she could have with Oliver? Because of course he didn't do anything partway. Each kiss was savored and returned with more. His thumbs trailed from her cheeks into her hair, sending delicious little shivers down her spine. Everything was warm, and rosy, and utter delight.

So this was what it was like to really be kissed. Nothing on the K-dramas came close.

When they slowly pulled apart, it wasn't a smirk on Oliver's face anymore or one of his charming dimpled smiles or cocky grins. He looked at her in awe. He tucked a piece of her hair behind her ear, his touch achingly tender and sweet. "Did you really kiss me?"

"Do you need some more convincing?"

Now he gave her a smile. A slow, devastating smolder. "You know, I might."

As he moved in, Bruce gave a deep bark at the sound of a car pulling up.

He groaned. "That would be my sister and daughter."

"Do you think they'll mind?"

"Are you kidding me? They'll be ecstatic. But are you ready for…all that?"

Good question. Nothing about her relationship with Oliver looked like what she'd thought a romantic relationship would look like. Was this just another fluke thing? Questions and doubts moved in, dissolving the heady rush from earlier.

"I don't know. I mean, how do I know this is real? Is it just a heightened emotional moment?" She never could trust her feelings.

He seemed to scramble for an answer. "Of course it's real. I'll take you out on a date."

"When?"

"Right now."

"That's not a date. I've waited a long time for this. I mean, you've probably dated a ton, but I haven't. I want to do this the right way."

He slowly nodded like he was taking it all in. "No problem. We can do that." So confident, and yet, did he really get it?

"Oliver, this is important. You need to plan out the date and ask me so I know what I'm agreeing to. And until then, why don't we"—she took a step back—"stay quiet about…us."

His puzzled and slightly disheartened expression was kinda cute. She held herself from reaching for him again.

"Okay…I mean, if it's important to you, I will. But you do realize this is a lot of pressure to put on a guy?"

"Like I said, I want to do it right. You up for it?"

"Of course! Especially if I know it will end with one of those kisses."

"No guarantees."

"You're gonna make me earn it, huh?" His smirk was back.

"Believe it or not, I don't go around kissing random guys like that."

"So you're saying I'm special." He puffed out his chest. His ego was probably growing at an exponential rate by the second. "Irresistible."

She shouldn't encourage him, but his wiggling eyebrows made her laugh.

Kiah came running. "Miss Lena? What are you doing here?"

"I was just leaving."

"But I just got here. Please stay? Daddy, make her stay."

The gleam in Oliver's eye was a dangerous one as he swept his daughter up in his arms. "You heard her, Doc. You wouldn't crush a little girl's hopes and dreams, would ya?"

Kiah batted her eyelashes and pouted. "You won't, will ya?" These two must've practiced this routine a few times. They were good. And she wouldn't say it out loud, but they *were* pretty irresistible.

"I guess I can stay for a bit." It sure beat a lonely afternoon alone. "Maybe you could help me walk the dogs. I have a young poodle who needs a lot of exercise."

"I thought you only had two rescue dogs after the adoption event." Oliver set Kiah down.

"That couple brought Darling back, and Birdie found another stray. Seems like as soon as we find a home for one, two more take its place. We need to get that shelter built."

"Until you do, Kiah and I can help. Right, kiddo?"

"Right." Kiah grinned.

"And you have the funding started now, don't you?" Oliver asked her as they crossed over to her yard.

"It's not a for sure thing yet. I'm waiting to see about the grant."

"But the adoption event was a big success. It had to have brought in a good chunk of change."

"It was enough to get some plans drawn up, which is a start. And Birdie is donating their lot. We want to build it in Howard's memory. But even after we have the funding, it will take a while to get the shelter built and running. So for now, I need to find homes for the strays as they come in. I have Oscar, Darling, Scamp, and the newbie. Maybe you can help me name the poodle."

Kiah tugged Lena's hand. "I'm good at picking out names."

"I bet you are. He needs a good name and hopefully a good energetic family who likes the outdoors." Lena looked over at Oliver. "I actually think Oscar would be the perfect match for Edith Draper, but when I brought it up once, she claimed she's not a pet person."

"If we work together, maybe we can convince her. Especially if we bring Oscar with us."

"You want to show up at Edith's door and persuade her to take a dog she doesn't want?"

"Sometimes people don't know what they want until it's right in their face. Besides, it's worth a shot, don't you think?"

Risk was not something Lena was comfortable with. But maybe for Oscar's sake, and with Oliver's help, she should try.

fourteen

. . .

"Are you sure this will work?" Lena asked Oliver as she carried her fluffy friend up to Edith Draper's door the next day after work. Because it had to. Sweet Oscar was a senior dog, but he still had some good years left. He deserved something better than the kennel in her garage. Especially since Harry the poodle had moved in. All that puppy energy was stressing Oscar out. He couldn't even eat until they took Harry on a walk.

Oliver lightly squeezed her elbow. "Relax. This will be great. We brought our secret weapon."

Kiah grinned. "Me!"

Right. Edith might've said no to Lena, but with Oliver and Kiah here, it would be hard to turn her down a second time.

At least, she hoped.

Ollie rang the doorbell.

Edith answered with a bright smile. "Well, to what do I owe the pleasure of this fine company?"

Lena's mind blanked. She looked to Oliver.

Say something. Please!

He must've received her silent message, since he gave Edith the dimpled smile, the one that had a way of weakening a woman's resolve. Lena knew it well.

"We have a proposition for you, Edith. And we think you're going to like it."

Yup. Charm and confidence. That was Oliver.

Edith laughed. "Oh, really?" Her gaze moved from Oliver to Kiah and landed on Oscar in Lena's arms. "Hmm. Why do I get the feeling you're going to try to talk me into a dog?" She quirked an eyebrow at Lena.

She tried to follow Oliver's example and gave Edith a charming smile. It probably looked more like a grimace.

Still, Edith waved them inside. "Good thing I made a batch of snickerdoodles earlier today. Does anyone here like cookies?" She held out a hand toward Kiah.

"I do!" Kiah took Edith's hand.

Lena and Oliver followed them inside through the entry and into a small living room. The little cottage was immaculately clean, even if there were more knickknacks than Lena preferred. The picture window had a beautiful view of a patch of birch trees in the backyard. Their golden leaves fluttered in the afternoon sunlight. And the smell of sweet cinnamon lingered in the room. But Lena's stomach knotted up too much to enjoy any of it.

Edith settled them on the sofa and came back with a plate of cookies. "All right, so what is this proposition, you three? Is this the same dog you thought I should adopt, Lena?"

Since the words were stuck somewhere inside, Lena nodded. She took a cookie and bit into it quickly, not really tasting anything, but at least she had a good excuse now for not talking.

Kiah didn't seem to have the same problem. "This is Oscar. He's a good doggy, Miss Edith." She sat next to Lena and nuzzled Oscar's face. He obliged the girl with a doggy kiss on her cheek. "See!"

"I see that he likes *you*. But I'm not much of a dog person."

"Do you like cats better? Cuz Miss Lena still has a cat too." Kiah munched on her cookie. "Her name is Gypsy."

"I like animals fine enough elsewhere. I just don't know that

I'm ready to live with one. And you told me he was a senior dog. That sounds like more work than I'm willing to commit to."

"Actually, in many ways, he'll be less work. He's not a puppy that requires a lot of training or has a lot of energy." Oliver nodded toward Lena. "The doc says he's in good health."

"Is that so?" Edith set the plate on the glass coffee table. The look on her face said she wasn't convinced.

Oliver looked at Lena and motioned for her to set Oscar on Edith's lap like they'd planned.

"Would you like to hold him at least?" Lena carefully held him out to the elderly lady.

Edith took him in her arms. As Lena expected, he cuddled right in.

"I'll give you this. He is very sweet and mellow." Edith ran her fingers through his short hair. "But I live on a fixed income. I don't think I could afford a dog."

This Lena could address. "I have a supplier for dog food that I can sell you at wholesale prices. It breaks down to about twenty dollars a month. Maybe less when I can find coupons. And I'm willing to give you free checkups for the rest of Oscar's life."

"Twenty dollars a month? And free checkups? Why are you so desperate to get rid of him?" Edith looked down at Oscar like she was inspecting him for flaws.

No. That wasn't what she meant! The deal was supposed to entice her.

Lena looked to Oliver. But instead of jumping in, he gave her a subtle nod. Like he wanted her to do this. Like he believed she *could* do this.

With Oliver's warm hand on her back encouraging her, she pushed through and found the words she wanted to say.

"I'm not desperate to get rid of him, Edith. I'm desperate to find the best home for him. I think this is it. He's ten, so he's probably got another four to five years, maybe more. But my dogs are too much for him. And the shelter was a lot of stress for him too. He enjoys walks in a stroller, a quiet environment but still being near people. I'm gone all day and my dogs are anything but quiet. And remember when you and Birdie were talking a few weeks ago? You said sometimes the nights are lonely. I think Oscar could be good for you too."

Oscar gave a little bark.

"Are you trying to tell me something, sir?" Edith finally broke into a smile.

Oscar reached up to give her a kiss on her chin.

"He must've spent time with you, Oliver. He's a charmer for sure." She chuckled. "But you might be right, Lena. It has been a little lonely here. My son, Ed, has been pestering me to get a dog, but his huskies are so much work, the idea didn't sound very appealing."

"Oscar is a Maltese. They don't have nearly the energy and exuberance of the Alaskan huskies. They're bred to run. Oscar here is bred for companionship. And he has an especially gentle nature. His last owner passed away, and I think he's been lonely ever since."

"Oh." Edith hugged Oscar a little closer. "Maybe we would be good for each other, then. Huh, boy?"

The pressure in Lena's chest eased.

Oscar had found his new home. And Edith had found the most loyal kind of companion she could ever hope to find. It was a perfect match.

After going over care instructions and leaving food, dishes, and the few toys Oscar had attached to, Oliver, Kiah, and Lena left, each with a cookie to go.

Kiah skipped ahead to the van. While she was momentarily distracted, Oliver wrapped his arm around Lena and lightly kissed her temple. "You did it."

Whether it was the secret display of affection, his whispered words, or his confidence in her, she couldn't say, but it broke something loose inside Lena.

"Thank you for helping me."

Oliver held the van door open for her. "I didn't do much. You were the one who convinced her."

"But it was your idea to offer the deal for free care."

"True, and as brilliant as that was, I think it was you sharing your heart that made a difference. Edith needed more than facts and deals. You connected with her emotionally, showed her what kind of impact she could have for Oscar. That was all you." He winked and closed her door.

Maybe sharing a little of her heart really had made a difference. Maybe that was why Oliver was so persuasive. He connected with people's emotions. He inspired them.

After checking Kiah's seat belt, he hopped in the driver's seat and they started toward home. "Now, ladies, are you ready for my famous mac-and-cheese dinner? This time I promised Robin I wouldn't try to burn the house down."

Kiah gave an enthusiastic cheer from the back seat.

Now that the worst part of the ordeal was over, Lena's stomach growled. "Dinner sounds good, but remember we need to get those invitations done tonight. And design the banner and photo book so we have time to print them."

"We'll get to all that. But first, we'll celebrate with a delicious dinner and ice cream," Oliver assured her.

But walking into Oliver's house killed the celebratory mood. They were assaulted with a strong odor that was anything but delicious. Kiah gagged as the three of them stood frozen at the edge of the living room.

Garbage was strewn throughout the area. One of the couch cushions lay in the middle of the room, gutted, with white cottony stuffing scattered all around. The houseplant in the corner was knocked over with black soil spilling out of the pot. Big muddy paw prints dotted the rugs and wood floor everywhere they could see. In the middle of it all was a pile of dog poo.

"Bruce!" Oliver yelled.

They soon found the culprit cowering under the dining room table.

Oliver's jaw clenched tightly as he moved one of the chairs and stared down at Bruce.

Lena reached for Ollie's arm. "Go easy on him. He knows he was naughty. Look at him."

"Go easy?! Look at the mess he made!" Oliver pointed at the disaster in the living room. "How am I supposed to fix that?"

Kiah burst into tears. "Are you going to get rid of him? Don't do it, Daddy!" She fell down and sobbed into Bruce's big neck. "Don't take him away!"

And at that exact moment, footsteps sounded from the entry way and a strange voice called out. "Hello?"

They must've left the front door open. Social worker Diane Wolfe stood with wide eyes, taking in what looked like the scene of a crime. "Uh, I'm here for a welfare check on Kiah Jackson."

🐺 🐺 🐺

INSTEAD OF GETTING SHORTER, OLIVER'S LIST HAD GROWN THANKS to the county social worker's untimely visit yesterday. He grunted as he lifted the sledgehammer and set it in the van. His muscles ached after a day of breaking up the concrete floor in the fire hall and running a new water line.

At least that job was almost done. And Peter Dahlquist was grateful.

Diane Wolfe, not so much.

The scene from last night played through his mind.

"You're lucky I'm the one who walked in on this and I know you two." Diane, who crazily enough used to babysit Oliver, had pulled out a tablet and started typing with one hand. "I'm going to assume this"—she made a circular motion with her finger over the living room—"is a case of bad timing and not the norm, but I do need to see Kiah's bedroom. And after she's calmed down, I'd like to have a visit with her."

Since Lena was with Kiah and Bruce, Oliver showed Diane the room.

Her pursed lips said it all. She wasn't impressed.

"Oliver, this looks like a teenage boy's room slash home gym and storage shed. Where's a dresser? And are you telling me that Kiah is into NFL players from the late 90s?" She stared at the poster of Randy Moss on the wall behind the headboard. "Are any of these trophies on the shelves Kiah's?"

Oliver shook his head.

"The stack of containers in the corner could cause some serious damage if they toppled. This is a hazard." Her finger made a check mark on the screen.

He scrambled for something to explain it all. "Those are Kiah's things. But I'll move them tonight. I've been meaning to, but we just moved back. I'm still working on the house and trying to get settled."

"According to my records you've been back for almost two months."

"Yeah, but it's been a really busy two months. I started a new job. I'm attending AA meetings and taking first responder classes. I just haven't gotten around to fixing up the room."

"Ollie, your first priority needs to be Kiah."

"It is. I promise." He caught sight of Kiah's flowery backpack. "And she's doing great. She loves school. You should talk to her teacher."

"We will, don't worry. But seriously, you've got to step it up here. The social worker from Iowa will be here at some point. She's going to want to see Kiah has a real bedroom, set up especially for her. She needs to see that Kiah feels safe and secure. So that living room disaster? Is that a normal occurrence?"

"No, of course not. The dog has a little separation anxiety. I guess we were gone longer than he was comfortable with."

"Then you probably need to find the dog a new home. At least for now."

"That will upset Kiah further. She loves Bruce."

"Do you want to risk someone else coming for a welfare check and walking into that scene? Garbage everywhere? Dog feces in the middle of the room?"

Oliver had clamped his mouth shut. Yeah. It'd been bad. He and Lena and Robin had spent the rest of the night cleaning it all up. But the worst of it had been when Lena had to take Bruce back to her house. His daughter's weeping had just about shattered him. It didn't matter to her the reason, or even telling her it was only temporary. She was devastated, and all the ground he'd made with her had crumbled. She wouldn't even give him a hug goodbye when he'd dropped her off at school this morning.

Oliver slammed the van door closed. What good was a job well done if his family was falling apart? He couldn't even make inroads with Grayson.

The one good thing was Lena. He'd sent her a big bouquet of roses at the clinic and asked her out on a date for Saturday. Her yes was the one thing holding him together today.

So maybe he should take her advice on dealing with Grayson too. Not that Oliver would send him flowers or anything, but her words rang true.

You're trying to make amends by doing all the things. But have you stopped to simply take responsibility and say you're sorry?

If it'd made a difference for Lena, maybe it would make a difference for Grayson too. Either way, he had to try. He loaded the last length of PVC and locked up the trailer on the job site. Time for the party was closing in. If he wanted Grayson's help reaching Grandpa, he needed to make progress now.

Oliver drove back out to Trinity Horse Camp and headed for the stables. He found Grayson lugging a big straw bale. He dropped it by one of the stalls.

"I gave my RSVP to Robin if that's why you're here."

Grayson cut the twine from the bale and started scooping fresh straw into a stall with a pitchfork.

Oliver grabbed another pitchfork from the wall and joined him.

His brother stopped and glared. "Been doing this a long time without you. I don't need your help."

"I know you don't. But I hope you'll accept an apology. A long overdue one."

Grayson said nothing. But he didn't turn away this time.

It was a start.

"Do you remember what Dad would tell us, when we were unsure about something, when we didn't think we could do it?" Oliver asked.

"The brave face thing? Yeah, I remember."

"I always thought he meant we shouldn't show weakness. And I always thought apologizing was the ultimate weakness."

"So now you're blaming Dad?"

"No. I—" Oliver blew out a short breath of frustration. "Dad counted on me to be strong for you and Robin, and I—" His throat thickened. "I failed you. I couldn't save them."

"That's what you're apologizing for?" Grayson's voice might've lost the biting tone, but accusation still hung in the air.

If only that was it. But there was so much more. "I failed you when I thought I could handle a few drinks and still drive. I'm sorry for hurting you, Gray. And most of all, I'm sorry for walking away." Ollie clenched his jaw tight, waiting for Grayson's response.

"Why didn't you just listen to me and let me drive that night?"

"I don't know. Because I was young and stupid. Trying to show off to my little brother how much I was living it up. I didn't want you to see how much I missed home while I was away at college."

"You? Homesick? I thought you couldn't wait to leave Deep Haven and you were never coming back."

"I was pretty messed up. Maybe I still am. But I'm trying, you know? I'm trying to be someone Mom and Dad could be proud of again. That you and Grandpa might at least be willing to acknowledge again."

Grayson sat on the stack of straw bales across the aisle. Some of the tension in his shoulders relaxed. "Did Grandpa really tell you that you didn't deserve to be a part of the family?"

Oliver toed the dirt underneath his work boots. "I can't blame him. I almost killed you."

"I didn't have to get in that car. Legally, I was an adult. It's not *all* on you."

"But I'm the big brother. I was supposed to be looking out for you, keeping you safe."

"We're supposed to look out for each other, period." Grayson tugged his leather work gloves off. "And…I guess I walked away too. I thought you didn't care. But maybe I was wrong?" He looked up at Oliver, a question in his last words.

Oliver looked at the brother he'd spent his childhood with. His best friend. For goodness' sake, they'd been through hell together when they watched their parents drown. They'd once been inseparable. And Oliver had walked away from it all. Regret ate at him, and now he was trying to find his way back. If he looked weak for saying so, so be it.

"I cared, Gray. I still do." He held out a hand. "Forgive me?"

Grayson shook his hand and gave him a nod. He looped his thumbs in his pockets. "So, tell me about this daughter of yours. How'd that come to be?"

The release of tension inside Oliver's chest allowed him to draw a full breath for the first time in forever as he helped fill the rest of the stalls with fresh straw and told Grayson about Kiah. "You should come over for dinner and meet her."

"That would be nice." Grayson leaned against the stall door and smirked. "Would you be inviting Lena to this dinner too? I hear you two spend a lot of time together."

"I hope so. I asked her out on a date and she accepted. That's as far as it's gone. But…I like her. A lot. Always have." He lugged another bale over from the pile. "I was actually jealous of you growing up."

"Of me? Why?"

"Because you and Lena were friends. She would actually laugh with you and Robin. She always scowled at me."

"Does she still do that?"

Oliver laughed. "Yeah."

"Sounds like it works for you, then." Grayson paused and leaned on his pitchfork. "Have you talked with Grandma and Grandpa? Do they know about Kiah?"

Oliver shook his head. "I know I need to. And I'll tell Grandma about Kiah this week before the party so it's not a complete surprise. But there are some things I want to settle first before facing Grandpa."

"I thought about what you said earlier, how he was harder on you. You might be right. I think it's because you remind him of Dad. Grandma always said you look just like him."

"I sure didn't act like him though. Everyone always talked about what a stand-up guy he was."

Grayson shrugged. "It's never too late to change."

"I hope not. And I hope this party can show Grandpa I *have* changed. For the better."

"I'll be there."

It was all Oliver hoped for and more than he deserved. But the hardest part about this whole ordeal was yet to come. Grandpa.

fifteen

· · ·

THINGS WERE GOING TOO WELL. LENA WAITED FOR SOMEONE TO JUMP out and tell her it was all a dream. That she only imagined the ridiculous display of red roses on her counter yesterday and Oliver asking her out. That all the time she spent getting to know her father was part of an elaborate science experiment.

But the furry chinchilla wiggling in Lena's hand was very real. Fiesty little guy. Handing it back to Maryann, she was pleased to see it coming out of the anesthesia without any adverse reactions.

But how long would all this smooth sailing last?

"Patient is making a good recovery. Send a picture to the Brinleys, and let them know they can pick him up tomorrow morning," Lena told her assistant. "And make note that they need to make hay the main staple of his diet, or we'll be seeing Wilbur in here again."

She finished her notes for Wilbur on the tablet and, together with Maryann, walked out of the surgical room.

Sheila met them in the hall with a strange look on her face. "Lena, there's a man here to see you." The whispered words held a hint of warning.

"What kind of animal does he have? And why are you whispering?"

"He doesn't have an animal. And he's nice and all, but—"

"But what?"

"He said he's your..." She looked behind her toward the lobby but didn't say anything.

"Goodness, Sheila, spit it out."

"He said he's your father."

Her father? The two techs stared at her.

Lena left them in the hall whispering and marched out to the lobby. Brad Fowler stood in the flesh, making himself a cup of coffee. And this time there were witnesses.

Her father was here. In Deep Haven. In her clinic.

And he was *telling* everyone he was her father.

Her brain scrambled for an explanation as he poured creamer into his cup.

"What are you doing here?" Maybe not the warmest welcome, but this was not what they had planned. See? She'd known it was only a matter of time until something blew up.

Brad, however, didn't seem to mind her blurted question. He turned and smiled at her. "I wanted to see where you work. What a great town too. This is where you grew up?"

"I thought we agreed on supper tomorrow—Silver Bay on Thursday." Had she missed something?

"We did. I wanted to surprise you."

She was surprised, no doubt.

This was a good thing though, right? A surprise? Most people seemed to enjoy them. They always threw her off and confused her. Just another reason she was weird.

But still...Brad was here.

She needed to shake off the unexpectedness of it and see it for the gesture it was.

He wanted to spend time with her.

"Is it okay that I'm here?" He walked toward her a little stiffly, like his legs were sore from the long drive.

"Of course. You took me by surprise is all."

"I don't want to keep you from your work, but I saw a nice-looking bistro on my way in and wondered if you'd like to have dinner with me when you're done."

It was so last minute. And in town, where everyone would see them and wonder who he was. She had hoped to keep this quiet until she knew where he fit in her life.

But he had driven all the way here.

For her.

He wanted to get to know her.

The suddenness wore off, and the weight of that truth broke through to the hidden, hungry spaces inside. It offered a sustenance she'd been dying for.

He was here.

Her mother might have barred the way for a long time, but he'd found her anyway. Sought her.

So yes, she could manage dinner.

"I need to finish a few things, and then I can meet you there."

"Is half an hour long enough?"

Because words were so inadequate, she nodded and tried on a smile for him.

"Great. I'll see you then."

She didn't need half an hour to finish her work, but it would hopefully be enough to calm the twisting in her stomach.

As soon as he left, Sheila and Maryann were at her side.

"Is he really your father?" Maryann asked. "You do resemble him, but that doesn't always mean anything."

Guess there was no use keeping it a secret now.

"Yes, he is my father. We've recently connected."

"Wow, Dr. Larson…that's…a lot. Are you doing okay?" Sheila asked.

"I'm great. This isn't a big deal." Okay, so it was a huge deal, but she needed to keep her business demeanor intact here. "Just keep this quiet, and I expect professional behavior from the both of you."

They nodded in unison, wide-eyed and tight-lipped.

"I'll lock up tonight. You two can go home."

Lena went through the motions of closing out her charts and finishing up her notes, but so many feelings and questions tangled up her thoughts. She brushed her hair in the bathroom and stared in the mirror.

She did look like him. Similar green eyes. Straight brown hair, where her mother's had been wavy and blonde. The features that had always looked so odd on her when she stood next to her mother were now something she was grateful for. She didn't have to be embarrassed anymore.

She looked like her father.

After everyone else left, she locked up and set the security alarm. She walked to the Trailside Bistro to find Brad already there, right in front at a window booth.

She'd imagined many versions of him over the years. At one point she'd compared him to Pa in the Little House books, traveling during the lean times to provide for his family. She'd pretended he was a famous actor staying away to shield her from the invasion of the paparazzi. Her favorite had been pretending he was Steve Irwin, the Crocodile Hunter, off at some exotic location saving animals. But he wasn't a figment of her imagination anymore.

The jaunty jingle of the bell on the door welcomed her, along with a blast of warm air and the distinct aroma of tomato basil soup. With a quick wave to her favorite server, Dina—a cat lady through and through—she joined Brad in the booth.

Thankfully Dina knew her usual turkey club wrap with sweet potato fries order, so she didn't have to decide on what to get. But since it had been a day of big surprises, why not shake it up a bit and order some pie for dessert too?

Brad grinned. "Peach pie is my favorite too." He looked at Dina. "I'll take a slice as well."

Over the meal, Brad asked about her work with animals. He

seemed to know exactly how to put her at ease. He told her more about his rescue dogs and their silly antics.

Was that a genetic thing? It would be an interesting study.

When Dina came out with dessert and decaf coffee for Lena and green tea for him, Brad slipped her his credit card. "Please put it all on here."

"You don't have to—" Lena rushed for her purse until he stopped her with a hand on her arm.

"Let me do this, Lena. It's not much, but please."

His hand was a little chilly, but it warmed her to the core. One meal wouldn't make up for a three-decade absence, but it was a nice start.

A really nice start. "All right."

Feeling content and full from her wrap, she took her time and savored the first bite of pie. The sweet flavor of peach burst on her tongue, followed by a hint of cinnamon, warm and bright. Perfect for a cozy evening.

With her father.

Brad watched her, then set down his mug. "Lena, I've enjoyed getting to know you. You're incredibly smart and ambitious. And I hate that we've missed out on so much."

A lump came to her throat. They *had* missed out on a lot. "I've enjoyed getting to know you too."

"I'm glad. And…I wasn't going to do this, but I wonder if you'll consider something for me."

"Of course." She laid down her fork.

Was he wanting to officially recognize her? It was still early in their acquaintance, but she'd heard of people being adopted as adults. Was that what this surprise trip was all about?

"I have end-stage kidney failure—"

Wait. "What?"

"I was born with some abnormalities that caused issues, and for a long time I've been able to manage, but recently the disease has progressed rapidly."

"What does that mean?"

He held his mug with both hands and stared at his tea for a breath. When he looked up, there was a very real sense of fear in his eyes—eyes so similar to the green eyes she had stared at in the mirror not an hour ago.

"I'm at the point where I need a transplant or I will be on dialysis for the rest of my life." He paused for a solemn moment, fiddling again with his tea bag, a habit she'd only begun to notice. "I know this is asking a lot. And you are under no obligation. But I was hoping you would consider being tested as a possible donor."

His words hit her in the chest. She finally had a dad in her life who'd shown up and taken her out to dinner and said how proud he was of her. And now the news that he was basically dying?

God, how is this fair? Why now?

No. She wasn't going to let this happen. She was a doctor. Sure, a doctor of veterinary medicine, but she knew how biology worked. She needed to start thinking like a medical professional if she was going to find a way to save him.

"What is your diagnosis?"

"Stage five renal failure."

The last stage? Already? Rather than reaching for the antiacids in her purse, Lena clasped her hands under the table and forced a steadiness in her voice. "And your treatment plan?"

"I'm currently doing hemodialysis. Doctors say I can keep going on for a good eight more years while we wait for a donor."

Eight years? But he was still young. Eight years wasn't going to be enough. He wouldn't win any Father of the Year awards, but that didn't mean they couldn't have a good relationship. She'd waited too long for this to simply let him die on her.

She pushed past the uncomfortable constriction in her throat and found words.

"I'd like to do some more research on your condition, but I can at least be tested while I consider."

Relief flooded his gaze. "I've got no right, but I have to say I'm so grateful. I'm practically a stranger—"

"No. You're my father. And I'm going to find a way to help you."

Brad looked at her with wet eyes. "Thank you."

Now that things were finally falling right into place, she wasn't going to let anything mess that up. Not even kidney failure.

🐺🐺🐺

IT'D SOUNDED SO EASY EARLIER IN THE WEEK. PLAN A DATE. NO BIG deal.

But now it was Saturday, and it kinda *was* a big deal. Oliver had a real shot here.

His whole life Lena had been a sturdy anchor, a fixed point that didn't waver and shift with the wind. But she was also a new adventure he didn't want to end. She had depths he'd only begun to discover.

And she knew the skeletons in his closet and somehow wasn't scared off by them.

This relationship could really go somewhere. *If* he could do this right.

"Is the great Oliver Fox actually nervous for this date?" Robin leaned over the kitchen counter with an amused look on her face.

"Of course not."

Her arched eyebrow said she didn't believe him, but she stayed quiet as she stirred the soup she was heating on the stove for lunch.

"You got the van cleaned, right?" He pulled out sandwiches and lemonade from the refrigerator.

"It's all ready, lover boy. Relax."

"I told you. I'm great."

She pointed at him with the spoon. "Then you meant to wear your shirt like that?"

What? He looked down. The thermal he wore under a flannel was inside out. He checked the clock. And he was running out of time. He ran upstairs and fixed the shirt.

He stopped in Kiah's room, now devoid of precarious towers of containers and exercise equipment, though he still needed to take down the posters and trophies from his childhood. Kiah sat on the bed surrounded by her growing family of stuffed animals.

"Hey, darlin'. I'm going out with Lena. Are you excited to pick out paint with Aunty Robin for your room?"

She shrugged.

"Still upset about Bruce?" He sat next to her on the bed.

Her gaze flicked up to his face for a mere second and then back to her Ellie-phant, but she didn't say anything.

"Maybe you and Robin could visit him before you go to the store."

"No, thank you." Her soft voice carried the weight of all the tears she'd shed over the last few days.

"Why not? Lena said you could go over any time you wanted."

"Bruce will be too sad when we leave again. It's better if I don't see him." She sniffed, still not looking Oliver in the eye.

So they were back to this, his daughter treating him like a friendly stranger.

But until he had full custody, he couldn't risk another living room Armageddon scene. He lingered a moment more, but she ignored him.

"If you change your mind, let Robin know, 'kay?" He dropped a kiss on her head and left the room.

"What's wrong?" Robin asked as soon as he walked back into the kitchen.

He looked toward the stairs. "Do you think I should stay? Kiah…she's hurting."

Robin shook her head. "I know she's missing Bruce, but you and Lena need this. It's long overdue. I think Kiah will be excited once we get to the store. We're going to find the perfect comforter, fun throw pillows. It will be good."

"Yeah, but"—he scrubbed his hands down his face—"I feel awful leaving her when she's like this. Like I'm abandoning her or something."

"You're not abandoning her. She's with me. And I could use a little girl time. Trust me. Interior decorating and a milkshake, and she'll be great." Robin handed him his pack with the lunch he'd prepared. "Now, go. I've got this. Lena's waiting."

Guess he'd have to trust Robin knew how to handle it.

With the bouquet of wildflowers he'd picked earlier, he stood on Lena's front porch and rang the bell.

Lena answered the door dressed in jeans, a fleece pullover, and hiking boots. Nothing out of the ordinary there. But her shy half smile had his heart soaring.

He handed her the flowers and watched her smile grow. "These are for you."

"*Helianthus tuberosus.* How sweet."

"Helio-what?"

"The common name is Jerusalem artichoke. They're basically a native sunflow—I'll stop talking now and go put them in water." She blushed and turned back into the house, leaving the front door wide open.

So maybe he wasn't the only one with a case of nerves.

Oliver gave Wentworth and Jane a few scratches while he waited for Lena in the entry. It gave his sweaty hands something to do. From his extra-large doggy bed in the living room, Bruce lifted his head for a moment but plopped it back down once he saw it was only Oliver.

He walked over to Bruce and knelt. "If it helps, she misses you too, buddy." He rubbed Bruce's forehead, trying to smooth out the wrinkles around his forlorn eyes.

The dog let out a long whine and looked away.

"What, did you two rehearse this act? Because it's working." Maybe he should ask for a raincheck.

"Ready to go." Lena sounded a little breathless as she walked into the living room. A stranger probably wouldn't notice that quickness in her step, the tiniest of smiles she was beginning to let show, or the way her hands clasped together like she did when she was nervous.

But he did.

I've waited a long time for this. I mean, you've probably dated a ton, but I haven't. I want to do this the right way.

And so did he. Because she deserved it. Because besides his daughter, this might be the most important thing to get right. Because he was very much in love with this woman. So he needed to push away the worry about Kiah and give Lena his full attention.

"Let's go." He offered her his arm.

Thick clouds overhead grew darker the farther they drove out of town. He could've sworn the weather app had predicted cloudy but no rain.

Lena pulled out her phone. "I found a list of songs for the party—"

"No party talk today, boss. We're here to enjoy nature and some good food and each other's company."

"Right." She paused a moment. "I hope you had Robin pack the meal."

"What are you talking about? I'm not bad in the kitchen."

"Really? Because I heard about the burnt mac and cheese. And the disaster at the bakery." She gave him her familiar scowl, but today it had a playful twist.

"I'll have you know I made everything myself. Just chicken salad sandwiches and lemonade. So we're safe from culinary disasters. I thought we could hike to Carlton Peak and eat there."

"That's a great spot. I'm surprised you didn't bring Kiah with you."

"I'm not her favorite person right now. And I didn't think a sullen kindergartener set the right mood for a date." But the fact that Lena would've been okay with it boosted his spirits.

"She's still upset about Bruce?"

"Big time."

"You could've brought her with you. She has to come first for you. I get that."

"I appreciate that. I do. But Robin is taking her shopping. And…I wanted you all to myself today."

She blushed and smiled at him.

That was more like it.

They parked at the trailhead, a pullover spot on the side of the highway. His was the only vehicle. Strange for a peak weekend of autumn colors, but having the trail to themselves would be nice. The wind kicked up leaves and shook the trees towering above them. The temperature must've dropped ten degrees since they'd left home. Oliver grabbed the blanket and his backpack with the meal packed in it.

Lena studied the sky. "Do you think it's going to rain?"

"Nothing was on the radar when I checked this morning." He reached for her hand. "Don't worry. I'll keep you warm."

Her touch certainly warmed him all right, until she had to pull away and use her arms for balancing on the planks of wood stretching over the muddy parts of the path. On the trail, red oak and maple trees sheltered them, but the air was frigid for mid-October. Lena took a beanie out of her pocket and pulled it down to cover her ears.

Once they passed the mud puddles and started climbing, it was easier to look up and enjoy the colors. In every direction gold, amber, and red hues from the ash and birch trees surrounded them. For one perfect moment the clouds released a short burst of sunlight. The canopy of leaves filtered the white rays like stained-glass windows, scattering colors everywhere. Oliver stopped and they took a selfie before the sun slipped back behind thick cloud cover, and they continued on the path.

An icy wind wound down through the trees, causing Oliver's

nose to run. Lena's cheeks were chapped and red by the time they hit the part of the trail where the evergreens outnumbered the deciduous trees. But they didn't need to talk. A contented silence tethered them together as they continued the cold climb. It was definitely good Kiah hadn't come along. She hated being cold.

"It will be worth it for the view," he told his date.

"I'm certainly working up an appetite." Her teeth chattered a little as she spoke.

"I hope that means you're not one of those women who won't eat in front of a guy." Oliver stopped and wrapped the blanket around Lena's shoulders.

"Believe me, I don't have that problem." She looked up at him, and everything stopped for a moment.

"Good." It was one of the things he loved about her. She was resilient. She didn't care about what other people thought. So even if the weather didn't want to cooperate, at least he had a great meal to offer her. Because he really wanted to show her he was all in. And while she might not care about others' opinions, she *did* want things to be done the right way. And he certainly didn't want to mess this up like he had with Jalisa. So instead of leaning in and kissing her here like everything inside him wanted, he tucked her hand in his, and they continued on the path.

By the time they reached the end of the trail and climbed out on the domed rocky peak, Oliver couldn't feel his extremities and his thighs burned. But this was the best part. He pushed aside all discomfort.

"Ready for this?"

She nodded, keeping her mouth and chin hidden in the collar of her jacket. Leaving the shelter of the trees, they stepped into the cleared area with a three-hundred-sixty-degree view of the surrounding hills. Instead of being wowed with a spectacular view, they were bombarded by a frigid lake wind.

"It's beautiful," Lena yelled over the gusts threatening to

blow them off the peak. Sweet of her to try to find something nice to say when her shoulders were hunched over her ears and she clung to the blanket he'd given her earlier.

While Lena took in what little they could see with the low clouds moving in, Oliver searched for a spot for their picnic. Squinting from the wind in his face, he slowly turned. The beauty was lost on him. There was no way they could eat here. The food he'd spent so much time preparing would be blown right off their plates. And Lena was shivering under the blanket.

But he'd promised her a meal. "Let's go back into the trees and find a place to sit."

Lena nodded. In a spot right off the trail, they huddled together on a small rocky ledge. Oliver set his pack down and pulled out the meal. "Hungry?"

"Oh yeah. Let's see if your cooking is as good as you say." She challenged him with a pointed look.

As much as everything else about this date wasn't working out, at least he had this. He pulled out the container of sandwiches. He lifted the top and groaned. Instead of soft white cottage bread fresh from the family bakery, the chicken salad had soaked through, resulting in a soggy mess. "I don't understand. I've made this recipe a thousand times. I've never had this happen."

"It's all right. I'm still hungry." Lena choked down a few bites but eventually put it aside. They couldn't even enjoy the potato chips since they'd been smashed to crumbs under the thermos he'd packed.

In a container he definitely had *not* packed, they found peanut butter chocolate chip cookies and a note from Robin wishing them a happy first date.

"Guess my sister knows me well." He handed a cookie to Lena. As the only edible things, they quickly disappeared, but it was too cold to linger much longer.

"How about a quick drink before we start back down?" Oliver poured the lemonade from the thermos and offered the cup to Lena. She brought it to her lips and took a big gulp. Her eyes went wide. She reached for her water bottle and downed most of it.

"What's wrong with it?" He tipped the thermos to his lips and immediately turned and spat the drink out. "That's disgusting."

"I can see why you're a plumber now and not a baker." She took another swig of water, swished it around, and spat it out on the leaves below them.

"I must've switched the sugar for baking soda. Robin has them both in those fancy glass jars and—"

His words were cut off by a crack of thunder.

Of course. A storm. Why not end this disaster of a date with a bang. "We'd better head down." The trail was bad enough as it was, but with the rain it would get dangerous fast.

The moisture in the air made for a slick descent. And sure enough, rain poured down before they made it halfway back to the van. He held Lena's freezing cold hand to keep her safe, but at this point he wouldn't have been surprised if a bear or mountain lion had attacked.

"We're almost to the—" Oliver slipped. His arms windmilled as he scrambled to find his balance, but there was no balance to be found. His feet flew out from under him, and he landed in the mud on his backside.

He closed his eyes as rain pelted his face and the wet mud seeped into his jeans.

So much for his perfect date. He couldn't even blame Bruce for this. If Lena knew what was good for her, she would run away and not look back. He sighed and looked up.

But she stood there still, towered over him, hands covering her mouth, hair dripping, eyes big. She was probably wondering how long she should stay before she could politely decline any possibility of a future date with him.

And then she laughed.

"You think it's funny?" He had to yell over the wind and rain to be heard.

She nodded and laughed even harder. She couldn't catch her breath and bent over, holding onto a tree trunk for balance. Suddenly the soggy sandwiches and the rain and cold couldn't stop the sunshine from flooding into his heart. This woman was something else.

He was falling for her big time.

Well, there was still one more thing a good date needed. Oliver reached up a muddy hand. "A little help, please."

Her hand was icy as she took his, but instead of letting her pull him up, Oliver tugged and caught her as she fell right into his lap. He chuckled at her shocked expression.

"That's what you get for laughing at my expense." He wiped at the smear of mud on her cheek.

"You told me I should laugh more often."

"I did, didn't I?" He caught her hand and held her closer. He stilled as she moved in and kissed him. It was slow and sweet and by far the best thing about this day. And if she could stick it out through an arctic hike, practically being blown off a peak, and a disaster of a meal, she might be the kind of woman who stuck around for a guy no matter what. And honestly, there was no one else he'd want anyway.

"Please tell me you'll give me another chance. I promise I can do better," he said.

"The date was perfect, Oliver. I got to spend the afternoon with you."

And her kiss gave him plenty of reasons to hope that at least he'd got this one thing right.

🐺🐺🐺

Lena couldn't stop smiling throughout the wet ride back to Deep Haven, the long hot shower at home, or while dressing in her thick fleece joggers and sweatshirt. Tonight she would eat dinner with Robin, Kiah, and Oliver like she was one of them. Like she belonged.

As she was rushing through the living room, her gaze caught the picture of her mother on a small decorative shelf. What would she think of all this?

While Lena was growing up, Mom hadn't minded Lena spending time with the Fox family. But she'd had little patience for anything to do with boys, dating, or romance in general. After she heard about Oliver and Grayson's accident, she'd warned Lena.

A man like that only brings trouble. You're better off alone.

If she'd known about Lena's high school crush, she'd never let on. But her warning hinted that she had. She probably would think Lena was making a foolish mistake dating that same man.

But Oliver was different now. He still possessed an impossible hold on her attention and her heart—one that never had made sense but that she couldn't deny. He deserved another chance.

Lena tried to shake off the haunting memory of her mother's disapproval as she said goodbye to the dogs and slipped out the back door, but the hint of doubt followed her. She strolled over to the Foxes' back deck and knocked on the glass door. She waited for Robin to wave her in before entering.

"You know you don't have to knock. Now, get in here and tell me everything." Robin patted the barstool at the kitchen counter. "Ollie took Kiah to pick up the pizzas, so while I make a salad, you can sit here and spill your guts about this date."

"What do you mean?"

"Come on. You can't hide that grin. And Ollie was even worse. But he wouldn't tell me a thing." Robin pulled out the cutting board and began to chop the romaine lettuce on the counter. She handed a peeler and a couple carrots to Lena. "How was his picnic lunch?"

"Awful. The sandwiches were soggy and squished by the time we ate them. And somehow he mixed up the baking soda and sugar when he made the lemonade—"

Robin looked horrified and started laughing. "No wonder he didn't tell me about the date. What was the deal with all the mud?"

"It rained." Lena grinned remembering. She started peeling her carrot. "Ollie slid on the trail and landed in a puddle." But she would be keeping the kissing part all to herself. It was too special to chat about, even with one of her best friends.

"Remind me to never allow him back in the kitchen. Ever." Robin chuckled. "For such a smooth guy, sounds like my brother's plans were a disaster."

"I know. The whole date was a complete flop."

Robin's eyes narrowed as she looked up from the lettuce. "But…?"

"But I don't know if I've ever been happier." Lena ran the peeler over the bumpy carrot skin. "I mean, the weather was miserable and the hike more treacherous than romantic. In so many ways it was a failure."

"Yeah, but he went out of his way to show you that you're important to him. And that makes up for a lot."

"He's an amazing dad. And he's working on buying out Mack and having his own business. He was a huge help to me with the adoption event." Lena threw away the carrot peels, her mother's warning whispering in her mind. "Do you think it's okay, that we're so different though?"

"Different can be good. When you're working on a project, you help him focus and direct his energy in a positive way. He helps you loosen up and enjoy the process. I've never seen either of you this happy."

"So…you don't think it's a bad thing? Me and Oliver together?"

Robin tossed the lettuce in a bowl. "It makes my heart glad to see you together. And I know it's early, but I always thought we'd be great sisters."

Early or not, Lena couldn't deny she'd already pictured it.

Finally she'd have a real family.

It wasn't the way she'd thought it would happen, but maybe that was okay too.

"Hey, speaking of the men in your life, I forgot to ask, weren't you supposed to meet Brad? How did that go?" Robin got up and grabbed glasses out of the cupboard.

"He showed up at the clinic and took me to dinner the other night."

"He just showed up unannounced? And you were okay with that?"

"Once we talked, I understood why. He's sick. So he really wanted to meet. I saw him Thursday too. He insisted on paying for my meal both times."

"So he's trying to make up for lost time or something?" Robin poured water from the refrigerator dispenser into the glasses.

Lena nodded. Until she did some more research, she didn't want to mention the kidney transplant. Oliver already didn't think highly of Brad. And if her labs came back that she wasn't compatible, it wasn't even an option, so why bring it up?

For now she would relish the fact that everything was finally going her way. A guy she was falling for willing to do things the right way. Well, he was trying his hardest. And a father coming into her life and wanting to be a real dad.

"So what about all that stuff your mom said about him?"

Lena took one of the glasses Robin offered. "I don't know. Maybe, like Oliver, he's changed too, because he's not this horrible monster she always made him out to be. He's funny. Kind. He showed me pictures of his dogs. He can't be all bad."

"Your mom was never one for second chances."

"No. She always said if you mix an alkali metal and water you will always get the same reaction. An explosion."

"But people are more than elements and chemistry. We grow and we are capable of change."

Lena sipped her water. She wasn't sure what to think of her mother these days. She'd always taken what she said about Brad as truth, but it wasn't lining up at all with her own experience. "I suppose there is room for scientific bias in her analogy. Brad left her and she didn't want it to happen again. So she focused on her work."

"Don't you think she was lonely? She never seemed really happy."

"She was content in her own way. Her job was her priority."

"You're her daughter. *You* should've been her priority."

"She tried. She wanted me to be strong and independent, to rely on facts and not be driven by emotions. It's not all bad. She just wasn't an affectionate woman."

"But she kept Brad out of your life."

"I know."

And while Mom had been right about a lot of things, definitely not everything. With Oliver, Lena felt more like herself, like she didn't have to wear a mask all the time or hide what she was feeling. And as scary as that was, she liked it.

So once Oliver and Kiah came back with pizza, she laughed when she wanted to laugh. She didn't hold back a smile when she wanted to smile. And when Oliver slipped extra sausage onto her plate because he knew it was her favorite, she squeezed his hand, not bothering to hide her pleasure at the small but sweet gesture.

She had to come to her own conclusions. No matter what her mother had told her growing up, some men were worth giving a second chance.

sixteen

. . .

MISTY ZIMMERMAN'S EMAIL THAT MORNING STILL ATE AT OLIVER AS he walked into the grocery store with Lena's list and grabbed a cart. Somehow he'd been able to redeem the disaster of a date a few days ago, but now he had other problems.

Kiah hasn't been acting herself lately. Is anything going on at home I should be aware of?

How did he respond? *My daughter is traumatized because I took her dog away?* That would go over well. He pushed the cart through the produce section. Lena needed fresh limes for her punch.

At least Kiah's bedroom was all hers now. Instead of posters and trophies, light-pink paint covered the walls. A yellow-and-orange bedding set, a white girly dresser that used to be Robin's, and more pillows than he could understand had transformed the space completely.

Not that Kiah seemed to care about any of it.

But Lena's suggestion of a family movie night with Bruce and popcorn and a pillow fort was the first thing to have sparked Kiah's interest since the whole social worker debacle. He needed to capitalize on it.

Where were the bananas? Kiah loved his strawberry-banana smoothies.

After finding bananas, Oliver moved to the pop aisle and started loading up two-liter bottles of lemon-lime pop. The familiar smell of whiskey hit him before a strong hand clamped down on his shoulder. He turned around to see Jeremy.

"Ollie, my man. Havin' a party?" He pointed to the shopping cart filled with bottles.

"Yup. My grandparents' fifty-fifth anniversary."

"No way!" He whistled. "Remember when we hijacked your grandpa's car and some liquor from that fiftieth anniversary party we crashed at the community center, and my brother puked in the back seat? Now that was a party."

He remembered all right. Not exactly fond memories. "Where is your brother now?"

"He's down in the Cities. Divorced. He's got a couple kids."

"So you're *Fun*cle Jeremy?" Oliver added another two-liter to the cart.

"Not really. His ex has custody. He doesn't see the kids much."

"What about your parents? They still in town?"

"Mom is. Dad bailed on us back in high school."

"Oh, right. Sorry."

"Don't be. We were better off without him."

How did Oliver not remember that? It made more sense now, though, how Jeremy always got away with stuff. Oliver had resented his grandfather's strict rules, but at least he'd been around. He was the one that'd taught him how to drive, how to shave, and how to tie a Windsor knot. Jeremy hadn't had that. And the few times Oliver had been at his house, he'd gotten the feeling Jeremy's mom wasn't home much or involved either. Back then he'd envied his friend's independence and freedom. Now, not so much.

"Hey, we should go get a drink and catch up," Jeremy said.

Oliver's mouth watered. "That would be fun, but—"

"Then let's go. We won't have to use my brother to get us beer now."

Oliver *was* hungry. He wouldn't have to drink to catch up with Jeremy. He could order food. And if Oliver was reading this right, the guy could use a positive influence in his life. He could help.

A text came through from Lena.

LENA

Don't forget the lemon sherbet for the punch.
And butter for the popcorn.

Right. Movie night. "I'd love to catch up with you, Jer, but I've got plans already. Maybe some other time?"

"Totally. Cuz I got plans too." Whatever tonight would hold, Jeremy probably wouldn't recall tomorrow morning.

Oliver remembered those days.

Actually, he didn't remember much from those days. That was the problem. But he remembered the hollowness he'd kept trying to fill and how it'd only expanded to the point it threatened to swallow him whole. Thank God Hezekiah found him. Maybe Oliver could help Jeremy.

"Jer, you know, I quit drinking actually. And I found a lot of help at AA meetings. If you ever want to talk or go—"

"Aw, that's good. Good for you, Ollie." He shifted his gaze to the slim brunette woman with a green scarf and skinny jeans walking toward them in the aisle. "I'm good though."

"You sure? If you ever need anything—a ride or, you know, anything—you've got my number."

"Yeah, yeah. I'll let you get back to your granny party. See you around." He gave him a wave and left to strike up a conversation with the woman.

Oliver sent up a quick prayer for the guy as he finished loading up his cart and paid for the groceries. Time to cheer up Kiah with a movie and popcorn. And he certainly wouldn't mind sitting close to Lena, maybe sneaking a kiss or two when Kiah wasn't looking.

As he hoisted the last double-layered bag into the van, his phone rang.

Grandma.

He stared at the screen a second. He always let it go to voice mail. But the party was this week. He was running out of time to tell them about Kiah.

He slid into the driver's seat, out of the wind, and answered the call. "Hey, Grandma." He didn't dare start the engine and try to drive. He was too distracted as it was.

"Oliver! You answered. I was all ready to leave a message." She must be on the road with the engine noise and quiet radio he could hear in the background.

"How's Florida?" he asked.

"We love it. But I'm so excited to see you, dear. I can't believe you're finally back home." He pictured her then, a hand over her heart like she always used to do when she was excited or touched by a thoughtful gesture.

"Yeah, it's a little crazy, but I'm back. I made a few changes to the house. I hope you'll like them."

"Ollie, it's your house now. You don't need to ask my permission for anything. And I figured you would want your space. Grandpa and I are bringing our camper and staying out at the Evergreen Resort, so we won't be encroaching on you for this visit. But Robin said we're having a little get together on Saturday? At the house?"

"Yeah, we want to celebrate your anniversary. We invited practically the whole town."

"That will be nice. Grandpa and I can't wait to see everyone."

Oliver blew out a quick breath and braced himself. "Good, because there's someone I'd like you to meet."

"Oh?" Grandma's voice raised an octave. "Have you got someone special with you?"

"I do. My...daughter."

"Your—I'm sorry, dear. Did you say daughter?"

Oliver could almost see her with a shocked expression on her face. Not a silver-blonde strand of hair would be out of place, but he knew there would be plenty of disappointment in her blue eyes if he were there. He swallowed hard, looking out the windshield at the lake stretching beyond the downtown area. His feet and hands had grown cold.

But he had to get this out.

"I did. I...I have a five-year-old daughter named Kiah."

"Five—" Grandma choked up. "Oh my."

"I know, I should've told you. I should've done a lot of things differently, and I don't have any excuses. I've made some really bad decisions. But Kiah, she's...amazing. She just started kindergarten and loves it. She's smart. Really smart. I can't imagine my life without her."

"Is her...mother...in the picture?"

"She passed away." He slid his free hand along the steering wheel, needing something solid to hold.

"Oliver, why would you not tell us? We could've been helping all this time. We've already missed so much—"

"It's a long story, and I will tell you everything once you're here, but I wanted to give you a heads-up. You have a great-granddaughter. And she's really excited to meet you." That might be a stretch since she wasn't excited about much of anything these days, but maybe things were looking up and by the time his grandparents arrived it would be true. "I'll send you some pictures."

"That would be nice." Grandma's voice was so soft he could barely hear, like she was trying not to cry. "Are you staying in Deep Haven for a while?"

Thinking of Lena, Robin, his job, he smiled. "Yeah, we're sticking around. Maybe Kiah and I can take a trip to see you this winter."

"I'd like that. Very much."

Grandpa's bass voice sounded muffled in the background.

Oliver started the car, hoping warmth from the heaters would thaw his hands. "Will you…will you tell Grandpa? About Kiah."

"You could talk to him—"

"I'll wait. Until you're here. I'm sure he's driving, so…"

"All right. We'll see you soon. And Oliver, I love you. Grandpa does too."

He said goodbye and ended the call. For a moment he closed his eyes, thankful to have escaped the temptation to go out with Jeremy and to have gotten the phone call over with. There would still be repercussions once Grandma and Grandpa arrived, but at least they were prepped to meet Kiah. They both had a soft spot for children. He didn't worry that they wouldn't be kind in front of her or anything. But they could now avoid an awkward surprise.

And hopefully he'd set the stage for rebuilding their family.

🐺 🐺 🐺

WALKING THE DOGS AFTER WORK WITH OLIVER AND KIAH WAS usually Lena's favorite part of the day, but this afternoon's news kept intruding on the late-October evening. Who else had applied for the Deep Haven funds? Not that she had time to worry about it with Jim and Elaine's party tomorrow, but ever since she'd run into Ed Draper at the clinic and he'd told her, she'd wondered.

But she still had so much to do. Why had she let Oliver convince her a little stroll in the brisk air would do them all good and get her mind off the worries of the day?

And who called thirty-four degrees and falling "brisk"? It was downright freezing.

"Did you hear me, Miss Lena?" Kiah held Bruce's leash. The dog might be quadruple her weight, but she had him completely in her control.

Quite unlike Lena's own thoughts, which she couldn't seem to rein in. "I'm sorry. I was distracted. What were you saying?"

"I was telling you about what Jack did."

"Oh, right. So what did Jack do?" Lena tried to listen to Kiah's chatter about Jack's latest escapades on the playground. According to Oliver, this was the only time she opened up and seemed happy, when she was walking Bruce.

Lena forced herself to push aside the discomfort of her frozen hands holding on to Jane's and Wentworth's leashes. The autumn colors were gone now. Bare limbs rattled in the cold wind while the spruce and pines above their heads swayed. Thankfully they were almost back to their houses.

But come to think of it, Oliver had been quiet tonight too.

She nudged his arm. "What's on your mind?"

"Not much." He paused. "Kiah, you and Bruce can go ahead. Wait at Lena's mailbox." He watched them run off.

"Nervous about tomorrow?" Lena asked.

"A little. I want it to go well."

"So you can prove to your grandfather that you've changed?"

"Something like that." He switched Scamp's leash to his other hand and gathered her hand in his. His warmth soaked into her fingers.

"Oh, and I think I found a home for Harry the poodle here. I'm going to have Seth and Ree Turnquist meet him. They were interested."

"They'd be a great couple." Lena looked over at Oliver's handsome face. His black Carhartt beanie tugged down low over his forehead only accentuated his dark eyes. "Thanks for helping me find homes for the dogs."

"It wasn't much. Thank *you* for helping organize the party. I admit, the green and gold look nice. Even if they are Packer colors."

They reached Kiah, waiting with Bruce at the mailbox. Lena handed her leashes to Oliver and grabbed the stack of mail inside. "I didn't pick the colors because of a dumb football team."

"You're right. They are a dumb team. Which is why I suggested we go purple and gold."

"Dad, you can't call people dumb. That's not nice."

"And it's their emerald anniversary. We can't have pur—" Lena's fingers stilled as she saw the logo on the corner of the top envelope of the stack.

"What is it?" Oliver looked over her shoulder.

"Just some lab work I was waiting on." She moved the envelope to the bottom.

Kiah pointed over toward their house. "Hey, whose car is that in our driveway?"

Oliver shrugged. "Dunno. Lena, want to leave your pups here and we can go find out?"

"Sure." She wasn't quite ready to see the results anyway. She left the mail on the hall table and Wentworth and Jane with fresh water and treats. They settled the other dogs in the garage kennel, except for Bruce. The more time he and Kiah had together in the evenings, the better they both did, even if Lena had to drag him back to her place at the end of it. She joined Oliver and Kiah as they walked with Bruce toward their back deck.

Voices drifted outside from an open window. Familiar voices.

Ollie stiffened. "They're early. I thought they weren't arriving until the party tomorrow."

"Who is it?" Kiah asked.

"Hey, pumpkin, why don't you do a quick check on Oreo and come right back to me. I'll wait here."

She ran off with Bruce to the goat pen.

"Maybe this is good." Lena took Oliver's free hand. It had gone cold. "You can start showing them how much you've changed. Kiah can meet them without all the party guests around. In fact, maybe I should go home—"

He tugged her closer. "No. They like you. They'll probably be more excited to see you than me."

He *was* nervous. Apparently, the man wasn't all confidence and swagger. And the fact that he was okay sharing his questions and doubts with her made her want to be with him even more.

She squeezed his hand. "They love you. They always have."

"Grandma, sure. But Grandpa?" Oliver's lips went tight.

"You want a second chance? It's only right that you give him one."

"Fine. But please say you'll come with us." His big brown eyes stared down at her, two deep grooves carved in his brow. Grooves she wanted to help soothe.

"Is the great Oliver Fox scared?"

He always responded better to a challenge than pity or sympathy.

"Never."

"All right, then, let's go."

Kiah ran back to them. "Oreo is all good."

Oliver knelt down. "Nice job, kiddo. So, you want to know who—"

"Ollie, is that you?" Elaine Fox stepped out on the deck.

Her thin frame and quick gait gave the impression of someone half her age. The dark-blue fleece jacket, practical yet stylish, set off her eyes. But it was the affection shining in them that Lena had always admired.

"Hey, Grandma." He walked up the steps with Kiah and hugged the sweet woman who had been a neighbor to Lena since she was three years old. "And you must be Kiah." Elaine looked down on the child with so much tenderness Lena choked up.

Lena stayed down in the grass, in the shadows, and watched the introductions as Robin joined the others on the deck. Maybe she should sneak away back home. She hated to intrude on the special family moment.

"Lena?" Elaine hurried down to her and squeezed her tight. The familiar floral perfume she wore brought back years of memories and sweet moments. "I've missed you, neighbor."

"Hi, Elaine. I've missed you too."

She moved close to Lena's ear. "And is it true? Are you and Oliver really dating?"

Lena nodded.

She clasped her hands and sighed. "I can't tell you how happy that makes me. I always knew you two were made for each other." She hooked her arm through Lena's. "Now, let's go inside. I need to hear all about it. And I want to get to know this great-granddaughter of mine."

"Where's Jim?"

"We're staying at the Christiansens' resort. Jim needed to rest after the long drive. But he'll be here tomorrow."

Oliver could breathe easy for another day. And tonight, Lena would walk into the Fox home as one of them, not as a neighbor or an outside friend.

They spent a cozy evening around the table with ice-cream sundaes, catching up until Kiah's bedtime came around.

"But I'm not sleepy." The stormy look on Kiah's face didn't bode well. Especially since part of the bedtime routine was saying goodbye to Bruce, which always involved tears. For both parties.

"It's my bedtime too, Kiah, so I better be going," Elaine said. "I want to be well rested for the party tomorrow."

Kiah studied her great-grandmother for a beat. "Well, if Gigi is going to bed, I guess I can too." She still cried saying goodbye to Bruce, but she allowed Robin to carry her upstairs without as much fuss as usual. Only after she convinced Robin to read three bedtime stories though. The little girl *was* her father's daughter after all.

Oliver saw his grandma out and then walked Lena and Bruce home. She hung up her coat in the entryway while Oliver played with the dogs. Bruce whined by the back door as he usually did when he had to be separated from Kiah.

Oliver tossed Wentworth's rope toy and Jane's squeaker into the living room, and as soon as they were distracted, he wrapped Lena in his arms.

It was quickly becoming her favorite place to be.

"See, that wasn't so bad, was it?" she asked.

He pulled her in closer. "Nothing seems bad when you're there." He dropped a kiss on her cheek and nuzzled the ticklish spot under her ear. Wentworth came and dropped his rope at their feet. He barked, demanding a game of tug-of-war.

Oliver looked down at him "I'm a little busy." He kissed her again, but Wentworth wouldn't take no for an answer.

"This is what you get for teaching him this game." She pulled away.

"He can wait—"

"I should get his meds anyway." She found the box with the once-a-month heartworm medication and called Wentworth and Jane to the kitchen.

"What's this?" Oliver picked up the envelope with her lab results. "Why didn't they send these to your office?"

Why wouldn't they send them by email in this digital age? would be a better question. Then she wouldn't have to deal with this right now.

She held out the square morsels for each dog. Jane gobbled hers up. "They're not for the clinic. They're for me."

"Is this like an ancestry thing or something?"

"Not exactly." Jane ran off. Wentworth turned up his nose, refusing to take the medication. "Bud, you need to eat this."

"Then what exactly is it?"

"Why does it matter? It's personal."

"It matters because you're being weird and secretive about it. Like you don't want to tell me."

"Maybe because I don't." Lena moved to the cupboard for peanut butter.

"Are you sick or something? You wouldn't keep that from me, right?" The worry in Oliver's face was real.

"I'm not sick. My father is."

"Brad? You're still in touch with him?"

"He's my father. Of course I'm still in touch with him." She smothered the medicine in Jiffy. Wentworth finally ate it and rushed out of the kitchen.

"Sperm donor would be more accurate. He's ignored you for the last thirty years. Why are you getting lab results when he's sick?"

"It really isn't your business."

"Not my—" His nostrils flared. "You are my business. At least, I thought you were. I know we haven't exactly defined this relationship, but give me a break here. What's going on?"

He did have a point. If both of these men were going to be in her life for the long haul, he probably should know. Maybe it was okay to let Ollie be a part of things she usually handled on her own. That was what couples did, right? Maybe hearing what Brad was going through would stir a little compassion in Oliver. Show him Brad wasn't a threat. "He has end-stage kidney failure."

Oliver's jaw dropped. "He wants one of your kidneys? Unbelievable."

"Why should that matter?" She snatched the envelope from Oliver's hand and walked into the dining room.

He followed. "He doesn't deserve you. Or your kidney. Please tell me you're not actually considering this."

Okay, this was *not* the reaction she'd been hoping for. She spun on her heel. "I gave you a second chance after you broke my heart, after you left your family, after you ignored me for the last however many years." She pointed at the sealed lab results. "Why shouldn't I give him a second chance at life? He's my dad."

"He's not a dad! He's never once tried to be a father to you until he needed something from you. Don't you find that at least a little suspicious?"

His words sliced through her. "So the only reason anyone would want to be with me is because they want something?" Lena wrapped her long cardigan closer to her, overlapping one side over the other. "What is it *you* want? Are you with me because it will make it look better for your grandparents? Because I helped you organize this party so you would be the hero once again?"

"What are you talking about? I'm with you because—"

"Because what?"

They stood toe to toe and glared at each other.

Please say it, please just say it.

"If you really don't know from everything I've done, I guess you don't understand. But I will say this. You don't need that man. You don't need him to feel worthy or loved or…legitimate. You want to give that guy a kidney, so be it. But don't do it to win his approval. You don't need it."

"That's easy for you to say." Wentworth started barking from the doorway. "You have no idea what it's like to be alone. To be taunted or bullied. Everyone loves you. They've always loved you."

"Right, and that's why my wife left me. Why I'm fighting to keep custody of my own daughter. Why I've had to spend the last two months trying to make it up to my own family for all my failures. Because I'm such a lovable guy, huh?"

Jane crowded around Lena's feet, whining, probably scared. Lena set the envelope on the table and picked up Jane.

"You grew up with an amazing father for twelve years and then a grandfather who gladly stepped into that role when he was gone. You had a loving mother, and you still have a sweet grandmother. You grew up with siblings who adored you, who still care. And now you have a daughter too. But me? Who do I have?"

"You have me." He thumped his chest. Not in an aggressive,

silverback gorilla way—his voice was too gentle for that. He looked at her with intensity, like he was desperate for her to believe him. Like he would scale any wall she tried to put between them.

It doused her initial flare of anger and left the lingering question.

"Are you going to stick around? I want to believe you, but you could still leave at any time. And like you said, we haven't defined this relationship."

"Is that what you're worried about?" He moved in closer and gently lifted Jane out of Lena's arms and set the pup on the floor. "If anything, I thought having a home, a daughter, a job here would show you."

"Show me what?"

"Lena, I'm not going anywhere." His deep bass rumbled in her ear. Strong arms wrapped around her, securing her close to his chest.

She rested her head against him, listening to his heartbeat.

Right. He was here. So maybe she could let herself lean into him, draw from his strength.

Maybe, for the first time in forever, she wasn't alone.

seventeen

. . .

WHILE IT WAS STILL DARK OUTSIDE HIS WINDOW, OLIVER THREW THE covers off, ready to build on yesterday's victories and conquer the day. The meeting with Grandma and Kiah had gone well last night. Although Lena had been upset about the whole Brad thing—which still didn't sit well with him—their kiss goodnight had ended the evening on a good note.

Good enough he'd had to force himself to leave her. It'd almost been as bad as one of Kiah and Bruce's goodbyes. But once he had everything situated with Grandpa, and Kiah's custody was set, convincing that woman to marry him would be next on his list.

Because he didn't want to say goodbye to her at the end of the day anymore. He wanted to build a life with Lena and Kiah. Build a business. And if his plan to help her get that shelter going worked, he might have a shot at convincing her he meant to settle in Deep Haven for good.

Oliver made an extra-strong cup of coffee. Robin and Kiah soon joined him in the kitchen as the first light of dawn peeked through the eastern windows.

"We're off to get the cupcakes and fresh flowers. Do you have your list?" Robin asked.

"Yup." He scooped up Kiah, trying to gauge her mood. "Are you ready for a party?"

She didn't give him a full-wattage grin or anything, but she nodded. "Uncle Grayson is coming, and Gigi, right?"

"That's right."

"And I get to meet my Grandpa Jim too."

The reminder sent a ripple of nervous energy through Oliver. Then again, it could be the coffee kicking in.

"You sure do." He carried Kiah out to Robin's car and buckled her in. "Now, guard those cupcakes and don't let anything happen to them, 'kay?"

"All right, Daddy." She kissed him sweetly on the cheek. He almost cried. Finally they were getting somewhere.

As they left, Grayson pulled in with Sammy Johnson, Seth Turnquist, and Peter Dahlquist in his truck. Together the men hauled the big marquee tent to the frosty backyard and began unfolding it. They set the corner stakes and poles using the ratchet sets provided. As they were setting the center pole, Lena arrived.

Oliver craned his neck around the tent flap for a better look.

She had on what she called her working jeans and a barn jacket with her cowgirl boots.

It definitely worked for her.

"Dude, you helping or watching your girlfriend?" Seth asked. He grunted as he helped push the pole into place.

Right. Oliver finished adjusting all the outside poles. Once the tent was in place, the guys began lugging tables and folding chairs from the trailer behind Grayson's truck. Lena was out of sight and even more help arrived. So much for sneaking in a good-morning kiss from his other girl.

With the trailer emptied of tables and Peter off to get the next load, Oliver could finally check in with Lena. He was looking for her out front when Robin pulled up and parked in Lena's driveway. He walked over to help her. As soon as Kiah was unbuckled, she ran off to see the big tent. Robin and Oliver soon followed with trays and boxes of green and gold cupcakes.

"It looks good, bro," Robin said. She set her load on one of the picnic tables off to the side of the tent.

He looked over the activity. It was all coming together. "Yeah, it does. Having the party here was a good idea."

Robin grinned. "I know. Now, if you don't mind, I see my handsome boyfriend over there, and I think I'll have him help me with the rest of the cake stuff."

Speaking of significant others...where was Lena? Before he could take two steps, Kiah ran over with Bruce.

"Did you help make that big tent?"

"I helped set it up. But, honey, Bruce shouldn't be here. How did he get out of Lena's house?"

"I heard him crying, so I let him out. He's lonely." She stuck her lip out and gave him the puppy-dog stare. "And Miss Lena said I could visit him any time."

"I know, but we're getting ready for the big party, remember? He's going to be in the way, and we don't want him to get—"

"Oliver, which direction do you want these tables set?" Peter Dahlquist stood by the stack of tables and chairs.

"Lena will know." He squatted down next to Kiah but was interrupted again.

"Any chance you have a long extension cord?" Seth asked. "Oh, and Beth was asking for soapy water to wash down the tables."

While Oliver tried to answer him, Kiah ran off with the dog. She was happy for the moment, so maybe he should just let them be. Hopefully she would keep him out of trouble.

Oliver found rags to wipe down the tables and chairs. By then Grayson was back with the propane tanks for the heaters. Eventually Robin took Kiah inside—with Bruce sticking close by—to get dressed. Finally, he could go talk to Lena himself.

He found her in the barn, directing Beth where to hang the

banner she'd had printed with Grandma and Grandpa's wedding photo.

Oliver scooched past the gift table and tugged Lena by the hand around the corner of a stall, giving them a modicum of privacy. "I've been waiting all morning to see you. It looks amazing in here."

"We still have a lot to do." She watched Beth secure the corner of the banner.

"I know, but you can take a minute or two to give me a proper good morning, can't you?"

Her focus finally landed on Oliver. Her green eyes brightened as an enticing blush bloomed on her cheeks. "Good morning."

"That's better." He looped his arms around her back. "If we didn't have an audience right now, I'd—"

"You would what?" Her shy, flirty look would be his undoing.

"I'd—"

His phone rang. Jeremy? Oliver frowned at the screen. What did he want?

"It's all right, Ollie. I should—"

"No, stay here."

But the moment was lost. "I'll see you later." Lena squeezed his hand before she moved across the room to Ree Turnquist, who was setting up napkins and eating utensils while her infant Anders slept against her chest in the baby carrier .

Fine. Since he couldn't talk to her, he answered his still ringing phone. "Hello?"

"Hey, Jolly Ollie." Why did Jeremy's voice sound so raspy? "Remember how you said if I ever needed anything you could help me out?"

"Yeah, but today is not a good time."

There was a pause on the line. "I didn't know who else to call."

Oh. That kind of help. This was more than needing a designated driver. "What's going on?"

"I'm at the hospital. I had a bit of a— You know what, I'm just gonna have the nurse explain it, cuz I'm..." Jeremy's words slurred and trailed off.

"Hello? Jeremy?"

"Is this Oliver Fox?" a female voice asked.

"Yes?"

"This is Carol at the hospital, and Mr. Stanly here said he could be released into your care. He needs a ride and supervision for the concussion he sustained."

"Concussion?"

"We need you to pick him up in the next hour. I'll have the doctor's instructions and can go over them when you get here. Thanks."

She hung up before Oliver could say anything. He grunted as he fisted his phone and walked out of the barn. Of all the days for Jeremy to take him up on the offer for help. But maybe this was the wakeup call he needed.

Oliver could still taste what rock bottom felt like—waking up in his own vomit, no recollection of the night before. The only thing he could recall was Jalisa telling him he was a father and she was coming back to town. With his two-year-old daughter.

The horrifying realization that he was nothing like what a good father should be had crushed him. Where would he even start? Yet God must've known what Oliver needed, because that was the moment Hezekiah had knocked on his door. He'd always been there in the background as a good boss, a patient friend, talking to him about the Lord while they worked. But that day, he'd taken Oliver to an AA meeting and agreed to be his sponsor. It'd changed his life.

And Jeremy could probably use some help right about now. Oliver could give him a ride from the hospital to his house and make sure he had what he needed for the day. Then maybe tomorrow, once all this party stuff was over, he'd invite him to church.

If he hurried back, he'd still have time to change before the guests started arriving.

Lena stood in his path with a smile. "Where are you going? I thought you were going to set up the heaters and lay out the tablecloths."

"I will. But Jeremy needs me. He's at the hospital—"

"Jeremy Stanly?"

"Yeah."

She lost the warm smile. "So it's okay for you to help him, but you don't think I should help my father?"

Her softly voiced question poked his conscience. "Look, I know Jeremy's not your favorite person, but he needs help right now. I'll be back as soon as I can. Will you keep an eye on Kiah, please?"

"Sure."

He watched her walk away, longing to call her back and remind her of how much he cared. But the sooner he could take care of whatever Jeremy needed, the sooner he'd be back. Oliver dodged tables and chairs and made his way across the lawn, around the house, and to the driveway. His van was blocked.

Of course it was.

He ran in to ask Robin—who'd been smart enough to park in Lena's driveway—for her keys but instead found his grandfather standing in the kitchen, glaring at the new kitchen sink while Bruce slobbered all over his feet.

"Grandpa?" Oliver stilled.

"I take it this is your work?" He pointed to the tiled backsplash. As always, his serious expression reeked of judgment.

"You're early."

"Yes, well, I thought we should talk before the festivities began. Your grandmother said you have some things you'd like to say." Grandpa's chin lifted and he stared down at Oliver, arms crossed in front of him.

Like a kid caught off guard, Oliver scrambled for words. "I

do have a lot to say, but someone needs my help right now, and I
have to go."

"Can't this person wait?"

The same judgmental look Oliver had faced for years set off
an instant urge for a strong drink. "Since it's been over ten years,
maybe we can hold off a few more hours. Trust me when I say
it's important."

"Who needs your help so badly you're going to walk out on
your family now?"

"Jeremy Stanly."

Grandpa's forehead wrinkled as he frowned. "He's always
been bad news."

"He's in the hospital."

"Then I guess some things never change."

Oliver braced himself and took a quick moment to hold his
temper back. "That's not true. *I* changed. I came back. And I do
want to talk to you. But Jeremy needs help right now. Can you
please give me a chance here?"

Grandpa stepped away. "I'm not the one leaving. I'll be here
when you get back." He left the kitchen with Bruce trying to
follow him.

Oliver called Bruce and gave him a rawhide to chew on.
Hopefully it would keep him occupied. Oliver should probably
get him settled in the pen with Oreo for the party so they didn't
have to hear the pathetic barking. But later.

He left Robin a quick note and snatched her keys from the
holder by the door. The sooner he could get Jeremy settled, the
sooner he could get back to the party and try to fit this family
back together again.

꼬리 꼬리 꼬리

Lena guessed it was up to her to spread out all the green tablecloths so they could decorate the tables, since Ollie wasn't around to do it.

Then again, he trusted her to watch Kiah. That was something. The girl colored in a notebook at the end of one of the tables, feet resting on Bruce's back under the chair.

Robin walked into the tent with the box of centerpieces. "Are you okay?"

"There's just a lot to do." Lena took the box and set it on the table. "People will be arriving soon. I still have to get Oliver's stupid chocolate fountain set, I need to cover all these tables, change my outfit. Then there's—"

"Hang on. Lena, look around. There's plenty of us here to help. And remember, this is supposed to be a party. Cheer up."

"How am I supposed to cheer up when"—she gave a quick glance to Kiah and dropped her voice to a whisper—"the one person I'm doing this for isn't even here. Instead, he's ditched me to go hang out with Jeremy Stanly." Oh, that'd come out way harsher than she'd meant. But she was tired of acting like it didn't matter. Oliver should be here.

"Wait a minute. Oliver left the party to hang out with Jeremy the Jerk?" Robin's indignant tone helped soothe Lena's ire a tad.

"Well, he's not exactly hanging out." Lena whipped the next tablecloth out of the box and unfolded it. She moved away from Kiah and started at the other end of the tent.

"Then what is he doing?"

"He said something about Jeremy being in the hospital."

"The hospital? Oh. I suppose Ollie has a good reason then. We should give him the benefit of the doubt. Don't you think?"

"I suppose." Of course she'd take her brother's side. Lena kept working, spreading out the cloths while Robin situated the centerpieces.

"So what's really bothering you?"

Robin knew her too well.

"We argued last night." Lena shoved one of the chairs back

under the table and moved on to the next row. "And I thought I was over it, but when he told me he was leaving and why, it all came rushing back."

"What did you argue about?" Robin followed with the box.

"He doesn't want me to help my father. Which is so hypocritical. Because Oliver begged me to give *him* a second chance." She whipped out the next green cloth. "Now he's running off to help Jeremy, and yet he doesn't think I should give Brad the time of day."

"Oliver can be a tad overprotective. Especially over those he cares about."

"Well, I don't need his protection." After being around Oliver so much, it was harder to hold back the growl from her words. She'd gotten used to revealing too much.

"What are you helping Brad with?" Robin sounded suspicious.

Rather than answer the question, Lena spread out the last tablecloth and moved to the table with the chocolate fountain, keeping Kiah in her sights. But Robin followed right behind her. "I know you heard me. What's going on with Brad? You said he was sick, but how sick?"

Robin had her trapped. The sooner Lena spit it out, the sooner she could get back to her checklist. "He has stage five renal failure."

"What does that mean?"

"He needs a kidney transplant."

Robin's eyes almost popped out of her head. "That's why he came here?"

"Why are you so quick to judge him? The man is sick. And I, for one, am thankful he put himself out there to find me."

Robin stared with her hands on her hips. "So you're going to give him one of your kidneys?"

"I agreed to be tested. That's all. I don't even know if I'm a match." She'd been too chicken to open the envelope last night. With so much riding on this party, she needed to compartmentalize everything, but here it was all crashing in at once and mixing together in the worst way.

"Yeah, but are you sure it's a good idea? You barely know him."

"How can you understand? You've always known exactly who you are and where you belong. You have no idea what it's like to not know where half your DNA comes from." Lena pushed back a sob. "You don't know what it means to be truly alone."

She hated that tears escaped and that she choked on the words, but maybe Robin would finally get it.

Robin pulled Lena in for a hug. "I'm so sorry."

Lena wiped her eyes. "It's fine."

"But it's not fine. And you're right. I don't know what it's been like for you to not have a father in your life. But, Lena, knowing who you share your DNA with isn't going to magically fix anything. And more importantly, you are not alone. You have us."

Nice words that maybe at a different time would help, but right now there were too many things that needed to be done, and she'd had enough of all the platitudes. Maybe Oliver was right to help his friend. But why did it have to happen at her expense? Lena leaned around Robin to check on Kiah. Elaine was with her, pointing at the notebook, probably fawning all over her great-granddaughter's artistic expression.

Gertie Thurber and another woman in black slacks and a gray wool coat walked into the tent. "Excuse me? Do you know where I can find Oliver Fox?"

Question of the day, lady.

Lena tried to slip out while Robin took care of it, but as she walked away, Mrs. Thurber followed her.

"Dr. Larson, I need to talk to you."

Lena tried not to cringe at the nasal voice trailing her. "This isn't a great time. Can we talk after the party—"

"It's about the grant."

Lena bit her tongue and counted slowly to three while she turned around to face Mrs. Thurber. "All right. What about the grant?"

"I was tasked to tell you that we've decided to give the funds to someone else."

"What? I thought the adoption event was a big hit."

"I'm sorry. But the committee can only choose a grant for a non-profit or a low-interest loan for a small business. We decided to go with a loan for Oliver." But the woman didn't look sorry at all. In fact, a smugness in her expression said she was enjoying this. Every second.

"Wait a minute. Oliver? You're giving the funds to Oliver Fox?"

"Yes. For his plumbing business. It was a difficult decision, but ultimately Deep Haven needs a plumber more than the animal shelter. You're welcome to apply next—"

But whatever words Gertie said, Lena couldn't hear over the roaring in her head.

She was such a fool. Of course they would give the funds to Oliver. Any time she went up against him, she always came out the loser.

eighteen

. . .

WHY WAS IT EVERY HOSPITAL SMELLED THE SAME? BIG ONES, SMALL ones, it didn't matter. Whether it was the soap or the cleaner, Oliver didn't know and didn't care. He just wanted to get away from it and the memories it evoked as soon as possible.

A nurse showed Oliver to an emergency department room where he found Jeremy lying in the hospital bed. Talk about being in rough shape. Wrinkled and stained clothes, a bandaged arm, and one eye completely swollen shut and bruised a dark purple.

Jeremy raised his water glass to him. "Hey, there's my ride." His voice was scratchy and groggy.

"What happened? You don't look so good."

"Things got a little out of hand. Wrecked my car."

"Have too much to drink?"

"Nah. That tree came out of nowhere." Jeremy started to laugh and then winced and grabbed his head. His moan was more pathetic than Bruce's.

A different nurse walked in with an empty wheelchair. "Are you Oliver Fox?"

"Yes."

"Here's the doctor's orders. This is the standard concussion protocol. You need to bring Mr. Stanly back immediately if he shows any of these symptoms. He should rest, but don't let him sleep longer than two to three hours without waking him up. If you can't wake him, call this number." She thrust a bunch of papers in his hand and then patted the wheelchair. "Time to go."

Oliver read down the list as she helped Jeremy into the chair.

"Wait, so he needs to stay at my house?"

The nurse gave him a *duh* look. "We discussed this on the phone. He needs supervision, so unless there's someone else who can watch over him for the next twenty-four hours, yeah."

Twenty-four hours? That was just great.

They settled Jeremy into Robin's car and left the hospital. As they drove out of the parking lot, Jeremy turned to him. "Hey, man, can we swing by my place? I need to change."

Oliver would have to bring him to the party at this point. Looking over at the blood-stained shirt with the smell of booze and smoke rolling off it, a change of clothing was probably a good idea.

"We need to make it quick. It's the anniversary party today."

"Right, the granny party. No worries, man. I'll be fine at my place. You can just drop me off."

Guilt slammed into Oliver. For Jeremy to call a guy he'd barely spoken to since high school probably meant he didn't have any better options. "No, it's fine. You can stay with me, come to the party. I just need to get there as soon as you change. So where am I going?"

Jeremy directed him to a rundown apartment complex outside of town that had been an old motel when they were in high school. Oliver looked out at the crumbling retaining wall on the side of the building. The concrete stoop right in front of them was cracked, the door dingy and stained with black scuff marks. Cobwebs hung thick from the porch light to the soffit above. Oliver so easily could've ended up here.

"I'll be back in a jif. Promise," Jeremy said.

It would probably be the fastest option. If he wasn't back in ten minutes, Oliver could go after him. But Jeremy was back in five with a small duffel bag, and they were on their way.

Back at his own house, Oliver situated Jeremy in the basement rec room, where hopefully he would just sleep. He set an alarm on his phone for three hours and left to get dressed.

As he came upstairs, he spotted Grayson standing in the stairwell.

"Oliver, what's going on? And was that Jeremy Stanly you brought home?"

"Yeah, long story. He needs a place to crash for the next twenty-four hours." He headed for his second-floor bedroom to change.

Grayson followed Oliver all the way up the stairs and down the hall. "Well, hurry up and get dressed. Guests are arriving any minute. And one of the guys ran into Oreo's pen with the trailer. A section of the fencing is down, so we just tied her up on a leash at the moment, since the barn is being used."

Oliver wiggled out of his flannel shirt. "Where's my daughter?"

"Outside with Beth and Lena. Oh, and Robin said some lady needed to talk to you and it was important."

"One thing at a time. I'll get dressed, take care of the goat, and then I will find Robin."

Oliver took a quick shower and dressed in the clothes Robin and Lena had picked out for him earlier in the week. He would try to keep them nice while he worked on the damaged goat pen. Couldn't have the goat in the barn bleating throughout the toasts, so he hauled a cattle panel and used some scrap wire to fasten it to the fencing. He left Oreo in the temporary pen and went to find his sister and the mystery woman.

He couldn't find them, but he did see Lena. Another thing he desperately needed to fix. Even as he watched Grandma and Grandpa start to greet the first guests now arriving, he ran over to where Lena was setting up party favors.

Oliver was tempted to take her and run away from the party and everyone else. Just the two of them.

"Where's Kiah?"

Lena didn't look up. "She's with Beth. She wanted her to meet Ingrid Christiansen's granddaughter."

"Good. We need to talk. Please?" He reached for her hand. She pulled away.

"Now you want to talk? What, to rub it in that you won. Again?"

But as he opened his mouth to explain what was going on with Jeremy, her words sank in. "Won? Again? What are you talking about?"

And why was she glaring at him like that and pulling away?

"You applied for the small business loan from the Deep Haven funds?" she asked. It sounded a lot more like an accusation than a question.

"I *am* buying a small business. What's the big deal?"

She folded her arms and glared. "Let me guess. Your plumbing class was your community event?"

Seriously, what was going on here? "Well, yeah. Why are you mad about that? I thought you wanted me to stay in Deep Haven. That means I need a job."

"That was *my* grant. What do you think the pet adoption event was for?"

Oh no. His body went cold. "You never said it was for the Deep Haven funds. I didn't even know they offered grants. I applied for a small business loan."

"Yeah. They come from the same funds." She stopped moving and looked him in the eye. "You didn't know?"

"I had no clue that was the funding you were talking about. You never once mentioned the grant. I wouldn't—"

"Ollie, someone is here to meet with you. And we need to get ready for the family pictures," Robin called from a few feet away. A woman he hadn't met before stood next to her.

"I'll go get Kiah," Lena said, and she left.

"This is Mrs. Walters, a social worker from Duluth. She's here for a welfare check." Robin stiffly nodded toward the woman next to her.

Okay, this just wasn't even funny anymore. A welfare check today of all days? If he didn't know better, he would've thought someone was pulling a prank on him. But no. This was his life. His girlfriend was hurt. His grandfather was already condemning him. He had a concussed and hungover friend in the basement, and now this.

"Hi." Oliver strode forward with an outstretched hand and manufactured smile. "You're just in time for a party."

The woman paused writing in a notebook to shake his hand. "Your sister explained that to me. But that's fine. I'm here as a favor for the Cerro Gordo county in Iowa. I'm going to observe you today. I'll try to stay out of the way, but at some point, I'd like to talk with Kiah and visit with you. For now, pretend I'm not here."

Yeah, right. It was only custody of his daughter on the line. "Of course. Make yourself at home."

Behind Mrs. Walters, a flash of red sneaking around the side of the barn caught Oliver's eye.

Nobody was supposed to be over there. He ignored Robin calling his name and jogged around milling groups of people to the back side of the barn. The one person he'd seen wearing red shouldn't be anywhere but resting right now. But when Oliver turned the corner, Jeremy was there, leaned against the wall of the barn, taking a swig from a bottle.

"What are you doing?"

Jeremy shrugged. "Needed some air. I didn't want to crash your party, so I came out here." He took another swig and then held it out to Oliver. "Want some?"

The no was on his lips. But the yes—oh, the yes was right behind it because suddenly, as he stared out at all of the things happening, at the woman that could take away his life, the fact that he'd hurt his girlfriend yet again, and the state of his grandfather staring at him with his arms folded in disapproval… yes seemed like the exact right answer.

He'd never wanted a drink so badly in his life.

A waft of whiskey met his nose. Sure, it was cheap, but it would do the trick. A sip to help take the edge off.

Jeremy wiggled the bottle. "A little liquid courage to get you through it all."

The brown bottle glinted in the sunlight. Oliver could practically taste it. The drink promised an escape from all the weight piling up on him. No one would have to know if he took one small sip.

Jeremy lifted the bottle to his mouth once more. Oliver watched him swallow and lick his lips.

Just one drink—

Wait. Oliver stepped back and looked at his friend. One arm in a sling. A black eye. There was still dried blood on his head right above the ear.

Jeremy had just wrapped his car around a tree and walked away, but he so easily could've died or killed someone. And yet here he was, back at it again. Oliver had been in his shoes. And he had hurt someone. His own brother.

Others could handle it just fine. But it would never be one drink for him. And a drink wasn't going to fix anything.

Oliver slapped the bottle away. The amber liquid splashed against the barn and onto Oliver's shirt.

"Dude, what was that for? You could just say 'No thank you.'"

"Jeremy, you need help." He snagged the bottle and poured it out onto the grass between them, drops of whiskey splattering on his shoes and pants. "You can't drink this with a concussion."

"It's a bump on the head. And I don't need you telling me what to do. That's not why I called you."

"I've been where you are. I can help. This"—he held out the bottle—"is not going to help."

"What's going on back here?" The deep voice startled them both. Oliver turned to see his brother.

"Nothing." Jeremy swiped the bottle out of Oliver's hand and walked away.

Oliver and Grayson watched him. Jeremy probably needed to cool off. At least there was nothing left in the bottle.

"What was that all about?" Grayson lifted his chin toward Jeremy.

"He's got a concussion from drinking and crashing his car. He's supposed to be resting in the basement, but I found him out here."

Grayson looked at him suspiciously. "I'm supposed to get you for the opening greeting and prayer, but maybe you should go change. You smell like whatever was in that bottle."

Oliver wasn't going to waste time explaining himself anymore. "We don't have time for that." The party was quickly turning out as bad as his date with Lena. He just had to get through the next few hours and a welfare interview.

By the time he and Grayson wound through the crowd, his family was seated at the table of honor under the tent. Kiah settled in next to Grandma. Many of the guests were also sitting. Lena, of course. picked the farthest spot, sitting by herself in a corner.

He wanted to go to her, but Grayson handed him the microphone. Right. It was time for the blessing.

Oliver was supposed to greet everyone and pray for the meal. And maybe while he was at it, he could try to make it up to Lena too and give her credit for the amazing party she'd organized.

Because, as he studied his surroundings, the aroma from the smoked turkey wafted from the barn where the caterers had set up the buffet. At the other end of the tent was the dessert table with Robin's cake and the chocolate fountain Lena had set up just for him, even though she'd said it would make a mess. And in between were all the people.

Coach Presley was there in his wheelchair with his daughter and son-in-law. And Peter Dahlquist and his wife. Pastor Dan. Birdie Dawson smiled at him. A whole community was gathered to celebrate, many of whom he'd taken for granted. People who'd welcomed him back and forgiven him. Especially his family and Lena. It was time to acknowledge them.

Oliver moved to the aisle across from his grandparents. A reverent hush settled on the crowd. Bruce barked in the background. A titter rolled through the crowd. Oliver ignored it and spoke into the microphone.

"On behalf of my brother and sister and myself, I want to welcome you all—" Bruce's barking grew louder. Oreo bleated.

Wait. They were close. Too close. Hadn't someone taken Bruce back to Lena's? Oliver swung around to see through the clear plastic window of the tent.

Bruce was chasing poor Oreo, who bleated in terror, running full speed toward the tent.

"BRUCE, STOP!!"

No! Oliver tried to move, but Edith Draper sat in a chair next to where he stood. She held Oscar against her chest. His grandfather was on the other side of him, and he couldn't rightly hurdle over the table of children in front of him.

He could only watch everything unravel in slow motion. Oreo ran under the tent wall and jumped onto the dessert table. She kicked the fountain over, splattering chocolate all over the white tent and the group of older ladies from church at the nearby tables. Grayson lunged for Oreo, but she jumped onto the next table and ran down the length of it, stopping between Grandma and Robin. Napkins and forks flew through the air. Grandma screamed. Oreo froze.

Then she fell stiff into his grandma's lap.

At that moment Bruce, who'd gotten caught in the tent, ripped through and jumped up on the same table. Oliver reached for his collar and tried to pull him off, but Bruce's back legs slid out and caught the edge of the table. It toppled over on Oliver. Bruce ran off with a yelp.

Oliver scrambled out from the mess. The kids at the table squealed, wiping off the mess the animals had made. Oliver tried to reach Grandma to get Oreo off her lap, but Grandpa blocked him.

He sniffed Oliver's shirt. "You've done quite enough."

Kiah started crying and tried to run after Bruce. Oliver caught her up before she slipped in the frosting and chocolate now covering the grass.

"Let me go! I need to see Bruce!" She kicked at him to be put down. "I told you he needed me."

"Kiah, listen—"

"I hate you!" she sobbed. "I don't want to be here anymore."

And out of the corner of his eye, Oliver watched the social worker taking notes.

🐺 🐺 🐺

LENA STOOD AT THE EDGE OF THE TENT. HER HEART WRENCHED AT Kiah's words. She must've stunned Oliver enough to loosen his hold, because the little girl wriggled out of his grasp and ran after Bruce. Lena was the closest person to go after her. She found Kiah and Bruce curled up in the corner of her own deck by the rabbit hutch. The girl wept, her arms around Bruce's thick neck.

"Hey, Kiah." Lena approached slowly.

"Leave me alone."

Oliver rushed up the deck steps. "Kiah, come on, darling. You're tired. There's been a lot going on. Maybe we should let you rest a bit."

Kiah lifted her head. "I'm not a baby! I don't need a nap. I just need Bruce. But you took him away. And you yelled at him."

"I was only trying to stop him from coming into the tent."

"Just go away with Lena! Like you always do."

What? Was Kiah hurt that Lena was taking too much of Oliver's time?

Bruce must've caught on that his little human was upset and it was directed at Oliver, as he stood and barked loudly.

Lena pulled Ollie back to give the dog room. She caught a wiff of strong alcohol and gasped. "Have you been drinking?" Maybe the stress of the day had gotten to him.

"Of course not!"

"Then why do you smell like you bathed in liquor? I can't believe you would drink—"

"I didn't!" Oliver balked.

"Are you sure about that, Mr. Fox?"

Both Oliver and Lena whipped around to see the same lady that had been with Robin earlier. She came closer, right up to the bottom step of the deck. "She's right. You do reek of whiskey. Have you been drinking?"

"I'm telling you both, I haven't had a drop in over three years. I spilled the whiskey while talking to a friend."

"I'll need you to take a breathalyzer test to confirm that," the woman said.

"Fine. Then maybe you'll believe me. I'm completely sober."

"And who is this 'Lena' Kiah mentioned?"

Lena didn't like the way the woman said her name, like it was a dirty word. And why was she invading their privacy in the first place? She had no business being here asking these questions.

"*I'm* Lena." She stepped in front of the woman, blocking her way up the steps. "And why are you encroaching on my property without permission? You need to leave."

Bruce barked at the woman too.

"Lena, stop," Oliver whispered. "You're not helping. This is Mrs. Walters. She's the social worker doing a welfare check."

Lena froze. Oh.

Mrs. Walters narrowed her eyes, staring at them all. "What is the nature of your relationship with this woman, Mr. Fox? Kiah is obviously upset by it, and she doesn't seem like a good influence on your daughter."

Lena waited for Oliver to explain, waited for him to turn on the charm and smooth things over. She waited for him to tell this woman that they were together as a couple, that Lena had a great relationship with Kiah. She was just out of sorts at the moment.

Instead, he stumbled over his words. "I…uh, she's…look, Lena's just the next-door neighbor here. She doesn't have anything to do with this."

Just the next-door neighbor? Didn't have anything to do with this?

Lena's chest squeezed to the point it hurt to breathe. Just beyond her deck, Seth, Peter, and Jensen Atwood stood in the grass with a hose and the overturned table, staring at them.

Bruce barked again. Oliver continued saying something to Mrs. Walters, but Lena had already heard all she needed to hear. She backed away from them all.

Oliver looked at her. "Lena, can you get ahold of Bruce? Help me out here, please."

Right. Because that was all she was good for. Cleaning up after his messes. Helping him out, making him look good.

"Let's go, Bruce." Somehow she managed to choke out the words. "We're not wanted here."

She opened her French doors to lure him in. Kiah started crying again. Oliver had to pry her fingers off Bruce's collar and carry her away while Lena held on to the dog. Oliver tried saying something, but Lena ignored him. She just needed to get inside before the tears fell.

"Bruce, come on, boy. Treat."

Once Oliver and Kiah crossed over to their own property with the social worker following close behind, Bruce came inside. Lena's hand shook as she offered him the promised treat.

He carried it away and plopped on his dog bed. Instead of eating the biscuit she'd given him, he dropped it on the rug and laid his big head on his paws.

"I know how you feel," she whispered.

How could Oliver do that to her? Just dismiss her like she was nothing to him? It was the letter and the football team all over again.

Lena went numb. How stupid was she to fall for him yet again? Her mother must be shaking her head in disgust.

Just as she was going to curl up on the couch, the envelope with the lab results on her kitchen counter caught her attention.

Oliver didn't want her, but her father did. Maybe even needed her.

Lena ripped open the envelope and pulled out the letter.

She read the words once. She read again and studied the numbers and the chart on the second page.

Her heart sank.

She wasn't a match?

But she was all Brad had. How could this be?

God, I thought this was my ticket in. The way I could forge a relationship with my father. First Oliver. Now this?

This wasn't the way it was supposed to go.

But Lena could fix this. So she wasn't a match for a transplant. A good daughter wouldn't give up. She could look into alternatives, second opinions, experimental trials. As she looked down at her phone, it was clear. This wasn't the kind of thing a person did with a call. She needed to go to Duluth.

She looked out her dining room windows across the lawn to the Fox backyard. She scooped up her keys and was soon on her way. She wiped the few tears that had already escaped as she got into her truck. The party was still in full swing next door, but no one would miss her. Oliver had plenty of family, plenty of people to help him out. He had his team and family to clean up after him.

She and Brad only had each other.

Yet how many times in the last few weeks had she turned Brad down when he'd wanted to meet with her because she'd chosen to work on the party?

Now she could surprise *him* this time. Show him he could count on her to be there through whatever he had to face.

Maybe she could even move her practice to Nevada. What did Deep Haven have to offer anymore? If she sold the clinic, she'd have enough money to build Birdie the animal shelter and start over somewhere close to Brad. If they only had five to eight years, she'd make the most of them.

Lena made good time to the hotel, reaching it in just under two hours. Striding into the lobby, she rehearsed what she would say. First, invite him to dinner. Then she could tell him about the lab results, and they could come up with a new plan of action.

"Lena?" Brad walked into the lobby with two bags from the restaurant across the street. So much for her dinner idea.

He looked around the lobby. "What are you doing here?"

"I wanted to return the favor and surprise you. I got the lab results back." She showed him the envelope.

His face lit. "You did?" He led her to the small sitting area off to the side of the front desk. He set his bags down and sat across from her. "So? What do they say?"

Anyone could see the anticipation on his face. He'd put so much hope in her, and her own cells had failed her. She hated to disappoint him. But if he could get past that, she would show him. She wasn't going to abandon him in his time of need.

A quaking in her middle made it hard to take a deep breath. "I wish I had better news, but the crossmatch is positive."

"You're not a match." He dropped his head down into his hands. His shoulders drooped.

She scrambled for the words to help. "This isn't it, though. We can fight this. And we'll find another way. I could even—"

"There you are. Hon, we're all waiting for the food—" A woman in dark jeans and a black sweater stepped up to Brad and stopped once her eyes landed on Lena. "Who is this?"

Lena started to speak but stopped when Brad shot to his feet. "Sweetie, I thought you were going to wait upstairs."

"I wanted to ask the front desk for more towels. Do you work here?" the woman asked Lena.

"I'm—"

Brad grabbed the woman's hand. "She's nobody. Just a doctor. She's...on my medical team and stopped by to give me some news. We thought we had a donor, but"—he ran his hands down her arms—"but it wasn't a match."

His words sent a heavy blow right to Lena's heart.

She's nobody. Just a doctor.

She looked at the woman's left hand. A ring.

Brad handed the restaurant bags to the woman. "Take this up. You and the kids can get started and I'll be right there."

Kids? The knife in her chest twisted.

His wife looked down at her. "But why is she here at the hotel? Did she come up from Mayo like you were hoping? I should hear what she has to say—"

"No, no. Don't worry about anything. Go eat. I know everyone's hungry. Le...uh, Dr. Larson and I will finish up here and I'll be right up."

"Are you sure?" The woman's brow knitted with concern. Brad kissed her cheek affectionately and assured her he'd be right behind her as she walked toward the elevator with the bags.

But Lena had heard enough. She stood and stiffly walked to the hotel exit.

"Lena! Wait."

She swallowed back the pressure in her throat to keep her voice even and quiet. "I've seen enough."

"I can explain."

And if you want to cry, you should. Or yell. Or cheer. Just let it all out.

Well, the cheering wouldn't be happening any time soon. But

why pretend she wasn't in excruciating pain? She spun on her heel and let the tears flow.

"No. I don't want any more lies. I don't need your explanations."

"I didn't lie. You are a doctor—"

"I'm a veterinarian! I'm not on your medical team!"

"You have to understand. My family, they—"

"I thought *we* were family. But the only reason you sought me out was for this!" She held up the envelope with the labs. "So let me fill in the blanks. You have a family. You have a wife. Kids. But none of them were a donor match. Is that about it?"

"I didn't lie. They're my stepchildren. I—"

"You led me to believe you were alone."

The front desk employee came up to them. "Excuse me, ma'am, you're blocking the door and disturbing the guests. You need to calm down—"

Forget staying calm. She didn't care if she was blocking the entrance. She would get this off her chest. "And what now? Now that you know I'm not a match, are you even going to tell them about me?"

Brad's mouth pinched shut fast.

She had her answer.

This was why he hadn't wanted to meet in Duluth before. Why he'd been so anxious for her to get tested. Why he'd "surprised" her in Deep Haven.

He didn't want to be seen with his illegitimate daughter.

She was a fool. And worse, Oliver had been right. She stuffed the envelope in the garbage receptacle outside the hotel doors and ran back to her car. The sobs hit before she started the engine and drove away.

She had done everything right.

And it meant absolutely nothing.

Because like always, she was still all alone. She should've listened to her mother. No man was worth giving her heart to.

nineteen

. . .

THEY'D TAKEN KIAH AWAY.

The social worker had talked with her for all of five minutes and said she had everything she needed.

How could she be gone?

Oliver drove as he replayed the discussion from earlier—in the garage, the one place that hadn't been overrun with people as the party had been going full blast outside.

Mrs. Walters had stood in her coat, a messenger bag hanging from her shoulder, arms crossed as she'd faced him. "Kiah's aunt is here. I was going to ask to arrange a visit for her, but after what I've just witnessed, Cassandra Freeby will be taking Kiah with her back to Iowa. Pack her bags."

"She's not going anywhere. She's my daughter."

"Obviously your daughter is not thriving here. What do you call that display out there?" Mrs. Walters pointed out toward the backyard.

"She's overtired and acting out. Kids do that. There's a lot going on."

"You heard her yourself. She doesn't want to be here. And I don't blame her when you've got a drunk, injured man in the basement. Animals running around and causing chaos. A rather aggressive girlfriend when you just barely moved here and should be focusing on Kiah. No wonder when I asked her if she wanted to leave and go stay with Cassandra she said yes."

"Of course she said yes. She wants to see her aunt and cousins. That doesn't mean she doesn't like it here. You caught her on a bad day. And that man is a friend I'm trying to help. He's only here for one night. Lena, my girlfriend, was only protective of Kiah because she didn't know who you were. She would never do anything to harm anyone. And she's more than just a girlfriend. She's part of the family." Or at least she had been. And as soon as this was situated, he desperately needed to talk to her, because that look in her eyes had said he'd injured her. And it was killing him. But first, he stared down Mrs. Walters. "You can't take Kiah away."

She adjusted the strap of her bag. "I have a judge's decree stating I can. She's clearly traumatized. She's coming with me."

"I'm not going to let you."

She pulled out her phone. "Then I'll get law enforcement involved. And how will that look at your custody hearing? How will Kiah feel about that, seeing policemen restraining you? So you can help her pack and send her off peacefully, or it can get ugly. Your choice."

And what kind of choice was that? But the social worker had him. It would traumatize Kiah more to have deputies holding him back from trying to fight to keep her. And maybe a little time with her aunt would help him clean up this mess of a life and figure out a way to convince the judge that she belonged with him.

When Cassandra had shown up, Kiah had run to her aunt without a glance back or hug goodbye.

Now she was gone, the party done, and he needed to get away.

He might've come back to Deep Haven to fix all the things he'd broken, but the truth was, Lena was right. He could never make up for all his mistakes.

He couldn't bring his parents back. He'd almost killed his brother. He'd pushed away the one woman he loved, and now he'd lost custody of his daughter. Obviously no matter how hard he tried, the truth was he was not a good man.

Storm clouds rolled in as he drove to the empty marina. No one was crazy enough to be on the water when it was this cold. No one but him. The bay frothed and foamed, tossed about by the wind. Oliver hiked along the edge of the shore to the breakwater guarding the town. He grabbed a handful of the ice-cold stones and chucked them into the waves one by one.

Not enough. Never enough.

He found a bigger rock, one as big as his head. He lifted it up to his shoulder and then hefted it out into the angry lake. Its splash barely made a difference with all the waves crashing on the jetty. Like a shot-putter, Oliver launched another stone, a primal cry ripping from his throat. Then another, and another, each boulder bigger than the last, until his shoulder and biceps screamed and he could barely breathe. It still wasn't enough.

"Oliver!" Robin stood on the shore and shouted over the wind. Grayson was with her, bundled in a thick sherpa jacket and his cowboy hat.

Completely spent, Oliver sank down to the wet rocks, sweat dripping down his back despite the arctic gusts bearing down on him. Waves crested and shattered at his feet as they hit the wall of huge stones protecting the bay. He stared at the rise and fall of the lake.

Robin and Grayson picked their way along the breakwater and sat next to him, one on each side. They didn't say anything for a moment. Just sat next to him and watched the storm, probably, like him, remembering the storm when they'd been huddled together on the boat so long ago. Picturing the boom when it swung loose, the sickening sound as it hit his mother's head, and her scream as it pitched her over the starboard side. Remembering his father's cry when he dove into the freezing waves to save her, waves so much bigger than these.

Robin's cold hand slipped into his. "You did everything you could."

He'd tried. Again and again he'd thrown the life ring out into the wind. Each time it'd missed his father's reach, and the fifteen-foot breakers had swept his parents farther out to sea.

"You've been fighting it your whole life, bro. But some things you can't fight." Grayson's steady voice cut through the wind. "You can only accept them."

"Accept that because of me our parents died?" He already knew that. He should've done more. Tried harder. Been stronger. But he'd failed.

Robin laid her head on Oliver's shoulder. "It wasn't your fault."

"Of course it was. I couldn't reach them." His voice cracked and broke like the weakling he was.

"That storm was bigger than you. Out of your control," Grayson said. "No one expected you to save them."

It sounded too much like defeat. He was supposed to simply accept that he'd never be good enough?

Because deep in his bones, he knew it was true. He'd always known.

But what was he supposed to do about that? Now he'd lost Kiah too.

"I let Mom and Dad die. I've tried so hard to make up for it. To fight it. But I can't. No wonder that lady didn't think I was fit to be a father."

There were times he thought he had the upper hand. Times he was able to ignore it for a while. Times he could pretend he wasn't such a bad guy. But it was all a farce. Take away his brave face and Oliver Fox was simply a weak, broken man. The social worker knew that.

Everything inside Oliver cracked and splintered. Released from its tentative dam, tears finally fell and mixed with the rain pelting his face. Robin huddled next to him. Grayson looked out at the water.

Oliver stood and wiped his face. "I have to leave."

"Where are you going?" Robin held out her hand. He helped her stand.

"I'm going back to Iowa to get my daughter."

🐾🐾🐾

THE DRIVE BACK FROM DULUTH HAD LEFT LENA COMPLETELY drained. Still, she had animals to care for.

As soon as she walked in the door, she held Jane close as the pup licked her salty cheeks. She needed to pull herself together before tomorrow, when she would have to see everyone at church. But for now, here she was on another rainy Saturday night, crying, with only her dogs for companionship.

Well, the dog part wasn't so bad. They were loyal, at least. They didn't leave her in the lurch or bolt at the first sign of trouble. They didn't lie to her or make promises they couldn't keep. They didn't care if she did everything right or completely fell apart.

Lena left Jane on the couch and walked into her garage. She'd managed to find homes for all the cats now, but Darling, Scamp, and Harry still remained. Darling pawed at her kennel door, begging to be picked up. Lena went through the motions of scooping food into their bowls and filling water dishes before picking Darling up. Poor things were never supposed to be here this long.

"I'm sorry, girl. I tried to find you a home and I couldn't. I tried to build a new shelter, but that fell through too. Guess we're both just a couple of strays without a family."

A pounding on the front door startled them both.

"It's probably Oliver, but you know what? I don't want to see him." And even though she rarely did this, since the cresti-pug was terrified of Wentworth, Lena carried Darling inside.

She'd made it this far alone. This was her life. And after thirty years, maybe she just needed to accept that.

Sure, she'd enjoyed the way Oliver had made her feel cherished for a little while. But in the end, he didn't want her. He'd probably try to smooth talk his way into her forgiving him, but he'd shown when it came down to it, she was just the next-door neighbor. Again. So why not skip further heartache and start setting realistic expectations? She was better off this way and so was he.

But the pounding continued. Wentworth kept barking. Even Jane joined in the chaos with her little yips.

Lena yanked open the door. "What do you want?"

Birdie stood in her doorway holding a pie. Rain pattered on the porch roof and splashed behind her. "It's key lime."

Oh. Lena shoved aside the disappointment that it wasn't Oliver. Which was so stupid, really. Not to mention completely illogical and not worth examining. Just add it to the stack of reasons she should forget him as soon as possible.

"Sorry. I thought you were someone else." Lena opened the door wider and held back Wentworth as Birdie stepped in and shook off her coat. Bruce, in the meantime, hadn't moved off his dog bed.

"That was quite the party you organized." Birdie hung up her coat and carried the pie into the kitchen. As soon as she set it down, she reached out for Darling.

Lena put the teakettle on. "Yeah, some party."

"It will go down in Deep Haven lore. I'll never forget the look on Elaine's face when that goat fell into her lap." Birdie chuckled. "But of course, she handled it with such grace. You probably didn't see it, since you and Oliver ran after Kiah, but Elaine made a joke, and soon, with everyone's help, the table and the messes were cleaned up and everyone enjoyed the meal."

Lena set out two dessert plates and forks. She wasn't in a

joking mood, plus she needed to tell Birdie the bad news about the grant.

Maybe after the pie.

"It looks like Florida has done wonders for Jim's health. Didn't he look good?" Birdie asked.

Lena nodded. Not that she'd seen much of Jim, but he looked like he'd lost a few pounds and gained a nice tan in the Florida sunshine.

As the two ladies settled in the living room with their tea and pie, Wentworth and Jane cuddled up at their feet with bones Birdie had brought for them. Darling lay across Birdie's lap, happy as could be. If only Birdie could take her home with her.

Just another failure of Lena's. She couldn't convince the senior center to accept Darling as a service animal for the residents, even though it would've been the perfect solution.

The tart-sweet lime curd of Lena's first taste of pie cooled the burning in her throat. She took her time with each bite. If she opened her mouth to say anything, she'd probably break down sobbing, and she was tired of crying. So tired.

And as her mother had been so fond of reminding her, crying didn't change anything.

"I looked for you after the party, but someone said you left?" Birdie asked.

Lena nodded. For once she hadn't worried about the cleanup, who was in charge, who would make sure the borrowed punch bowl got back to Sheila, or if the tablecloths were laundered. She'd been worried about Brad.

What a joke. He had plenty of family to take care of him.

"You worked so hard on Jim and Elaine's party. It really was gorgeous."

"Thank you." Lena stared into her mug of tea.

"Nothing to say about what happened? About Oliver? Poor man."

"What is there to say?"

Sipping her tea, Birdie studied her intently. Wentworth

nudged his big nose under her hand, begging for a good scratch. Lena kept her own hands busy stroking Jane, who had somehow made it into her lap once more.

Finally, Birdie set her mug down. "So, you never said where you went after the party."

A change in subject? Great. Better than talking about Oliver. "I went to Duluth."

"You've been to Duluth and back? Whatever for?"

"I went to see…my father." Okay, so maybe this wasn't better. She held her chin up as best she could, but the tears broke through and her voice wobbled. She grabbed a tissue from the box on the coffee table. It turned soggy in an instant.

"Oh, Lena. What did that man do to you?"

The sympathy and warmth in Birdie's gaze shattered the thin veil of reserve she'd tried so hard to hold up. "I thought he really cared. That after all this time he wanted to get to know me. But it was even more of a disaster than the party."

"What happened?"

"Just like with Oliver, I trusted him. Turns out he only wanted my kidney, and when I wasn't a match, he—" She left her words hanging between them and shrugged.

"He what?" The lethal tone in Birdie's voice was almost comical. Lena had never heard the sweet woman so angry. Even Wentworth gave a low growl.

"He went back to his *real* family. He wouldn't even admit to his wife who I was. Said I was…a nobody." Being ignored would've hurt less than being tossed aside like dirty laundry the way he'd done.

Birdie's hands fisted. "A nobody? I'd like to show him a thing or two. That man has been a cad from the first."

"You knew him?"

"I only know what your mother told me. The first time he wanted to come back to her, she believed him when he said he wanted to be a good father and husband. You were just a baby. But as soon as he had access to her accounts, he wiped them out and left. She eventually moved here just to get away from him and start over."

"She actually admitted all this to you? Why wouldn't she tell me?"

"She told me nothing until close to the end. She wanted me to be on the lookout in case he ever came around. And I think, I think she was ashamed to admit to you what she'd done. That she fell for such a man."

All that time, her mother hadn't been trying to keep Lena from him for selfish reasons or out of bitterness? She'd been trying to protect her?

"Your mother tried, Lena. She wasn't the most affectionate person. But she did love you in her way. And I know you probably don't want to hear this, but from what I've seen, Oliver does too. He's gone above and beyond to help us with the dogs here. Don't lump him in with the likes of Brad Fowler."

"Oliver is heartache and disaster waiting to happen. Oh, wait. It already did happen."

"That little ruckus at the party wasn't completely his fault. You can't hold that against him."

"I know. But it doesn't matter. I tried following my heart instead of my head and look where it got me. I'm done."

Even if she did love him.

Because Oliver Fox would always have a piece of her heart. Kiah too. But what little she had left, the small part that was intact, she needed to protect. If her mom had been right about Brad, she was probably right about wasting time pining away for the boy next door too.

Lena looked Birdie in the eye. "I'm better off alone."

Lena expected Birdie to have a comeback. What she didn't expect was her to laugh in her face.

Birdie threw her head back and howled.

"I don't see what's so funny about me being alone." Lena held Jane closer and waited until Birdie was done.

"Oh, you looked just like your mother when you said that.

She would be proud." Birdie wiped her eyes and focused on Lena once more. "And as much as I respected her, I have one thing to say about that. That, my dear, is a load of horse doodie! No one is better off alone. Even you, as capable as you are. That is fear talking."

"No, it's logic. I gave Oliver a chance. I gave Brad a chance. And where did that leave me? Here. Alone."

"But you're not alone. Like the psalm says, 'A father to the fatherless, a defender of widows, is God in his holy dwelling. God sets the lonely in families.' This verse has brought me a lot of comfort since losing Howard."

"But you're alone too now." Where was the hope in that?

"The problem is not the earthly family you think you lack. This verse reminds us that we have a Father who will never abandon us. A Savior who rescued us, wants to be with us. That's real love. It's courageous and persistent."

"But it's not that easy."

"Love is never easy, Lena. Life together will be muddled and difficult at times. Relationships *are* risk. And I miss Howard every single day. But the benefits of loving him far outweigh the costs. I wouldn't give up the years I had with him for anything."

"Birdie, you don't understand. I have so little left to give. I've tried. But everything I've done for Brad, for Oliver, for the shelter, it's all fallen to pieces. There's nothing left."

The hollowness in her chest attested to it. It echoed with loss and pain, and she simply couldn't handle any more.

"You say you don't have much to give. I say you know the source of all love. You've known it since you prayed at Vacation Bible School when you were seven years old. All the love and acceptance you've been hungry for is yours for the taking."

"So, what? I'm supposed to sing 'Jesus Loves Me' and call it good? I've done that. I know God loves me."

"Do you?" Birdie leaned forward and brushed Lena's hair behind her ears. "I think you know it here. In your head. But what about down here?" Birdie pointed to her heart. "Because love that is invested and cultivated in the right place multiplies and grows. You don't know the amazing fruit that will come of it if you stay closed off and alone, like your mother did."

"But look at what Brad did to her."

"I know. And it was courageous of you to try to help him, Lena. Now you know he doesn't really want a place in your life, and you can move on. But I've seen you come alive these last months with Oliver. And it's only the beginning. Can you imagine what would happen if you went all in?"

No. She wouldn't let herself imagine that anymore. Lena sighed and leaned back against the cushions. "I don't know, Birdie." Oliver had his own family, and really, what did he need her for? She was uptight and weird. There were plenty of Misty Zimmermans around that would gladly give him all the attention and warmth he wanted.

Birdie stood. "Just remember, with or without Oliver, you're not alone, Lena. But with him you'll be able to experience so much more than you could ever imagine. It just takes some faith and a whole lot of courage. Besides, he could probably use that about now."

Lena set her mug down. "So you think I should give him another chance."

"I think you should give *yourself* the chance."

God sets the lonely in families.

What had Oliver said when Kiah wanted to adopt her into their family?

Lena might not have a family, but she's got some great next-door neighbors.

He wasn't wrong. The Foxes had always welcomed her like one of their own. And Birdie and Howard had been closer to her than her own grandparents. Robin and Beth had always treated her like sisters. Oliver had done a lot for her over the last couple of months. The adoption event, the little home projects, the date he'd tried so hard to get right.

A haphazard mix of kooky neighbors didn't look the way she thought a family should look, but maybe Birdie was right.

Lord, I always tried to do the right thing, but I think I was wrong. I've been looking for the perfect guy to care about me, whether that was my father or Oliver or someone else. All this time I thought that was what I lacked. But I've been searching for perfection in others when it can only be found in You. What I really need is You.

A stirring in her soul spoke to the cracked and desolate places of her heart.

She wasn't alone. She already belonged.

Birdie carried the mugs to the kitchen. "So, are you going to go see Oliver? He could use your encouragement right about now."

"You mean because of the party disaster?" Lena set the plates and forks in the dishwasher.

Birdie looked up from rinsing the mugs. "No. Didn't you hear?"

"Hear what?"

"The social worker took Kiah."

twenty

· · ·

I<small>F HE PACKED QUICKLY, HE COULD MAKE IT AS FAR AS</small> D<small>ULUTH</small> tonight.

After Oliver had sped home from the marina, soaked and shivering, he'd showered quickly, but the hot water beating down on him had failed to thaw his frozen core. He found the same duffel bag he'd brought with him from Iowa in the closet.

Because bright and early Monday morning, he would be at Monica Emiliano's office in Mason City, fighting to get his baby back.

He stuffed a stack of T-shirts from the drawer into the bag.

"Oliver?" Grandpa stood in the doorway of what'd used to be Grayson's old room. "You and I are long overdue for a talk, son."

Oliver grabbed a pile of pants. "I'm sorry, Grandpa, but I don't have time to hear all the ways I've failed you right now. I need to get my daughter back."

"Things have gone unsaid for far too long. Can you give me a few minutes?" His tone bristled.

Ollie fought for patience and a steady voice. "Yes, sir." He still owed Grandpa an apology. Even if it killed him. Because part of this sobriety journey was taking responsibility for his actions. And Grandpa was right. This was long overdue. Even if Grandpa didn't accept his apology, he needed to do his part. Not just for the sake of gaining custody of Kiah. He needed to do what he could to bring this family back together.

Oliver closed the open dresser drawer and faced his grandfather. "I should've said this a long time ago, but I'm sorry."

Grandpa looked taken aback. "What exactly are you sorry for?"

"I'm sorry I couldn't…save them. I'm sorry for almost killing Grayson. For—"

"Oliver, stop." Something cracked in his grandfather's demeanor. He stepped into the room. "I came to apologize to you."

"To me?"

Grandpa sank down on the bed. He'd aged in the last twelve years, sure, but Oliver had never before witnessed the pain etched in his face or the sorrow in his cloudy blue eyes. "I failed you."

Huh?

"I have a feeling your father would be ashamed of me. Your grandmother certainly is. And for good reason."

Oliver could hear each word, but they weren't computing.

His grandfather continued. "I never gave you a chance. I preached being a good neighbor, expected politeness and respect to all, showing mercy and kindness. But when it came down to it, I failed to extend those things to my own grandson."

Ollie shifted his weight from foot to foot, unsure of what to say. All his reasons and arguments he'd prepared for this conversation were swept away.

Grandpa looked Oliver in the eye. "I'm sorry, Ollie. You are so much like your father, and I'm afraid I pushed you too hard because of it. I should've never let you walk out of that hospital the way I did. I said things in my anger that never should've been said. And I'm sorry I wasn't there for you." He stood. "Will you forgive me?"

With the words choking up his windpipe and eyes stinging, Oliver could only nod and offer a hand. Grandpa pulled him in and hugged him tight. Somehow Ollie managed to squeeze out, "I'm sorry too. I really am."

When Grandpa stepped away, he swiped his eyes quickly. "I know. I think it's time we started over. I know you're going to get Kiah back, but you're not going alone. I've already talked to your grandmother. We're coming with you."

At his first AA meeting after accepting he couldn't fix himself, Oliver had fallen on his face and cried out for help. The Lord had met him there. He remembered that moment of being freed from the crushing weight of his burden—the freedom when he stopped fighting and let God take it from him. But somewhere along the way, he'd forgotten that it wasn't up to him to restore everything else to its rightful place and had started to take on himself a task he could never accomplish.

He guessed the same could be said for putting his family back together again. Even the situation with Kiah.

Lord, I can't do it. I couldn't rescue my parents. I couldn't even save myself from my own addiction. Why I ever thought I could earn my way into Your presence or the family You gave me, I don't know. I've been trying to battle into Your good grace, when all along its been a gift. Help me to receive it.

Maybe he didn't have to wage war to be a part of this family again. Maybe he simply needed to accept the fact that he already was one of them. Despite his failures. Despite his weakness. Despite his inability to save his mom and dad. Maybe he needed to take his place among them instead of running away.

"You sure you want to come?" Oliver asked. "I don't know how long this will take."

"It doesn't matter. We're in this with you. Family sticks together."

"I'm coming too," a voice said from the hall.

Oliver looked up to see Grayson in the doorway.

Robin peeked in from the other side. "You're not going anywhere without me. I'm already packed, so hurry up."

"On it." Oliver opened up his sock drawer.

"So, what is this I hear about you and Lena Larson?" Grandpa asked, moving out of Oliver's path between the dresser and the bed.

"I don't know that there's anything there anymore. I messed it up. I was worried what the social worker thought and said she was just the neighbor."

"She is your neighbor. Are you saying there's more to it?"

Oliver added a handful of socks to his duffel. "A lot more. I love her, but maybe we're just too different. I don't know that I'll ever measure up to her idea of the perfect guy."

"That's a good place to start."

Oliver stopped in his tracks. "Huh?"

"You might as well go into a relationship knowing neither one of you is perfect. You need to decide if she's still worth going after."

Oliver wanted to. Because the picture of family and home wasn't complete without her. But did she even want anything to do with him after everything he'd said?

She'd forgiven him once. How much more could he ask of her? And the timing couldn't be worse.

"But…Kiah."

Grandpa sighed. "Right. First things first."

🐾 🐾 🐾

OLIVER WAS GONE. RIGHTLY SO. KIAH NEEDED HIM. BUT LEAVING things broken the way she had kept Lena up all night. She knocked on the Fox door first thing the next morning.

No one answered.

At church, the empty Fox pew distracted her from the worship time. She heard little of the sermon. Sammy Johnson sat with his mother, but no Robin was in sight. Grayson was gone too. But Beth would know what was going on.

As soon as the service was over, she beelined for her friend.

"Where are the Foxes? Jim and Elaine aren't even here this morning."

Beth tucked her sermon notes into her Bible before looking up. "They left late last night."

"Were they that angry at Oliver that they left town?"

"No. They went *with* Oliver. Robin and Grayson went too. They're going to fight for custody of Kiah. Ollie didn't waste any time. He's determined to be at his lawyer's office as soon as it opens tomorrow morning."

She couldn't blame him. "He must be going crazy over it all."

"Grayson said his court date is Wednesday. They're hoping to push it up, but they'll be there as long as it takes."

"He's been updating you?"

Beth nodded. "He asked if I could check in on Oreo until they get back."

Right. Because why would Ollie think he could ask Lena for anything after she scared the social worker away? Got his daughter taken away.

He probably didn't want anything to do with her.

It hurt. She couldn't pretend it didn't.

Had it only been a few nights ago she'd been in his arms with Oliver insisting he wasn't going anywhere? Now he was on his way to a different state. Who knew when he'd be back? If he'd be back.

But Oliver was doing the right thing. He needed to focus on Kiah. In the meantime, Lena had a business to run, animals of her own to take care of. And no matter what happened with him, she would hold on to the truth that she already belonged.

Seth and Ree Turnquist approached as Beth left to speak to Vivien Buckam.

Seth carried his son in the baby car seat carrier. "Hey, Lena, we were wondering if we could meet the dog Oliver mentioned. I think he said you've been calling him Harry."

"You're interested in Harry?" For a moment Lena was speechless. "I'd love to introduce you. He's a sweet dog."

"Is now a good time?" Ree asked. "I just fed Anders so he'll sleep for the next hour."

"This would be a great time."

The Turnquists followed Lena home. As soon as Harry was released from his kennel, he ran right over to them, but Scamp insisted on playing too. He wagged his tail and sat next to Harry. Feeling badly for Darling, Lena carried her while she watched the couple fawn over the other two. Anders slept in a stroller oblivious to it all.

"Scamp loves to play fetch." Lena offered Seth a well-worn tennis ball. "Harry is more of a Frisbee guy."

Seth pitched the ball to the front yard. The terrier mix ran after it and brought it back, dropping it at Seth's feet. Harry waited politely for a Frisbee toss and caught it midair.

"Wow, they're both well-trained." Ree took a turn throwing the ball. "How old are they?"

"I estimate Scamp about two years old. Harry is one. Both young, but not in the puppy stage anymore."

"That's the hardest part for us," Seth said. "With as busy as we are with a baby, we don't want to train a puppy, but I'd really like to have a dog around the house."

"Both these guys are crate trained and potty trained. They've always been well-mannered, but both have a lot of energy."

Ree bent to rub down Scamp's body. "I don't mind energy. That will be good for us. We can take him hiking, on the biking trails. We'll have a blast." She looked up at Seth. "What do you say?"

"I don't know. Harry here looks like he'd be great on our camping trips." He grinned down at his wife. "Let's get both."

"Good, because I wouldn't know which one to pick anyway. And now they won't be lonely while we're gone at work."

Lena's chest swelled. A home. Finally. She cuddled Darling closer to her chest. "I can get their paperwork right away and a week's worth of food for them."

"And while we're here, maybe you can get the plans for the new animal shelter for me. I'll need a copy for my order." Seth threw the tennis ball again for Scamp.

"Your order?" What was he talking about? "I don't have funding lined up yet. I'm nowhere near being able to pay for the building or put down deposits."

Seth looked confused. "I didn't expect you to pay. I'm donating the lumber and siding materials. I need the plans to know the amounts."

"You're what?" Having recently gone over the construction plans, Lena knew the staggering cost of that portion of the project.

"Didn't Oliver tell you?"

Lena shook her head.

"He convinced me it would be a good tax write-off. And he offered free plumbing for the remodeling project we're planning on for our own house. We're building an addition."

Lena's head was spinning. "When did he do that?"

"When we were setting up for the party yesterday. I think he lined up the whole first responder crew to donate labor. With the simple pole shed design, we figure the raising will go pretty fast. He was working on lining up the excavation and cement work. Knowing him, it won't take long."

No, it probably wouldn't. Because Oliver had a way of making people feel like part of the winning team. He brought people on board, made connections. Sure, she'd never leave him on his own to pick out decor or organize all the nitty-gritty details, but this was what he did well. And he'd done it because it was important to her.

twenty-one

. . .

ONCE AGAIN OLIVER FACED THE COURT. HE WAS ANXIOUS TO SEE Kiah with his own eyes, to hold her again after an agonizing three days, but he couldn't yet. However, Monica had assured him she was waiting nearby with a social worker until the hearing was over.

He turned around to see Grandma and Grandpa and his siblings in the gallery seats behind him. Sammy Johnson sat with Robin, and Beth Strauss with Grayson. Blanche had even flown in from Florida to be here. She and Grandma Elaine couldn't be more different in appearance, but they were already swapping recipes and planning to meet up when they were back south.

Grandpa gave him an encouraging nod. They'd covered a lot of ground on this road trip. But now Oliver's fate as a father rested in the hands of the judge.

Besides Kiah's, the other face he longed to see was Lena's. He'd thought about calling, but he wasn't sure she'd answer. Besides, what was it she'd once said?

You're harder to ignore in person.

Picturing her face as she'd said those words sent an ache straight to his heart. As much as he wanted her here, he didn't deserve her. Monica wanted a testimony from her, but he couldn't ask it. Not of Lena. Not when he hadn't stood up for her when he should've. Hers was the only written statement from his list he hadn't gotten. He would be completely at the mercy of the court.

"All rise," the bailiff's voice boomed.

Judge Clancy entered the room from her chambers. "Well, well. Mr. Fox. Here we are again."

"Yes, Your Honor." Oliver resisted the urge to crack his knuckles. It was too quiet in the room.

"Looks like you have a cheering section with you. I'll take that as a good sign." The judge settled into her chair. "So you've done the work? You made amends?"

Monica stayed him with a hand on his arm. "Your Honor, if I may, my client has made excellent progress in repairing the relationships of people he felt like he'd harmed."

"I see. So, Mr. Fox, I have statements from everyone on the list you gave me?"

Oliver's mouth went dry, but the judge looked to him for the answer to her question, not his lawyer. "Almost. I'm missing one."

Judge Clancy adjusted her glasses. "And whose statement are you missing?"

"Lena Larson's."

"And who is Lena Larson in relationship to you? Could you not track her down?"

She was giving him an out here. But he couldn't take it.

"She lives next door to me in Deep Haven. I've known her since we were kids. But I really messed things up with her. I couldn't ask her for a statement after hurting her the way I did."

"I see. I appreciate your honesty." She flipped through a stack of papers. "I read all these statements. Rather impressive." She pulled one sheet out of a file. "Unfortunately, though, I have a rather disturbing eye-witness account from a Beverly Walters. Her assessment is that you are unfit to father Kiah. And by not having a statement from *every* person on your list, you haven't met the requirements I gave you back in August."

Monica stood. "Your—"

The large doors in the back of the room squeaked open. As tempting as it was, Oliver didn't turn to see who came in. He wouldn't drop his gaze as the judge stared him down. But she shifted her focus to whatever was going on behind Oliver's back.

Shuffling footsteps, lots of footsteps, and a quiet electric motor sounded.

"Excuse me," the judge said. "Who are you?"

"I'm here to testify on behalf of Oliver Fox. He's a good man, Your Honor."

Now Oliver looked. Coach Presley rolled in on his electric wheelchair with his daughter Izzy Knight right behind him.

Coach was here? Testifying on his behalf? Seb Brewster walked in with them, followed by Peter Dahlquist and Edith Draper. Misty Zimmerman's high heels clicked on her way to sit next to Robin. Mack Hill, along with Pastor Dan and his wife Ellie, all squeezed into the seats with Oliver's family.

"Am I to assume you are all here to testify on Mr. Fox's behalf?" the judge asked.

They all answered in unison. "Yes, Your Honor."

"Are these people all from your hometown?" the judge asked Oliver.

Unable to speak from the emotion lodged in his throat, he simply nodded.

"Well, as much as I can appreciate the sentiment that almost everyone in Deep Haven wants to come forth, we simply don't have time. I'll allow one person to come and testify—"

"I will, Your honor."

Oliver whipped around. Lena stood in the aisle, waiting to approach the bench. To anyone else she might look calm, but her fingers were clasped together so tightly her knuckles were white.

"And you are?" The judge glared down at Lena.

"Lena Larson."

Judge Clancy's eyes widened. "By all means, Ms. Larson, please approach."

After placing her hand on the Bible and swearing to tell the truth, Lena sat in the witness stand.

Monica leaned toward Oliver. "Did you know?" she whispered.

He shook his head. He'd had no clue.

"Please tell me, Ms. Larson. What would you like to say in regard to Mr. Fox's ability to care for his daughter?"

Lena took a quick breath, like she was preparing for battle—and for her it probably felt like it. Her cheeks already blushed bright red. "Oliver is an excellent father. And I would know. Because growing up without a dad, I always imagined what a good father would be like. Ollie exceeds anything I imagined."

"And are you the kind of person prone to exaggerating?"

"No, Your Honor. If you asked me to list Oliver's faults, I could. He's impetuous, at times impulsive. Don't ever let him bake for you."

Robin and others in the crowd laughed.

But up on the stand, Lena didn't crack a smile. "But Oliver also cares about people. Deeply. And he loves Kiah. He's patient with her. He listens to her. He once danced with a goat, just to make Kiah laugh. And he's protective of the people he cares about too. I have no doubt he would give his life for her if need be. Because Oliver is a good man. And I know Kiah has been through a lot this last year, but I'm begging you, Your Honor. Let her grow up with her father. Let her be a part of this amazing Fox family. I've known them my whole life and wanted to be one of them. She couldn't have a better home."

Her words choked him up immediately. After everything he'd done to her, the ways he'd messed up, she still saw him as a good man? She'd still stood up for him?

"Thank you, Ms. Larson. You can step down." Lena stood and moved toward the gallery.

Oliver shot to his feet. "Wait. Please, Your honor, I would like to say something."

"And what is that?"

"Earlier you asked about my relationship to this woman. And I wasn't completely honest, because I know I don't deserve her. But I want it stated for the record. I love her. If I have any kind of shot here, I hope one day she *will* officially be part of our family."

Judge Clancy smiled. "Let the court show Oliver Fox is in love with you, Ms. Larson."

Lena gave him a wobbly smile with tears coursing down her face.

"Now back to the matter at hand. Custody of Kiah Louise Jackson. Truth of the matter is, I spoke with Kiah myself. She's a lucky little girl to have so many people who care about her. So this decision isn't easy, but—"

"Wait, Your Honor. Please." Cassandra stood. She closed her eyes a moment before looking up at the judge.

Judge Clancy motioned for her to continue.

"I've loved being with Kiah these last few days. The girl has so much of her mother in her. But she couldn't stop talking about her father or her new home in Deep Haven. She told me how Oliver helped her when she was scared to go to the first day of school. How he reads her bedtime stories and they take walks with the dogs. She cries every night and asks when she can go back home. And he obviously has a wonderful community she can grow up in. I don't want to take her away from that. I hope I can still have some visits with Kiah, but I give up any custodial rights I might have. She belongs with Oliver."

The courtroom fell silent.

"Are you certain, Ms. Freeby?"

"I am, Your Honor."

The judge picked up her gavel. "Mr. Fox, having also received your request for a name change, I hearby grant you full and complete custody of Kiah Louise Jackson Fox." She tapped the gavel and the crowd from the gallery cheered.

The doors in the back of the room opened again and Kiah ran in. Oliver caught her in his arms.

"Daddy!"

"Oh, Kiah, darlin', I missed you so much." He didn't bother to stop the tears that fell. "I love you."

"I love you too, Daddy."

He would never tire of hearing those words from her lips. They were surrounded by family and friends instantly. Kiah insisted on being passed around from Robin to Grayson to Sammy and Grandma—even Grandpa, much to his delight. Oliver craned his neck, looking for Lena, but he couldn't see her over the crowd. Knowing Kiah was fully and officially his, he left his daughter with the rest of his family and excused himself from the room.

But Lena wasn't in the hall. He ran and caught a glimpse of her in the marble-floored lobby. "Lena!"

People stopped to stare at him, but he didn't care what they thought. He ran up to the woman he loved. "Where are you going?"

"I didn't want to bother you. This is your time with Kiah. With your family."

"Then you should be in that courtroom, because you're one of us. Maybe one day, once I've made it up to you, you might even make it official and marry me, because I can't live without you. The last three days have been absolute torture."

"You…meant it, what you said?"

"It's on the official court record. Of course I meant it. And I know I was such a jerk, but—" He pulled out his wallet and showed her the folded piece of paper he carried with him always.

Lena's hand covered her mouth. "That's my letter. You still have it?"

"It reminded me that no matter where I went, who I was,

what I was doing, at one time this really amazing girl loved me. And it pushed me to keep trying to be the man that she could be proud of one day. I'm not there yet. And I'm so sorry I didn't stand up for you with the social worker at the party. And I'll shout it here in this lobby if I have to prove it, but I love you, Lena Larson. I really do."

He was clueless about a lot, but he took it as a good sign when she came willingly into his arms, laughing and crying at the same time, not holding back a thing.

"I love you too, Oliver Fox," she whispered right before she kissed him in front of the applauding crowd.

epilogue

· · ·

LENA AND BIRDIE LAUGHED, TRYING TO BOTH GAIN HOLD OF THE large unwieldy scissors. As the crowd counted down, the January sunshine sparkled off the mounds of snow surrounding the new metal-sided building like glittery confetti.

"Three, two, one!"

Together they cut the red ribbon.

Oliver stood on the makeshift dais, arms opened wide. "Welcome to the new Howard Dawson Rescue Shelter!"

Probably eager to get out of the single-digit temps, the crowd cheered and walked through the double doors.

Once Lena entered the building, her hands were caught up by Kiah. "Did you see the doggy playground, Lena? It's inside!"

"I know, isn't that great? Now the dogs have a place to play all year long."

Kiah ran off with Bruce right behind her. They passed the new kennels and the visiting rooms where families could bond with potential rescues and Birdie's front desk where she would watch over all the comings and goings. For now, Birdie stood under a portrait of Howard, handing out goodies for both human and canine open-house visitors.

On the edge of the play area, Gertie Thurber watched some of the dogs next to Elaine and Jim. She had a tight grip on the handle of her doggy stroller, where Charles rested alongside another dog.

"I bet you don't see them at the clinic much these days, do you?" Oliver asked as he wrapped a strong arm around Lena's shoulders.

"Nope." She leaned into his chest. "Who knew Gertie would be the perfect dog-mom for Darling? Or that Charles would thrive with a companion and not get into so much trouble."

Oliver's chuckle rumbled through her, sending warmth all the way down to her toes. "Uh, if I remember correctly, you did. But I was the one that had to convince her to give it a try."

"What can I say? We make a good team."

"That we do." He gently kissed her temple.

"Thanks for giving the speech, by the way. And you remembered to thank all the donors."

"I had your list so I wouldn't forget anyone. But if you really want to thank me"—he pulled her toward one of the family bonding rooms—"you'll help plan another event."

Lena groaned. "Another event? Don't get me wrong, I like planning, but it's been nonstop since you came back to town. First the pet adoption, then the anniversary party, and now the shelter open house."

"Yeah, but this will be even better than all of those."

The way his brown eyes flashed with excitement, it must be something big. And she had to be honest—the man could talk her into just about anything. "What kind of timeline are we looking at?"

"That would be up to you." Oliver stood outside the closed door of the room, one hand on the doorknob. "But if I have my way, it will be a pretty short one."

"Why are the curtains over these windows closed? I want everyone to see how cozy and cute these rooms are."

"No, I don't think you do." He opened the door and ushered

her into a dimly lit room glowing with soft twinkle lights that hung from the ceiling.

Kiah waited inside with Bruce, Wentworth, and Jane. All of them were freshly bathed. Wentworth sported a dapper polka-dot bowtie, while Jane wore a frilly tutu.

"What is this?" Lena asked. "And how did these guys get here?"

Instead of answering, Kiah motioned to Jane. "Go ahead, Janey."

Jane sauntered over and dropped a little box at Lena's feet. Oliver came from behind and stood in front of Lena.

"Ollie, what's going on?"

He'd opened his mouth to speak when a commotion sounded at the door.

"We didn't miss it yet, did we?" Robin sneaked in with Sammy, followed by Grayson and Beth and finally Jim and Elaine.

"Not yet, but it took ya long enough." Oliver leaned around her to scowl at them.

Elaine's eyes already shimmered wet. "Go ahead, dear. We're all here now."

"Good, because I don't want to waste any more time." Ollie knelt down and opened Jane's box.

Lena's breath hitched at the sight of the white-gold band with a princess-cut diamond, resting on a velvet cushion.

"I'm here to ask you a very important question. And I wanted to share this moment with the most important people in our lives, because if there's one thing I've learned, it's that life is so much richer and better when it's shared with those we love. These are the people that have carried us through good times and bad and will always be on our side. And I know there's no one else I want at *my* side for the rest of my life. So"—Oliver took her left hand—"will you, Lena Joy Larson, do me the honor of being my wife and joining our family?"

After all the ways Oliver loved her—everything from

remembering how she liked her coffee, to finding community members to donate the building they now stood in, to shouting it in a county courthouse lobby—there was only one answer she could give him.

"Yes!"

🦊 🦊 🦊

THANK YOU FOR READING *THE WAY YOU LOVE ME*! HAVE YOU READ the other Fox Family siblings' stories? Turn the page to discover more . . .

DISCOVER ROBIN FOX'S LOVE STORY IN
HOW SWEET IT IS BY ANDREA CHRISTENSEN.

Sometimes the sweetest moments in life are made from the most familiar and ordinary ingredients.

Robin Fox is living out her dreams working in a gourmet bakery in Paris. She thought she'd live there forever, but when her relationship with her boss sours, those dreams crumble. She finds herself back home in Deep Haven, Minnesota, caring for her grandparents' rundown bakery while they're away. But she vows that when they return in six weeks, she'll trade this ordinary life for the one she left behind.

Sammy Johnson has never gotten traction in any area of his life. This hasn't improved in the almost two years since the accident which nearly killed him. Although his heart is still beating, it contains little passion for the life he's living in Deep Haven. But that begins to change when he offers to help his former high school friend, Robin.

Working together to keep Fox Bakery from going under, they find more than friendship is simmering between them. But when the six weeks are up, will Robin follow her old dreams back to the glamor of Paris or will she discover how sweet it is to be loved in Deep Haven?

Return to Deep Haven with the Fox Family, where Robin and Sammy find that small town life isn't ordinary after all.

Get your copy now!

Don't miss Grayson fox's second chance romance in
It's Your Love by Rachel D. Russell.

When Grayson Fox is asked to return home to Deep Haven and run the wrangler activities for the local camp, the last thing he expects is to run into the one woman he never wanted to see again. Worse…she's his boss. But Grayson has big hopes for a life back in Oregon, and he must keep the promise to the camp in order to keep his dreams alive.

Just because Beth Strauss has stuck around Deep Haven doesn't mean she doesn't want a bigger life. And becoming the camp assistant director is the first step to that bigger life. Of course, standing in her way happens to be the one man who has always managed to derail her dreams, way too arrogant Grayson Fox.

But if they want to keep the camp afloat and their dreams alive, these two must learn to work together. But will these enemies become sweethearts, and if they do, will they find something better than the dreams they're striving for?

The next delightful installment of the Fox Family series!

Available now

She's doesn't want any trouble…

Former soldier Veronica "Ronnie" Morales isn't going to let her kid brother, Tiago, get pulled into the gangs of Minneapolis, so, seeking safety and a fresh start, she heads to sleepy Deep Haven on the north shore of Minnesota. She's hoping to put down roots as the paramedic for the new Crisis Response Team, but it's not easy to be the outsider.

He can't seem to escape it…

It's also not easy being the guy related to everyone in town. Especially when you're the holdout vote for a landmark project. Fire Chief Peter Dahlquist might be the loneliest guy in town when both sides of his massive family—the Hatfields and McCoys of Deep Haven—demand that he pick sides. The only one who seems to understand is the newcomer in town…his new, albeit street-tough paramedic.

Can trouble bring them together?

When Tiago finds himself caught up in small town shenanigans and the town blames Ronnie for tragedy, Peter is forced to pick sides. But this choice just might cost him the home—and the woman—he loves.

Start this sweet contemporary romance today!

Sled dog musher and blogger, Nick Dalquist has some simple goals—teach outdoor survival, run the Iditarod...and chat with online friend, LadyJHawk. Sure, he's starting to like her more than he'd like to admit. But he has no time—or room—for a IRL relationship.

Chopper pilot Jae Washington has been an avid follower of Nick's DogQuest vlog since inheriting a military working dog. Now, his online friendship has made her wonder if he could be more than a friend. What if she moved to Deep Haven? Would that be stalking, even if she got a job on the Crisis Response Team?

Nick is pretty sure petite Jae won't last a moment in the brutal cold—a fear he shares with LadyJHawk. Meanwhile, Jae decides to keep her avatar a secret until she can prove to Nick she's not a stalker. But as he trains her—and the chill between them begins to thaw—what if he discovers the truth she's hiding?

When a blizzard strikes, and the CRT is deployed, more than just their relationship is at risk...

Cozy up to this delightful twist on You've Got Mail set in the snowy escape of Deep Haven.

Get your copy now!

Join USA Today best-selling author Susan May Warren, award-winning author, Rachel D. Russell, and best-selling Minnesota authors Michelle Sass Aleckson and Andrea Christenson in this delightful twist on Bing Crosby's holiday favorite song, Winter Wonderland.

A Deep Haven wedding at Christmas? With snow glistening in the lane, sleigh bells ringing, and all the world a winter wonderland—magical, right?

Or maybe not, because the snowstorm of the century has buried their small town, and as Vivien Calhoun and Boone Buckam fight the sleet, snow, and ice, just about everything can—and does—happen to skid their big day into the ditch. It'll take all their friends—and a few strangers—to turn this Christmas wedding from a blizzard to a beautiful sight in this charming collection of novellas.

Discover four enchanting stories featuring old friends, and new, who discover that there just might be a happy ending waiting in this winter wonderland—if only they can shovel their way out of trouble.

Buy now!

acknowledgments

You might not realize this, but it takes a lot of people to write a book! Between emotional support, prayer support, and general keep-Michelle-sane-while-on-deadline support there are so many I need to thank. And that's not even counting the technical side of things. And I know I will forget people. So, to you who helped me on this journey in everything from coffee treats, writing outings, meals, prayers, etc THANK YOU!

To my family who gets the brunt of this burden, I love you and am grateful every day for you. Jesse, you are an unfailing support, the best part of my day, my inspiration for every hero ever, and the true love I always hoped and dreamed for. Anders, Evie, Lucy, and Trygg, your laughter, smiles, cheers, and hugs are my fuel for this writing journey. I'm so blessed to be your mom.

To Karen Hoffman, thank you so much for help with the legal side of things. Any errors are completely my fault. When are we taking over the conference room for board games next?

To Susie, Rachel, and Andrea who know and love Deep Haven the most, I think we need another trip to World's Best to celebrate. You gals are the best writing partners a girl could have!

To Mollie who is still my friend even after listening to me whine and moan throughout the various stages of writer's angst with this book. You're so quick to help and support, and I will forever be thankful for writing because it brought us together.

To the amazing support at Sunrise. From our fearless leaders

Susie and Lindsay, to the marketing peeps, editors, to proofreaders, to the Sunrise Support Team, y'all ROCK!

To my prayer huddles, mom-friends, friend-friends, extended family, and more, thank you for keeping me going. Your love, prayers, and support mean the world to me.

connect with sunrise

Thank you so much for reading *The Way You Love Me*. We hope you enjoyed the story. If you did, would you be willing to do us a favor and leave a review? It doesn't have to be long—just a few words to help other readers know what they're getting. (But no spoilers! We don't want to wreck the fun!) Thank you again for reading!

We'd love to hear from you—not only about this story, but about any characters or stories you'd like to read in the future. Contact us at www.sunrisepublishing.com/contact.

We also have weekly updates that contains sneak peeks, reviews, upcoming releases, and fun stuff for our reader friends. Sign up at www.sunrisepublishing.com or scan our QR code.

about michelle sass aleckson

 After growing up on both the east and west coasts, **Michelle Sass Aleckson** now lives the country life in central Minnesota with her own hero and their four kids. She loves rocking out to 80's music on a Saturday night, playing Balderdash with the fam, and getting lost in good stories. Especially stories that shine grace. And if you're wondering, yes, Sass is her maiden name.

Visit her at www.michellealeckson.com.

- facebook.com/AuthorMichelleAleckson
- instagram.com/michelle_aleckson
- x.com/MchelleAleckson
- goodreads.com/michellealeckson
- bookbub.com/authors/michelle-sass-aleckson
- amazon.com/stores/Michelle-Sass-Aleckson/author/B08M8P51B7

other deep haven novels

Fox Family Collection

How Sweet It Is

It's Your Love

The Way You Love Me

Deep Haven Collection

Only You

Still the One

Can't Buy Me Love

Crazy for You

Then Came You

Hangin' by a Moment

Right Here Waiting

Once Upon a Winter Wonderland

Deep Haven Series

Happily Ever After

Tying the Knot

The Perfect Match

My Foolish Heart

Hook, Line, & Sinker

The Shadow of Your Smile

You Don't Know Me

Christiansen Family Series

The Way You Love Me: A Deep Haven Novel
Fox Family Series, Book 3
Published by Sunrise Media Group LLC
Copyright © 2024 by Sunrise Media Group LLC

For more information about Michelle Sass Aleckson, please access the author's website at the following address: www.michellealeckson.com.

Published in the United States of America.
Cover Design: Jenny Zemanek, jennyzemanek.com
Editing: Susan May Warren and Barbara Curtis